THE LOVE POSITION

EVIE ALEXANDER

EMLIN
PRESS

ISBN (eBook) 978-1-914473-32-6

ISBN (Print) 978-1-914473-33-3

ISBN (Audiobook) 978-1-914473-46-3

A CIP catalogue record for this book is available from the British Library.

www.emlinpress.com

*For Jennifer Peterson
& the class of May 2009*

ALSO BY EVIE ALEXANDER

THE KINLOCH SERIES

Highland Games

Hollywood Games

Kissing Games

Musical Games

Wedding Games

Christmas Games

THE FOXBROOKE SERIES

One Night in Foxbrooke

Love ad Lib

An Unholy Affair

The Upper Crush

The Love Position

Christmas off Script

One Night Only

Righting Mr Wrong

Under the Influencer

Foxbrooke Extras

By Evie Alexander and Kelly Kay

EVIE & KELLY'S HOLIDAY DISASTERS SERIES

Cupid Calamity

Cookout Carnage

Christmas Chaos

Get Evie's books in all formats as well as special offers, early releases, and exclusive deals direct from her website:

www.eviealexanderbooks.com

EMLIN
PRESS

CONTENT NOTES
(INCLUDING SPOILERS)

Dear lovely reader,

All of us have different life experiences and find certain topics upsetting. Whilst it is impossible for me to know what these might be for you, I want you to be aware that this book mentions the following subjects, which may be triggering for some:

- Injury requiring treatment at a hospital (full recovery made)
- An attempted (and thwarted) sexual assault

There may be other subjects in The Love Position that you might find difficult to read, but I want you to feel safe in the knowledge that good always triumphs over bad and true love always wins!

Big love,

Evie ♡

JANUARY

Heart thumping, Sophia squinted at the coin in the half-light.

'It's Iceni, isn't it?' Maggie asked, the lines around her eyes creasing deeper.

Sophia nodded, running the pad of her thumb across the inscription. '*Saenv*. From the late denominational period.' An excited giggle escaped her. 'Maggie, this could be it.'

The older woman glanced around the empty landscape and lowered her voice. 'You think?'

Sophia nodded again. 'The walkover survey I did indicates a settlement might have been here, and the raised area at the edge of the field could be a burial mound. Is this the eighth coin you've found this weekend?'

Laying her metal detector on the ground, Maggie rummaged in a battered leather satchel around her neck, then handed Sophia another two. 'Now it's ten. I've logged the locations using my GPS tracker.'

'Superstar. If it's a hoard, it must have been scattered by ploughing, but it's a sign we could find even more here.'

The two women gazed out at the view from the vantage point at the edge of the escarpment, high above the plain below. The cool January sun was sinking towards the horizon on their left, but Sophia faced east, her mind two thousand years in the past.

Are you here?

No-one knew what happened to Boudica, Queen of the Iceni tribe, after the Romans quelled her uprising in AD 60. She simply disappeared from the historical record.

I would have fled west.

'Aren't you meant to be at some fancy dinner in York this evening?' Maggie asked, interrupting her thoughts.

Sophia pulled a face. 'You know I'm not great with big groups of people. Especially ones I don't really know.'

'But aren't you the guest of honour?'

'I'm *one* of them.'

'So, you bailed on the entire weekend and drove five hours just to meet me in a muddy field?'

Anxiety prickled in Sophia's stomach, and she rubbed the coin for reassurance. It felt warm and alive.

'My lecture was the first one this morning,' she replied breezily. 'I didn't really need to stay after that. And anyway, this is more important.'

'Searching for a needle in a haystack.'

'Maybe...' She shrugged. 'But to find this amount of Iceni coinage so far from East Anglia? The only accounts we have of Boudica after the battle is one saying she died of injuries and the other that she took poison. If she came this way, either dying or already dead, then where would she have been buried?'

'Stonehenge? Avebury? Silbury Hill? One of the countless

barrows?' Maggie gestured to the landscape below them. 'They're all in spitting distance.'

'They've been dug already, and Iron age people didn't have the same attachment to Neolithic sites. I don't think she's there.'

'But you think she's here?'

Sophia's anxiety about skipping out of the conference turned to fizzing excitement. 'I could say it's an educated guess... But I also feel it in my gut.'

Maggie's eyes twinkled. 'Nowadays my guts just grumble. You know I've been a detectorist longer than you've been alive, and I've never found the motherlode when out fieldwalking. It's always ring pulls and toy cars, not treasure.'

'But what if it was? Just imagine!'

'Oh, I do. It's what gets me tramping fields on my own all day.'

'You're the best there is.'

'Humph. I don't know about that. I'm just a persistent old bugger.'

Sophia squeezed the coin tighter, as if it held all the secrets of the universe as well as her fortune.

'Can I...?' She let the question hang in the air.

Maggie chuckled. 'You can have it on loan. Just don't start muttering "my precious" to it.'

Snorting with laughter, Sophia held it up in the dying light. 'My preshhhhhhhus!' she hissed.

'I'll report what I've found to the Finds Liaison Officer in the morning,' Maggie said. 'Do you think it's enough to get a dig?'

'I'm going to drive straight home and show this one to Marcus. It's ultimately his decision what we do in the department, but after the research I've already done on this site, hopefully the coins will be the tipping point to get the green light.'

'Even though they're not Roman?'

'He's not *that* biased.'

Maggie gave her the side eye. She wasn't a fan of Sophia's boyfriend, archaeology professor Marcus, and he openly despised detectorists.

'I'll sell them as "Roman adjacent".'

Turning away from the view, they strolled back through the field towards their cars.

'He'll be pleased you're back early,' said Maggie.

'Yes. He *was* a little grumpy that the conference was over his birthday weekend.'

'The big six-o?'

'Maggie! It's his fiftieth and you know it.'

The older woman smirked. 'So, what have you got him?'

'A framed silver denarius of Marcus Aurelius and a weekend away in Rome.'

'He'll love that.'

'I hope so. Anyway, it'll be nice to surprise him. I'm going to pop into Tesco on the way home and grab a takeaway.'

'Italian?'

'Of course.'

SOPHIA SWUNG HER CAR THROUGH THE GAP IN THE LAUREL hedge and came to a halt outside the house she shared with Marcus. As well as his Alfa Romeo, there was a shabby Vauxhall Corsa parked on the drive. It was vaguely familiar, but Sophia couldn't place where she'd seen it before.

Marcus had guests?

She'd rung him to say she was coming home early, but the

call had gone to voicemail. Taking a fortifying breath, she got out of the car.

Sociable face on and make an effort.

It didn't matter how tired she was, or how much she wanted to tell him about Maggie's finds. Today was Marcus's birthday so everything needed to be about him. Luckily, Sophia had bought enough food to share with whoever he was with, and she could always eat toast if there wasn't enough for everyone.

Opening the front door, she was hit by the smell of burning and vinegar, and music from Marcus's favourite CD. The musicians were playing copies of ancient Roman instruments and Sophia always thought it sounded like the percussion section of an orchestra had been taken over by enthusiastic ducks.

'Hi!' she called out over the sound of honking reed instruments and cymbals. 'Only me.'

'Magis! Ita!' Marcus roared through the living room door.

Sophia's heart sank. Her boyfriend yelling 'more' and 'yes' in Latin meant he'd reached the obnoxious stage of drunkenness, where he truly believed he was the reincarnation of Marcus Aurelius.

Please don't ask me to be your slave girl later...

Gritting her teeth, she carried the shopping bags to the kitchen. There was no sign of what could be causing the awful burning smell, but a roll of tinfoil was out on the worktop. Putting it away, she took out the takeaway boxes, turned the oven on, then went to wash her hands, thinking of any task she could do to delay facing a drunk Marcus and his friends when she was completely sober.

She froze as a shriek of female laughter carried along the corridor.

Who on earth is in there with him?

Then there was a high-pitched yelp of... pleasure?

Adrenaline prickling the back of her neck, she moved towards the living room. Pausing, her hand on the door knob, she heard Marcus groaning loudly from the other side. He only ever made that noise when they were together in bed. Alone.

Pulse pounding in her temples, she entered the room.

The people inside were so caught up in their activities, they didn't notice Sophia's arrival. Shock turned her blood to ice as she took in the tableau.

Marcus, her boyfriend of the past ten years, and the only man she'd ever slept with, was facing away from her, kneeling on the floor in front of the sofa, and rutting a woman from behind. His only clothing was a purple bed sheet tied haphazardly around him like a toga, and a laurel wreath on his head.

Sophia's gaze fixed on his pale buttocks as they clenched and wobbled with every thrust.

Is this what he looks like when we make love?

She couldn't see anything of the woman he was having sex with apart from her legs, but did recognise the other woman in the room. Holding a lighter underneath a sheet of tinfoil, she was inhaling noxious brown smoke coming off a substance on the top.

'Kiera?' Sophia asked, her voice thin and dry.

The young woman glanced up, her pupils blown out and her eyes glassy.

'Oh, shit!' she gasped, dropping what was in her hands and fumbling to pull a white bedsheet around her naked body.

The foil landed on the carpet, burning side down, and the smoke intensified.

'Fuck!' Kiera cried, bum-shuffling away.

Marcus didn't notice, his backside pounding faster as he cried 'slave girl' in Latin.

Dashing forward, Sophia grabbed a throw cushion from the floor and smothered the flames.

'What were you smoking?' she asked, her heart thumping against the inside of her ribcage.

Please let it not be what I think it is...

The young woman stared at Sophia, eyes wide like a rabbit in headlights.

'Kiera!'

She blinked. 'Opium.'

Marcus was grunting 'ancilla' louder and louder. He roared as if victorious in battle, and the woman beneath him screamed like a banshee.

Then the only sounds left were heaving gasps of recovery and discordant reed instruments.

Every one of Sophia's senses was assaulted. This was her house, her sanctuary, and it was being defiled on every level. Hands trembling, she flicked the music off.

'Huh?' Marcus said, his gaze moving to Kiera.

Kiera looked at Sophia.

Marcus turned, eyes bulging in his red face as he clocked her.

Sophia's breath came faster, her chest tightening as if being crushed by a snake. She couldn't find any words inside a head filled with white noise.

The thread veins in Marcus's cheeks were as purple as his makeshift toga. Sweat beaded on his forehead and his irises had been swallowed by the darkness of his pupils.

'It's my birthday,' he said, as if those three words explained everything away.

The woman bent over the sofa shifted to see who Marcus was talking to.

'Darcie?' Sophia stuttered.

'Fuck!' Darcie gasped, struggling to move away from Marcus. However, she was currently pinned between the sofa and his cock.

'Er...' Marcus began, his gaze swinging drunkenly around the room.

'Can you get off her, please,' Sophia said, her voice a whisper.

Marcus pulled out of Darcie and faced Sophia. Her gaze fell to his wet cock, rapidly deflating along with the man it was attached to, as if needing confirmation he'd been doing considerably more than dry-humping one of his nineteen-year-old students.

Scrabbling off the sofa, Darcie lurched across the room and grabbed her clothes.

'Sorry,' she muttered to Sophia, then tugged her friend's arm. 'Kiera, come on!'

Marcus stood and straightened his toga, his movements unsteady. 'Wait!'

Sophia ignored him. 'You can't drive home,' she said to Darcie.

Kiera started crying.

'I'll take you.'

'But—' Marcus began.

'Come on, quickly now,' Sophia continued, her voice wobbling as she tried to ignore her boyfriend's whine.

Darcie and Kiera ran from the room and Sophia followed, snatching her keys from the bowl by the front door and unlocking her car.

Marcus followed them outside into the chilly night air. 'Soph—'

'Get back in the house,' she said to him, then bundled the two women into the car, got in the driver's seat and reversed out onto the main road.

. . .

'WHERE AM I GOING?' SOPHIA ASKED AS SHE DROVE TOWARDS the centre of Salisbury, her jaw tight with pain as she tried to keep her emotions under control.

'Bishopdown,' Darcie replied. 'Miss—'

'Don't. Please don't say anything.'

'I'm sorry, Miss Hunter-Savage,' Kiera snuffled.

'It's *Ms* Hunter-Savage,' she ground out.

'I thought you said they weren't married,' Kiera whispered loudly to Darcie.

Sophia gripped the steering wheel as if it were her only link to sanity. 'The title *Ms* refers to an adult woman without her being defined by her marital status.'

'So, you're *not* married to Marcus then?' Kiera continued.

Pain lanced Sophia's chest. She'd spent nine of the last ten years hoping for a marriage proposal that had yet to arrive.

'It's Professor Thwaites to you,' she replied, her world smashing into pieces around her. 'Is this your first time having unprotected sex with him?'

Silence from the back seat.

I'll take that as a 'no,' then... 'And do you usually smoke heroin at the same time?'

'What?' Kiera asked.

Sophia's eyes briefly closed, then she focused on the road ahead, driving as fast as the speed limit would allow.

'Heroin. The class A drug you were taking.'

'That's opium, not heroin,' Darcie replied. 'It's part of the reenactment.'

'Heroin is derived from Opium,' Sophia said, her throat tightening with every word.

'I feel sick,' Kiera moaned. 'Can you slow down?'

Sophia sped up. She needed to get them out of her car before she broke down. The two girls were first-year students, barely legal.

Just like you were, ten years ago.

What if they told other people what they'd been doing? Would someone contact the police? Would she be arrested if they found drugs in the house?

'Miss—' Kiera began.

Sophia turned left. 'I'm nearly there. Darcie, how far along—'

She was interrupted by retching noises.

'Oh, my god!' Darcie cried.

Slamming her foot on the brake, Sophia screeched the car to a halt and dashed to open the back door. Vomit coated the back of her seat, dripping into the footwell.

Kiera stumbled onto the pavement and threw up again.

Darcie came to her friend's side and held onto her.

'Which one is yours?' Sophia asked, glancing up the street.

'This one,' Darcie replied, dragging Kiera towards a small terraced house.

Sophia waited till they were inside, then got back in her car, wound the windows down and drove away.

The winter air cut into the car like a knife, but the violent shivers wracking her body were not due to the cold. Her life had been a beautiful stained-glass window, years in the creation, but had just been smashed within the blink of an eye. The sharp-edged pieces now lay on the floor around her, and she didn't know if they could ever be put back together again.

Calm down!

But her breath was coming too fast to control. Swerving the car to a stop at the side of the road, she cut the engine and clutched her head as her vision began to go.

Come on! Come on!

Throwing open the door, she staggered out of the car, made it to the pavement and dropped to her knees, welcoming the cold, hard reality of the tarmac.

'Breathe with me!'

Her brother's voice cut through the cacophony, and she clung to the thought of him.

'You can do this.'

Even though he wasn't there, she felt his strength. Four years older than her, James had always had her back. Sophia loved her parents, but it was her brother she went to first with any problem.

But now?

Breathing slowly in and out, she stared at the pavement, glowing orange under the streetlamps. James would kick Marcus's arse to Rome and back, but that would only land her brother in even deeper shit than he was already in. Last year, he'd lost his job in London and been barred from working in financial services. Now he was living with their parents in Somerset and struggling to run an entertainment company.

One step at a time.

Pushing to her feet, Sophia got back in the car and drove the rest of the way home. The bigger picture could wait. Right now, she needed to find a pair of rubber gloves and scrub away all traces of the night.

'Marcus?'

No reply.

Closing the front door behind her, Sophia went into the living room.

Her boyfriend was sprawled on the sofa, asleep, his penis creating a damp patch on a scatter cushion that had the letter 'S' embroidered onto it. It had been a housewarming gift from her mother when Sophia had moved in, along with a cushion with the initial 'M' for Marcus.

Donning an apron and rubber gloves, Sophia set about

clearing the living room whilst her longtime partner snored and drooled. He'd mentioned using opium before in his quest to emulate Marcus Aurelius, but Sophia had shut the idea down. She'd indulged his fantasy of her being his slave girl a couple of times when they'd had sex, but it had made her deeply uncomfortable.

On the coffee table was a polaroid camera and shots of Darcie and Kiera doing things she'd refused to.

I wasn't enough for him.

Her stomach turned. How many times had he had sex with them? And had there been anyone else? She'd always ignored students flirting with Marcus. Had she been blind?

Running upstairs, she entered his study and rifled through the desk drawers. At the very back of one she found more polaroids, these featuring several former students. Dressed in togas or naked, they had various orifices around the cock Sophia believed was for her use only.

Backing out of the room, she stood in the hallway, desperate to collapse to the floor, but not wanting to touch anything more than she had to. Everything that was so familiar about her home now felt dirty.

Where will I live? What about work? Have I got an STD? How many people know about this? How have I been so stupid?

Her mind was fracturing into a million thoughts and she didn't know which one to pay attention to first.

Clean the car. Then you can leave.

SWEATING WITH EXERTION, HER NERVOUS SYSTEM RUNNING on empty, Sophia hauled the last suitcase into the boot of her car. She'd lived with Marcus for nearly a decade, and one night wasn't enough time to unpick the tapestry of their life together. She had the essentials packed. Everything else could wait.

'Soph?'

Marcus was in the doorway, his face puffy and his slate-grey hair defying gravity. He was still wearing the purple bedsheet, but it was crumpled and stained.

'Come inside and we can talk.'

She straightened. 'About what?'

He sighed, his expression irritated. 'Don't be like that. Let's be adults about this, okay? There's no need to be so reactionary.'

Reactionary? 'So, how exactly *would* you like me to behave after finding my boyfriend smoking heroin and having sex with his—and *my* university students?'

Marcus rolled his bloodshot eyes. 'It's *opium*. Plant medicine.'

'It's illegal.'

'And the girls mean nothing. It's just a bit of birthday fun. When you turn fifty, you can do the same if you like?'

Sophia's stomach lurched. When she reached fifty, Marcus would be seventy-one. Would they have had children?

'Why did you come back early?' he asked.

'Maggie's found ten Iceni coins at the site on the escarpment. I thought...' She trailed off. What did it matter? He wasn't going to support her now.

Marcus scratched his balls through the sheet. 'Ten?'

Sophia nodded, staring at him as if for the first time. Had she really given this man a decade of her life?

'Might be worth doing geophysics now then. And didn't you say there was a structure that might be a barrow? I'll take another look at your dig proposal next week.'

'You'd support it?'

He shrugged. 'Maybe? Be a good project for the undergrads

and we'd get another paper out of it. Now, come on back inside.'

She shook her head.

'Look, I'm sorry, Soph. It was a one-off. It won't happen again.'

'I found more photos in your desk drawer,' she choked out.

'What were you doing poking around my office?'

'What were *you* doing, poking around with at least ten of your students?'

Marcus ran a hand through his grey hair. 'It's nothing.'

'Nothing? You might have given me an STD!'

He rolled his eyes again. 'It's fine. Don't throw the baby out with the bathwater.'

Sophia stepped back, a hand reflexively touching her stomach.

'Where are you going to go?'

She swallowed. 'My parents' new place in Somerset. I can commute to work from there.'

'So, I'll see you at the staff meeting tomorrow?'

'It's in four hours, Marcus. And no, I won't be there.'

He glanced up at the pale sky with a frown. 'It's Sunday.'

'No, it's not. Today is Monday.'

'It can't be.'

Sophia got in the car.

Marcus stepped forward. 'Soph! Wait!'

She ignored him, slamming the engine into first gear and driving away. She didn't know what was going to happen next in her life, but she knew with utter certainty that her relationship with Marcus was over.

2

FEBRUARY

Sophia ran a finger over the glossy surface of the Valentine's card, tracing the cartoon of a fluffy dog holding an outsized heart.

Inside, the words '*From ?*' had been written by her mum using her left hand in a traditional, and futile, attempt to disguise who'd sent it.

Ever since Sophia had been a little girl, her parents had given Sophia and her brother cards on Valentine's day. They'd stopped when she got together with Marcus.

Now they'd started up again.

Hearing footsteps outside of her bedroom door, Sophia wiped her eyes. She had to put on her big-girl pants. What she was going through with Marcus was nothing compared to what her mother was currently having to handle.

'You in there, babe?' her mum called through the door.

'Yes, come in.'

Beverley Hunter-Savage entered the room and Sophia drew her in for a hug. 'How are you holding up?'

'I don't know what to do with myself,' her mother replied.

The two women sat on the edge of the bed, hands intertwined. Apart from the same brown eyes and cupid's bow lips, they couldn't have appeared more different. Sophia's thick brown hair was unstyled and tied in a ponytail, whereas her mother's had been bleached to within an inch of its life then carefully coiffed into a donut bun.

Sophia rarely wore make-up, however Beverley had never gone a day in her adult life without a full face of war paint. And whilst Sophia lived in off-the-peg jeans, her mum favoured animal-print designer clothes.

Beverley's manicured nails flicked the edges of Sophia's bitten ones. 'You need to get a set of acrylics done. Then you won't bite them.'

'Not great for work, Mum.'

'You could bring a bit of glam to archaeology. You're so pretty. You should be on the telly.'

Sophia repressed a shudder. It had taken her long enough just to deliver a lecture without an anxiety attack. The last thing she wanted was to be the centre of attention like that.

Beverley squeezed her hand. 'I don't know where we went wrong, babes. Your brother's got confidence flying out his arse, but you...'

'We're just very different, Mum.'

'Yeah... You sure I can't do you a makeover?'

Sophia shook her head. Growing up with crippling shyness, she'd wanted to fade into the background. However, her mother dreamed of creating a little princess in her own image. Luckily, Beverley loved her daughter more than her desire to create an 'it girl'.

'You seen Marcus?'

'At work.'

'You sure you're not going to get back with him?'

'I'm sure.'

Sophia hadn't told her parents the details of what went wrong. It was too mortifying. She also didn't trust her father not to call in a favour from an old gangster friend and have Marcus beaten up. Or worse...

'I just don't understand, babe. We thought you were so settled.'

An image of Marcus pounding into Darcie flashed into Sophia's mind, and she tensed. It was now an open secret in the archaeology department of Salisbury University that Professor Marcus Thwaites was in a polyamorous relationship with two of his students. But rather than this news creating uproar and condemnation, he'd received envious back slaps from men and offers of sex from other women.

Sophia, on the other hand, was treated like a morbidly fascinating train wreck, or someone who'd got what they deserved for having the gall to take up Marcus's precious time over the last ten years.

Anxiety pricked her chest like a thousand tiny needles, and her heart quickened.

'Soph?'

She shook her head rapidly, gulping in breaths. 'I'm okay. I'm okay.'

Beverley put her arms around her. 'I'm here, babe. Do your breathing thing.'

Squeezing her eyes tightly closed, Sophia pursed her lips and exhaled a slow, steady breath. Then did it again. Her doctor had suggested breathing techniques to control her anxiety, but they didn't always work. Held in her mother's embrace, she got herself back under control.

'Are the pills helping?'

Sophia nodded, even though the packet lay unopened in the bottom of her wash bag. She hated taking any medication, and after reading the small print about potential side effects, had chickened out of taking the drugs the doctor had prescribed for her anxiety.

'Good. And you're going to try that yoga class later with Estelle?'

'Only if you're okay with being on your own for a couple of hours?'

'I'll be fine, babes. I've got a couple of episodes of *The Real Housewives of Chelsea,* and Estelle's doggies to keep me company.'

'You *sure* you'll be alright?'

'Yeah, yeah, of course I will. I'm tough as old boots.'

Beverley's smile was bright, but Sophia could see the anguish behind it. Her husband and Sophia's father, Kevin Hunter-Savage, was currently detained in China. James had left two days ago to try and secure his release. The situation was terrifying and Sophia knew just how helpless and alone her mother felt. It was up to her to be strong, but it only took one look, overheard comment, or thought, for her anxiety to kick in. She was ashamed at her inability to handle her emotions, and sick of the negative thoughts running through her brain on an endless loop. Her doctor had recommended yoga, so she was giving it a go.

'Are you sure what I'm wearing is suitable?' Sophia asked, a hand twisting in the fabric of her oversized jogging bottoms as she met Estelle by the front door of her parents' home.

Estelle was working with James from a wing of the manor house. Now that he was abroad, she'd been staying over whenever Sophia was away and couldn't keep Beverley company.

'God, yes. Some women wear pyjamas.'

'Okay.'

'Although, I think it's just so they can imagine they're in bed with Isaac when they do corpse pose.'

'What?'

'The lying down bit at the end.'

'Oh.'

'He might be talking about chakras and white light but I swear to god all they hear is "Mmm, yeah, baby". One of them moaned once.'

Sophia snorted with laughter. The movement felt strange on her face, as if the muscles were out of practice.

Estelle winked. 'Full disclosure, it was me.'

'Is he really that attractive?'

'One hundred and sixty-nine per cent. That's why I'm giving you fair warning. You'll probably pop a lady-boner when you meet him.'

'A *what*?'

Estelle gave her the side eye. 'You've never heard that phrase before?'

She shook her head.

'Ah well, it'll all make sense when you meet him.'

Pushing open the manor door, Estelle led the way to a battered Land Rover Defender. 'I've cleaned her up, I promise.'

Sophia got in the passenger side. Her seat was clear, but the footwell was full of receipts, empty food wrappers and dog chew-toys.

'Just kick it to one side,' Estelle said, leaping into the car.

'You sure?'

'Yeah. Unless you want to start an excavation?'

'Can you promise me a warrior queen's final resting place?'

Estelle's eyes lit up. 'That I can.'

'Huh?'

Leaning into the footwell, Estelle rummaged around, finally pulling a DVD from the floor.

'*Xena: Warrior Princess*. I got it from the charity shop the other day.'

Sophia giggled. 'Is she one of your heroines?'

'Yep, along with Scary Spice, Wonder Woman and Buffy the Vampire Slayer.'

Lady Estelle Foxbrooke was unlike anyone Sophia had ever met. Confident and stunningly beautiful, her hobbies included mounted archery and driving James Hunter-Savage to the edge of reason. Sophia could see how her brother had fallen for her. Estelle was gloriously and effortlessly herself.

'I wish I was more like you.' Sophia's thoughts were out of her mouth before she could stop them.

'Really? You want to be the human equivalent of Marmite?'

'You're amazing. I wish I had some of your confidence.'

'You should steal some from your brother. He's got way too much of the stuff.'

Sophia suppressed a smile. She wasn't sure if anything had happened yet between James and Estelle, but the two of them were made for each other.

'Yoga will give you confidence,' Estelle continued, pulling out of the drive. 'Or at least help keep you calm under stress. Isaac's big into pranayama.'

'Prana...?'

'The breathing bit.'

Sophia's mind flashed her an image of Marcus panting in bed above her, his wine-soaked breath filling her lungs.

'He's not creepy or anything, is he?'

Estelle's eyes snapped from the road to glance at her. 'Isaac?

Fuck, no. He's one of the nicest guys I've ever met. He's painfully professional, and as far as I know, no-one's been able to get him into bed. And believe you me, I've tried.'

'I just.... I don't feel great around people I don't know, especially men.'

Estelle leaned across the console and squeezed Sophia's knee. 'I promise it'll be fine.'

Sophia had told Estelle about the break-up with Marcus, just not the gory details.

'Is it really bad having to work with your ex?'

Sophia shrugged. 'I try to keep things professional, but he's either trying to get me back or flaunting his latest... But I've got the dig to plan, so I'm focusing on that.'

'When do you start?'

'We're doing surveys this month, and fingers crossed we can break ground in April once it's warmed up a bit.'

'You excited?'

'Yes. It's something I've been working towards my entire career.'

'Well, I hope you find her.'

Estelle pulled the Defender to a stop outside a prefabricated building with a corrugated metal roof. A sign reading 'Foxbrooke Scout Hut' was above the door.

'It's not exactly a temple at the foothills of the Himalayas,' Estelle said. 'But it's the best option until the church hall gets a refurb.'

Getting out of the car, Estelle led the way. 'I've brought you early so you can do the paperwork and get settled. Isaac's got all the equipment you need, so don't worry about any of that.'

Inside were men's and women's toilets on one side of a corridor, and a kitchen on the other. In front of them was a set of double doors. Sophia followed Estelle into a large, open space.

Facing away, and pushing an industrial-sized flat mop across the floor, was a tall, tanned, and muscled man dressed in blue shorts and a white vest top.

So this is Isaac Hayward.

He had the body of a gymnast, with lean, defined muscles, and a mop of curly dark brown hair. Sophia hadn't seen the front of him, but the back was enough to make her heart beat faster.

'Isaac!' Estelle called out. 'I've brought Sophia, the one I emailed you about.'

Isaac turned, his smile finding Estelle, then moving to Sophia.

The moment his green eyes locked on hers, the world seemed to stutter, as if fumbling for words. Isaac had the timeless beauty and physical perfection of a Greek statue, but the warmth and heat of a man who was very much alive.

He stared at her as if confused, his tanned cheeks darkening.

Sophia shrank back.

'I know you got my email,' Estelle continued. 'You replied to it and said to come fifteen minutes early.'

Isaac blinked. 'Yes, sorry. Hi, Sophia. I'm Isaac. Estelle, can you show her where the forms are? I need to finish cleaning the floor.'

He turned away.

Estelle frowned, then quickly replaced it with a smile. 'He's got them in a folder on the table over there next to the cash box.'

Sophia followed her to the back of the room. Estelle's description of how hot Isaac was had been spot on. He looked like the kind of rock star or actor usually found on the cover of a magazine pulling an orgasm face.

'I did warn you,' Estelle whispered as she took a new student form from a folder.

Sophia nodded and pressed the backs of her hands against her flaming cheeks.

'Do you want me to grab you a mat and we can hide at the back?'

'Yes, please.'

'Okay. I'll sort that and you fill this in. Don't forget the bit about your favourite sexual position.'

'What?'

Estelle snorted. 'I added mine to the bottom of the form when I filled it out.'

'Oh, my god! You didn't!'

She winked at Sophia. 'You want to be more like me? Do that. Go on, I dare you.'

'No way!'

'You're no fun.'

'I know.'

Estelle's face fell. 'I didn't mean it like that. Sorry.'

'Don't be. I don't think I'll be much fun for quite a while.'

Estelle gave her a squeeze. 'As my sweet friend, Eveline, would say, "You're perfect just the way you are". And she should know. She's got a direct line to God.'

Sophia managed a smile. 'She came to the house to see how Mum was doing after Dad… She's really lovely.'

'That she is. I only have nice friends, and now you're one of them, whether you like it or not. Now fill that in and I'll get us set up.'

After putting in her contact details and answering the health questionnaire, Sophia sat on a yoga mat next to Estelle as people arrived. The other students were mainly women and were of all ages. Even though many were young and dressed in tight Lycra, there were plenty in their fifties and sixties, and one or two did indeed seem to be wearing pyjamas.

Sophia watched Isaac interacting with each person as they came in. He was friendly and clearly well-liked.

'He seems really nice,' she whispered to Estelle. 'Does he have any faults?'

'Yes, one massive one.'

He does? 'What?'

'He won't shag me.'

Someone cleared their throat loudly next to them, and Sophia stifled a giggle.

'Okay, everyone,' Isaac said, sitting cross-legged on a mat at the front of the room. 'Let's start in easy pose. Make sure you're sitting on at least one block. Crossing the legs at the mid-calf point, extend the heels away. Now lift the flesh of the buttocks out and apart so you're on your sit-bones.'

Sophia followed his directions.

'Closing the eyes, bring your awareness to the lower abdomen...'

Sophia's eyes didn't want to close. Everything was new and her subconscious didn't trust a roomful of strangers.

'Bringing the hands into prayer position, let's begin with three oms and the opening chant.'

Isaac took in a deep breath, his chest expanding, then sang a deep om that resounded through the wooden floor. Everyone else apart from Sophia joined in.

After the oms, he began a chant in Sanskrit that those around her seemed to know off by heart. It was a beautiful sound, but anxiety was shifting around inside her stomach. Was this what yoga was all about?

Isaac's eyes flicked open and found hers. As he sang, he smiled as if to reassure her and she smiled back. She knew she should make more of an effort to close her eyes, but he was so gorgeous her eyelids refused to shut. The chant continued, filling the air around them, and everything else about the room slipped away. There was just her and him.

Something shifted in his expression, and heat pulsed between her thighs. She was suddenly aware of what Estelle had meant by a 'lady boner'. Sophia hadn't felt this level of sexual desire before. Ever.

As the chant finished, Isaac's gaze moved away, and he dropped his hands into his lap.

'I wanted to begin by speaking a little about the Yamas and Niyamas, the first two limbs of Raja yoga, so we can start to think about how we might use them in our practice. But before I do that, let's change the cross of our legs.'

Sophia followed his lead.

'Yamas and Niyamas can be thought of as precepts, or ways to live in yoga, and the first of the Yamas is ahimsa, the principle of non-violence. So, when you're in a pose, be gentle with yourself. Yoga is a path of internal discovery, not an exercise system to endure. If you need to come out of a posture before anyone else, then please do so.'

A wave of relief flooded through Sophia.

'The second Yama is satya, which translates as truthfulness. So, whilst you should respect the principle of ahimsa in your body, also employ satya. Ask yourself if you're being truthful to the pose, or simply going through the motions. Then take what you learn about your own inner truth out of the class and into your life.'

Despite the grief at the end of her relationship with Marcus, Sophia knew she'd been true to herself by leaving him. She was lucky to have grown up with parents who loved and respected each other, and she knew in her guts she could never take Marcus back after his betrayal, no matter how much she'd loved him.

'The third Yama is brahmacharya, which is traditionally thought of as the sublimation of sexual energy, or chastity.'

Sophia was suddenly far too hot. Isaac seemed to be the embodiment of sexual energy. The women in front of her sat up straighter as they listened.

'Sometimes brahmacharya can mean sexual abstinence. In my case, I took a vow of chastity twelve years ago—'

'Fucking *knew* it,' Estelle hissed under her breath.

'But if you think of it as the "right use of energy", then you can use the concept to think about where you put your focus and attention. In yoga, we direct our energy from external satisfaction, to instead finding peace and contentment within ourselves.'

Wow. This god of a man hadn't had sex for over a decade? Whereas Marcus had been whoring it up with whoever he could get his hands on.

'So, in today's class, think about how you can bring ahimsa, satya, and brahmacharya into your practice. Okay, let's start with parvatasana. Interlock your fingers, press the palms away and inhale, bringing your arms above your head.'

Isaac demonstrated every posture, pointing at his various muscles to explain each pose, and Sophia copied him, her mind reeling. She tried to keep her thoughts academic, however she'd never been invited or encouraged to stare at a man so intently before, and there was a party going on in her pants.

As Isaac did a perfect headstand, the bottom of his vest top came untucked from his shorts, falling down to reveal a six-pack dusted with dark brown hair.

Oh. My. God.

Estelle leaned over. 'See what I mean?' she murmured.

Sophia nodded. Isaac Hayward was off-the-scale hot. 'But I can't do a headstand,' she whispered.

'It's okay, he'll help you.'

Isaac lowered his legs to the floor as if they defied gravity. 'Okay everyone, come up into headstand. Remember to use any props you need, as well as the wall. Sophia, we're going to look at the foundations of the pose.'

Estelle winked at her as Isaac brought his mat over and showed Sophia how to position her arms and head.

'Now, you have a go.'

Feeling awkward and ungainly, she tucked her t-shirt into her joggers, then put her head on the mat with her hands interlocked behind it.

'That's great. Lift your shoulders away from your ears, putting weight through your forearms. Now tuck your toes under and walk your feet closer in.'

Upside down, blood rushed to her head. Everything felt too heavy.

'Do you want me to kick up?'

'No, not this time. Just get used to the feeling.'

Of what? You standing next to me?

Lowering to the floor, she rested, her pulse pounding as Isaac returned to the front of the room.

'Why didn't he give you a hand?' Estelle whispered as she came back to Sophia's side.

'Huh?'

'He always asks first, but he usually helps people get up into headstand if they've never done it before.'

Oh.

'You've done brilliantly, by the way,' Estelle continued, 'and your reward is almost here.'

'Reward?'

'Yoga bedtime stories and sleep.'

Isaac cleared his throat. 'So, moving onto sarvangasana, also known as shoulder stand...'

After a few more postures, Sophia lay on her mat and Isaac

talked them through a breathing exercise. No matter how hard she tried, she still couldn't close her eyes and her heart raced. Emotion squeezed her throat, and she blinked back tears.

You cannot cry!

Estelle reached across and took her hand, giving it a squeeze. The connection helped calm Sophia, and her eyelids finally closed.

'Bringing your awareness now to your right-hand thumb, index finger, middle finger...'

Isaac's voice was deep and soothing as he named different parts of the body to focus on.

Sophia lost herself in his words, her mind letting go of all the stress of Marcus, her job, her family. The doctor's advice had been spot on. Yoga was the right thing for her to be doing.

'Sophia?'

The voice was Estelle's, but it sounded very far away.

'Sophia?'

Her eyes snapped open.

Estelle was smiling down at her. 'Wakey-wakey, Princess.'

'What?' Sophia scrambled to a seated position. The hall was empty apart from the two of them and Isaac, who was putting props into a cupboard.

'Was I asleep? Oh no, please don't tell me I snored?'

'You were as quiet as a baby.'

'I didn't think babies were that quiet.'

Estelle grinned. 'Most people nod off at the end, but you were out for the count. Let's get you home.'

Sophia got to her feet, her limbs tired and uncooperative.

'Thanks, Isaac,' Estelle called over.

He turned and gave them a wave. 'Thank you both for coming.'

Estelle hesitated, as if expecting him to come over, then turned for the door, Sophia following.

'Holy shit!' Estelle cried as soon as they got back in the car. 'Celibate? Well, that helps explain why my seduction of him was such an abject failure. Anyway, how did you find it? Relaxing?'

'Yes. I mean, I don't know what I'm doing, but I can see the benefits, and it's much better in person than watching a video.'

'Well, he runs classes most days, so whenever you're here, you can go.'

Sophia nodded. She knew Isaac would never be interested in her, but knowing he'd taken a vow of chastity made her feel safe around him, and right now, that was what she desperately needed.

❧ 3 ❧

'Come in, come in!' Eveline, Foxbrooke's vicar, said as she opened the back door of the rectory. 'You've arrived at the perfect time!'

The smell of baking and spices filled Isaac's nostrils. 'It smells like Christmas.'

'It's mainly ginger. Let's go into the kitchen.'

He followed Eveline through the ground floor. 'Where's Jack?'

'Shopping, AA meeting, then he's going to pop into Foxbrooke Haven to see Robert and Shirley.'

Entering the kitchen, Eveline flicked on the kettle. 'Take a seat and tell me how the yoga classes are going over there. I keep forgetting to ask.'

Isaac sat at a round wooden table. 'Really great. I'm doing two a week now at Foxbrooke Haven and one is entirely chair-based for those with limited balance and mobility.'

'And are the ladies behaving?'

He rubbed his stubble to hide his smile, then chuckled when Eveline gave him a look.

'Doris pinched my bum last week.'

'Oh no... I'm so sorry. I'll have a word.'

'No need. She's eighty-five, and it made everyone laugh like hyenas.'

'But it's sexual harassment.'

'Hardly. She did it when I was looking, and to be honest, her hands are so arthritic, I didn't exactly feel anything.'

'They are so naughty sometimes.'

'I know. That's why I like them so much.'

Eveline grinned. 'Me, too.' She made two mugs of tea and brought them to the table, along with a plate of biscuits. 'Tuck in. They're ginger snaps.'

'For the morning sickness?'

She nodded and pulled a face. 'It's not that bad. It's the tiredness that's the worst.'

'Does anyone else know you're pregnant?'

'Only Jack, you and Estelle. I'm not even going to tell my mum until I'm into the second trimester. I don't want to jinx it.'

Isaac took a sheaf of papers from his bag. 'I've been going back over my notes for pregnancy yoga and written a few sequences down. But only do them if you feel up to it.'

'Thank you, that's so kind.'

'There are a few pregnancy classes in and around Bath you can try when you're past the twelve-week mark.'

'I will.' She stifled a yawn. 'I'm looking forward to feeling a little more myself again.'

'Are you sure you're alright with me here? Wouldn't you rather rest?'

Reaching across the table, Eveline squeezed his hand. 'I'd much rather spend some time with you. It feels like ages since we've had a proper catch-up.'

'Well, you have been a little busy...'

She laughed, her face glowing. 'Yes, I have. A whirlwind romance, a brush with death, an unexpected marriage, Christmas, then getting pregnant. It *has* been an eventful few months.'

Isaac's heart was full. Eveline was his closest friend and the sister he'd never had. He was so happy she'd found her happy-ever-after with Jack.

'So, enough about me,' she said. 'I want to know what's going on in *your* life.'

He paused. On the surface, things were almost the same as they'd been for years. However, on a deeper level, they weren't. Eveline knew him better than anyone, and he valued the fact he could always be upfront and honest with her.

'There have been a few changes.'

'Go on...'

'Last night I told the class about my celibacy.'

Eveline's eyes widened.

'It felt like the right thing to do.'

'Oh dear, has Estelle been pursuing you again?'

'No, she seems to have backed off.'

'Ah. Did anyone else prompt this declaration?'

Thinking of Sophia, Isaac's heart thumped faster in his chest. He'd been around beautiful women all his life and was used to students showing an interest. In the past, it had been easy to say no. But last night, his body had had an immediate and visceral reaction to the woman Estelle had brought with her.

He cleared his throat. 'What was it like? The moment you met Jack?'

Eveline's face lit up. 'It was like I already knew him on a soul level, as if we'd known each other in another life. It was more of a *connection* at first sight, rather than love, although I was so attracted to him I nearly fainted.'

Isaac nodded. Meeting Sophia had also made him light-headed, but mainly because all the blood supplying his brain had decided to head south.

'Have you met someone?'

Isaac shifted in his chair, his skin prickling. 'Estelle brought a friend with her last night.'

'Sophia?'

'You know her?'

'Yes. She's absolutely lovely. Did... Did she *flirt* with you?'

'No, not in the slightest.'

'So... If she didn't appear attracted to you...?'

He passed a hand over his face. 'The moment I saw her, my body reacted.'

'Has this ever happened before?'

'Never. I flicked that switch off years ago.'

'And now Sophia's turned it back on?'

Had she? 'I don't think so...' He let out a heavy breath. 'I don't know.'

'Did you tell your students you were celibate so she wouldn't think to make a move?'

He shook his head. 'I'm not that vain. I think I said it more to remind myself of the path I've chosen.'

'The path isn't always easy.'

'No. And recently I've been feeling... I don't know... Distracted? Even lost, maybe?'

She squeezed his hand again. 'You need more friends in your life.'

'I'm going back to India this summer to spend time with my guru.'

'That's not what I'm talking about.'

'I meet people all the time in my classes. And I've got you.'

'Isaac, you know I love you very deeply...'

He sat back in his chair, preparing for one of Eveline's truth bombs. 'Go on. Tell me what I don't want to hear.'

She passed him another biscuit. 'When I visit Taizé, I'm surrounded by Christians of all denominations. I feel connected, uplifted, and surrounded by divine love. But when I come home, I'm challenged at every turn. People attack me for wanting to remove the pews from the church, or because I'm a vicar, or a female vicar, or there's a dispute between parishioners they expect me to sort out. When you're detached from everyday life, it's easy to hold on to your truth, but when you're living in the middle of it, it's far more challenging.'

'So, you think I'm taking the easy way out?'

'I think you're playing safe with your life.'

'And Sophia is what? Some kind of test?'

'She might be a gift? Sometimes the people and situations that seem the hardest to deal with can enrich us beyond all imagining. They give us a different perspective. A deeper insight and understanding.'

'I don't want a girlfriend.'

'And you don't have to have one. But Sophia isn't Daniella. And you're not the man you were, thirteen years ago.'

Isaac rubbed the centre of his chest as an old ache resurfaced.

'Sophia's going through a lot right now. And I know she's not looking for a relationship. Maybe a friendship with her is what you need?'

He nodded, but he wasn't convinced. Life was easier and safer for everyone if he stayed in his lane. But even that was now under threat. Taking a letter from his bag, he handed it to Eveline.

'This arrived last week.'

She scanned the contents. 'Oh, my goodness! Can they do that?'

'Yes. My land is in the middle of the proposed bypass around Foxbrooke. So, if it goes ahead, my home will be under a compulsory purchase order.'

'Can you challenge it?'

He nodded. 'But there's no guarantee I'll win.'

'I'm so sorry. Have you taken any legal advice?'

'Not yet. It's still sinking in, to be honest.'

'And after all the work you've put into your house. Oh, Isaac.'

'It's not a done deal, and I don't want you to worry. I think this is partly why I've been so unsettled.'

'Maybe. Well, if there is anything I can do, please just ask.'

'I will.'

'And even though it won't solve any of your problems, I do have something for you that I know will put a smile on your face.'

'Sausages?'

She grinned. 'And a packet of home-cured bacon.'

LEAVING THE RECTORY, HIS BAG HEAVY WITH SAUSAGES AND bacon from Eveline's pigs, Isaac made his way through Foxbrooke village. It was a crisp and clear February day and normally he would have treated the walk home as an exercise in mindfulness, noting everything his senses took in as he moved through the ever-unfolding present.

But today he wasn't grounded in the here and now. He was living in an uncertain future. He knew he was playing safe with his life. After his world broke apart in his twenties, he'd set out to smash every piece of who he was to dust, and create something better and more sustainable. Yes, that involved a simpler life, but what was wrong with that? Why should shallow connections and conspicuous consumerism be the cornerstone of one's life?

Eveline isn't like that. And she's married and starting a family. In the heart of the community.

He shook the thoughts away. Eveline also didn't have the capacity for uncontrollable rage that he had. Him being romantically unattached was better for everyone.

But I can't get Sophia out of my head.

Turning off a minor road at the very edge of the village onto a track, he checked the mailbox by the locked five-bar gate marking the entrance to his property. Large signs were stuck to it reading 'Private Property', 'Keep Out', 'No Right of Access'.

Apart from Eveline, no-one knew where he lived and he'd been happy to keep things that way. His home was his sanctuary and the last thing he wanted was to have his privacy invaded in the way that Eveline's constantly was.

He stared at the signs, printed in angry red letters as if seeing them for the first time.

That's pretty aggressive for a yoga teacher.

His phone rang. *Benjamin.* The eldest of his three older brothers.

'Hi Ben, thanks for ringing me back.'

'No worries. I've got a few minutes between meetings. Just getting a bit of air.'

Isaac listened to his brother's breathing change as he sucked on a cigarette, and the traffic noise in the background. Taking in the silent trees around him, gratitude filled his heart at how different his life was from when he'd lived in London.

'How are you? Rachel? The kids?'

'All good, all good. Quieter now the last little bugger's at boarding school.'

Isaac winced. Ben's youngest, Edwin, was seven. 'You must miss them.'

'Yeah, of course. But with our long hours, it's the best place for them. And we're quids in now we've been able to ditch the nanny. The money we're saving pays his fees with enough left over for us to go to Verbier in half term.'

Isaac didn't know what to say in response, but luckily his brother was used to filling silences.

'Anyway, I've had a squizz at that letter you sent over. Not my area of expertise, I'm afraid, but I'm going to ask one of the guys at my club. Best thing you can do is contact anyone else affected by the plans and coordinate your response. But there's no guarantee you'll fight it off.'

'Okay, thanks.'

'Look, gotta run, but you might want to think about finding somewhere else to live. Or cut your losses and come back to London. Plenty of yummy mummies here to keep you busy. I'll ping you if I've got anything else.'

The line went dead.

Isaac stood in the clearing outside his house. Set in two acres of woodland, it had been derelict when he'd bought it at auction a decade ago. Razing it to the ground, he'd rebuilt a different home from scratch, living in a static caravan whilst he did the work. It had taken the best part of eight years, but now he had an off-grid sanctuary.

Covering a footprint twice the size of the original property, the building was single-storey and super insulated. Built primarily from wood, it had a green roof and blended into its surroundings. The biggest extravagance had been the windows. Almost an entire side of the building was glass, and when the enormous triple-glazed panels were open, the main living area continued outside onto a covered deck. No matter what the weather, Isaac could practise yoga or meditate surrounded by nature.

Putting the sausages and bacon in the fridge, he went outside to split logs for the burner. The rhythmic movement of the axe was meditation as well as exercise.

His body was filled with a restless energy that only physical labour could touch. He'd thought his life was perfect, but his happy-ever-after wasn't giving him the same peace and contentment as it had done in the past.

Take longer off over summer. Spend time with Guruji. He'll get your head straight even if you can't.

$$ \maltese \; 4 \; \maltese $$

APRIL

‘Nadia, could you mark out this section of the dig, please?’

Sophia handed the student a map of the site with the areas for excavation marked on it. Finally, after three months of site surveys, they were about to break ground.

Marcus had supported the project, but she didn't know whether it was out of guilt or in the hope she'd take him back. The field was busy with university students and volunteers, but Marcus hadn't shown up and Sophia was glad.

The last few months had been hell. Her brother was still in China trying to get their dad home, and when she wasn't supporting her mother, Sophia was negotiating a department where she had to be civil to her ex and his new girlfriends on a daily basis. The only respite came from surveying the dig site and the yoga classes she'd started attending.

Spotting Maggie arriving, she went over and gave her a hug. ‘I'm so glad you're here. Thank you for coming.’

'Wouldn't miss it for the world. Is Britain's biggest arsehole here?'

'Not yet. And remember. I'm in charge and I want you here. We should get going in the next hour and I want you leading the team when we've got a spoil heap.'

Maggie glanced at Nadia, marking out a rectangular strip on the side of a small hillock. 'Why are you starting there?'

Sophia followed her gaze. 'We're not. I've got no idea what she's doing. Sorry, Maggie. Let me sort this out.'

Striding back across the field, Sophia's heart thumped louder. Yoga was helping her anxiety attacks, but she'd been breathless far too many times to count. The doctor said it was stress-related, but that didn't help the panic she felt when she became light-headed and struggled to breathe.

'Nadia! That's the wrong area.'

The young woman looked up, her cheeks colouring. 'I... I was told to do this bit instead.'

'By whom?'

Nadia glanced towards Darcie, who was posing whilst Kiera took a photo of her.

Sophia gritted her teeth. 'Well, I'm the one running this dig and I'm telling you to mark out the first trench over there.'

Nadia didn't move.

Panic tightened Sophia's throat, and she opened her mouth to breathe quicker. Day one, and she was already being contradicted by her own students.

'Stay there,' she said, then marched up to Darcie and Kiera. 'Why did you tell Nadia to dig in the wrong place?'

Darcie shrugged. 'Marcus said you've interpreted the data wrong, so he's changing the location of the trenches.'

'But... This is what was agreed in the excavation brief! He can't do this! It's *my* dig!'

Darcie gave her a sympathetic smile. 'It's the *department's* dig.'

Turning her back, hands trembling, Sophia pulled out her phone and rang Marcus.

'How's it going?' he drawled when the call connected.

'You can't change my plan. I've spent months surveying the site, going over the data and submitting the grant proposal. I—'

'You're wrong, and I'm not wasting public money proving it. *I'm* the Head of Department and I'm changing the dig locations and research objectives. I can't believe you didn't want to excavate the barrow. That's a schoolgirl error I can't overlook.'

'It's *not* a barrow, Marcus! Richard told me it's a pile of rubble from when he levelled the ground in the next field to build a barn. Have you lost your mind?'

'Don't take that tone with me. Do you want to be a laughingstock? I'm doing you a favour here.'

Sophia bit the inside of her cheek to stop her tears from flowing.

'Honestly, Soph? It would be nice if you could show some gratitude. I'm the one giving you the opportunity to pursue a passion project and helping you save face. You need to back-off and respect my experience. You can remain on site to oversee the excavation, or hand it over to Darcie—'

'Are you insane?' Sophia choked out. 'She's a first-year student, for goodness sake!'

'And also capable of following directions. Look, I've spent my precious time going over the raw data and your conclusions are wrong. Dig where I say, or hand the job over.'

Sophia cut the call, lights flashing in her vision.

Get a hold of yourself! Don't fall apart!

A warm hand took hers and walked her to the edge of the field. 'Don't talk, just breathe,' Maggie said.

Sophia stared numbly at her wellies as she stumbled over the ground. When they were a distance from the group, Maggie handed her a hip flask.

'Brandy. Drink as much as you can.'

Sophia took a sip, then coughed as it burnt its way to her stomach.

'Have some more and listen to me. You will not allow that pitiful excuse for a human and his barely legal fuck-buddies to get to you.'

'He's changing the dig sites.'

'Of course he is. Honestly, that man needs a team of people to find his own dick. But we still could get lucky. You've come this far. Don't walk away.'

'I'm really struggling to hold it together, Maggie.'

'I know, love, but I'm here for you, as are the rest of the volunteers. We've got your back. Now have some more brandy, take a deep breath and go do your job, okay?'

Sophia nodded. 'Thank you. I will.'

May

Sitting on the edge of a trench, Sophia stared into space, the evening sun warming her skin. Nearly a month had passed and all they'd uncovered was an old wall, some broken crockery, and a few more Iceni coins. She'd sent everyone home an hour before, but couldn't find the energy to move. This was meant to be the highlight of her career, but it was a big fat failure.

Gazing across the field, she thought of the places she'd wanted to dig, but that Marcus had vetoed. The fact that his supposed 'burial mound' had indeed turned out to be a pile of rubble didn't fill her with any satisfaction. Instead of admitting he was wrong, Marcus had doubled down, claiming that the landowner had disturbed the site, and insisting they continue excavating nearby.

Had opium overuse addled his brain? Or was he too preoccupied with keeping two girlfriends happy to do a proper job as an archaeologist?

Sophia rubbed her face. *What does it matter? He's pulling the plug and there's nothing I can do about it.*

Getting to her feet, she gathered her tools, ready to head back to Maggie's, her eyes still drawn to the land that lay untouched. The one place she'd always wanted to excavate was at the edge of the escarpment, but the site was tricky to access. However, the spot where she'd planned to put in a trench on the very first day of the dig was on level ground.

Her hand tightened around the handle of her spade. *Could I?*

Without allowing a second thought to usurp the first, she strode over, her tummy prickling with excitement and nerves. Double checking the site surveys, she marked a small section and removed the turf. She may have been going over Marcus's head, but she was still going to do this properly, even if it was just a test pit.

With only two and a half hours of light left, Sophia moved quickly but carefully, inspecting the ground each time she lifted out more soil, and using her trowel as she went deeper.

Was there something there?

The sun was now low in the sky, creating deep shadows in the hole, so she crouched down, her body blocking the light, and blinked at the soil.

Yes!

The earth here was a slightly different texture and colour,

indicating human involvement at some point in the past. Her breath quickening, she used the point of her trowel to remove a thin layer of dirt.

Oh, my god.

It was the cross guard and blade of a sword, stained reddy-brown with rust. Heart thumping, Sophia grabbed her smallest tool and excavated around the edge of the metal.

There was more.

Holding her breath, she carefully moved the soil away, shrieking with shock and excitement when she found human bone and a gold coin glinting in the darkness of the pit.

Had she found her? What now?

Do the right thing.

She rang Marcus.

He didn't pick up, so she sent a text.

Sophia: I've found a grave. Please ring me

Her phone rang almost immediately.

'Marcus! I—'

'What are you talking about? You there now?'

'Yes, I decided to put another trench in, and—'

'What? You did *what*? When?'

She cringed at the anger in his voice. 'An hour or so ago. I'm the only one here—'

'What have you found?'

'A sword, human remains and a coin so far. I—'

'Don't move and don't touch anything else. I'm on my way.'

He cut the call.

Sophia took a quick breath, then another.

Calm down. It's okay.

Sitting on the cold ground, she dropped her head.

Remember what Isaac said. Try to breathe through your nose.

Usually, it was her brother's voice that came to mind when she was experiencing anxiety, but now it was Isaac's.

You've done nothing wrong. This is your dig.

But no matter how she tried to convince herself everything would be fine, butterflies with razor-sharp wings flapped inside her, cutting the inside of her chest until she was drowning in a sea of adrenaline.

Come on!

She rang Maggie.

'You still staying at mine tonight? Are you on your way?'

'I've done something bad and Marcus is going to kill me.'

'What's going on?'

Sophia told her.

Maggie blew out a breath. 'Good for you, Soph. You trusted your instinct. He can't stay mad when you've discovered something this incredible. Want me to come down?'

'I'd love that, but you know how he can be with you...'

'Yeah, you're right. No point in poking the rat.'

Sophia giggled. 'Don't you mean "bear"?'

'Nope. Now take photos before he starts clomping about in his size sevens, banging on about the bloody Roman Empire.'

'Maggie, you are naughty, but that's good advice. I'll ring you when I'm on my way to yours.'

Over the next hour, Sophia documented everything she'd unearthed, but left it in situ. A discovery like this happened maybe once a lifetime and changed the entire focus of the dig. She couldn't wait for the team to get back onsite the next day so they could see what else was buried there.

The sun was heading for the horizon when Marcus arrived,

stomping across the field, his black coat flapping behind him like broken wings.

He didn't even bother greeting Sophia, going straight to the test pit and dropping to a crouch.

Her pulse rocketed as his body froze. Then he stood and faced her, his eyes bright.

'This is big, Soph.'

She nodded.

Taking out his phone, he fiddled with it, then passed it to her. 'We need to record this.'

Sophia held it up and pressed the button. 'I'm filming.'

Marcus stood straighter, his expression earnest. 'I'm Professor Marcus Thwaites, head of the archaeology department at Salisbury University, and I've just made the archaeological find of the decade.'

The phone jolted in Sophia's hand. 'What do you mean "I've"?' she asked, anxiety rising.

'Hold the phone still.'

She stopped filming. 'Marcus. This is *my* proposal, *my* dig, *my* find!'

His expression hardened. 'There's no "I" in "team", Sophia. The University of Salisbury is paying for this excavation *and* your salary. It's a group effort. Stop being so childish and selfish. If it hadn't been for me, you wouldn't be standing here now. Would you?'

Her throat was too tight to reply.

'Now start filming again, or I'm taking the entire dig off your hands.'

She lifted the phone and pressed record.

'That's my girl.' Marcus tilted his head and raised his hands as he looked down the lens, as if he was a politician auditioning for a role as a TV presenter. 'Picture the scene. Ancient Britain nearly two thousand years ago...'

Sophia zoned out as he continued talking. She knew how much Marcus wanted to be on television. He'd pitched archaeology show ideas to TV networks with him as the star over the last few years, but nothing had ever come of it.

Focus on what's important. You've found something. That's all that matters.

❧ 5 ❧

JUNE

'Sophia?'

The voice was comforting, but very far away. She was stuck in treacly fog, trying to find her way out.

'Sophia?'

Her eyes snapped open, and she pushed up to sit, glancing around the Scout hut. Everyone else in the class had gone, and Isaac was sitting on the floor a few feet away.

'I fell asleep again.'

He smiled. 'You must have needed it.'

'I'm so sorry. I can't believe I keep doing this. Usually Estelle wakes me up, but...'

'She's too busy organising the festival.'

Sophia nodded. 'I'm so embarrassed.'

'Don't be. It's all good.'

'Your voice just seems to send me to sleep.' She clapped a hand to her mouth. 'Oh my god, I didn't mean it like that.'

Isaac laughed. 'I've spent years perfecting a delivery this boring—'

'You're not boring.'

'When you teach yoga nidra, it's important to keep the pitch, volume, and speed of your voice level and even, so students can focus on the words and not be distracted by how you say them.'

'I feel very safe with you. I think that's also why I keep dropping off.'

Something flickered in his expression, but she couldn't work out what he was thinking.

'How's your father doing?'

She blinked as her eyes suddenly pricked with tears. 'Good. It's such a relief that he's home, and Mum's overjoyed to have him and James back. Dad seems a bit slower, and he's lost weight, but she's fattening him up.'

'And the dig?'

Sophia hesitated. 'We're finishing up the documentation and preparing the finds for a special exhibition at the Salisbury Museum as they're affiliated with the University. The osteologist says there's an eighty per cent chance the skeleton is male, and radio-carbon dating shows he's from the early first century AD. It's likely he's Iceni from the coinage and other artefacts we found.'

'That's exciting.'

She nodded, although she didn't feel that excited. After her discovery, Marcus had been more hands-on, taking over the excavation of her trench. On paper, she was still in charge, but in actuality, she felt like one of his minions.

'Sophia...'

Her pulse quickened as she stared into Isaac's emerald-green eyes. 'Yes?'

'I know we've spoken about your breathing before, but

we've never had a chance to go into it in detail during the class. I'm concerned you're chronically hyperventilating. If you can find the time, I'd like to offer you a free one-to-one so we can explore some different techniques and strategies to help.'

'You don't need to do that.'

'I want to.'

'I'm fine, honestly.'

He smiled. 'Okay, but the offer's there, so text me if you change your mind.'

Sophia nodded and rolled up her yoga mat, a present from Estelle. 'Thank you. I'd better go. Sorry again for falling asleep.'

Isaac held up his hands. 'Honestly, no problem at all. I really don't mind if you need to sleep through the whole class.'

What?

He chuckled. 'It's happened before. Often this is the only time in the week women get to themselves and know they can relax without interruption or listening out for a child. If sleep is what you need from my class, then that's more important than any posture.'

'Wow. Is that why so many people come here in their pyjamas?'

Isaac let out a belly laugh, and Sophia's tummy turned over. He was ridiculously good-looking at the best of times, but right now...?

Don't let your silly crush turn into full-blown infatuation.

'I hadn't thought of that.'

She nodded and tucked a strand of hair behind her ear, focusing on her mat.

'Have a great weekend, Sophia. Will we see you next week?'

'Thanks, you too. And yes, I'll be there.'

· · ·

Smoothing her hands over her skirt, Sophia entered the university archaeology department. Today was a meeting with the curators of the museum to discuss the exhibition and she wanted to make a good impression.

Inside the largest classroom, lying on a table, were the principal finds from the dig. Sophia's gaze went from the sword, pottery, a horse bridle bit and coins, to the room of people.

As well as Marcus, Darcie, Kiera, and other students who'd stayed on after the end of term, the admin team for the department were there, staff from the museum, faces she didn't recognise, and—journalists? A man stood to one side with a camera over his shoulder and a notepad in his hand.

She took a seat at the back as Marcus clapped to get everyone's attention.

'Hello everyone, thanks so much for coming today. I've prepared some information about the discovery for you. This is an opportunity for us to plan the exhibition and make an official statement to the press.'

Sophia picked up the press release she'd helped write from the table in front of her and scanned it.

What? He's changed *it?*

Her heart sank. This could not be happening.

'For those of you who don't yet know me, I'm Professor Marcus Thwaites, head of the archaeology department at Salisbury University and a world-leading expert in Roman history. Two thousand years ago, the Romans arrived in ancient Britain to find a tribal and, some might say, *primitive* society.'

Sophia shook her head.

Marcus's eyes narrowed as he glanced at her, then his smile was back. 'We live in a culturally-rich landscape and after gold coins were found not far from here, I knew we had to explore what might be hidden beneath the soil.'

He paused, as if for dramatic effect, and spread his arms

wide. 'And my hunch paid off. In one of the most significant finds of a generation, I discovered the grave of a Roman soldier, complete with a sword from his vanquished enemy.'

Everyone clapped, and Marcus nodded, bathing in the applause.

'No,' Sophia said, her voice cracking.

A few heads swivelled in her direction.

'No.' Her head was pounding, but she didn't stop. 'It's not the grave of a Roman soldier. It's most likely the grave of an Iceni male.'

All the other people in the room blurred as she stared Marcus down.

'The pottery isn't imported Belgic, it's middle Iron Age and shell-tempered. The bridle-bit and sword are non-Roman, the coinage is almost exclusively Iceni, and the isotope analysis shows he was native to the UK, most likely from the east where the Iceni were. It makes no sense for him to be Roman. And it's *not* your discovery, it's mine.'

Marcus laughed and held up his hands in a placatory gesture. 'I apologise, ladies and gentlemen, for this distasteful interruption. Unfortunately, Miss Hunter-Savage and I were involved romantically, and she's been a little unstable since I broke off our relationship.'

'You... You...' Sophia shook, her breath coming faster and faster. Everyone was staring at her as if she were an animal hurling its own shit at the fence of their enclosure.

'Darcie, do you mind escorting Miss Hunter-Savage out? I think she needs a little help.'

Pushing to her feet, Sophia dashed from the room. She didn't stop, running along the corridor and down the stairs. She had to get out.

Reaching the street, she sat on a bench, clutching her pounding head.

It can't get any worse. It can't.

Her phone rang. It was Elyse, her father's assistant.

She picked up, using all her strength to keep her voice even. 'Hello?'

'Sophia, it's Elyse. Your dad's in the hospital.'

'Oh, my god.'

'He's adamant I shouldn't tell you, but I disagree. He's been suffering from chest pains but has been hiding it from everyone.'

Sophia pressed a hand against her heart as if to stop it from exiting her ribs. 'I'll leave now.'

Elyse told her which ward he was in, then ended the call. Standing, her limbs stiff, Sophia walked slowly towards where she'd parked her car.

A text came through.

> Elyse: Drive safe. James is about ten minutes away from the hospital and your mum is here too

Lights were flashing behind Sophia's eyes, and her fingers were tingling. She knew how important it was to control her breathing, but every time she gulped in a breath, she had a panicked urge to take another one.

She fumbled to text Isaac.

> Sophia: Hi, this is Sophia. I'm really struggling and would like to accept your offer of a breathing class if you have time?

Her phone pinged almost immediately with his reply.

> Isaac: Absolutely. Let me know when you're free over the next few days/week and I'll book the hall and get back to you

Sophia: Will do. And thank you

Isaac: No problem. Looking forward to it

Pocketing her phone, Sophia stood, wobbly on her feet.

You've got this. Just focus on getting to Dad without crashing the car. Everything's going to be okay.

A few days later

'EXCUSE ME, SORRY, EXCUSE ME...'

Sophia moved against the flow of people as they made their way down Foxbrooke high street toward the music and arts festival taking place at the manor. It was blisteringly hot and she could feel her stress levels rising along with the temperature.

She wasn't sure what she should wear for her private class with Isaac, so had worn a t-shirt with spaghetti straps and her jogging bottoms. By the time she reached the Scout hut, she was so hot she felt she might faint.

Isaac was waiting outside, a frown on his face as he stared at his phone.

'Everything okay?'

He turned with a jolt. 'Er, hi. Sorry, there's been a bit of a cock up.'

'What's happened?'

He ran a hand through his curly hair. 'They've double booked us with a rummage sale.'

'Oh.'

A wave of disappointment crashed through Sophia's chest. Was *anything* going to go right for her?

'I've been trying to find another solution, but I'm not having much luck.'

She forced a smile. 'It's okay. Another time?'

Isaac shook his head. 'No, this is important.' He ran a hand through his hair again. 'Look, we could always do it at my place? If you don't mind, that is?'

'Not at all. Should I get my car?'

'We could walk if you have time? It's about ten minutes from here, on the outskirts of the village.'

'Yes, that's fine. I don't have anything on for the rest of the day.'

He nodded, extended an arm, and they set off.

Sophia's heart beat faster. Estelle had told her that no-one apart from Eveline knew where Isaac lived. He may have been friendly in class, but it was clear he valued his privacy. What was his house like? Estelle had many theories, ranging from a tree house made from macrame, to a cave filled with incense.

'How's your dad doing? Eveline told me he was out of hospital?'

'Much better. Weaker, but still as belligerent as ever.'

Isaac smiled. 'I'm glad he's home. That must have been a huge worry for you.'

'Yes, it was.'

'And the festival seems to be going well?'

She nodded. After all the trials and tribulations, Foxbrooke's first music and arts festival was in full swing, and Estelle and her brother seemed to be taking their business partnership to a personal level.

Even though Sophia knew her family loved her, she didn't feel as needed as she'd been when James and her father were in China. She was now facing the long summer break with no idea what she might do with her time off.

'Do you have any siblings?' she asked.

'Er, yes. Three older brothers: Benjamin, Samuel and Jacob. All living in London and married with kids. My parents are retired and live nearby.'

'Do you see them much?'

'A few times a year.'

'Are they like you?'

Isaac smiled and shook his head. 'I think it's easier to say I was once like them.'

Oh. Does he have an ex-wife? Children?

'They're all lawyers. I was one for a City firm until my mid-twenties.'

'So, no kids then?'

He shook his head.

'What made you want to be a yoga teacher?'

For a second, Isaac's posture changed, his shoulders stiffening, then he relaxed. 'I was burned out by the corporate world and took a sabbatical that turned out to be permanent. I travelled for nearly a year and ended up in India at an ashram where I met my guru.'

'Had you done yoga before?'

He shook his head. 'I was a gym rat.'

Sophia sneaked a glance at his arms. Isaac still looked like he worked out, but his muscles were lean and defined, not bulky.

'Yoga filled all the spaces in my life that were empty and gave me peace. It completely changed my life for the better.'

'How long did you stay in India for?'

'Nearly two years. I pledged my life to my guru, Swami Vishnu, but he said I should return to England and spread the teaching of yoga. I found a bit of land outside Foxbrooke to live on and moved here almost a decade ago.'

'Do you still see him? Your guru?'

'Yes, I visit every summer.'

'In your last newsletter, you said you were taking August off.'

He nodded. 'It's the best month to go, as so many people are away.'

Sophia spread her fingers in a futile attempt to cool down. The Bath stone buildings and the grey pavement radiated heat around her to almost unbearable levels, even on the shady side of the street. It was like being in an oven.

'Is India as hot as this?'

'Sometimes. The headquarters of the Devanandara organisation are in the foothills of the Himalayas, but it can get pretty humid in the summer.'

Sophia wanted to know everything about Isaac but wasn't sure if he wanted an interrogation, so fell silent. Walking next to him and knowing she was about to visit his house was thrilling.

She was an inch taller than Marcus and he often made jokes about her height, or commented on how useful she was at reaching high shelves. Taking the yoga classes with Isaac had made Sophia realise how much she'd hunched her shoulders and slouched, just to fit in and make her ex feel better about himself.

Isaac, on the other hand, had at least three inches on her, and carried himself with the quiet confidence of someone who was happy in their own skin and had nothing to prove.

'What drew you to archaeology?'

She paused before replying. This year she'd almost completely lost sight of why she loved her job.

'When I was at primary school, we learnt about the stone age. The class book was *The Boy with the Bronze Axe*. Do you know it?'

He shook his head.

'It's a story based on the settlement of Skara Brae on Orkney.'

'That vaguely rings a bell. Isn't it called "the Scottish Pompei"?'

'Yes! It's five thousand years old, but was only uncovered after a storm in eighteen-fifty. In class, we made our own versions out of clay, and I just lost myself in the project. As a kid, even ten years seemed like a lifetime, but here were people thousands of years ago who looked like us, living in houses with what we would recognise as dressers, beds, fireplaces. It made me see the landscape completely differently, and I wanted to discover what else was hidden below the surface.'

'What period are you most interested in?'

'It all fascinates me, but I'm most drawn to pre-industrial civilisations. We're so used to electricity, cars, phones, and modern houses. It's easy to forget that for most of human history we haven't had anything like that. I love finding out how people took what they could find and shaped these incredibly rich and diverse cultures. And I love being in nature, feeling the earth in my hands and connecting with people across millennia.'

As Isaac smiled at her, Sophia's heart sang. She felt seen and heard in a way she hadn't done for years. Marcus used to love her enthusiasm, but as she became more knowledgeable and experienced, he would find ways to put her down, as if they were in some kind of winner-takes-all competition where he had to come first.

And he always did come first...

Sophia's happy balloon deflated at the thought of sex with Marcus. Would she ever be intimate with a man again? She hoped she would, but right now, she couldn't imagine it.

Well... She *could* imagine it, but sex with Isaac was only ever going to happen in her dreams. Not only had he taken a vow of chastity, but he was also completely and utterly out of her league.

'When's the exhibition opening in Salisbury? I'd love to visit and see what you found.'

Sophia bit the inside of her cheek as pain flared in her chest.

Isaac's expression changed, his brow furrowing. 'What's happened?'

She shrugged.

'Sophia?'

His voice was so gentle she wanted to weep.

They stopped by the side of the main road into Foxbrooke, then crossed and continued down a narrow lane lined with old hedges.

'You don't have to tell me. But I want you to see me as a friend. And I'll never betray your confidence.'

The traffic noises were receding, and the air was filled with birdsong. Sophia felt the edges of her anxiety soften. She could do with a friend. Someone who didn't know Marcus, her family, her life. Isaac had no agenda. He could just be an incredibly kind and extremely hot human worry-doll.

'I don't think you really want to hear about my drama.'

'I do. I want to know what's been making your light dim. Apart from everything to do with your dad, of course.'

Had Marcus dimmed her light? Or was she just the same old dull Sophia with her nose in a book that she'd always been?

She took a deep breath. 'When I went to uni, I fell in love with my professor. We've been living together for the past ten years and are now colleagues. Only in January, I found him with...' Her stomach turned at the memories from that night.

'Another woman?'

She glanced at him. '*Women...*'

The look of shock on Isaac's face was almost comical.

'I didn't know at the time, but he's been cheating on me for years. Now he's in a relationship with two first-year students. I know I can't judge, as I was once like them.'

'Was he in a relationship when you got together?'

'God no! I'd never have gone anywhere near him if that was the case.'

'Then you're not like the women he's with now.'

Sophia shook her head. 'I guess you're right. And I haven't smoked heroin, either.'

Isaac's eyes widened.

'My boy—*ex* boyfriend, Marcus, believes he's the reincarnation of Marcus Aurelius, who was addicted to opium. That night I came home early, they'd been burning heroin on tinfoil.' She let out a hollow laugh. 'You must think I'm stupid.'

'Why would I think that?'

'I should have known.'

Isaac was silent, his normally relaxed face tight with tension. 'No. People who are doing wrong are often incredibly good at hiding it. And if you're a good person, you wouldn't think to look for trouble where none should be found.'

Sophia was suddenly desperate for a hug, but she knew she couldn't ask that of Isaac, so she wrapped her arms around her body instead.

'What's happened with your project?'

She shook her head. 'It's not my project anymore.'

'How come?'

'When we started the dig, Marcus refused to allow me to open trenches where I believed we had the best chance of finding something. We only found the grave because I went behind his back one night and dug a new test pit.'

Isaac's face lit up. 'That's brilliant!'

A smile tugged at her mouth, then disappeared. 'Marcus

took sole credit for the find, and has decided the man is Roman.'

'And is he?'

'If he's Roman, then I'm Cleopatra.'

'You might be.'

'Huh?'

'You're both clever, powerful, and beautiful women. If your ex thinks he's the reincarnation of Marcus Aurelius, then why can't you be the reincarnation of Cleopatra?'

Sophia rolled her eyes. 'He's *not* the reincarnation of Marcus Aurelius.'

'That's true. He's only one step up from pond life, but my money's still on you being Cleopatra mark two.'

She grinned. 'And who were *you* in a former life?'

He puffed out his cheeks. 'No idea.'

'Gandhi? Shakespeare? Boudica?'

'Nah. I bet they've already broken the cycle of death and rebirth by now. If reincarnation is a thing, then I don't think I was anyone exceptional before.'

'Well you're making up for it in this life.'

'That's very kind, but I'm definitely nothing special. I'm just trying to lead a useful life.'

'And you are. Your classes have already helped me so much.'

'I'm glad.'

Isaac turned off the narrow lane onto a track lined with ancient and sprawling hedges. A few yards further on was a wooden gate with signs in shouty red capital letters reading: 'Private Property', 'Keep Out', 'No Right of Access'.

Sophia's feet faltered and she glanced at him.

Cheeks darkening, he pulled a face. 'I apologise. They were there when I bought the plot and I've never got around to taking them down.'

'Are you sure about this? We can wait for another time?'

He opened the gate. 'If you're going to work on your breathing, then I can work on my social skills.' He extended an arm. 'Please, after you.'

Stepping through, the air was cooler under the trees. In front of her, the track wound through the wood.

'Where's your house?'

'A short walk. It's pretty tucked away.'

'Estelle thinks you live in a tree.'

He burst out laughing. 'That's pretty cool, but a bit impractical. I live in a bungalow.'

Sophia thought about all the bungalows she'd ever seen and tried to imagine Isaac living in one. She couldn't.

'I lived in a cave for a bit when I was in India.'

'You did?'

'Yes. I spent a couple of months on my own in silence.'

'No way! What was that like?'

'Intense. You can't hide from yourself.'

'How did you get food?'

'It was brought for me every day and left in a box a short distance from the cave so I wouldn't have to talk to anyone.'

'Wow. I'm pretty quiet, but I can't imagine going even a day without talking to someone. Were you lonely?'

He shrugged. 'At certain points, yes. It was a rollercoaster of emotions, but at the end I felt as if I'd ordered things in my mind a bit more.'

'Did you achieve enlightenment?'

'Not in the slightest. I'm a pretty unevolved soul. It'll take me many more lifetimes before I get there.'

Sophia wasn't sure if she believed in reincarnation, but Isaac seemed the most altogether man she'd ever met. Someone who'd done the work on themselves and knew who they were. She thought she knew herself well, but she'd missed every sign with Marcus and sold herself short.

The track curved around to the right, their destination hidden behind a cluster of thick holly and yew trees. Isaac slowed as they approached the bend, as if delaying the moment when she saw where he lived.

She stopped. 'Has anyone else ever visited you before?'

He shook his head. 'Not even Eveline, and she's my closest friend.'

'Well, I won't judge and I won't tell anyone I've been here if that makes you feel any better.'

'It's only a house. I think I've been protecting my privacy more than I need to.'

'Maybe. But it's still your life, so it's your choice how you live it.'

Isaac's smile was dazzling. 'You're a very wise woman.'

Sophia scrunched up her nose. 'I don't feel like I've been very wise in my love life. Maybe I should take a leaf out of your book and join a nunnery.'

He raised an eyebrow.

'You know what I mean. I can't really see you in a nunnery.'

'I tried to join, but they told me I had too many bad habits.'

A giggle burst out. 'Was that a joke?'

'Was it second to nun?'

She shook her head. 'They're dad-level.'

He grinned. 'My nephew bought me a joke book one Christmas, so we trade jokes when we see each other.'

'What are his favourite ones?'

'Anything involving inappropriate bodily functions...'

'His parents must be thrilled.'

'I'm sure you can imagine. My brothers call me the hippy uncle. Or the fun one, if they're in a good mood.'

'You're definitely the fun one. So, you think I'm ready to see Casa Hayward? I'll keep my opinions to myself.'

He drew his shoulders back as if steeling himself, then extended an arm.

Bracing herself, Sophia strolled around the corner, then stopped dead, her mouth falling open. She'd expected a post-war prefab, but found herself staring at a house that belonged on the cover of a magazine.

'Oh, my god!'

Almost the whole of one side was glass and reflected the trees around the building. Along with the weathered timbers and the green roof, the house felt like a living, breathing part of its surroundings.

Sophia blinked to make sure the vision was real, then her gaze snapped back to Isaac. He looked relieved.

'Isaac, this is like my ultimate dream house. You actually live here?'

He nodded.

'Holy shit! I mean, just look at it!'

To the left was an open-sided building with a car parked inside and a pile of chopped wood against one wall. To the right, a short distance away and partly hidden by the trees, was a dilapidated stone building, a tree growing up from the inside where the roof once was.

'Is that yours too?'

'Yes. That's an old barn I haven't got around to renovating yet.'

'This place is unbelievable.' She glanced around. 'Are you off-grid?'

He nodded. 'I've got a septic tank for waste, a spring for water, and a small wind turbine and solar panels for electricity. It's super insulated, so doesn't need much heating, but I've also got a couple of wood burners.'

'Did you build it?'

'Mostly. Some jobs I'm not legally allowed to do, but everything else I did myself. That's why it's only single storey. It makes it easier.'

'It's...' She shook her head. 'I don't think I've ever seen anything more beautiful.'

Something changed in Isaac's expression as she held his gaze, and the ground suddenly felt a little less solid than before.

He turned away, breaking the connection. 'Do you want to go inside?'

$$\maltese \quad 6 \quad \maltese$$

'**C**an I look around *outside* a bit more?' Sophia asked. 'I feel like I've just dropped into paradise.'

Isaac nodded, the butterflies in his tummy now whirling like leaves caught by the wind. His house and land had been private for so long that having Sophia here felt like she'd wandered into his bathroom when he was having a shower.

But her delight was also a drug, and he wanted more.

'When I bought the place, there was already a house on it, but it was derelict so I knocked it down and started from scratch.'

'Did you demolish it yourself?'

He grinned. 'Yes, with a digger. I felt like a little kid.' He led her to the right of the house. 'There was a large garden at the back when I moved in, but I decided to do something different with it. Although it was also an excuse to play with heavy machinery again.'

Behind the house had been a market garden. He'd kept a small vegetable patch and beds for cut flowers, then had planted fruit and nut trees in the rest of the space and created a natural swimming pool fed by the spring.

Sophia gasped when she saw it, her hands flying to her face. 'Oh, my god!'

Isaac's cheeks hurt from smiling so much.

'I just...' She glanced at the back of the house, her gaze falling to the wood-fired sauna and hot tub. 'No freaking way!' She shrieked with laughter. 'This is too much! No wonder you don't ever have guests. They'd never leave.'

Isaac knew his house and garden were special, but seeing them through Sophia's eyes made him appreciate them even more.

'And perfect for weather like this. If I had my swimming togs, you wouldn't be able to get me out of there. Do you swim every day?'

'Most days, yes. If it's really cold, then it's combined with a sauna.'

Throwing back her head, Sophia laughed with joy.

Isaac had never seen her so happy before. In class she'd always seemed shy, unsure, and as if the weight of the world was on her shoulders. Now she seemed lighter and bubblier than champagne.

'Honestly, I wasn't joking, Isaac. You've created heaven on earth.' She gazed up at the clear blue sky. 'What's the light pollution like?'

'Not bad. It's far enough from the village that you can still see a lot of stars if it's a clear night.'

'Do you sit in the hot tub and look up at them?'

'Yes.'

His mind immediately and inconveniently supplied an image of a naked Sophia in the hot tub, her long legs entangled with his.

This is a mistake.

No, it's not. When have you seen her like this before? Doesn't she deserve to be this joyful?

But...

Eveline said Sophia needed a friend. You can do that. Be her friend.

'And you grow your own food?'

'A lot of it, yes. Although I've tried to create a permaculture forest garden. Something that can more or less look after itself.'

She shook her head. 'Honestly, this is the most beautiful place I've ever seen.'

Isaac's heart swelled with pride, then it stopped for a beat as he remembered the letter about the compulsory purchase order. If that went through, then all of this would be gone. He blinked as if his eyelids were a camera shutter and he was committing this moment to memory. Sophia was achingly lovely, and the most beautiful creature to have ever been in his garden.

He cleared his throat. 'Would you like a drink?'

'Yes, thank you. I'll have a white wine spritzer, please. Or a mimosa. Whatever you've got to hand.'

'Um—'

She burst out laughing. 'I'm joking. I'm absolutely parched and would love a glass of water.'

'Give me a moment.'

Turning, Isaac made his way into the house. He could have invited her in, but when he set out that morning, he'd never intended on Sophia coming back with him.

Casting his gaze around the open-plan living area, he tried to see it through her eyes. Luckily, he had few possessions and was naturally tidy. Would she like it? *Does it matter?*

This was the first time since he'd taken his vow of chastity that a woman had affected him in this way. He'd been slowly getting to know Sophia over the last few months and each time he'd met her, he liked her even more. He just had to divorce his mind from his body. Liking her as a friend was allowed, but his body needed to learn how to switch off the deep physical attraction.

Exiting the back door, he stopped in the shade of the house and watched her at the edge of the pool. Her shoes were off and she was paddling in the shallows. His cock twitched as he imagined her stripping off and diving in.

Briefly shutting his eyes, he took himself back to the cave in India. If that had been a test, then it was nothing compared to hanging out with Sophia and not craving her touch.

You can do this.

She noticed him and waved. 'It's colder than I expected!'

Stepping forward, he handed her the glass, making sure their fingers didn't touch.

'Once you're in, you get used to it.'

She downed the water in one. 'Thank you. That's just what I needed. And it tastes lovely.'

'It's from the spring.'

She rolled her eyes, but they were sparkling. 'Of course it is.'

'Do you want some more?'

'Actually, yes, thank you.'

He took the glass from her. This time, his fingers made contact with hers and a zap of electricity travelled up his arm.

Sophia took a sharp breath in. 'I was going to ask... Where did you want to do it?'

Huh?

Her cheeks burst into flames, and she took a step back. 'The breathing class.'

'Er, up to you? Maybe the front deck? It's sheltered from the sun but still outside.'

'Sounds great.'

He turned abruptly, the back of his neck prickling and she followed him back towards the house.

Inside, he went into the open-plan living space and pulled the glass doors to one side on their runners, opening up the front so the wooden floorboards inside merged into the decking outside.

He didn't look at Sophia, but her excitement felt like popping candy in his chest.

'Oh Isaac, this is incredible! I know I'm sounding like a stuck record, but this is beautiful. You've got such amazing taste. And the roof extends over the deck so you can still have these doors open if it rains! Ooh! Books!'

Isaac tried to stop smiling, but the effort was too much. He'd never experienced such pride and pleasure in his own home. Gathering a pile of sheepskins and pillows, he took them onto the deck as Sophia continued her monologue.

'I'm presuming you made these bookshelves? Of course you did. You can't pick up something this lovely in IKEA. Ah, the wood feels like glass. And my mother would be proud of your cleaning skills, as there isn't a speck of dust. Hang on, let me wipe away my finger marks.'

Going to the kitchen area, he refilled her glass.

Sophia sighed happily behind him. 'I could stay here forever. I mean, of course I *won't*. This is a one-off, and I promise your secret is safe with me. What happens in Frank Lloyd Wright's Hobbit house stays in Frank Lloyd Wright's Hobbit house.'

Turning, he passed the drink to her. 'I like the new name.'

'What was the original house called when you bought it?'

'Shady Acres.'

She drank the water and put the empty glass on the side. 'That sounds like the name of a West Country rapper.'

A laugh burst out. 'I love it.' He held her gaze, their smiles filling the space between them. 'I've never seen you this happy before.'

Her expression cracked, and she took a shallow breath. 'It's been a tough year.'

'There. Your breathing just changed.'

'It did?'

'Yes, you're breathing from the upper chest, not the abdomen.'

'Oh.'

The sunshine left her face and the clouds returned.

'It's alright. We can fix it. Do you want to start now?'

She nodded.

'Okay. I've set up on the deck.'

Sophia followed him out and sat opposite him. Her thick brown hair was tied in a bun, but a few loose curls hung down, grazing her shoulders. Isaac wanted to feel them between his fingers, brush kisses across her skin, hear her whimper with desire.

This is a bad idea. A very bad idea.

She was looking uncertain again, chewing on her bottom lip.

Just focus and do your job.

Placing one hand over his belly, he put the other in the centre of his chest. 'We're going to start by looking at gentle abdominal breathing, activating the diaphragm and not the rib cage.'

He risked a glance up. Sophia was staring intently at his chest.

Please don't get hard.

He cleared his throat. 'If you put your hands on your body like I am, I want you to see if you can breathe in and out through your nose, with only your tummy moving.'

She tried, but her movements were jerky and uneven.

'I'm sorry! I'm really trying.'

'You're doing great.'

Letting out a frustrated huff, she rubbed her face. 'I've been thinking recently that I should just go to an ashram for a few weeks to try and crack this breathing thing.'

'You don't need to. You've already made significant progress over the last few months.'

Her eyebrows raised, and she gazed at him sceptically. 'I was looking at the Devanandara website. They've got month-long teacher trainer courses which they say are suitable for complete beginners. I've got the entire summer off with no plans anymore, so I might give it a go. I don't want to teach yoga, but it looked like it might be a helpful thing for me to do?'

Isaac hesitated. The Teacher Trainer Course was immersive but also intensive, and he wasn't sure if it was right for someone as fragile as Sophia currently was.

'I threw myself into mine and it changed my life for the better,' he began. 'But it's not for the faint-hearted.'

Her expression tightened, as if his words were a criticism of her ability to handle it.

Shit!

He cleared his throat. 'I mean, it's pretty full-on, and er—'

'I'm used to studying,' she interrupted. 'I know it's all new, but I'm sure I could pick it all up fairly quickly.'

Isaac didn't know how to reply without continuing to put his foot in it, so he nodded.

'And I didn't realise there was an ashram in the Caribbean,' she said, her expression bright. 'On its own private island! If I was going to study yoga, then I couldn't think of anywhere nicer to do it than on a white sandy beach.'

He smiled. 'It's a beautiful place to do the course.'

'I bet it's not as lovely as here.'

'Maybe not.'

'Anyway, it was just an idea. I doubt I'll actually do it.' Taking a deep breath, she squared her shoulders. 'Let me try breathing abdominally again. Can you look at my chest and make sure it doesn't move?'

Jesus…

Isaac nodded, even though he wanted to run in the opposite direction. Sophia's breasts were magnificent and he wanted to bury his face in them.

Don't be a creeper!

But it was easier said than done. Sophia's brow was furrowed in concentration, but all Isaac could think about was laying her down on the sheepskins and kissing every part of her body.

He hadn't touched himself for years, his celibacy extending to masturbation. However, after meeting Sophia for the first time, he'd woken from sleep multiple times to find he'd climaxed during the night.

Next time, it's the Scout hut or nothing.

He couldn't teach her here ever again. It was too intimate.

'I'm still not doing it right!' She sighed. 'It feels so strange, and the more I think about it, the worse it seems to get.'

'It's all good. Don't worry. Why don't we strip things back even further? Let your hands rest in your lap and see if you can sync your breathing with mine. Don't think about an objective or a goal. Just stay in the present moment.'

She nodded decisively and sat up straighter. However, rather than staring at his chest, she looked into his left eye, the gateway to his soul.

His heart beat faster, but he held her gaze, his breath flowing gently in and out.

After a few moments, the tension in her face released, and her breathing matched his.

This is good. She's getting it.

The air was still around them, so warm Isaac couldn't feel the boundary of his skin anymore. The birdsong and rustling of leaves faded into the background until it disappeared. All that was left in his sphere of awareness was Sophia. He didn't want to break eye contact and wasn't sure he could even if he tried. They were breathing as if they were one being, connected in a bubble with energy flowing around and between them.

Then it began.

The air around Sophia shimmered into fractals of light, and a wave of bliss moved up from the base of his spine. Her eyes widened, but she kept breathing with him.

Now her face was morphing, dissolving into an image of the great goddess, Devī, then back into Sophia again.

The small part of Isaac's rational mind that remained, knew he was experiencing the tantric awakening of his kundalinī energy and that Sophia was experiencing it, too. This knowledge had been theoretical to him until this moment, but now they were being swept into a limitless ocean of divine energy.

Time became a fluid construct as the universe unfolded around and within them. They were separate beings on the deck but also entwined in multiple dimensions. Every cell in his body was vibrating with bliss, his energy and hers connected as one in a full-body cosmic orgasm that rippled through him in never-ending waves. It was an all-knowing rapture where they were the centre of the universe, transcending space and time. Bound together by a sexual energy that went beyond the physical.

And Sophia didn't seem scared by the overwhelming power of what was happening. Her eyes were fixed on his, holding his gaze with an intensity that matched the ecstasy pulsing through his body.

Isaac had no idea how long they'd been bound up in this shared experience, but at the very edge of his consciousness, his watching, critical mind asserted itself.

You can't do this. Make it stop.

He closed his eyes, his heart racing, drawing his soul back into his body and settling into the physical realm. It felt like being in a spaceship, coming into land.

And after the transcendental high, now came the very earthly low.

What have I done?

'What—What was that?'

Reluctantly, Isaac dragged his eyes open. Sophia was staring at him, her expression utterly dazed.

'Did you... Did you feel that?'

How could he explain what had happened? How could he tell her they'd had a divine sexual experience? He was her teacher. He was celibate. Everything about this was wrong.

'Feel what?'

Confusion clouded her features, and she blushed. 'I, er... I felt... Um, I think I might have had some kind of experience.'

He forced a professional smile. 'I think you're just learning how to relax your breathing. Why don't you go home and practise?'

'I... Oh... I'm not sure what I've just learnt.'

Isaac stood, grabbing the cushions he'd been sitting on and holding them in front of his trousers. He needed to get Sophia off his property before his entire world unravelled.

'You did great.'

He turned back into the house, raw fear rapidly deflating his cock.

Sophia followed him, going to the back door to grab her shoes. She was flustered, her fingers patting her hair as if to make sure her head was still in one piece.

'Should I head off now, then?'

He nodded, his attention anywhere but on her.

'Oh... Okay.'

Going back through the house, she sat on the edge of the decking and slipped on her shoes.

Isaac stayed inside, his fingers gripping the edge of the kitchen island, his knuckles white.

Sophia glanced back at him. 'Thank you.'

He raised a hand. 'No worries.'

'So, I'll see you in class next week?'

He nodded, then took her glass to the sink and turned on the tap. By the time he'd finished washing it, she'd gone.

To: All students

From: Isaac Hayward

Subject: Cancellation of classes

Dear all,

I apologise, but I'm cancelling my classes for the rest of the summer and leaving for India earlier than planned.

If you've bought a pass, it will be extended so you can use it when I'm back in September.

Don't forget I've got videos available on my website so you can continue your home practice.

Have a great summer,

Isaac

P.S. - I will not be checking my email when I'm away.

❦ 7 ❦

Nose pressed against the glass, Sophia drank in the view as the aeroplane descended.

Rocky green islands, fringed with white sand, rose from sapphire deep waters, and the surface of the sea sparkled in the sunshine. Despite the exhaustion from the journey, excitement flickered in her tummy. She might have been running away from her problems, but where better to run to than paradise?

And the fact it took her four thousand miles away from Marcus? Even better.

The small plane banked, beginning the final descent to Beef Island and Sophia checked the seat pocket in front of her for the umpteenth time.

Heart beating faster, she focused on her breathing. Her family may have been worried about her abrupt decision to spend the summer at an ashram, but she hoped the experience would help with her anxiety and breathing, as well as provide respite from the most stressful year of her life.

Gripping the armrests as the wheels touched down with a

judder, she pursed her lips and let out a long breath. She'd never liked flying, and this journey had involved three aeroplanes and had taken nearly twenty-four hours. Sophia was shattered and her stomach was growling at her for food.

'Ladies and gentlemen, welcome to the British Virgin Islands. The temperature may be thirty-one degrees, but the drinks are ice cold...'

Sophia smiled. She wasn't big into booze, but right now she wanted a pitcher of fruit punch and a kip on a sunbed in the shade of a palm tree. She doubted there would be alcohol at the ashram, but the pictures online had shown multiple pristine beaches and she couldn't wait to do a bit of yoga and a lot of relaxing.

Stepping off the plane, she paused for a moment, squinting in the bright sunlight as the heat enveloped her. England may have been enjoying an uncharacteristically hot summer, but this was something else. Securing her bag over her shoulder, she gripped the handrail of the stairs and descended to the tarmac, her free hand flapping the top of her t-shirt to cool down.

Inside the airport, waiting for her suitcase, Sophia checked the information she'd printed out about getting to the ashram. There was a ferry dock a short walk from the terminal, and the ashram had its own dedicated boat that ran six times per day.

Making her way there, she found the right dock extending out into the bay and a wooden sign halfway down that read 'Tranquillity Island Ashram'.

There was a small bench, but she didn't sit, peering instead at the water. It wasn't the clear blue she'd seen from the plane. The surface was covered with brown seaweed that choked the entire area, and the smell of rotting eggs filled the air.

'It's sargassum,' an American voice said behind her.

Sophia whipped around to see a woman who looked to be

in her twenties with a smiling freckled face, wavy auburn hair, and a large duffel bag slung over her shoulder.

'It's a real problem this time of year,' the woman continued. She dropped her bag and held out a hand. 'I'm Jessica. You going to the ashram?'

Sophia took it. 'For a month. I'm Sophia.'

'Teacher Training Course?'

'Yes, although more for the experience than anything else. You?'

Jessica sat on the bench and unzipped her bag, pulling out a baseball cap and jamming it onto her head.

She shrugged. 'Something different? And it'll be good for my résumé. I was owed vacation time and was in the area, so... Why not?'

Sophia sat next to her. 'Are you a therapist?'

'Hell no, I'd be goddam terrible. My advice is usually "go bother someone else with your problems". I work in the yachting industry as a stewardess. I've just come off a boat in Saint Martin.'

'That sounds very glamorous.'

Jessica pulled a face. 'If you like being nice to rich assholes all day and sharing a cabin with a dude who snores and farts in his sleep.'

'You have to share with a man?'

'Sometimes. The boat I was just on is only a hundred and fifty feet, so crew quarters are a little cramped. I wanna get on a billionaire's boat. Tips will be better there, too.' Jessica frowned at her. 'Hey, have you done much yoga before?'

Sophia shook her head. 'I started a class earlier in the year, but I'm not very good. You?'

'Nah. I've followed a few videos online, that's all.' Jessica held up her hand for Sophia to high-five her. 'We can hide at the back together.'

The tension in Sophia's stomach eased. She'd found a friend with even less yoga experience than her and wouldn't be the odd one out.

'So, whadda you do in the UK?'

'I'm an archaeologist.'

'Cool. Digging up old bones and shit?'

Sophia grinned. 'Usually shit. You can learn a lot about a culture from a midden.'

'Is that like a trash pile?'

'Yep. Everything from human waste, to animal bones, to potsherds.'

'What's the coolest thing you've ever found?'

Pain lanced Sophia's chest as the wound Marcus had made tore open again.

She forced a smile. 'Earlier in the year, I was part of a team that discovered the grave of an Iceni warrior.'

'No way? When was he alive?'

'Around two thousand years ago.'

'That's awesome. Any treasure?'

'A bridle-bit, coins, a sword, pottery. It's going to a local museum.'

'Neat.'

In the distance, coming towards the jetty, was a wooden boat with a small cabin up front, and the rest of the deck open with an awning to protect people from the sun.

Sophia glanced at her watch. 'This must be it.'

They stood as it approached, the brown seaweed parting before it.

It slowed to a stop beside the dock and a heavyset man wearing white baggy trousers and an orange t-shirt hopped out and secured the bow line. A handful of people climbed out with their luggage, then started making their way towards the airport terminal.

'Hi,' Jessica called out. 'Can we come aboard?'

The man nodded and reached to take her bag. Jessica passed it to him, then helped Sophia get her suitcase onto the boat.

Sophia stood at the edge of the dock, suddenly aware that getting herself onto a small boat was yet another life skill that had passed her by. She knew how clumsy she was at the best of times and didn't want to start her trip by pitching into the harbour.

'Take my hand,' Jessica said.

Sophia did, holding her breath as she stepped onboard, then allowing Jessica to pull her into the centre.

'Thank you.'

'No problem. You gonna be sick? I know the smell from the sargassum doesn't help.'

'I don't know. I've never been on a boat before.'

'What, never?'

She shook her head.

'Well, if you need to barf, just do it over the side and I'll hold your hair back.' Jessica turned to the man. 'Sir? How long is the crossing?'

He pointed at a sticky label on his chest with the word 'Mauna' written on it.

'O-kay... How long is the crossing, Mauna?'

The man rolled his eyes, pointed aggressively at the label, then mimed zipping his lips shut.

'You can't talk? Sorry, let me try to remember my ASL.'

Sophia watched as Jessica's hands moved, making signs. The man got angrier, shaking his head and gesticulating between the label and his mouth.

'I'm sorry, Mr Mauna. I'm doing my best here.'

Sophia took her phone out, quickly googled 'Mauna', then showed Jessica the screen.

'You've taken a vow of silence? Why didn't you say?'

The man threw his hands in the air, turned and stomped into the small cabin.

'Well, namaste to you, too,' Jessica said under her breath.

Sophia giggled. 'He doesn't seem very happy,' she whispered.

'If there's ever a man who needs a bit of yoga in his life, it's him. I hope the rest of the staff have a better attitude.'

'Me too.'

The two women sat in the shade as the captain waited for more passengers, Sophia feeling more nauseous every minute from the smell of the seaweed.

No-one else came, so the man untied the bow line and reversed away from the dock.

Sophia gripped the side of the boat.

'Can you swim?' Jessica asked.

'Am I going to need to?'

Jessica shuffled closer, putting her hand over Sophia's. 'Highly unlikely, but I can ask our friendly captain for a life-jacket if you like?'

'I think I'll be okay. It's the smell and sight of all that—' she gestured to the water around the boat, '—that's making me feel queasy. It was never in the pictures.'

'It never is, and it's becoming more of an issue every year.'

'Where does it come from?'

'The mid-Atlantic. It's natural, but it's been getting bigger each year. When it hits land, it chokes life under the water, makes nesting for sea turtles almost impossible, clogs propellers and desalination plant intakes, and ruins it for tourists.'

The boat chugged past the brown line of sargassum and suddenly they were surrounded by cobalt blue water and the fresh smell of the sea. The boat picked up speed, cutting smoothly through the small waves. Sophia took a big breath, her anxiety and nausea receding.

'Better now?'

'Yes, thank you. I'm a bit of a scaredy-cat about a lot of things.'

'Think of it as a good instinct for survival. You're not like my stupid brothers. My mom spent so much time in the ER when we were kids she knew all the staff by name.'

'What did they do?'

'Everything. And with no sense of self-preservation.'

'What do they do now? Something safe?'

Jessica rolled her eyes. 'They're firefighters.'

Sophia smiled. 'That's amazing. My brother wasn't wild growing up, but he's super-competitive. He was an Olympic-standard rower.'

'That sounds very British. Does he still do it?'

'Every day, but on a rowing machine. Plus running and weights. He's the athletic one.'

'Well, give it a month and we'll both be bendy-Wendy yoga bunnies.'

'You think?'

Jessica smirked. 'Probably not, but I hope we have fun.' She glanced at the boat captain, staring at the ocean as if in a stand-off, then back at Sophia. 'Do you think they'll be any hot guys at the ashram? My girlfriend does yoga retreats in Hawaii every year, mainly for the hook-ups.'

Sophia's mind went straight to Isaac. He was the hottest guy she'd ever known, but was currently eight thousand miles away in India. 'I hadn't really thought about it.'

'You haven't? I'm single and hoping to mingle. You?'

'I split up with my long-term boyfriend back in January. I don't think I'll be ready for anything new for a long time.'

Jessica gave her a sympathetic smile. 'Was he a douche canoe?'

'A what?' Sophia spluttered.

'A grade-A fuckwad. Someone so douchey they no longer fit in a bag.'

Sophia smiled. Even though it still hurt, being so far away from Marcus helped dull the pain.

'He's a professor who heads up our archaeology department. Over the ten years we were together, he had multiple affairs with his students. I only found out when I came home earlier than planned and found him smoking heroin with two of them, and also...'

'Get outta town! What an A-hole! Holy hell, Sophia. He's not a douche canoe, he's a douche *barge*.'

Sophia nodded. There were so many ways that Marcus had treated her terribly, culminating in the dig. How had she managed to normalise his behaviour for so long?

'And you're a good person,' Jessica continued. 'I'm an excellent judge of character. You have to be if you're working in the hospitality industry and living in such close-quarters with people. Is that why you've come to the ashram? To get away?'

'Yes, but I also hope it'll help with my breathing and anxiety.'

'Okay then, we've got a plan. You'll get chill, and if there's any cute dudes about, I'll get laid.'

'Are you in a single room?'

'Nah, I'm in a dormitory as it was the cheapest option without having to camp.'

'Me too!'

Jessica high-fived her again. 'Hey, roomie! Don't worry, I'll save my hook-ups for somewhere other than the single bed next to yours.'

'Thank you for your consideration.'

'You're so British, it's goddamn adorable. I'm glad I met you, Sophia. We're gonna have the best time.'

THE BOAT SAILED ON PAST ISLANDS, HEADING FOR ONE IN the distance. They'd been travelling for forty-five minutes by the time they reached a small jetty extending out into a mat of sargassum. Sophia's heart sank. There was a beach to the right, but it was covered in stinky seaweed.

'Gross,' Jessica muttered. 'Let's hope the other ones aren't affected.'

Getting off the boat, they went along the jetty to the shore. The buildings on the island were all lower than palm tree height, so from a distance the place looked unpopulated. However, there were two buildings underneath the first trees. The one on the left was marked 'Tranquillity Island Ashram Reception', and the one on the right had a sign reading 'Shop'.

As they approached, a man stepped out of a side door of the reception, dressed in baggy white trousers and a tight orange vest. His hair was chestnut brown with sun-kissed high-lights and tied back in a man-bun.

He waved at them. 'Namaste, mademoiselles,' he called out in a French accent. 'Welcome to Tranquillity Island.'

'Namast-hey, hey, hey...' Jessica murmured under her breath. 'I call dibs on Monsieur hot-pants.'

Sophia smothered her grin. 'Hello. I'm Sophia Hunter-Savage, and this is...'

'Jessica Pedersson. We're starting the Teacher Training Course tomorrow.'

His eyes lit up. 'So, you're here for a month?'

'Sure am... And you are?'

'Mohan.' He extended his arm, his gaze raking appreciatively over Jessica's curves. 'I'm here to make sure your stay is très agréable.'

Jessica took his hand. 'I'm liking the sound of that. Can I get a massage?'

He gave a half shrug. 'If we can find the time, anything is possible...'

'Très bon, Mohan. I'll definitely find the time *and* the possible.'

Seeming reluctant to release Jessica's hand, Mohan turned to Sophia and gave her a nod of greeting. 'Can I get you a drink?'

'Yes, please, that would be lovely.'

'I'd like sex on the beach,' Jessica added.

Mohan released her hand and gave a flirtatious frown. 'Unfortunately, we have a little problem with the seaweed at present...'

'Mohan!'

He stumbled back at the sound of an American voice, his posture stiffening.

Sophia turned to see a young woman stomping down a concrete path towards them, her blonde ponytail swishing angrily from side to side. She was also wearing baggy white trousers, but it was paired with a shapeless orange t-shirt. Out of breath, she reached their side and glared at the three of them.

'Er, hi—' Sophia began.

'You here for the TTC?'

'Yes. I'm Soph—'

'Passports,' she snapped, then turned to Mohan. 'Have you fixed the washing machine yet? Swami Saraswati is asking again.'

She didn't wait for a reply, brushing past him and entering the side door of the reception building.

Mohan strode briskly away without a second glance.

The woman poked her head through the large opening that faced the path. 'I'm Anisha,' she said, 'and that is my boyfriend, Mohan.'

She thrust two pieces of paper through the window. 'Sign and date these.'

'What are they?' Sophia asked, taking them and passing one to Jessica.

Anisha huffed. 'Just a standard liability release and acceptance of the ashram rules. No drinking, no smoking, no drugs, no meat, no fish, no eggs, no caffeine, no chocolate, no swearing, no sex, no mobile phones. Attendance at morning and evening Satsang is mandatory, as well as all your classes.'

Sophia glanced at the piece of paper, covered front and back with dense type.

'No sex?' Jessica asked, gazing up the path in the direction that Mohan had fled. 'So how do you and your boyfriend get it on? Does the rule just cover penetration? What about oral?'

There was an excruciating pause.

'Passports,' Anisha spat, holding out her hand.

Sophia quickly found and handed hers over, then turned to read through the form. She thought yoga was all about peace, love and relaxation, but the ashram seemed to have more rules than a prison. She hastily scrawled her name at the bottom, then gave it back.

'Can you tell us what time lunch is, please? And if there's somewhere I can fill my water bottle?'

'There's no lunch,' Anisha replied.

'What?' Jessica interjected.

'Breakfast is at ten a.m., and dinner is at six. You may purchase granola bars from the shop and fill your bottle at the station by the dining area.'

Anisha passed Sophia a piece of paper containing a map of the island. 'I'll take you to your dormitory now.'

Jessica handed her signed form and passport over, then Anisha emerged from the small building and set off up the path.

Following her, and trying to keep pace whilst wheeling her suitcase, Sophia caught Jessica's eye and the two women exchanged bemused grins.

There wasn't time to take in the surroundings as they jogged to keep up with Anisha, finally coming to a halt when she stopped in front of a two-storey building with steep, narrow wooden steps leading up to the first floor.

'The women's dormitory is up there. Tomorrow, after morning Satsang, you'll have the course orientation.' She turned and stomped off.

'Ommmmmm...' Jessica deadpanned as soon as Anisha was out of sight.

Sophia burst into giggles. 'This isn't quite what I expected.'

'Hell no. What with Captain Asshole, fuckboy Mohan, his pissy-as-hell girlfriend and no freaking lunch? The only thing stopping me from turning around is the fact I've paid four thousand dollars to be here.'

Sophia knew what Jessica meant. She'd dug deep into her own savings for the course and flights and was determined to stick it out.

Her stomach growled. 'I'm so hungry. I didn't think to bring any food with me.'

'I've got some trail bars you can have. Wanna dump our stuff and explore?'

Sophia nodded, and they hauled their belongings up the steep steps.

At the top was a small balcony and a door. Jessica pushed it open, and they entered a large room with six single beds, a nightstand by the side of each one.

'You choose which one you want,' Jessica said. 'I'm easy.'

Sophia wheeled her suitcase to the bed in the furthest corner of the room and sat on the mattress. It was about as soft as a bag of rocks, but she was so shattered, she knew she could probably sleep standing up.

'You know, there's no lock,' Jessica said, dropping her duffle bag on the bed next to Sophia and casting her eyes around the room. 'And only two plug sockets between six women. It's gonna be like Lord of the freaking Flies.'

'Well, they did say no phones.'

'And I say they can fuck off.' Jessica took her mobile out. 'I've got no signal here and there's no wi-fi, either. We can check if there's a sweet spot anywhere.'

Sophia took the map Anisha had given her of the island. In the centre was a rocky hill they'd spied earlier from the boat.

Smothering a yawn, she handed it to Jessica. 'Maybe here?'

'Hey, you wanna sleep for a bit?'

A wave of tiredness rolled through her. 'I've been travelling for nearly twenty-four hours and jet lag is hitting me hard. I'm sorry.'

'Don't be silly. I'll wake you before dinner.'

Jessica went to her bag, pulled out a bottle of water and two granola bars, and handed them to Sophia. 'Here. Eat, drink, sleep.'

'Thank you so much.'

'I'm gonna explore and check out if there's a phone signal or a hot dude who doesn't have a girlfriend. Hopefully, I'll find both.'

'And a beach that isn't covered in seaweed?'

'Good call. Now get some shut-eye.'

Jessica left the dorm and Sophia ate both bars and

drank the bottle of water. She thought she might be too wired to sleep, but as soon as her head hit the pillow, she was gone.

'SOPHIA? WAKE UP, GIRL. IT'S TIME FOR DINNER.'

Pushing herself up to sit, Sophia rubbed her eyes. Her limbs were leaden, and she was even more exhausted than before. Looking around the room, she noticed the rest of the beds had bags on them.

'Our new roomies have arrived,' Jessica said with a glint in her eye.

'What are they like?'

'A mix of hippies and Lululemon models. Two from my country and two from yours. I'll let you make up your own mind about them.'

Sophia swung her legs out of bed. 'That sounds ominous.'

Jessica smirked. 'Let's just say I'm glad I've met you. Come on, let's grab food and I'll fill you in.'

Outside the dorm, they descended the narrow stairs, Sophia holding tight to the handrail as she still felt unsteady on her feet.

'So, I've done a recce and there's good news and bad news,' Jessica began.

'Can we start with the bad news?'

'Sure thing. Okay, there are four beaches and three of them are almost completely covered in sargassum.'

'And the fourth?'

'Is out of bounds. It's marked no entry and is behind this big building which I presume is for the head swami. I tried to sneak in, but there's a gate with a key code lock. I also found a wi-fi signal that's strongest in that area, but it's password protected.'

Sophia followed Jessica down a path, palms on either side of them, with pretty flowers at their bases.

'Any mobile reception?'

'Yup. That's part of the good news. It's patchy, but I managed to get online and ring my mom to let her know I was here. The shop is crazy expensive. Trail bars are five dollars each! As soon as we can get off the island, we can go to Tortula and stock up with snacks as there is no way I'm gonna last with only two vegetarian meals a day.'

'Why don't they eat eggs?'

'I dunno, some yoga thing? Anyhoo, I've checked everything out and even though it's almost sunset, I'll take you on a tour after dinner. But wanna know the best news of all?'

'Am I guessing it involves hot men?'

Jessica snorted with laughter, and two people walking sedately in front of them turned their heads and frowned.

'It sure does...' Jessica lowered her voice. 'I don't know how many are spoken for or swing the lady way, but ma hoo-hah has been yelling yee-ha if you know what I mean...'

Sophia clapped her hand to her mouth to stifle a giggle. Jessica reminded her so much of Estelle, and even though she didn't share both women's confidence, she felt very comfortable in their company.

Circling the hilly and rocky centre of the island, they reached the kitchens. In front of the buildings was an open space with wooden tables and benches. The scent of fragrant food filled the air, almost completely covering the sulphurous smell of sargassum coming from the beach beyond.

The place was packed with people and Sophia moved closer to Jessica, her social anxiety kicking in.

'You okay?'

Sophia shook her head. 'I'm not great with large groups of people, and people I don't know.'

Jessica took her arm. 'You okay with me?'

She nodded.

'Alrighty then. I'll stick by your side until you get tired of me, and I'll give you fair warning if I sneak off to bone a dude.'

Sophia gazed at the crowds whilst waiting with Jessica in line for food. There were lots of people dressed in white trousers and different shades of orange t-shirts, and some were dressed head-to-toe in orange robes. She spotted a group of younger women in tight Lycra outfits and wondered if any of them were her roommates.

She also noticed plenty of good-looking men. Most weren't wearing white or orange and were obviously checking some of the women out. When their eyes came to her, she looked away. She wasn't interested. Having a casual hook-up wasn't her style, nor an effective way of erasing Marcus from her mind.

After filling her plate with food, Sophia followed Jessica to a small picnic bench near the beach.

'Did you see all the hot guys?'

Sophia nodded. 'And they're either single, or have the same level of fidelity as Mohan and my ex.'

Jessica laughed. 'So true. I think I'm gonna ask them straight up if they're unattached. It's skeezy to go for someone with a girlfriend.' She leaned forward. 'But I tell you something, these dudes ain't nothing compared to a guy I saw earlier. He's not here now, but I tell you, one sight of him and I was sweating like a whore in church.'

Sophia choked on her mouthful and grabbed a glass of water.

'I think he might be one of the staff. He was rocking the whole baggy white pants look.'

'More handsome than Mohan?'

'This guy shares the same gene pool as a Brazilian supermodel.'

Sounds like Isaac…

The thought made Sophia's heart skip a beat, and she glanced around the dining area.

'I told you, he's not here. All the important people eat in a private area over there, but you can't see all of it from here. Hey, you okay? Not feeling sick again from the sargassum smell? I picked here to sit because I thought you might like to be away from everyone else, but it is a bit stinky.'

'I'm fine. Just jet-lagged, I think. What time is the Satsang thing we have to go to?'

'Not until eight.'

Sophia slumped in her seat and let out a sigh. 'I'd much rather be in bed.'

'Skip it then. No-one will notice.'

'I can't. I'm not very good at breaking rules. If I did, then I'd be too anxious.'

'Well, we can rest in the dorm beforehand.'

Sophia nodded, then lowered her voice. 'Our roommates, are they the women on the table to my right? One of them is wearing a pink t-shirt that says "Hot Yoga Bitch" on it.'

Jessica snorted. 'You guessed it. I'm sure they're lovely, but they just rub me up the wrong way.'

'I think I'll just take a wander before Satsang, then. I don't have the strength to meet them yet. They remind me too much of my ex's current girlfriends.'

'You want company? I can show you around the island or we can hike up the hill at the centre? It's a bit of a scramble, but it should be quieter up there.'

'Thank you, a tour would be really good.'

After finishing their meal, the two women stayed at the table chatting, then Jessica led Sophia along the maze of paths meandering through the trees of the island. There were areas for tents, bathroom blocks, and several large open-sided wooden structures which they presumed were for yoga classes. There was also a small spa that offered massages for eye-watering prices.

Jessica huffed. 'For a hundred and fifty dollars, they'd better rub me down with essential oil of angels, then finish with a happy ending.'

'What's a happy ending?'

Her new friend's eyes sparkled under the lights shining from the building in front of them. 'You for real?'

Embarrassment flushed Sophia's cheeks. 'Sorry, I don't know what that is.'

Jessica giggled and squeezed her arm. 'You're too sweet for your own damn good. A happy ending is when the masseuse gets you off at the end.'

'What?!'

'I've never heard of it being done for women, but in some parts of the world, it's common for men. I've heard guys call it a "banana massage" because, well, you can imagine...'

Sophia shook her head. 'I feel so naïve sometimes.'

'Hey, you're not naïve, you're sweet. And you haven't had much contact with the seedier side of life.'

The memories of burning heroin and Marcus's flabby backside as he rutted Darcie rolled through Sophia's stomach.

Jessica touched her arm. 'You okay?'

She puffed out her cheeks. 'Sometimes I think I'm doing fine, but then I get flashbacks and suddenly I'm there again, watching my life implode like some kind of nightmare made real.'

'I'm so sorry. Hopefully, being here will help clear your head.'

A bell sounded loudly from the other end of the island.

Sophia smiled. 'Starting with meditation?'

'Is that what Satsang is?'

'I think it's like school assembly twice a day. But to be honest, I'm not sure. I only decided to book the course a few days ago.'

'No shit?' Jessica laughed. 'Well, come on then. The temple's at the other end of the island, so we'd better get going.'

She set off and Sophia followed, weaving along a path that ran behind a bank of luxury villas. The buildings overlooked the south beach, but the stench of sargassum that coated the sand marred their appeal.

As they got closer to the end of the island where the jetty was, others joined them, everyone moving in the same direction. Sophia shuffled closer to Jessica, the press of unfamiliar people making adrenaline prickle in her belly.

Lights were placed every few yards, but it wasn't enough to see clearly and she stumbled a couple of times on the uneven ground. Sophia liked routine and seeing the same faces. Everything about this experience was new, and therefore unsettling.

Keeping her gaze on the shadowy movement of her feet, she didn't notice the path had joined a new one until it was too late and she crashed into someone.

Her eyes jerked up, her mouth opening to apologise, but the sight of the person in front of her stopped her words as well as her heart.

Isaac's jaw hung slack as he stared at her. 'Sophia?'

'Isaac! Wha—what are you doing here?'

'I, er... What are *you* doing here?'

Sophia felt Jessica close beside her. The three of them were boulders in a stream, interrupting the flow of people moving towards the temple. But Isaac didn't seem to notice, staring at Sophia as if she were a ghost.

'I'm doing the teacher course,' she began, trying to keep her voice steady as her breath instinctively quickened.

He blinked as if trying to reset himself. Sophia had never seen him so flustered before.

Jessica leaned forward, holding out her hand. 'Hi, I'm Jessica, Sophia's brand-new BFF. Isaac, right?'

Isaac's gaze flicked to Jessica as if shocked to discover there was another human in their vicinity.

His mouth opened and closed, then he took her hand. 'I'm... Hanuman.'

'Hanuman?' Sophia repeated.

Even in the half light, she could see his cheeks darken.

He dropped Jessica's hand and cleared his throat. 'In the organisation, I go by my yoga name: Hanuman.'

Sophia had been getting to know Isaac for months now, and felt like they had the beginnings of a friendship, even though they were still teacher and student. But now, an ocean away from Foxbrooke, was he a completely different person?

'Please excuse me,' he said, dipping his head. 'I have to go.'

Without another word, he turned, striding off down the path.

Sophia's gaze stayed with him, becoming unfocused when he passed out of view.

'Well, smack my ass and call me Sally,' Jessica said. 'You wanna tell me how you know Mr tasty-pants?'

'He's... He's my yoga teacher,' Sophia replied, her throat dry.

'And he has got the *hots* for you, Missy.'

'No, he, er, hasn't.'

'You think I'm a member of the forty-watt club? If it wasn't already thirty degrees, you two just set the place on fire.'

'Shush! Please! Don't say anything.' Sophia twisted her

fingers in the fabric of her trousers. 'It's not like that, honestly. He's taken a vow of chastity.'

Jessica's eyes widened. 'Oh...'

'And he was meant to be in India with his guru for the whole of the summer.'

'But... Now you're both here...'

The anxiety that had reared its head was currently galloping across the plains of wretchedness towards misery town.

Jessica took hold of Sophia's hands. 'Hey, it's gonna be okay. I won't say a word to anyone. I promise. But we need to get going or we're going to be late.'

Sophia nodded and let Jessica pull her down the path.

It shouldn't matter that Isaac was here or not. Apart from the experience in his house that she still couldn't explain, he was her friend. And anyway, she was about to undertake an intensive, month-long course. It would be unlikely she'd even get to speak to him again.

❈ 8 ❈

As the echoes of the last 'om' still hung in the air, Isaac was on his feet, his hand proffered to his guru, Swami Vishnu, who was sitting on an ornate golden chair.

The older man raised an eyebrow, but allowed Isaac to help him up.

Everyone nearby bowed their heads and bum-shuffled out of the way so they could pass, and the two men took the back gate out of the temple that led to the private beach and accommodation for the leaders of the ashram and Devanandara organisation.

Satsang had always been a joy to Isaac. Collective meditation, chanting, and a teaching from a spiritual text, or visiting speaker. It centred him twice a day and provided inspiration, peace and comfort.

But this evening? Torture.

In the silence of meditation, his mantra became the word 'Sophia'. Every Sanskrit word of the chants turned into her name, and Swami Saraswati's reading became white noise in his head.

Sophia had been sitting at the back of the temple and Isaac had forced himself not to look her way, but it was as if she'd seeped under his skin.

He led Swami Vishnu towards the accommodation block, the moon glittering silver on the surface of the water to their left.

'Guruji...'

'Hanuman...'

'I need to...'

'Come.' The older man patted Isaac's arm. 'Let's sit and enjoy the evening and you can tell me what's troubling you.'

There were a few rattan chairs under the palm trees at the edge of the sand. Isaac pulled one out for his guru, then sat in the one next to him, his head bowed and his hands clasped as if in prayer.

'Hanuman. What has happened? Are your family okay?'

Isaac's gaze snapped up. 'They're fine, as far as I know.'

'Then what is it?'

The compassion in his guru's eyes filled him with shame. This was an embarrassing fuss about nothing. Here he was, monopolising the time of the leader of the Devanandara organisation with an uncontrollable infatuation.

He owed Swami Vishnu everything. Twelve years ago, Isaac had arrived at the ashram in the Himalayas after a year of travelling, still as lost and broken as he'd been when he'd left London. He'd only planned to stay a few days before moving on, but when he met Swami Vishnu, his new life began.

His guru was a British native, twenty years older than him, and understood the culture that Isaac had walked away from. Intensely charismatic, he'd had his own journey, leaving behind a career as a sports coach in the UK to embrace a life of spirituality and chastity. Renouncing attachments, he now had the honorific title of 'Swami', and led the other Swamis who each ran a Devanandara ashram across the globe.

'Guruji... You know me better than anyone.'

'Not better than you know yourself, Hanuman.'

Isaac shook his head. 'I've recently been worried that I don't know myself at all anymore.'

His guru reached across and patted Isaac's knee. 'Is the issue with your land disturbing you? That's completely understandable.'

'It *is* worrying me, but that's not why I need to speak to you.'

Isaac gazed out across the pristine sand. It was bright under the moonlight and utterly magical. He was grateful at least one beach on the island had escaped the tide of sargassum.

Just rip the plaster off.

'It's about a woman...'

Swami Vishnu lifted his hand from Isaac's knee. 'Ah. The ultimate test!'

'Guruji?'

The older man's eyes were sparkling. 'I'm only surprised this hasn't happened sooner.'

'You are?'

'Hanuman. I see the way women look at you. You're a handsome man. And it's only natural to experience primal urges.'

Isaac shook his head. 'But I don't want to. I have my path.'

'Which is not always straight or bump free. You know why I haven't had every track here set with concrete? Because it's a way to stay in the moment, having to focus on each and every step as you take it. And it's also a reminder that life is always putting grit in your sandals.'

Isaac smiled. 'Guruji, you are very wise.'

Swami Vishnu raised a shoulder in a half shrug. 'I'm only passing on what I've learnt, as you do to your students. So, tell me. Who is she?'

'Her name is Sophia. She's been coming to my classes since the start of the year.'

'And has she thrown herself at you like all the others in their hot pants?'

'No. Not at all. She had a bad break-up in January and lots of stress with work and her family. A relationship is the last thing on her mind.'

'But what about sex?'

'Definitely not. She's very shy and has never flirted with me. She's not interested in me like that.'

'So, what's the problem here?'

Isaac rubbed his face with his hands. 'Even before she appeared, I've been feeling restless and out of sorts. I don't seem as content with my life anymore. Maybe because the house and garden are finally finished? I don't know. But no woman has ever affected me the way Sophia does. And now I've got the threat of the compulsory purchase order hanging over me. I think I should just cut my losses and come to live with you in India.'

'Hanuman. We've spoken about this. That's not your dharma. Spreading the word of yoga in the UK is your mission. And Sophia is just a woman. Sexual desire is fleeting. When you return to Foxbrooke, you'll see that.'

'But she's here, Guruji.'

'Here?' He straightened in his chair. 'Did you know she would be?'

Isaac shook his head. 'She's been struggling with her breathing and anxiety and mentioned she'd been looking into doing the TTC. I had no idea she would actually do it, but I bumped into her just before Satsang.'

'And?'

'She looked shocked to see me. And now I can't get her out of my head.'

'But before she arrived, your mind was clear?'

'Not really, but I was managing my thoughts of her better.'

'Hanuman. Recognise that they are Maya; a beautiful illusion. That which is truly not, yet appears to be, is Maya. Your feelings for this woman are illusory, an appearance. They veil the truth of Brahman.'

'But—'

'Her being here is a gift. You must spend more time with her. Then you'll discover your infatuation is ignorant. She's just a woman. Nothing special. The more you're in her company, the less you will feel.'

Isaac stayed silent. He trusted Swami Vishnu, but also knew once the man had made up his mind, there was no swaying him.

Logically, Isaac knew Sophia was just like Eveline, Estelle, and the other ladies in his classes. But she'd touched his body, heart and soul in a way that no other woman had before. Not even Daniella.

But he would follow his guru's lead and trust that his guidance would steer him away from temptation and back to a place of inner peace and stillness.

BONG! BONG! BONG! BONG!

Sophia woke disorientated, an arm flailing across the top of her nightstand, trying to silence an alarm clock that wasn't there.

Bong! Bong! Bong! Bong!

'Jesus wept. What time is it?' Jessica muttered from the bed next to hers.

The lights went on in the dorm, and Sophia shielded her eyes, the reality of where she was collapsing on her like a ton of bricks.

'Five thirty?' Jessica exclaimed. 'Is this an ashram or a boot camp?'

'Satsang is in half an hour,' another American voice said.

Sophia pushed herself up to sit, reaching for a scrunchie to tie up her long hair. Still jet lagged, she hadn't slept well, and her limbs were even more uncooperative than usual.

After Satsang and Isaac's abrupt departure the previous evening, Sophia hadn't had time to chat to Jessica. Suddenly she'd been meeting the four other women sharing their dormitory and queuing to use the communal bathrooms before bed.

Khloe-Narcisse and Paisley were in their early twenties and friends from Los Angeles. Fearne and Tyger were mid-twenties and knew each other from an ashtanga yoga class they attended in London.

All the women made Sophia want to crawl under her bed and hide. They looked like fitness models, each one wearing yoga clothes that were more hole than Lycra and designed to showcase just how little body fat they possessed.

The women had been friendly, however Sophia couldn't help but notice how assessing their gazes had been. Luckily for her, it seemed they'd decided she was no threat to them and relegated her in their minds to 'small and inoffensive animal' status.

Rushing back from the bathroom, she made her way down the stairs with Jessica, slipping off the bottom step to the ground.

Jessica grabbed her arm. 'You okay?'

'Yes, thanks. I'm super clumsy at the best of times, but

when I'm tired, it makes everything worse.'

'Bambi on ice?'

'More like a bull in a china shop.'

A couple of people passed them, shushing loudly.

'Good morning!' Jessica called out to them.

They turned and mimed zipping their lips shut.

'It's okay. We're not doing mauna.'

Shaking their heads, they continued on.

'Well, top of the morning to you, too,' Jessica muttered. 'Honestly, this—'

'Quiet!' hissed Anisha, striding down the path from the tent area with Mohan. 'You should be observing complete silence before Satsang.'

'No-one told us that.'

'It was on the piece of paper you signed yesterday.'

'I didn't read that bit. I was more concerned about the no sex rule. Do people check up on you? Listen outside your tent? Because, girl, that wouldn't work for me. When I'm coming, I sound like a hyena on a roller coaster.' Jessica threw back her head, yipping and screeching.

Sophia slapped a hand to her mouth, but it didn't stop the snort from escaping.

'And Sophia sounds like a warthog at an all-you-can-eat buffet.'

Anisha gave them both a death stare and stomped away, pulling on Mohan's arm.

Shoulders shaking with laughter, Sophia wiped the corners of her eyes. 'You make me laugh so much. You remind me of my friend Estelle.'

'Well, your friend picker ain't broke, even if your boyfriend one needs a reboot. Come on, let's go meditate.'

They strolled together in the darkness towards the ashram, Jessica whispering out of the corner of her mouth.

'As soon as we get a bit of privacy, you gonna give me all the deets on Hanu-he's-so-your-man?'

'He's not my man.'

'If my grandmother had wheels, she would have been a bike.'

'What?'

'The way he looked at you, he almost made *me* pregnant.'

'It's impossible for him to be attracted to me!'

'Because of the chastity thing? Girl, that vow's got about as much strength as a piece of overcooked spaghetti.'

Sophia opened her mouth to reply, but they were shushed from front and behind, so she continued on in silence, arms away from her sides to balance in case she tripped on the uneven ground. The sun hadn't yet risen, and under the trees it still felt like the middle of the night.

Outside the temple, Sophia toed off her flip-flops and entered the building. It was situated behind the reception block, two of the open sides facing the pristine, and out of bounds, beach. Inside, the floor was terraced so more people could see where the swamis sat.

Anisha, Mohan and others dressed in orange and white were already in position, hands resting on their knees and eyes closed.

Edging past a large metal statue of a Hindu deity in the half-light, Sophia and Jessica took cushions from shelves along the far wall and sat on the floor. The previous night she'd been comfortable for ten minutes, but then her knees, hips and back had been screaming at her for a chair. She gazed across the crowds. How did they sit like this for hours?

A movement outside caught her eye, and her breath quickened.

Isaac.

He was walking alongside his guru towards the temple.

The previous evening, Khloe-Narcisse had spoken in hushed tones about Swami Vishnu, the head of the Devanandara organisation, and how lucky they were that he was visiting the ashram from India.

Dressed in orange robes, he had piercing blue eyes and closely cropped fine grey hair that ran around the sides and back of his head, framing a bronzed bald spot. He appeared to be in his late fifties and had a commanding presence, even though he was a few inches shorter than Isaac and had yet to say a word.

Isaac opened a low gate at the back of the building for the Swami, then followed him to the front of the temple. Everyone else was sitting on the floor, but an ornate gold chair with an intricately embroidered seat pad and garlands of flowers hanging off the arms was waiting for Swami Vishnu. Pulling his robes to one side, the older man sat, his eyes going to the back of the room where Sophia and the other people new to the ashram were seated.

The man's gaze was searching, and a shiver ran across Sophia's skin. She had the sudden thought that he was the eye of Sauron and she was an oversized Hobbit trying to avoid detection.

Dipping her head, she stared at the white tiles of the temple floor, only looking up again when she heard a bell.

Isaac was holding it out for his guru to strike. After the third chime, Isaac carefully placed it on a cushion and sat back, eyes closing. This was the cue to meditate, but Sophia didn't feel relaxed enough to close her eyes. Everything was uncomfortably unfamiliar. And no amount of mental preparation for the trip could have prepared her for Isaac being there, too.

Gaze unfocused, her mind went back to what had happened the last time she'd seen him in Foxbrooke. His house and garden had been heaven on earth. Sure, he'd seemed uncertain about her being there, but then he'd loosened up. Smiled. He'd even cracked jokes. Even though she wasn't silly enough to imagine her crush would be reciprocated, she'd been so happy in his company and felt he was comfortable around her.

But then *it* had happened.

Something so extraordinary, so otherworldly, so utterly bizarre that even now she couldn't explain or understand it. She'd never taken LSD before, nor had a religious experience, but she imagined both things might have been similar to what had occurred when she was sitting opposite Isaac on the deck.

And accompanying those experiences had been an even bigger component that had nothing to do with drugs or religion.

Shifting on her cushion, memories passed through her, leaving ghosts of feelings in their wake—feelings of extreme arousal.

To begin with, Isaac's face had swirled and changed, as if he were a surrealist painting come to life. But then the swells of pleasure had begun, until it felt like every cell in her body was orgasming, over and over again like waves moving across the surface of an endless ocean.

It had been scary at first, but she trusted Isaac implicitly, so went with it, holding his gaze, feeling the two of them wrapped up so intimately in an experience that went beyond sex, beyond pleasure, to a place she never wanted to leave.

But then he'd broken the spell, and everything had changed. He wouldn't look at her. Wanted her off his property. Denied that anything had just happened between them.

Had she imagined it?

The bell sounded again, then a chant in Sanskrit started and everyone dressed in orange and white joined in.

Sophia didn't know any of the words and there were no books to follow in the temple, so she let the sounds wash over her and thought about how many years Marcus had successfully gaslighted her. Whether it was about his relationships with students, her abilities as an archaeologist, or her theories about their most recent dig, her ex had lied and manipulated her until she felt she couldn't trust her own judgement.

Had Isaac done the same thing at his house? And if so, why?

Shifting a little to the right so she could look around the person in front of her, Sophia sought him out. As he sang, his gaze passed over the other people in the room, but kept missing the very back where she sat, as if that part of the temple simply didn't exist.

Her throat tightened. What had she done wrong? Eveline, Foxbrooke's lovely vicar, was Isaac's best friend. Everyone in his classes adored him, and before she'd been to his house, Sophia believed he'd thought of her as a friend.

But now?

She frowned as she stared at him, trying to find a solution to a puzzle where the answer wasn't Jessica's theory that Isaac was fighting an attraction to her.

The back of her neck suddenly prickled and her focus snapped from him to find the shrewd and assessing eyes of Swami Vishnu staring her way.

Heart thumping, she wrenched her attention back to the floor. Did he know who she was? Had Isaac told him about her schoolgirl crush?

Jessica placed her hand on Sophia's knee and squeezed. 'You okay?'

She nodded in return. Seeing Isaac would get easier, especially as it would only be twice a day. Plus, he didn't seem to want to acknowledge her existence.

She needed to take a leaf out of his book. Concentrate on the course she'd come to do and pretend he wasn't here.

❅ 9 ❅

'Those starting the TTC this morning, please go to Asana Hall One which is located behind the shop,' Anisha said loudly as morning Satsang finished.

Getting to her feet, Sophia stretched then held her stomach as it growled angrily at her.

'Only another two and a half hours until kibble time,' Jessica muttered. 'I could murder a burger.'

'Have you got any granola bars left?'

'Four, but I'm rationing them until I know when I can return to the mainland and stock up. This is nothing like the yoga retreats my girlfriend told me about.'

'I'm already feeling a little light-headed,' Sophia murmured. 'I know I should see this is an opportunity to lose a bit of weight, but—'

'Why do you want to do that?'

Sophia's gaze slid to their roommates, who were bending at the waist to pick their cushions off the floor, demonstrating how flexible they were, and also showing off their pert backsides to the small group of men taking the course.

Jessica rolled her eyes. 'God gave me curves, and I sure as shit ain't gonna starve myself just so some jackass wants to bang me. And you shouldn't, either. You're hot AF. If I had a dick, I'd do you.'

Sophia giggled. 'Thank you for cheering me up.'

'Anytime.'

They made their way out of the temple, along the path towards the asana hall, then up the two steps to the covered wooden platform. At one end sat Anisha and Mohan, with piles of clothing and spiral-bound manuals beside them.

'Take a seat, everyone,' Anisha said, 'then we'll take a roll call.'

There weren't any cushions available, so Sophia sat on the floor at the back with Jessica. From about thirty people on the course, nearly all of them were women.

The four men were in their twenties and gazed around the room as if they'd just landed on a planet devoid of males and where every female was desperate to be impregnated.

'Jeez-Louise,' said Jessica. 'They're hot, but they're not *that* hot.'

'Do you think you'll make a move?' Sophia whispered.

'Nah. I'm not getting in line to beg for a bone. These motherfuckers can come to me if they want a taste of Jessica juice.'

Anisha cleared her throat loudly, throwing daggers their way.

Jessica waved back.

'Okay everyone, settle down,' Anisha began. 'For those of you who don't know me, I'm Anisha and I head up the admin team for Swami Saraswati who runs Tranquillity Island Ashram. This is my boyfriend, Mohan, who is the main asana teacher for the TTC. I'm going to start by making sure every-one's here.'

Lifting a clipboard, she read out a list of names, placing a tick against each one as people acknowledged their presence.

'Good,' she said as she finished. 'There will be a roll call at the beginning and end of each activity, including morning and evening Satsang. Attendance is mandatory, and failure to comply will mean you are removed from the ashram.'

A murmur went around the room.

'But what if we're sick?' Jessica asked.

Anisha gazed coldly at her. 'Attendance is non-negotiable. If anyone is unable to leave their beds, then someone must summon either myself or Mohan to assess the situation. In order to get the most from your course and the ashram experience, participation in all activities is required.'

Getting to her feet, Anisha went to the pile of clothes and began handing out bundles to each person.

Mohan followed, giving everyone a large spiral-bound manual with an orange cover and the logo for the Devanandara organisation on the front.

'Your manual has your name on it,' Anisha said. 'If you lose it, there is a fifty-dollar replacement fee. These are your uniforms and must be worn at all times.'

Sophia held up a pair of baggy white trousers and an over-sized orange t-shirt with the same logo as on the front of the manual.

'You have two outfits and they must be kept pristine. There are laundry facilities beside the main tent area, and tokens for the machines can be bought from the shop. If your uniform is lost or damaged, then you can buy new ones. T-shirts are thirty dollars and trousers are forty.'

'Whatta they made of?' Jessica grumbled under her breath. 'Silk?'

Sophia smothered her smile and nudged her new friend, inclining her head towards their roommates. The four women were looking at the clothes with expressions of utter disdain, as if they'd been asked to wear sackcloth and ashes.

Jessica snorted loudly, then coughed to cover it up.

'Inside your manual,' Anisha continued, 'is the timetable for the day. Wake-up is at five thirty, followed by morning Satsang at six, then your first asana class of the day at eight o'clock. Breakfast is at ten, followed by two hours of karma yoga. At one p.m. you have a chanting or a Bhagavad Gita class, then your main lecture, which runs until three forty-five. At four you have your second asana class, followed by dinner at six, then evening Satsang at eight o'clock.'

Sophia was exhausted just thinking about it.

'Each day you're expected to produce a summary of the main lecture and hand it in the following day to be marked. You have one day off each week when you're allowed to leave the island, however attendance at morning and evening Satsang is still mandatory.'

'Four trail bars to last six days,' Jessica murmured. 'I'm gonna die.'

'I'd like to take this opportunity to remind you of the main ashram rules you agreed to when you completed your online booking, as well as again when you arrived at the ashram. No drinking, no smoking, no drugs, no meat, no fish, no eggs, no caffeine, no chocolate, no swearing, no sex, no mobile phones. There—'

'What's the wi-fi password?' Jessica interrupted.

'That is for staff use only,' Anisha replied. 'If anyone would like to see the full ashram rules, we have a book of them in reception.'

'You've got a freaking *book*?'

There were a few titters.

Anisha glared at Jessica. 'The ashram is a harmonious and tranquil environment—'

'Clearly.'

'That is kept so by adherence to the rules,' Anisha continued, her voice rising. 'Anyone not willing to follow them is free to leave at any time.'

'After spending four thousand dollars? I think I'll stick it out.'

Anisha ignored Jessica, picking up her clipboard and turning the page.

'Now I'm going to give you your karma yoga allocations, which you will be doing for two hours over the next thirty days, starting after breakfast this morning. Blake, Xander, Zane and Colby, you're removing sargassum from the beaches. Ellie and Miriam will take the register at the start and end of every activity. Garden duties are assigned to Christine, Sonia, Holly and Emma. Lauren B and Lauren G will assist me with admin. Grace will clean the temple and Lulu and Kaleese will work in the shop. Washing up after breakfast will be done by Marla and Piper, after dinner by Caroline and Lina, and the cleaning of communal areas such as walkways and asana halls will be done by Joan, Lila, Kasey with a K and Casey with a C. Rubbish collection and removal is to be handled by Arabella and Chanelle, wash basins and showers will be cleaned by Fearne and Khloe-Narcisse, and toilets will be cleaned by Paisley, Tyger, Sophia and Jessica.'

Silence.

'Okay, let me get this straight,' Jessica began. 'I paid four *thousand* dollars for a yoga teacher training course, and you're expecting me to clean frikking *toilets* for two hours a day?'

'Karma yoga is an integral part of the TTC,' Anisha replied, her face a mask. 'By renouncing your own selfish needs and desires and working for the greater good, the ego is destroyed and union with the divine realised.'

'So, after breathing in Clorox for sixty hours, I'm gonna be Buddha?'

There were a few more snickers and Sophia bit the inside of her cheek to stop her smile. The last thing she wanted during an already over-scheduled day was to spend two hours of it on her hands and knees cleaning toilets.

Anisha gave Jessica a thin smile. 'Like I said, you've already agreed twice to the ashram's terms and conditions. If you change your mind at any point, the ferry to the mainland runs six times a day. Now, I'm going to run you through the manuals, then Mohan and I will take you to the person overseeing your karma yoga, or show you how to do it.'

BY THE TIME THE BELL RANG FOR BREAKFAST AT TEN o'clock, Sophia was sure her stomach had eaten itself. Anisha had told everyone to be mindful of each movement they made and not run when moving around the ashram, however she jogged after Jessica in order to be near the front of the line for food, then piled her plate as high as she could.

On the whole, the meals were tasty. But beans and vegetables weren't as filling, and didn't give the same nutritional punch, as one of her mother's Sunday roasts. Sophia doubted she could eat enough to last her eight hours until the next meal.

'I'm making a shopping list for our day off,' Jessica said in between huge mouthfuls. 'Plastic boxes we can fill with food for eating later, coffee granules, sugar, powdered milk, and a travel kettle. Beef jerky, trail bars and chocolate.'

'Is there a shop near the airport?'

'I think so, but if not, we can take a taxi into Tortula. If I don't get more food and coffee, I'm going to be even pissier than I am right now.'

'I don't think anyone's happy about their karma yoga.'

'Except the lucky fuckers helping in the shop or doing admin. The moment I figured Anisha was making the decisions, I knew we'd be scrubbing toilets.'

'The other girls in our dorm are, too. Well, Paisley and Tyger are, Khloe-Narcisse and Fearne are cleaning the showers and sinks.'

'It's because we're hot and she can't trust Mohan. It's punishment for looking at her boyfriend.'

'It doesn't seem very fair.'

'There's not much about the ashram that is.' Jessica fixed Sophia with a look. 'All animals are equal, but some animals are more equal than others...'

'Is that from *Animal Farm*?'

'Yup. See that area over there? Where the swamis and people in charge eat their meals?'

'Uh-huh.'

'As well as the island's wi-fi password, they get different food to us.'

'They do?'

'And *lemons*.'

'Lemons?'

'I start every morning with a glass of warm water and freshly-squeezed lemon juice. Sets me up for the day. That, and black coffee. Anyway, I asked one of the kitchen staff earlier if I could have one and she shut me down.' Jessica gesticulated with her cutlery. 'I tell you, Sophia. I'll clean frigging toilets all day, but deprive me of lemons while those fuckers get 'em and it's war.'

'Already? On day one?'

Jessica threw her head back and cackled. 'It'll be the straw that breaks the camel's back.'

'Are you going to try and pick some up in town on our day off?'

'Sure thing. And maybe some garlic. The food here is so bland.'

'I read in the manual that onions and garlic are considered too stimulating and stop us from having calm minds.'

'For real? Jeez. They really *are* trying to turn us into sheep. I wanted to learn how to teach yoga, not join a cult.' Jessica glanced at her watch. 'We've got twenty minutes before slave labour—sorry, *karma yoga* starts. Whaddya wanna do?'

'Can you show me the best spot for a signal? I messaged my parents when I got to the airport telling them I'd arrived safe and sound, but I want to let them know everything's still okay and that we're not really allowed to use our phones.'

'Sure thing. And I'll act as a lookout so the yoga police don't spot you.'

'Oh no, are you okay?'

Sophia closed the dormitory door behind her and went to Fearne's side. The young woman was sitting on her bed, gulping in breaths as tears streamed down her pretty face.

'H-how are we meant to keep these clean when there's only two washing machines?' she sobbed, gesturing to her white trousers streaked with dirt. 'And they're both being used at the moment!'

Sophia looked down at her own clothes, the knees muddy from the wet toilet floor. 'I'm not sure. Maybe we'll have to roll them up?'

'And Anisha shouted at me and split me up from Tyger. It's not *my* fault I've never cleaned a toilet before and that Mohan fancies me. I've been to other ashrams before, and they never made us do work like this.'

The door banged open, and Jessica entered. 'Only two freaking washers! Oh shit, what's happened?'

Sophia glanced up. 'Fearne's also wondering how we're going to keep our uniforms clean. And Anisha made her scrub a different block to Tyger.'

'Course she did. Page one of *Cult Leadership for Dummies*—separate y'all so you can't talk, and no free time so you can't think.'

Sophia looked around the room. The other women's dirty trousers and t-shirts were already draped over the ends of their beds.

'I think the others have already been and gone.' She turned back to Fearne. 'Do you want me to say you're ill? We've got to go now or we'll be late for class.'

Fearne shook her head. 'I'll be okay. Thank you.'

'And Fearne,' Jessica said. 'Don't worry about the clothes. Just dry them out, then give them to me. I've got a plan.'

THE WOMEN QUICKLY CHANGED, THEN RAN BACK TO THE same asana hall they'd been in earlier. At the entrance stood Miriam with a clipboard, ticking everyone off as they arrived. Whilst it was the easiest job to have been given, she looked awkward in her role, and Sophia, Jessica, and Fearne were late.

Next to Anisha, sitting on a pile of cushions at one end of the hall, her long orange robes draped around her, was Swami Saraswati, the leader of the ashram. She was French, in her seventies, with long grey hair tied back in a neat braid. Her thin lips pursed with disapproval and Sophia had a brief thought that she must love sucking the lemons Jessica coveted.

The staff at the ashram seemed in awe of their leader, but she appeared to have as much warmth as an arctic winter, and her presence made Sophia miss her mum.

'Turn to page one hundred and eighty-nine of your manuals,' she began. 'Here you will find the opening chant. You will sing this with your teacher at the start of every asana class and are expected to memorise it for your final exam at the end of the course.'

Sophia ran her eyes down the page of text. The long Sanskrit words bore no resemblance to English or any Latin-based language. She knew she was intelligent and used to studying, but this would have to be learnt by rote. Luckily, she was used to hearing Isaac singing it, so she hoped there was some part of her brain that had started to assimilate the words.

AT THE END OF THE HOUR, ANOTHER OF THE STUDENTS, Ellie, stood at the exit and checked off everyone's names again.

'This is ridiculous,' Jessica muttered. 'We're not in kindergarten.'

'Cinq minutes!' Swami Saraswati called from behind them. 'Five minutes until the main lecture of the day.'

Jessica was glancing between her water bottle and the nearest toilets, which were in the opposite direction from the drinking water tap.

Sophia took the bottle from her. 'I'll do it. I don't need the loo.'

'Thanks. See you in a bit.' Jessica dashed off.

'No running in the ashram!' Anisha shouted.

Jessica didn't stop.

Turning towards the dining area, Sophia walked quickly, trying to bring the blood flowing back to her stiff legs. She was desperate for sleep. Could she take a nap between dinner and Satsang?

Up ahead was the main door to the kitchen. Her heart

skipped a beat as Isaac exited, holding a lemon. With a broad smile on his face, he was saying goodbye to someone inside.

Sophia dithered. He hadn't noticed her yet. What should she do?

Going to the water station opposite the door, she turned her back and started filling Jessica's bottle.

Isaac laughed, and her tummy sparkled.

When both her and Jessica's bottles had been refilled, she took a fortifying breath and turned around.

Isaac had gone.

Sophia's throat squeezed painfully. There was no way he hadn't noticed she was there, but he'd chosen to ignore her.

Like Marcus, maybe Isaac just wasn't the person she thought he was.

Two hours later, Sophia laid out the yoga mat Estelle had bought for her at the back of the asana hall as Mohan did a complicated sun salutation. Her head, along with the first eight pages of her notebook, were filled with information from the lecture they'd just had, and now she was facing a long yoga class before dinner.

She wasn't sure if Mohan was warming up or showing off. His gaze was focused on the far wall, but Sophia was sure he was aware of the admiring glances flying his way from the majority of people in the room.

Lying back on her mat, her fingers rubbing the surface for reassurance, Sophia closed her eyes and listened to the murmur of voices and the birds in the trees. The sounds morphed in and out of each other as they retreated, getting quieter and quieter.

'Hey! Wake up!' Jessica hissed.

Sophia's eyes snapped open.

'Mohan's been dismissed. He's not teaching the class anymore.'

Huh? Rolling sleepily to her side, Sophia pushed up to sit, her head turning to the front of the class... where Isaac was now sitting.

'Close your mouth, you look like a guppy!'

'What happened?' she whispered to Jessica.

'He showed up a couple of minutes ago and spoke to Mohan, who then grabbed his mat and left.'

'Oh.'

'So it's our lucky day. We get the hottest dude in the ashram. Khloe-Narcisse and Paisley have already pushed their way to the front, and check out what they've done with their uniforms!'

Sophia glanced at the two women. They'd pulled the bottom of their t-shirts up, twisting the fabric, then knotting it under their breasts, leaving the entirety of their midriffs bare. They'd also tugged their trousers so low, their hip bones were showing.

Xander and Blake were busy rolling the sleeves of their t-shirts to their shoulders to better show off their upper arms.

'Seriously?'

Jessica sniggered. 'This is too funny. Should we tell them it's never going to work?'

'No, don't say anything. I don't know if he wants anyone else to know about his celibacy.'

'Fair enough. And anyway, watching them peacock is hilarious.'

'Okay, everyone,' Isaac said, 'let's get started. My name is Hanuman, and I'm going to be your main asana teacher for this TTC.'

Anisha and Mohan entered the back of the hall carrying bags filled with foam blocks.

'I appreciate that some of you might not have done any yoga before and most of you won't be used to sitting cross-legged for long periods of time,' Isaac continued. 'It's important you're comfortable and you don't injure yourselves, so Anisha and Mohan have brought blocks for you to sit on. If you're experienced and open in your hips, then you'll probably only need one. However, some of you may need three or more. You can also create a stack lengthways and kneel with the blocks between your legs and under your bottom like this.'

He demonstrated the position, then stood, took the bag Anisha was carrying, and began handing out the blocks.

'Decide on the right amount for you and hold on to them for the duration of the course. You can hand them back at reception when you leave.'

'I can't believe they're not charging us to hire them,' Jessica murmured to Sophia.

She nodded in agreement, noticing Anisha's frowning face as if she was thinking the same.

'How's everyone getting on?' Isaac asked.

He walked around the class, making slight adjustments to some people's set-ups and making other recommendations.

'I'm almost as in love with him as you are,' Jessica whispered out of the corner of her mouth.

Heat whooshed into Sophia's cheeks and she pressed her palms against them, petrified that people would notice.

Jessica leaned closer. 'Chillax. We're at the back. And believe you me, no-one is looking at us.'

Sophia glanced around. Without exception, everyone was gazing at Isaac as if he'd just floated down from heaven and was handing out hot chocolate with whipped cream and mini marshmallows.

Pride filled her chest. *This* was the Isaac she remembered.

Someone thoughtful and kind, who gave each person in the room the same amount of care, respect, and attention.

Well, almost. He'd made eye contact with everyone except for her.

'Fantastic,' Isaac said, taking his seat at the front of the class. 'Let's start with "easy pose", which is known in Sanskrit as sukhasana. Cross your legs at the mid-calf point and extend the heels away. Now lift the flesh of the buttocks out and apart so you're on your sit-bones. Roll your shoulders up as you inhale, then back and down as you exhale. Your spine should be comfortably straight without arching in the lower back, so you might need to tuck your tailbone under. Elongate the back of the neck and close your eyes if you feel comfortable doing so. We're going to begin with the opening chant.'

❧ 10 ❧

'Guruji, are you sure this is a good idea?' The weather had changed, turning the air thick with moisture, but that was not why Isaac was sweating.

The older man took his arm as they strolled away from breakfast.

'Hanuman. Whenever have I steered you wrong?'

Guilt tugged inside Isaac's chest. 'Never, Guruji.'

'Well then. It's been four days now and you have not done as I've asked.'

'But Guruji, I—'

'Hanuman, your body is present, but your mind is elsewhere. I've seen you teaching. The woman hides at the back and you ignore her completely.'

Isaac was silent. As ever, Swami Vishnu was speaking the truth. Isaac had taught Sophia twice a day since the start of the TTC, yet she may as well have been invisible for all the attention he gave her.

What would Eveline say about his behaviour if she knew? Shame flooded through him.

And despite all his attempts to block Sophia from his mind, she still filled his waking thoughts and fevered dreams. Whenever she wasn't looking his way, his eyes were drawn to her. He knew the course was hard, but she seemed exhausted, her face paler than normal and her eyes sunken. He'd done the TTC when he was younger than she was and he'd had the advantage of being strong and fit. Watching Sophia was like experiencing it again through a completely different lens.

How had he never truly noticed the pressure put on the students before? The lack of time to rest and assimilate the information being thrown at them? The fact so many of the asanas suited men's physiques better than women's?

'How do you expect to deal with your feelings towards her if you hide from them, Hanuman? By spending time with her, you will see they are shallow. Baseless. The construction of an unquiet mind. Soon the physical attraction will pass, and you will return to a state of equanimity.'

Isaac nodded, but no part of him believed his guru's words, and his restless feelings of dissatisfaction with his life had started before he'd met Sophia. Yes, he was drawn to her on every level, but removing those feelings wouldn't make the other ones disappear.

'Guruji, when can we return to India?'

The older man paused before replying. 'It is important you are here.'

'Why did we have to leave? You never explained.'

'There is nothing to explain. We are here, and now God has revealed why.'

'But I want to go back.'

They paused outside the entrance to the temple and Swami Vishnu patted Isaac's hand. 'And that is why you must stay.'

Isaac bit his tongue to stop complaints pouring out of him like a dissatisfied child.

'Now go and wait for her. I have explained to Anisha what is to happen.'

Swami Vishnu dropped Isaac's arm. 'I will see you later at the main lecture.'

'You're teaching it?' Isaac failed to keep the surprise from his voice.

The older man inclined his head. 'It is good to lessen the burden of Swami Saraswati and her team. And I am keen to understand what it is about this woman that has affected you so much.'

Shifting his robe further over one shoulder, Swami Vishnu turned and ambled away towards his villa.

Isaac stood at the entrance to the temple, unwilling to go inside. He'd always embraced every aspect of ashram life, but now his stomach knotted with resistance.

Was it time to renounce modernity entirely? Give up hope of saving his land in Foxbrooke and return to India to live forever in a cave? He had enough money to do that for the rest of his life. Was that now what his dharma needed to be?

'Isaac?'

He turned. Sophia was standing a short distance away, fingers clutching the sides of her trousers.

'Sorry, I mean Hanuman.' Her cheeks flushed. 'I, er...'

Heat rose in his own face.

'Anisha told me to come here for my karma yoga.'

He cleared his throat. 'Yes, your assignment is changing.'

'Why?'

Great. What lie can I tell her?

'Isa—Hanuman?'

'My guru wanted you to work with me.'

'You?' Her frown deepened. 'Why?'

He rubbed the back of his neck. 'He thinks I've been ignoring you.'

'And?'

Oh god. Has it been that obvious?

'Um...'

'So now Grace has to clean toilets for two hours a day instead of me?'

'That was your karma yoga?'

Sophia huffed. 'Don't sound so surprised. Anisha gave our entire dorm the worst jobs.'

'Why?'

She rolled her eyes. 'Because she thinks we all fancy Mohan.'

An unexpected stab of jealousy pierced his chest. 'Do you?' The words ran out of his mouth before he could stop them.

'I can't speak for the rest of them, but *I* certainly don't.' She crossed her arms. 'Anyway, it doesn't matter. I need to go back.'

'You want to clean toilets?'

'Of course not! But I doubt it's top of Grace's wish list either. And how's it going to look when people ask how I got out of my shitty job when they can't get out of theirs?'

Isaac had never seen Sophia so angry before. Part of him was glad. When he'd first met her, she'd been so quiet and unsure about everything.

'I'm sorry. This is Swami Vishnu's decision.'

'Well, I disagree.'

'You can't.'

'Of course not. I forgot what a rules-driven dictatorship this is.' She let out a deflated sigh and held up a hand. 'Sorry, that was disrespectful and unnecessary. Okay. What do I have to do?'

Toeing off his flip-flops, Isaac entered the temple, Sophia following.

'There are lots of jobs, but the main ones each day are

sweeping and cleaning the statues,' he began, moving to the back of the building. 'There's a cupboard here with everything you need.'

'And what are *you* going to be doing?'

'Helping.'

'Why?'

'Because… Like I said, my guru wants me to.'

Sophia took a tin of brass cleaner and a cloth from the cupboard and strode over to a many-armed statue of Shiva by the entrance to the temple. 'But what about what *you* want?'

'What do you mean?'

Shaking a blob of fluid onto her cloth, she rubbed the sharp brass edges. 'Look, I apologise for being so belligerent and unpleasant right now, but I'm so tired I want to cry all the time, I'm constantly hungry, and the last thing I want is to be forced to hang out with someone who hates me as much as you do.'

'What? I don't—'

'Yes, you do. If you see me walking towards you, you suddenly veer off in the opposite direction. If I'm nearby, I might as well be invisible, and in class you never look at me or help when I need it. It's like you're a completely different person than the one I met in Foxbrooke. What on earth have I done wrong?'

He swallowed. 'Nothing. You've done nothing wrong.'

'And why did you lie to me?'

'What?'

She dropped the tin and cloth to the floor and stuck her hands on her hips.

'I know I don't know much about yoga, but something happened when I was at your house and you pretended it hadn't. I've spent ten years of my life being lied to and gaslighted by Marcus and I'm not putting up with it anymore from anyone.'

Sitting on the floor with a thump, Sophia sank her head into her hands and burst into tears.

Fuck.

If Isaac had been feeling bad before, now he felt like the lowliest worm ever to crawl the earth.

Grabbing a box of tissues from the cupboard, he sat next to Sophia and held it out. He desperately wanted to touch her, comfort her, but didn't want to overstep a boundary, especially when she was so angry with him.

'I'm sorry, Sophia.'

'I wouldn't be so upset,' she gulped, 'if I wasn't so exhausted. This course is nothing like I thought it would be. I hate nearly everything about it.'

As if ashamed of her admission, her sobs intensified.

Guilt ate at him. As if Sophia's life hadn't been catastrophic enough this year, she'd travelled halfway across the world to spend a month doing something she hated. He should have told her more about what was involved when they'd been in Foxbrooke, but he'd had no idea how serious she was about doing the TTC.

Or had she made the decision because of his dismissal of the experience they'd shared at his house, then his premature departure for India? Had she come to the ashram looking for answers that he'd denied her?

'You're right,' he said quietly. 'Something *did* happen that afternoon. I'm so sorry I lied about it, and I'm mortified by my behaviour towards you here.'

Her head lifted, and she gazed at him, her eyes wide. 'W-what?'

Knowing he'd caused the tears that streaked down her face was a sucker punch, knocking out his breath.

'Sophia, I'm so sorry.'

She took a tissue to blow her nose, her tears still flowing.

'What happened at your house? And why are you being so distant?'

Was the way forward to be honest with her as well as with himself? Would this give him relief from the feelings tightening around his heart with every beat?

He moved further away, as if that would stop the urge to reach across the gap between them and pull her into his arms.

Sophia's eyes refilled with tears as she stared at him.

She probably thinks I can't stand being near her.

Letting out a strangled cry, he ran his hands into his hair.

'Hanuman?'

His head shot up. 'No.'

That name coming from Sophia's lips felt utterly wrong. With her, he was Isaac, not Hanuman.

'Please, call me Isaac.'

She nodded, but her forehead furrowed with confusion.

He took a deep breath. 'Explaining to you what happened means a much harder conversation. But it's only fair to you that I'm honest.'

'Okay.'

Drawing on all his reserves, he held eye contact, fully aware that the last time they'd gazed at each other like this, he'd had the most profound occurrence of his life.

'That afternoon, our kundalīnī shakti was awakened, and we shared a tantric experience.'

'Oh. Is that normal?'

Isaac wanted to laugh out loud at the idea, but instead shook his head.

'Not at all. I've been practising yoga for years and I've never even got off the spiritual starting-blocks. I knew in theory what I might expect, but it didn't touch how it felt.'

'So, we meditate in order to try and make that happen?'

'Yes, and also one hundred per cent not.'

'What do you mean?'

He let out a heavy sigh. 'Sophia, I don't know if it was the same for you, but what I felt was not peaceful or chaste. It was sexual bliss, as if every cell in my body was orgasming, over and over again.'

Her pale cheeks flushed red.

'You won't learn about this on the course, and the Devanandara organisation is totally against this form of yoga. But it's real, and it happened to us.'

Sophia was silent for a moment, then asked the one question he hoped she wouldn't.

'Why? Why did it happen to us?'

Resisting the urge to move even further away from her, he cleared his throat.

'The very first time we met, I was strongly attracted to you, and this attraction only grew the more time I spent in your company. I've never had this prob—this *situation* occur since I took my vow, and it has been deeply unsettling.'

Apart from the movement of her breath, Sophia appeared frozen, her liquid eyes holding his without blinking.

'When we were on the decking, it was the most incredible experience of my life, but I knew it wasn't what you were there for, so I shut it down. I was your teacher and yet I'd allowed it to happen. Everything about that moment freaked me out. Then I panicked about seeing you again and ran away to India. I had no idea my guru would bring us to this ashram, nor that I would find you here. I've been avoiding you because the feelings I have for you are overwhelming and...'

He stopped talking. He didn't want to add 'and I don't want to break my vow', because that would have arrogantly implied that Sophia would have wanted to break it with him.

She swallowed. 'Why?'

'Why what?'

'Why on earth do you like *me*?'

The shock at her question stopped all thoughts in their tracks. Sophia appeared genuinely confused. Had her ex made her think so little of herself that she didn't see what was self-evident?

'Because you're the loveliest person I've ever met,' he said, truth spilling out of him as if desperate to escape the prison of his mind. 'You're sweet, kind, clever, caring, resourceful, honest, and determined. You're also utterly beautiful, and I can't stop thinking about you. I want you with every breath.'

'*Me?*' Her voice was filled with disbelief.

Isaac wanted nothing more than to reach for Sophia and demonstrate exactly *how* much he desired her, but he forced himself to remain still.

'Yes, you. And only you.'

She pressed her palms against her reddened cheeks as if to cool them down.

'But you don't want to, er, do anything about it,' she said hesitantly. 'Because of your vow.'

His body was utterly paralysed. In that moment, he knew without a shadow of a doubt that he *did* want to do something about it. He wanted to do everything.

But instead, he willed his head to nod.

'Does your guru know how you feel?'

'Yes.'

'Then why does he want you to spend time with me?'

Isaac huffed. 'He believes the more I'm in your company, the less I'll feel for you. That my attraction is an ignorant illusion and will soon disappear.'

'And do you agree with him?'

'No.'

Her lips parted in a perfect 'o' shape, but no sound came out.

What a mess.

Even as his heart thumped in his chest with awareness of her, Isaac knew nothing about it was right and nothing was going to happen.

He'd taken a vow of chastity. He was her teacher. They were in an ashram. And if that wasn't enough, she'd given no sign she liked him more than as a friend and was also processing a terrible breakup.

'I deeply regret how I've treated you, Sophia. I've tried very hard over the last twelve years to be a good person, yet with you, I've failed spectacularly. I'm sorry.'

'You haven't.'

Unable to meet her eyes, he shook his head.

Silence filled the space.

She swallowed. 'So, er, what do we do now?'

He shrugged. 'We clean the temple and I make more of an effort to be less of a dick.'

As soon as Sophia entered the dorm, Paisley was in her face.

'How did you get out of karma yoga?' she demanded. 'Grace has been in tears all morning because she's now doing *your* job cleaning toilets.'

Side-stepping Paisley, Sophia went to her bed, heart pounding.

'We have a right to know,' Khloe-Narcisse added. 'Have you slept with Mohan? Is that it? I've seen you checking him out.'

Sophia shook her head.

Fearne and Tyger were also in the room, their arms crossed as they stared at her.

Jessica was nowhere to be seen.

What could she say? *Well, here's the thing. Know Hanuman, the hottest guy on the island? The one you keep shaking your arses at? He's my yoga teacher from back home and wants to break his twelve-year vow of celibacy with me. You know, cos I'm so hot and all that. But because he's trying to be a good yogi, he's doing his best to ignore me, so the head honcho is forcing us together to prove I'm not worth his time. Such fun!*

She cleared her throat. 'I don't know why and I didn't ask. Please don't get angry with me for something that isn't my fault.'

'Bullshit,' Paisley retorted. 'You must have done *something*.'

The four women's eyes flicked up and down Sophia's body as if scanning to determine how someone like her managed the seemingly impossible. It was like being back at school, the mean girls wanting to know why the super-hot Blaise Ponsonby-Urquhart was spending time with her, even though it was only because she allowed him to copy her homework.

Sophia's breath quickened, adrenaline rushing into her blood.

'Well?' Khloe-Narcisse spat.

The door opened, and Jessica entered. 'What's going on?'

Paisley glanced over her shoulder. 'Sophia got out of karma yoga and won't tell us why.'

'And you think bullying her will get you an answer?' Jessica replied, her tone sharpening. 'Get the fuck away from her. Now.'

The women reluctantly moved.

Sophia sat with a thump on the bed, her head spinning.

'And she hasn't got out of karma yoga. She's swapped with Grace.'

Khloe-Narcisse huffed. 'She says she doesn't know why.'

'Then leave her alone.'

'It's because she's slept with Mohan,' Khloe-Narcisse continued. 'We've seen him looking at her.'

Paisley nodded in agreement, and Fearne and Tyger exchanged glances.

'You have *got* to be kidding me!' Jessica cried. 'Apart from the fact Sophia wouldn't touch that fuckboy with a ten-foot pole, when do you think she's had the opportunity? The schedule doesn't give us time to fart, let alone fornicate.'

Khloe-Narcisse and Paisley looked at each other.

'She must have done *something*,' Tyger said defensively.

'Then go ask Anisha,' Jessica said, glaring at them all. 'If you run along now, you've got—' she looked at her watch, '—a whole *seven minutes* before chanting class. I'm sure Mohan could bone y'all twice in that time.'

She waved her hands as if shooing children away. 'Bye-bye now.'

They hurried from the room.

As soon as the door closed behind them, Sophia slumped forward, gasping for breath.

Jessica rushed to her side. 'Hey, hey. Breathe, honey.' She stroked down Sophia's back, soothing her. 'Don't let them get to you.'

Sophia rested her head against Jessica's shoulder. 'Thank you. I was so scared.'

'I could see. You were like a rabbit in headlights. I know they're exhausted and stressed, but it's no excuse for treating you like that.'

'No,' she replied quietly, wiping tears from the corners of her eyes.

'Do you have any idea why Anisha swapped you with Grace?' Jessica asked softly.

Sophia nodded in return, then told Jessica what had happened. When she finished, there was a brief pause, then her new friend screeched with laughter.

'Hoo-ee! If only our roomies knew!'

Panic cut through Sophia. 'Oh god! Please don't—'

'Cool your boots. I ain't gonna say a word.'

Sophia let out a sigh. 'Thank you.'

Jessica rubbed her back. 'Apart from the fact I'd never break your confidence, it's far better entertainment when no-one's got a clue what's really going on.'

'What?'

'Oh, come on. The way they strut about in front of your man, it's hilarious.'

Jessica pouted, her voice becoming high-pitched and breathy. 'Oh, Hanuman, you need to show me exactly where my diaphragm is. I'm still *so* confused. Look, I've pulled my t-shirt up so you can touch me more easily.'

Sophia giggled.

'That's better. Don't let the bastards get you down and don't let them bully you into telling them the real reason.'

'No way.'

Jessica glanced at her watch. 'We'd better run or we'll be late.'

Sophia nodded and got to her feet.

'So,' Jessica whispered as they made their way down the stairs outside the dorm. 'When you get back to England, do you think anything will happen with Hanuman?'

Sophia slipped off the bottom step and flailed for the handrail.

Jessica grabbed her before she crashed to the ground. 'You need to remember there's one more step than you think.'

'And you need to stop asking me awkward questions when I'm navigating uneven surfaces.'

Jessica smirked. 'Sorry about that.'

They set off at a fast pace towards the asana hall.

'So?'

Sophia shook her head. 'Nothing can ever happen because he wants to stay celibate.'

'But if he changed his mind...?'

Fire coursed through Sophia, exiting through her cheeks. The thought of being with Isaac was so incendiary she could barely allow herself to contemplate it.

'I'll take that as a "yes" then,' Jessica said. 'And I don't blame you. If Mohan's an eight, Hanuman's a ten million...'

Arriving at the asana hall, Grace was outside, her face pinched and red as she argued with Anisha. As soon as the two women noticed Sophia, the conversation stopped, and they glared at her.

'Grace,' Sophia began. 'Can I speak with you for a moment?'

'Don't bother,' Grace hissed, then ran into the hall, plonked herself on the floor next to a group of women, and started whispering to them.

Sophia bit the inside of her cheek, tears building again in her throat. Right now, she just wanted to go home.

'You're late,' Anisha said coldly.

'No, we're not,' Jessica replied. 'And nama-fucking-ste to you, too.'

Grabbing Sophia's arm, she led her into the building to the back of the group, as far away from their roommates and Grace as possible.

AFTER AN HOUR OF CHANTING, SOPHIA'S VOICE WAS HOARSE, and she had a headache. She wanted to go for a stroll in the five minutes they had between classes, but didn't want to get ambushed by one of the other students.

Jessica took her water bottle. 'I'll go fill it for you. If you need the toilet, duck out of the main lecture ten minutes in. That way no-one can hassle you.'

'Thanks. That's a good idea.'

Sophia rolled out her yoga mat at the back of the hall, lay down on it, and closed her eyes. She'd come to the ashram hoping to find peace, tranquillity, and an improved ability to handle stress.

What she'd actually discovered was...

Letting out a sigh, she squeezed her eyes tightly shut, pushing the tears back down. Every part of her body ached, and her brain buzzed with information overload. Even though she liked the yoga classes they were doing with Isaac, without enough food or sleep to recover properly, it was all too much.

The chatter of other students stopped abruptly. Turning her head, Sophia opened her eyes.

Isaac was entering the hall, Swami Vishnu by his side.

Scrambling to a seated position, her heart accelerated and her tummy turned over. Isaac was so beautiful it took her breath away. How on earth did someone that gorgeous find *her* attractive?

In the back of her mind, Sophia could hear her mother, Estelle, Jessica, and everyone else who fought her corner, yelling that she was beautiful. But it didn't seem to make a difference what they said. She'd been unconfident enough when she'd got together with Marcus, and now, after everything that had happened this year, her self-esteem was at rock bottom.

Anisha and Mohan carried the gold chair from the temple into the hall and placed it at the front, then Swami Vishnu swept the back of his robe out of the way and sat.

All the students were sitting up extra straight as they gazed at him, like meerkats on high alert. Anisha and Mohan were to one side of Swami Vishnu, glaring at everyone as if to force them into perfect behaviour, Isaac on the other.

The swami's eyes travelled around the room. Sophia turned away before they reached her, rolling up her mat as an excuse not to look at him.

Jessica dashed to her side. 'What's he doing here?' she murmured as she passed Sophia her water bottle.

'No clue,' she whispered back.

'Is everyone present?' Swami Vishnu asked Miriam.

Miriam nodded and took her seat.

'Very well.' He opened his arms and smiled benevolently at everyone. 'It's been a while since I taught a TTC. However, as I'm here, I wanted to lend a hand, starting with today's lecture on the chakras.'

Sophia opened her manual to the right page. She'd been a student for years and a lecturer for nearly as long. She knew all the tricks to avoid interaction with the teacher, and number one was assuming the role of the most diligent pupil. Someone who wrote copious notes with their eyes firmly down.

Swami Vishnu spoke genially about energy centres, vibrations and nadis, as if he were describing the hall where they were, rather than things beyond the scope of most people's comprehension.

Whenever Sophia glanced up, his attention seemed drawn to her, so she dipped her head back to her notebook.

This was the man who'd caused her no end of trouble with the other people on her course by changing her karma yoga. The man who thought Isaac's feelings for her would pass like a morning mist. Maybe they would? But that didn't give him the right to push the two of them together and make Sophia's life even harder than it already was.

Guilt nagged at her. Swami Vishnu headed up the entire Devanandara organisation, and Isaac, along with everyone else, it seemed, worshipped him. She knew she should be similarly obsequious, but just couldn't summon the feelings.

All her life she'd been the model student, never putting a foot wrong. When Marcus had singled her out in her first year at uni, she'd been so blinded by his light it never crossed her mind to question his behaviour.

But now she saw Marcus for who he truly was: someone who'd taken advantage of a vulnerable and virginal eighteen-year-old, then continued his pattern of predatory behaviour with other students throughout their ten-year relationship.

Swami Vishnu wasn't a predator, but there was something about him that made Sophia uncomfortable. Maybe it was the way people fussed around him like worker bees attending to their queen. In that way, he was all too similar to Marcus. A few years ago, she would have been as adoring of Swami Vishnu as Isaac was, but now she just saw him as a man at the centre of a web, pulling on people's strings as he saw fit.

'Let us look now at Manipura, the solar plexus chakra, located just below the diaphragm,' Swami Vishnu said. He gestured at Paisley in the front row. 'Would you like to come and help me?'

Paisley sprang up faster than a Jack-in-the-box, her head nodding and her cheeks pinking at the perceived honour. Her t-shirt was still tied up underneath her breasts, showing off the entirety of her abdomen.

'What is your given name, child?'

'Paisley, Swami Vishnu.'

'You may call me Guruji,' he said with a smile. 'Swami Vishnu sometimes feels so formal, don't you think?'

He turned his head, spreading his smile around the group to make sure everyone knew he was making a joke. Most people were deferentially compliant, providing the requisite amount of laughter, however Sophia and Jessica stayed silent.

Swami Vishnu held out a hand. 'Come closer, Paisley, so I can show people the correct location of Manipura.'

She did, and he placed his palm on her stomach, just above her pierced belly button.

'This is where the fire element is. The colour is yellow and the bija mantra is "ram". Place your hand on your body now, everyone, and close your eyes... Repeat ram, ram, ram, over in your mind, bringing your awareness to this region... By balancing this chakra, we are more confident and focused. We have more energy and freedom from disease.'

Sophia kept her eyes open. Paisley had an expression of bliss on her face, as if she was achieving enlightenment through the power of Swami Vishnu's touch alone.

'Very good,' he continued. 'Thank you, Paisley. Can I have another volunteer for Anahata, the heart chakra?'

Twenty-nine hands shot up.

'Such sattvic students!' he cried. 'This is wonderful.'

He beckoned to Tyger, who'd also modified her t shirt, so it framed her breasts and displayed acres of toned skin.

'What is your name, child?'

'Tyger. With a Y.'

'With a Y...' Swami Vishnu raised his eyebrows as he gazed across the faces of his rapt audience. 'Maybe you should visit our Indian ashram, Tyger. There are places where you can meet tigers without Y's if you're unlucky.'

Another round of fawning laughter rippled around the hall, and Tyger blushed.

'Come closer, child. Kneel for me.'

The hairs on the back of Sophia's neck rose and Jessica stiffened next to her.

Tyger dropped to her knees and Swami Vishnu put a hand on her shoulder.

'Good. Now we know that our physical heart is to the left

of the chest, however the heart centre, known as Anahata chakra, is located here.'

He placed the palm of his other hand between Tyger's breasts.

'The element of Anahata is air, and the colour is a pale green. The bija mantra is "yam", and when the heart chakra is out of balance, we may deal with feelings of anger, anxiety, fear or jealousy. Put your left hand on Anahata chakra now and close your eyes... Repeat yam, yam, yam, over and over as you meditate on feelings of love and compassion...'

Sophia shifted, so she had a clear sight line to Isaac. Surely he could see how dodgy this looked?

But his eyes were closed, his face serene.

Jessica nudged Sophia's leg, then pointed at her notepad where she'd written the letters *WTAF?*

Sophia nodded. Thank god she wasn't the only one who thought this wasn't right.

'Thank you, Tyger with a Y, you may sit back down,' Swami Vishnu said. 'Now, why don't we have someone from the back... Sophia! Please come here.'

Sophia's gaze flicked to Isaac. He was smiling encouragingly and hadn't seemed to notice that half the room had clocked the fact Swami Vishnu already knew her name.

Brilliant. Another reason for them to jump to all kinds of wrong conclusions.

Getting to her feet, she picked her way forward and stood in front of the older man, towering over him.

'Now kneel and face everyone, child.'

Again, she looked at Isaac.

Big mistake. The women in front of Sophia followed her sight line, then frowned.

'Come along, Sophia. We've only got another hour of this class left,' Swami Vishnu said, prompting sniggers.

Sophia moved to the right of the chair closest to Isaac and knelt so she could still see him out of the corner of her eye. Her heart was racing, adrenaline turning her stomach and making her muscles twitch in anticipation of running.

She couldn't see Swami Vishnu, but she could feel him, and her mouth watered as if she was about to vomit.

I'm safe. I'm in public. Isaac and Jessica would never allow anything to happen to me.

Swami Vishnu's hands touched her shoulders, and she flinched.

'Vishuddha chakra is found at the base of the throat,' he began, 'and the colour is a lapis lazuli blue…'

His hands encircled her neck, and she swallowed, trying to regulate her breathing.

He chuckled. 'You can relax, Sophia. I'm not going to strangle you.'

People laughed.

'The element associated with Vishuddha chakra is ether and the bija mantra is "ham"…'

Sweat was forming under his hands and running down Sophia's neck. Even though she was kneeling, she was so dizzy she was about to keel over. In panicked desperation, she turned her head to find Isaac.

Swami Vishnu's hands tightened slightly, holding her in place. 'An imbalance may be associated with timidity and the inability to express oneself. Does this sound familiar, Sophia?'

She took a breath, about to tell him to stop, when he spoke again.

'Now, everyone close your eyes and repeat the word "ham", focusing on your throat chakra.'

In her peripheral vision, Sophia saw Jessica stand.

Suddenly, her neck was released, and she fell forward, her hands finding the floor.

To her right, Isaac's eyes snapped open. He looked questioningly at her, concern etched into his brow.

Shaking her head, Sophia got to her feet and stumbled back to Jessica's side, sitting on the floor with a thump.

'Thank you, Sophia!' Swami Vishnu called over. 'Now, who would like to help me next?'

Jessica grabbed Sophia's hand, tugged her to her feet, and dragged her from the hall.

'Quick toilet break!' she called to Anisha. 'Back in a sec!'

Pulling Sophia along the path, Jessica didn't stop until they were by their accommodation block and the asana hall was out of sight.

Sophia collapsed onto the bottom step, shaking from head to toe.

'What the fuck was that?' Jessica growled. 'Creepy, letchy, pervy asshole. What kind of sick game is he playing?'

'I—I'm just being over-s-sensitive,' Sophia managed, her voice stuttering.

'The fuck you're not. I don't care if he's the head of the organisation, or if Hanuman thinks he farts fucking rainbows. That was all kinds of wrong.' Sitting next to Sophia, Jessica took her hand. 'What do you want to do?'

'I don't know.'

Right now, Sophia wanted to close her eyes and find herself transported back to her parents' house, her mum bringing her a hot chocolate and a plate of French Fancies.

She let out a sigh. 'The thing is, we've spent so much money and haven't even got to the end of the first week. And if I leave now, I'll have to spend even more money changing my flights.'

Jessica huffed. 'You're right, and I don't want to give Anisha the pleasure of seeing the back of me.'

'What a mess...'

'Ommmmmm,' Jessica intoned, and the two of them cracked up.

'I'm so bloody grateful I've got you,' Sophia said, wiping the tears of laughter away.

'And me you. We can get through this. Just promise me one thing.'

'Of course.'

'You won't ever be alone with Swami Smarmy-pants…'

❀ 12 ❀

Bong! Bong! Bong! Bong! Bong! Bong! Bong! Bong!
Sophia awoke from her half-sleep, her heart racing.

'Alright, alright! We get the message,' Jessica grumbled.

The dorm light flicked on and Sophia rolled onto her side, facing the wall, her body aching with exhaustion.

'The bell's late!' Fearne cried. 'It's already five forty-five!'

The floor vibrated as people ran for the bathrooms.

Sophia pushed herself up to sit. She'd hardly slept, her nervous system still on edge after everything that had happened the previous day. Now she was too tired to even make her limbs work.

Picking up her wash bag, she stumbled to join the queue outside.

By the time she'd had a quick wash, brushed her teeth and returned to the dorm, Khloe-Narcisse and Paisley had already left.

'Come on, ladies!' Jessica said, holding open her duffle bag.

'Put your dirties in here and I'll get them in the washer before Satsang.'

Ever practical, Jessica's solution for keeping their uniforms clean was to put them on to wash before Satsang each morning, then leave the temple to 'go to the toilet' forty-five minutes later in order to put them in the dryer. It was a genius solution and meant they always had a new set of clean clothes by the start of the first asana class of the day.

Sophia dropped her dirty t-shirt and trousers in the bag after Fearne and Tyger.

Jessica hoisted it to her shoulder. 'I'm gonna have to leave now,' she said to Sophia.

'It's okay, I'll see you in there.'

Jessica ran out and Sophia quickly dressed, dragged a brush through her hair, then left.

Hurrying along the path, she was relieved to see she wasn't the only person who was late, as she was jostled by people with harried expressions, all rushing towards the temple.

The ashram may have promoted community and tranquillity, but Sophia felt like she was in a race for the last lifeboat on a sinking ship.

In the distance, the ferry was pulling away from the jetty. She glanced at her watch. Six o'clock. *Late!* She'd been on the island less than a full week and she'd already been conditioned to conform.

Outside the temple was a bottleneck of people trying to enter. A flustered Miriam was by the door with her clipboard, trying to check everyone in as quickly as she could. However, it was still dark, and she was struggling to read the names on the sheet and tick off the right ones.

'Hurry up!' a voice said behind Sophia.

She turned to see Grace, whose face was scrunched up with annoyance.

'I'm trying,' she replied. 'I can't go any faster.'

Pressed between bodies, Sophia's anxiety had already sprinted off the blocks and was around the first bend. Taking a deep breath to calm herself, she got a lungful of body odour from the man in front and her stomach heaved.

Grace was tutting and huffing behind her, as if the delay was entirely Sophia's fault.

Breathe! You're nearly there.

The man in front moved, and she got to Miriam's side.

'Sophia. My name's about two-thirds of the way down on the right-hand side.'

'Okay, hang on a sec.'

'Get on with it!' Grace hissed.

Miriam's pen slid down the sheet, then finally stopped. 'Got you.'

'Thanks.'

As Sophia went to move, she was shoved sharply from behind. Stumbling, she missed the first step, lost her balance and tipped forward.

Trying to avoid crashing into the man in front, she twisted to the side, but her foot slipped from under her.

Arms flailing, she reached for the statue of Shiva, but it wasn't heavy enough to stop her fall and toppled towards her.

She pivoted again, her knee buckling with a violent stab of pain.

Instinctively, she let go of the statue and grabbed her knee as she hit the floor, the statue crashing down, straight onto her head.

There were cries and screams, but Sophia wasn't sure if any had come from her. Assaulted by blinding pain in her head, her knee, her hand and her hip, her mind didn't know what to focus on.

The statue was lifted off, and she tried to sit up.

'I'm sorry,' she slurred.

Embarrassment fought with pain for Sophia's attention and she moved, crying out as her knee shrieked at her. The room was still dark and blurry and everything she touched felt wet. Did she knock over a vase of flowers as well as the statue?

'Turn on the lights! Get out of the way!'

Isaac?

Sophia blinked liquid from her eyes. Had someone poured a glass of water over her head?

The lights went on and someone screamed.

Glancing down, Sophia saw why. Blood was everywhere, smeared across the white tiles, soaking her trousers, dripping from her head and hands.

Oh, my god.

'Sophia! Look at me.'

Isaac was by her side.

She sagged against him, fear, pain and adrenaline winding around her heart until it threatened to burst.

'Mohan! Get the keys for the speedboat! Anisha! The first aid box!'

'Isaac,' she whispered.

'I'm here. Can you tell me if anywhere else hurts?'

'My knee. I can't...'

Her breath was coming faster, lights flashing on and off behind her eyes, the pain escalating like an approaching storm.

She gripped Isaac's hand as she felt herself sinking.

'Sophia. Listen to my voice. Stay with me.'

But she couldn't. She sucked in a panicked breath. 'Don't leave me,' she gasped.

Then everything went black.

ENGINE NOISE. VIBRATION. PAIN. *ISAAC.*

Sophia didn't need to open her eyes to know it was his arms around her. Despite all the physical agony, she felt utterly safe.

She was curled in his lap, her head tucked against his chest, his arms cradling and protecting her. Sophia remembered a small speedboat moored up at the jetty when she'd first arrived at the island. Were they in that?

Opening her eyes, she saw Mohan standing at the helm, one hand on the wheel, the other on the throttle as he stared at the horizon.

'Sophia?'

She slowly turned her head, wincing at the movement.

Isaac looked like he'd been dragged through the gates of hell and back. Blood streaked his skin, his hair was bedraggled, and his expression was one of utter torment.

'Isaac,' she murmured.

His face collapsed with relief. 'Thank god.' He stroked her hair. 'I...' He took a breath. 'How are you doing?'

She looked past him. They were on the floor of the boat and she couldn't see out.

'Where are we going?'

'To the hospital. We're going straight to the marina on Tortula. Then we'll take a taxi to the Peebles hospital. It should only take another half hour at this speed.'

'But I don't have my insurance details. Money.'

'Shhh, it's okay. I've got your passport and plenty of money. We'll be alright.'

Isaac smiled reassuringly at her.

Tears flooded her eyes. 'Everything hurts so much.'

'I bet it does. You had a nasty fight with Shiva.'

Sophia tried to smile. 'Did I win?'

'Unfortunately not. He's got four arms, so it wasn't a fair fight.'

'How did I get to the boat? I don't think I can put any weight on my left knee.'

'I carried you.'

'But... I'm so heavy.'

'You're not. And anyway, I practise yoga every day and can lift far more than I weigh, which is considerably heavier than you.'

'Thank you.'

'Any time.'

Isaac swept away a trail of fresh blood from her forehead, then wiped his fingers on his t-shirt.

'Am I still bleeding?'

He nodded. 'I patched you up as best I could, but you need a professional to look at it. I didn't see you fall, so I don't know all the places you might have been injured. Can you remember how you did it?'

Sophia paused. 'The bell was late, so we were all stressed and rushing to get into the temple on time. Miriam couldn't see the register very well because it was so dark. Then...'

'Yes?'

'It was an accident.'

Isaac's gaze was intent. '*What* was an accident?'

'People were just trying to get in quickly. She didn't mean it.'

'*Who* didn't mean *what*?'

'It's nothing, honestly. It's my fault for being so clumsy.'

Fresh tears came to her eyes.

'Sophia, I'm not going to do or say anything if you don't want me to, but please tell me what happened.'

She took a shaky breath. 'I think Grace pushed me. She must have been mad about her karma yoga being changed and lashed out because she thought I was being slow and holding everyone up. But everything after that *was* my fault as I'm not the most coordinated at the best of times, and when I'm tired and it's dark, I'm even more unsteady on my feet.'

Isaac's eyes closed briefly, then opened, searing into hers. 'You're *not* clumsy.'

'Oh, I am. Really I am.'

Tension lined his face. 'Would you have fallen and injured yourself this badly if she hadn't pushed you?'

Sophia hesitated, not wanting to acknowledge the truth in Isaac's question.

The boat hit a wave and lifted for a second before thumping back down.

She winced with pain.

Isaac wiped more blood from her face. 'It won't be long. I know it's not very comfortable, but try to rest if you can.'

Utterly exhausted, she nodded, then closed her eyes.

⌘

THE WATER BECAME CHOPPIER, AND ISAAC BRACED AGAINST the seats to absorb as much of the impact from the boat as he could.

Sophia had fallen asleep again, her body curled in the cradle of his arms.

Despite his mind's constant rationalisation of the situation, his heart still thumped in his chest.

Sophia on the temple floor. Her cry of pain. The sight of her now.

Each memory slashed his skin until he was bleeding emotion and didn't know how to stem the flow.

You've done this. This is your fault. It's just like with Daniella.

It's not the same.

Physical or mental, pain is still pain.

If he hadn't told Guruji about Sophia, her karma yoga wouldn't have been changed. Grace wouldn't have pushed her and she wouldn't be here now. He'd got her into this situation and he would make sure he helped her recover from it in any way he could.

He carefully wiped a new trickle of blood from her forehead. He'd bandaged the wound to the best of his ability, but it was deep. Shiva's hands were beaten from a sheet of metal, and the edges were razor sharp. Moving the statue to the side of the temple would be one of the first things he did when they got back.

Cash, ashram credit card, phone, passport, water.

Isaac had the essentials. However, Sophia's uniform was trashed, and she was barefoot. Should he ring Anisha and get Sophia's next of kin details?

Wait.

She was alive, and Isaac knew he'd give up his own life to make sure she remained that way.

The boat slowed, and tall masts came into view beyond the edge of the speedboat.

Sophia stirred in his arms.

'Don't try to move. Mohan's just mooring the boat, then he's going to get a taxi.'

She nodded. 'What time is it?'

'A little after seven. Can I get you some water?'

'Yes, please.'

Lifting an arm from her back, she moved closer to him as if scared he was going somewhere. Another bolt of pain lanced his chest. Grabbing the bottle from his bag, Isaac unscrewed the lid and held it to Sophia's lips. She took it, blood from her palms smearing against the sides, the sight magnified by the water through the clear plastic.

His stomach lurched. *This is your fault.*

'Thank you. I was so thirsty.' She lifted the bottle. 'There's still some for you. I'm sorry I've made such a mess.'

'It's fine and I'm fine. You finish it.'

'Are you sure?'

'Absolutely. Please.'

Sophia drained the bottle, then settled back against his chest.

'Isaac...'

'Yes.'

'Are you leaving once we get to the hospital?'

Jesus Christ. 'No.'

'Thank you. I'm not great with new situations. Or people I don't know. Or hospitals.'

'I'll stay with you the whole time.'

'Promise?'

He gently squeezed his arms around her a little tighter. 'Promise.'

'HANUMAN!'

Isaac lifted his head.

Mohan was beside the boat. 'There's a taxi waiting at the entrance. I'll give you the boat keys for later, then take the ferry back to the island. Can I help carry her?'

The sensible answer to Mohan's question was 'yes', however some primal part of Isaac growled 'no'. He'd got Sophia into this state, and it was his responsibility to get her out of it.

And, much as he didn't want to admit it, the caveman side of him was beating his chest and roaring that Sophia was *his* woman and no-one would touch her but him.

'Hanuman?'

Get a hold of yourself.

'Thanks, Mohan, that would be great. I'm not sure if my legs have gone to sleep or not.'

Sophia went to move and Mohan leapt into the boat to help her up.

Getting to his feet, Isaac rubbed his legs as pins and needles pricked his muscles. As soon as he could trust them to work properly, he helped lift Sophia onto the dock.

Waiting for them was a trolley.

'I thought we could push her on that?' Mohan suggested.

Sophia stiffened, then took a breath. 'Great idea.'

'No,' Isaac replied, sweeping her into his arms. 'The dock is uneven and there's nothing to absorb any of the impact.'

Sophia relaxed, and his own stress eased a little.

Setting off carefully, Isaac followed Mohan out of the marina.

'OH, MY GOODNESS, WHAT HAPPENED TO YOU!'

The nurse clicked her fingers at a porter who dashed forward with a wheelchair.

'I fell,' Sophia said, her arms tightening around the back of Isaac's neck.

The woman's eyebrows raised.

'Into a statue of Shiva,' Sophia continued, showing the laceration to her palm, where she'd tried to stop her fall. 'Two of his hands are very sharp. And I've done something to my knee as well.'

There was a pause as the woman looked between them.

Isaac's heart sank. *She thinks* I *did this to her*.

'Well, my dear, let's get you checked in, then take you through for assessment.'

Isaac carefully lowered Sophia into the wheelchair, then the nurse firmly elbowed him out of the way.

'What's your name, sweetie?' she asked her.

'Sophia. And this is—'

'Well, I'm Doreen, and we're going to take good care of you, honey,' she replied, setting off across the reception area.

Sophia turned in her seat, reaching for Isaac.

Rushing to her side, he took her hand.

'It's okay, sir, we can take it from here.'

'No,' Sophia said, panic creeping into her tone. 'He has to come with me.'

They'd already reached a set of locked double doors.

Doreen pulled a keycard from a lanyard on her waist. 'I'm sorry, sweetie, but only family members—'

'I'm her husband,' Isaac interrupted.

Doreen's gaze snapped to Sophia.

She didn't miss a beat. 'Yes, this is my husband, Isaac. We've been staying at the ashram on Tranquillity Island.'

Sophia tugged the hem of her bloodstained t-shirt down to show Doreen the Devanandara logo. 'I was very tired this morning and not looking where I was going when I entered the temple for Satsang. I slipped and didn't want to crash into the person in front of me, so I pivoted and instead had an unfortunate encounter with a Hindu deity.'

She gave Doreen a sunny smile. 'As well as being inherently clumsy, I also struggle with panic attacks and have a deep fear of hospitals. I'm sorry if it's inconvenient, but if my husband can't stay with me, then I'm going to have to leave.'

Isaac tried to stay calm as Doreen glanced between the two of them. Sophia was squeezing his hand hard enough to cut off the blood supply to his fingers.

'Okay, honey, let's get the two of you through.'

Doreen unlocked the doors and pushed Sophia into the assessment area, wheeling her into a bay and up to a bed.

'When you're out of the chair, I'll get the doctor and the forms.'

Isaac helped her lift Sophia onto the bed. Then Doreen left, swishing the curtain across to give them privacy.

As soon as she'd gone, Sophia's head hit the pillow, all the energy that had animated her with Doreen draining away.

'I'm so sorry,' she whispered. 'I just don't want to do this on my own.'

Isaac took her hand. 'It's fine. I'm not going anywhere.'

Sophia's forehead creased. 'I think she thought *you'd* done this to me.'

Bile rose in his throat. 'Unfortunately, that's not an irrational thought.'

Her eyes became liquid. 'That's so awful.'

'I know.'

Reaching forward, he wiped her tears away with the pad of his thumb. 'I'm so sorry this has happened.'

Sophia tried to smile, but her lower lip was wobbling. 'This year has been the absolute worst. I'd like to think things came in threes, but this is the fifth awful thing that's happened and it's still only July.'

Isaac clenched his jaw, holding back his own emotion. Like Eveline, Sophia was one of the kindest souls he'd ever met and didn't deserve the hand she'd been dealt.

She swallowed. 'Isaac...'

'Yes, love.'

The endearment slipped out without him realising, but Sophia's expression didn't change. Had she even noticed?

'Am I to blame for all the awful things that have happened to me this year?'

'No! Of course not.'

'But... What about my prarabdha? The karma from my past lives that I'm meant to reap in this one.'

Isaac knew about the different forms of karma, but when someone as lovely as Sophia was suffering, he struggled to understand it.

'When people have been breaking down and crying, Swami Saraswati, Mohan and Anisha say it's because we're burning off negative karma,' she continued. 'But I think it's more to do with the fact we're hungry, sleep-deprived, and overwhelmed with information.'

Isaac had heard the 'burning off negative karma' explanation given for people's tears so many times, but had never questioned it before.

'But if karma is real, was I a truly terrible person in a past life? How Marcus treated me; the affairs, the drugs, the dig. And what happened to my dad this year? Is it all my fault?'

Isaac knew he should talk to Sophia about resilience and fortitude. About having a strong yoga practice to neutralise negative prarabdha and build positive agami karma for the future. But his throat was dry.

He swallowed. 'Maybe you're so lovely in this life, your next one will be perfect.'

'But I don't care about my next life. I'm living in this one. *This* is what's real to me.'

Isaac's heart twisted as he gazed at the tears tracking down Sophia's blood-stained cheeks, the dark hollows under her eyes. He'd been so sure about every aspect of yoga he'd been taught, but now questions were forming like tiny cracks on the surface of a frozen lake in the springtime.

'Maybe,' he began, his voice low as he spoke his heresy, 'the idea of karma is there to help us understand why bad things happen to good people and good things happen to bad people.'

'Do you really believe that?' she whispered.

He squeezed her hand. 'I believe that none of this is your

fault and you don't deserve any of it. You're the best of people, Sophia, and... and I—'

The curtain was swept aside, and a woman entered the cubicle, pushing a small trolley.

'Oh dear, you *are* in a pickle,' she said, then snapped on a pair of latex gloves. 'My name's Tonya. I'm one of the doctors here.'

Doreen arrived and passed Isaac a clipboard and pen. 'Can you fill this out while the doctor's taking care of your wife?'

Your wife...

He cleared his throat. 'Of course.'

Releasing Sophia's hand, Isaac took the forms and got off the bed.

'Don't go!' Sophia's voice was panicked.

'I won't, love. I'm right here. I just need to give the doctor some space. Alright?'

Sophia nodded, then glanced at Tonya. 'Sorry. I'm not great with hospitals and it's been a bit of a morning.'

Tonya smiled. 'And it's not even nine o'clock. Don't worry, Sophia, you're in good hands. Now, why don't you talk me through what happened and we can do a full injury assessment.'

Taking Sophia's passport from his bag, Isaac filled in the form as she talked, putting his mobile number down as well as his address in Foxbrooke, as Sophia's home. He knew they were in an abnormal situation and were only pretending to be married. However, the thought of her living in his home didn't evoke feelings of revulsion. Quite the opposite. In his mind, her presence there was natural, as if she was an intrinsic part of his happy place.

'Oof, that's a nasty cut you've got there,' Tonya said as she lifted the bandage. 'But it'll stop bleeding as soon as I've stapled it up.'

The clipboard dropped from Isaac's hands, and Sophia's face paled.

Tonya chuckled. 'Oh, don't worry, it's a medical stapler. I apologise. I forget how that must sound.' She took a small white device from the trolley. 'It's sterile and remarkably effective. You'll be able to have the staples out in about a week, and as the scar is by your hairline, hopefully it'll be pretty unnoticeable.'

Sophia gave her an unsteady nod.

'If people ask you how you got it, you have to have a very exciting story ready.'

'I had a fight with lord Shiva.'

Tonya laughed. 'That trumps a shark attack any day.'

ISAAC STAYED WITH SOPHIA WHILST THE GASH ON HER HEAD was stapled and the one on her hand bandaged, then followed as she was wheeled to have an X-ray, then CT scan.

After the scan, Sophia's bed was pushed into a private room overlooking the bay.

'Rest now while the doctor looks at the results,' Doreen said to Sophia, before turning to Isaac. 'Can you get her fresh clothes and a pair of shoes? I don't want to get Sophia cleaned up properly until she's got something else to change into.'

Isaac nodded. 'As soon as she's asleep, I'll—'

'Are you going back to the ashram?' Sophia interrupted, her voice rising.

He took her hand. 'No, love, just into town. I won't be long and I don't need to go right now.'

'Can I get you anything to eat?' Doreen asked her.

'Yes, please. I'm absolutely starving.'

'Okay, let me get you a menu.'

As soon as Doreen left the room, Sophia's face crinkled with concern.

'Isaac, how can I pay for this? I don't think my travel insurance will cover a private room and god knows how much a CT scan costs.'

Even though they didn't have to put on a show of being married now, he didn't want to relinquish her hand.

He smiled. 'You won't even need to worry about putting in a claim. The ashram is paying for all of it.'

Sophia's mouth dropped open. 'But how?'

'None of the ashram staff get a wage, so there's plenty of money for emergencies like this.'

'Anisha and Mohan work for nothing?'

He nodded. 'We all do. It's our calling. Our karma yoga.'

'Wow.'

'Long-term staff don't pay to stay at the ashram and they get their food and a tent space for free. If they've been part of the organisation for a few years, their flights are also covered from their home countries.'

'Gosh.'

Isaac squeezed her hand. 'So, when the menu comes, knock yourself out.'

'What about you?'

'I'll grab something in town later. Don't worry about me, just focus on you.'

Sophia's eyes welled up again. 'Thank you so much, Isaac. And thank you for pretending to be my...'

'Anytime.'

In the pause that followed his words, her pale cheeks flushed red and his heart thumped louder in his chest.

There was a knock at the door and Doreen re-entered. 'I've got the menu, sweetie.'

Isaac stood, his hand still holding Sophia's. 'Are you okay if I go into town now?' he asked her.

She nodded, her cheeks still coloured. 'Yes, thank you. I'll see you later.'

He hesitated, not wanting to break the connection between them.

Then, before he could talk himself out of it, he leaned forward and pressed a soft kiss to her forehead.

Heat flushing through his face, he stepped back, gave Doreen a quick nod, and left the room.

$$\text{❧ 13 ❧}$$

Sophia's eyes blinked open at the knock on the door.

Have I been asleep?

'Come in,' she called out, then glanced at her watch.

Isaac entered, carrying bags. 'How are you feeling?'

'A little more human. I had a sandwich, then nodded off. How are *you* doing?'

'All good, although I received a few odd looks in town.'

She gazed at his blood-spattered clothes. 'You didn't get yourself some new ones?'

'I did. I just thought I might clean myself up first here.'

'The en suite has a shower and Doreen left me a pile of towels, so knock yourself out.'

'Has the doctor been back yet?'

'Yes. Luckily the knee is just a sprain, no torn or broken bits, so I've been given crutches and painkillers and just need to rest and elevate it as much as possible. She's given me a sheet of information to refer to, and I've got an appointment in a week to have the staples removed. Apparently, the room is mine all day and we can leave when we want. You just need to fill out a few more bits of paperwork.'

'I can do that now.'

'Why don't you wash and change first?'

'If you're sure?'

'Yes! Or do you need to get back to the ashram?'

Isaac shook his head, and Sophia relaxed. Her injuries were still painful, but she was in no hurry to leave. Even being in a hospital felt like a holiday from the daily grind of the TTC.

She nodded her head at the bags he was holding. 'What did you get me?'

He froze, his cheeks darkening. 'I, er...'

Even though butterflies were partying in her tummy, Sophia attempted to act cool.

'Have you got me a pair of board shorts and a t-shirt that says "My parents went to the Caribbean and all I got was this lousy t-shirt"?'

'I bought that outfit for myself.'

'Oh my god, *did* you?'

He grinned. 'You'll have to wait and find out.'

'Spoilsport. So then, what am I wearing?'

Isaac took a big breath. 'There wasn't a lot of choice and I had to guess your size.'

His head dipped, looking at the bags. 'I don't want to come across as a sleaze, but I wasn't sure if you needed new under-wear, so—' He swallowed, '—I bought you some... As well as sandals rather than flip-flops so they'll stay on your feet better.'

The butterflies in Sophia's stomach stepped up a gear, dancing wildly to the pounding beat of her heart.

Gaze still lowered, Isaac placed every bag bar one on the end of her bed then backed away as if they contained unstable bombs.

'I won't be long,' he said, before disappearing into the bathroom.

Letting her breath go with a whoosh, Sophia stared at the closed door.

'I can't stop thinking about you. I want you with every breath.'

Isaac's words from the day before were a mirror reflecting her feelings for him. Many years ago, she'd been infatuated with Marcus, but it had been an immature fantasy.

Isaac had affected her down to her bones.

At the start of the year, she'd known she was attracted to him on a physical level, but she was still grieving the sudden end of her relationship and believed her attraction was merely a rebound, a distraction from thinking about her ex.

But now... Sophia knew enough about Isaac to know she liked everything about him. And 'like' didn't even begin to cover the depths of her feelings.

Taking a shoe box from the first bag, she opened it.

Inside were a pair of flat, Grecian-style sandals in soft tan leather. Her parents lived in designer clothes, and Sophia could see these sandals were of the same quality. They were beautiful, and she'd never owned a pair so special.

And they were the right size.

Letting out a little squeak of excitement, she looked at the box, trying to find the price.

It wasn't marked, nor was there a receipt.

Putting them carefully to one side, and feeling like a child opening their stocking on Christmas Day morning, she lifted tissue-wrapped packages from another bag.

Carefully peeling off circular stickers with a golden logo, she opened them up.

Oh, my god.

Fingers trembling, she held up a white bra, embroidered with pale blue flowers. The material was so soft, the design utterly exquisite, and she knew without checking that it would fit. Alongside the bra were—*two!*—pairs of matching knickers. Again, large enough to fit perfectly.

Sophia pressed a palm to her chest. No matter which way she tried to spin it, Isaac Hayward had bought her underwear...

She checked the bag, but there was no receipt and the price had been removed from the tags.

How much did they cost? And is the ashram really going to foot the bill for them?

Inside a third bag she found a hairbrush, a flannel, toothbrush and toothpaste, sun cream, a pair of sunglasses, and a wide-brimmed straw hat with a silk band inside so the straw wouldn't scratch against her skin.

And in the last bag was a scoop-necked maxi sundress with a blue hibiscus pattern on a white background.

Oh. My. God.

Sophia blinked a few times, as if needing to make sure this wasn't a figment of a pharmaceutically medicated mind, then replaced each item in their bag.

Isaac Hayward likes me. Me!

But the giddy excitement was tempered by the knowledge that he would never act on his feelings. The clothes were necessary, the shoes imperative. Isaac was just being his usual kind self and she would be silly if she read any more into his actions than that.

The shower shut off in the bathroom and Sophia carefully lifted her bad leg off the side of the bed and reached for the crutches. She'd been given a brace to support her knee but could take it off to wash. If she was mindful, she could clean the rest of herself without soaking the bandage on her hand and the stapled cut on her forehead. She remembered the flannel Isaac had bought. Had he already been thinking ahead?

After a few minutes, Isaac exited the bathroom, dressed in

loose, cream linen trousers and a navy t-shirt, his damp hair curlier than when it was dry.

Sophia bit back a whimper.

His gaze went from the bags to her as if wondering if she'd checked out what he'd bought.

'How much did it all cost? Will the ashram really pay for it? Are you going to get in trouble?' The words tumbled out of her mouth.

'Are they okay?'

'What? Yes! It's all perfect. Beautiful. Far too posh for me.'

'Well, you *are* a Lady.'

'Huh?'

'Your passport. Your name's Lady Sophia Hunter-Savage.'

Dropping her head, she let out a groan. 'I'm not titled. That's my dad's fault.'

'Is he the King?'

Sophia rolled her eyes. 'He thinks he is. Please don't tell anyone. I was going to change it when I—'

She broke off. *When I married Marcus...*

'The thing is, I was born Chardonnay Skinner.'

Isaac's eyes widened.

'I know, I know. You're thinking it suits me much better than "Sophia".'

He grinned.

'Anyway, when I was two, Dad's businesses really took off, and he decided to change my brother's name from Kevin to Lord James, mine from Chardonnay to Lady Sophia, and our surname from Skinner to Hunter-Savage.'

'Wow.'

'Yeah. My brother still calls me Char, but to everyone else, I'm Sophia. I don't talk about it much. Not that I'm embarrassed by what he did, more that I can't remember ever having a different name. But I never use the "Lady" part. I'll change it when... At some point in the future.'

Isaac was looking at her in a way that made her skin tingle. The air between them seemed to crackle with electricity.

He may fancy you, but nothing's going to happen!

Grabbing the crutches, Sophia pushed to her feet.

Isaac rushed forward as if to help but she shook her head.

'I'm okay, and I need to be able to get about unaided. Could you bring the bags, please?'

He took them into the bathroom, then came back out. 'Are you sure you're alright in there on your own?'

Heat flared through her, and she stopped, a crutch squeaking on the floor.

'Oh god, no! I didn't mean me. I—' Isaac ran a hand through his hair, his face on fire. 'I meant I could call for Doreen, or one of the other nurses.'

'Oh.' *See? Nothing's going to happen.*

Mortified at where her mind had gone, Sophia shook her head and hobbled to the door. 'I'll be fine. Can you do the paperwork please?'

Hesitating, he gazed at the brace around her knee and the crutches.

'I'm fine, Isaac. I'll pull the emergency cord if I need to.'

Giving her a brief nod, he grabbed his bag and left the room.

Sophia puffed out her flaming cheeks, then sighed. This was rapidly becoming torture. Like staring through the glass of the fanciest patisserie, knowing you could never taste any of it.

TWENTY MINUTES LATER, CLEAN AND FEELING LIKE A BOHO princess, Sophia exited the bathroom.

Isaac was sitting on the bed, looking at his phone. Standing, he pocketed it and stared at her as if he knew he shouldn't but couldn't look away.

'Do you like it?' she asked shyly.

His gaze was reverential but hungry. 'You're so beautiful...'

Sophia's mouth ran dry and her expensive panties ran wet. Her body ached for him.

Clearing his throat, Isaac glanced away. 'All the paperwork's done. We're in no hurry to get back, so I didn't know if you wanted to go for lunch. You said you'd eaten a sandwich, but that doesn't sound much.'

'That would be great. I'm still a bit hungry. Is there somewhere close by?'

'There's an amazing barbeque place just over the road.'

'Meat?'

Isaac looked embarrassed. 'In the interests of full disclosure, I had a burger an hour ago.'

Sophia burst out laughing. 'And my sandwich had chicken and bacon in it... So, what happens on Tortula stays on Tortula?'

He nodded. 'This is one rule I don't have a problem breaking.'

'So, YOU NEVER WENT ALL-IN WITH THE VEGETARIAN THING, then?' Sophia asked as she demolished a family-sized meat platter with Isaac.

The sun was gentler in the mid-afternoon, but they still sat under an awning, the sparkling sea just a stone's throw away.

'I did it in India for a couple of years, but it's not a diet I thrive on,' he replied. 'And if the Dalai Lama eats meat, then I don't think vegetarianism is necessary for a strong spiritual practice. I know plenty of people who are perfectly fine without meat. I'm just not one of them.'

'And you *are* friends with Eveline, who's famous for her bacon sandwiches.'

Isaac let out a happy sigh. 'They're the best. I didn't think they could get any more sublime, but then Eveline started using sourdough bread made by Libby, Henry Foxbrooke's girl-friend, and now they're...' He shook his head. 'I try not to become too attached to things that elicit extreme emotion, whether positive or negative, but her sandwiches are an exception to that rule.'

Even though her head still ached, Sophia's cheeks hurt more from how much she'd been smiling. Conversation with Isaac was effortless, and she couldn't remember the last time she'd felt so free.

Whether it was the warm air and sunshine, the fresh breeze coming off the ocean, the fact she was now well-fed and far away from Foxbrooke, or the man she was hanging out with, Sophia was utterly content.

Isaac seemed happy, too. Anyone strolling past them would have presumed they were a couple on holiday. Sophia felt beautiful in her dress, and knowing what was underneath it gave her a confidence she'd never experienced before. She was wearing gorgeous clothes, in a picture-perfect location, and spending time with a man who should have been on the cover of a magazine.

'I spoke to Swami Saraswati earlier,' Isaac began.

Worry spiked in Sophia's guts. 'Is everything okay? The money?'

'It's all fine. We were discussing your accommodation. There's no way you'll be able to get up and down those stairs safely with the crutches.'

'I can barely get up and down *without* crutches.' Sophia pulled a face. 'I've lost count of the times I've slipped.'

Isaac frowned. 'They're too steep and the tread's too

narrow. I've already spoken to her about getting them replaced, but it won't be in the next couple of hours, so we've arranged for you to move to a ground floor room.'

'Oh. Is it expensive?'

'There's no cost. It's usually used for visiting speakers, or high-level members of the organisation, and it's free at the moment.'

'Is she sure?'

'Absolutely. She can come across as a little, er... *severe*, but she's a wonderful person. And, to be perfectly frank, there's always the worry you'll sue.'

'Sue? For what?'

Isaac smiled. 'I know we Brits aren't particularly litigious, but you do have a strong case.'

Holding up a hand, he ticked off each point in turn. 'Inadequate lighting. Steps not marked and no anti-slip tape on them. Incredibly sharp statue not secured and right next to a public walkway. Overcrowding of a public space.' He sighed. 'And you could easily argue that you've been deprived of sleep that has affected your awareness and mobility.'

'Oh.'

'So, we're sorting you a room with easy access for the rest of your stay and covering all medical and other expenses. I'll also grab you another uniform from the shop, and no, you won't have to pay for it.'

'Thank you. I appreciate this so much. Would you be able to find Jessica for me when we get back? She can bring my things down from the dorm.'

'Will do. She reminds me of Estelle.'

'Me too! Can you imagine the two of them in the same room?'

Isaac laughed. 'It would be very loud and very funny.'

Sophia buzzed with happiness, but she knew they couldn't put off returning to the ashram forever.

'Isaac...'

'Yes, lo—yes?'

She tried to ignore what he'd almost said, even as her heart jumped. 'Before we take the boat back, can we find a supermarket?'

'Sure. Is there anything in particular you need?'

Sophia grinned. 'There is...'

'LEMONS!' JESSICA SCREECHED. 'NO WAY!'

Sophia's smile split her face at her friend's excitement.

'And that's not all...'

'Oh yeah, you found me a hot single dude to bang?'

'Hmmm, not exactly. Instead, I've found you the World...'

'Huh?'

'Wide... Web... Check out the information sheet on the inside of the door.'

Jessica went over and peered at the sign.

'Holy shit!' She turned around, her shrieks turning to whispers. 'The freaking *wi-fi* password!'

'Just don't tell anyone you've got it.'

'No siree! That's proprietary information. Only available to residents of the gated community and their new best friends.'

Sophia giggled. 'Every cloud and all that?'

Jessica turned in a circle, taking in the space.

The wooden, chalet-like structure overlooked the sargassum-free private beach and had its own porch. Inside was a single bed and nightstand, chest of drawers, wardrobe, desk and chair, and an attached bathroom.

'Hoo-ee, this is something else. If that bed was a double, I'd be moving in.'

'I'll give you the code for the gate so you can come and go whenever you like.'

'As if we've got loads of down time... Hey, you gonna be okay tomorrow? As soon as Satsang's over, I'm outta here.'

'I'll be fine. Isaac—*Hanuman* said he'd look after me.'

'I bet he did...'

Blushing, Sophia attempted to deflect. 'We went to an amazing barbeque place near the marina. You should check it out if you have time.'

Jessica sat on the end of the bed, carefully avoiding Sophia's outstretched leg, and grinned at her.

'So that's why you're looking so perky. You've had a big portion of meat this afternoon...'

A snort of laughter escaped. 'Behave! He's been very clear about the celibacy thing.'

'While buying you a fancy new outfit...' Jessica paused, a frown wrinkling her forehead. 'You still wearing your old underwear?'

If Sophia's face was hot before, now it was on fire.

Jessica howled with laughter. 'If I ever commit a crime, I ain't never getting you to cover for me. Your face can't lie.'

Sophia rolled her eyes. 'How was today?'

'At any given point at least one person was crying, and Grace practically didn't stop. She went from "oh Sophia's such a bitch", to "if she dies, I'll kill myself". Ugh. It was tedious.'

Sophia kept quiet. She didn't want Jessica to kick off if she discovered Grace had pushed her.

'And Swami Saraswati came into class and tore all the fashionistas a new one. Because they'd got away with turning their t-shirts into bikinis, Blake and Xander cut the sleeves of their t-shirts off, and the girls hacked theirs into crop tops and turned the baggy pants into hot ones. Swami Saraswati made them all buy new uniforms.'

'Oh dear.'

Jessica shrugged. 'Honestly, I don't give a shit. I'm just looking forward to getting outta dodge tomorrow and stuffing my pie hole.'

There was a knock at the door.

Jessica went to open it. 'Oh, hey, Hanuman. How's it going?'

'Great, thanks.' He looked past Jessica to Sophia. 'I've got your new uniform.'

'Thank you.' She went to get up.

'No, don't move. I also wanted you to know I'm arranging two chairs at the back of the temple so you can put your leg up during Satsang.'

Jessica took the bundle of clothes from him. 'I'll make sure she gets there in one piece.'

Isaac gave her a relieved smile. 'I really appreciate it.' He glanced at Sophia again, as if he wanted to say more.

Jessica smirked. 'Okay, thank you. See you later!'

He nodded, then left.

Jessica closed the door and made a show of fanning herself. 'Is it me, or did this island just get a whole lot hotter?'

Sophia rolled her eyes.

'Tomorrow's a day off and I'm planning on breaking as many ashram rules as I possibly can. How about you, chickadee?'

Sophia didn't reply. In her mind, she and Isaac were already breaking the biggest one of all.

'Hello, this is the Rectory. Eveline Newton speaking.'

'Hey, it's me.'

'Oh, my goodness! Isaac!'

'I tried your mobile, but it rang out.'

'I think I left it in the kitchen. What an absolute pleasure to hear your voice! How are you? And how's India?'

'I'm not there anymore.'

'Are you back?'

'No. My guru wanted to visit another ashram, so we came to the one in the British Virgin Islands.'

'How lovely! The weather must be a step up from the Himalayas. But what on earth is the time there now?'

Isaac looked out into the darkness, the moonlight glittering on the surface of the sea.

'Five a.m.'

'Good grief. I want to yawn thinking about it. Although in a few weeks I expect I'll be awake then.'

'How's pregnancy going? How are you feeling?'

'Every day is a little different, but it's manageable at the moment and I'm not as tired as I was at the beginning. Oh, and my belly button popped out the other day!'

Fear flashed through him. 'What?'

She laughed. 'Not literally. I got into a bath, and as I lay down, my inny became an outy! It was quite a surprise.'

He let out a relieved sigh. 'I bet it was.'

In the silence that followed, Isaac thought about Eveline. How her life had changed since meeting Jack. It was evolving. Growing. Were his feelings of unsettled dissatisfaction because he was stuck in a rut? If he needed to move on, none of his attempts so far were working.

'Have you heard anything about the compulsory purchase order?'

'No, not yet.' He rubbed the lines on his forehead. 'I've reached out to everyone else who's affected, including Erica at Foxbrooke Haven, so we can coordinate our response, so that's a start.'

'I had a thought that might help.'

'Yes?'

'Would it strengthen your case if you also ran a business from your home?'

'I don't know. What kind of business?'

There was a short pause.

'Quilting classes.'

'What?'

Eveline let out a peal of laughter. 'I'm joking! Yoga of course.'

'How?'

'The usual way? You must have space to teach a couple of people at least? It wouldn't have to be much, but you could then argue that the compulsory purchase order would affect your business as well as your home.'

Isaac tried to imagine the women from his class in his

house and couldn't. Apart from him, the only person he could see there was Sophia.

'Thanks. I'll speak to my brother and see what he has to say.'

'I know it's not an ideal solution. I'm just trying to think of anything that might help.'

'And I really appreciate it.'

'So then, how's the sunny Caribbean? I know an ashram isn't meant to be "fun" per se. But are you enjoying yourself?'

'It's... complicated.'

'That doesn't sound good.'

Isaac took a deep breath, trying to find the right words.

'Sophia! Oh my baby-brain! I completely forgot! She's at that ashram now, isn't she?'

He nodded.

'Isaac?'

'Sorry, I forgot you can't see me. Yes, she's here.'

'Ohhhhhh...'

'Yep.'

'My prayers have been answered.'

'Huh?'

'I asked God to help you.'

'With Sophia?'

'No, in general. But it would appear he wants you to spend more time with her.'

'So does my guru.'

'Really?'

'He thinks the more I'm with her, the less I'll feel.'

Eveline's laughter was so loud, Isaac had to hold the phone away from his ear. He couldn't help but grin at his friend's reaction.

'Oh, Isaac, what a silly man! That's the opposite of what's going to happen. Sophia's an absolute delight.'

He stared at the sand, scuffing it with his toe. 'I know.'

'You and her, stuck together on a tropical island. This is just like one of my Polly Hart novels!'

'The ones with really long titles?'

'Yes. I'm just trying to think of one for your situation... Hang on... It would be something like "Stolen Kisses and Moonlight Wishes at the Pineapple Ashram on Palm Tree Island". Yes! That's perfect.'

Lifting his gaze to the moon, Isaac imagined kissing Sophia. Every cell in his body lit up.

'Is it difficult being there with her?'

Isaac had always been honest with Eveline and now wasn't the time to stop.

'It's agony. It feels like we're one person, and when we're apart, everything inside me aches. Then, when I'm with her... I want to...'

'Do everything?'

He let out a held breath. 'Yes. But it's more than lust. It feels like—' He couldn't allow himself to say, or even think, the word that his soul cried out. 'It's just more.'

'Isaac, remember me telling you about my early twenties, before I found God?'

'Yes.'

'So, just like your life changed radically when you left your job in London, mine is the polar opposite of how it once was.'

'Uh-huh.'

'And now, since Jack, it's changing for me again. My point is that life never stands still. And just because we think we've got it where we want it, doesn't mean the status quo will be appropriate for a year down the line, or even a day. Events change us. *People* change us. And we also have the power to remake ourselves at any time.'

Eveline sighed. 'I know we like to think we're flexible, but most people are stiffer than steel girders. Even if someone's circumstances are simply terrible, they're often too scared to do anything different because they're too comfortable with what they know. And then there's the perceived social embarrassment if we've taken a certain position and go back on it.'

Isaac was silent. He'd been so sure of his path for so many years, but was now facing a fork in the road he could never have anticipated.

'It's like the staunch vegan who now eats meat. The evangelical Christian who renounces God. The man who comes out as gay, years after marrying a woman. We create these personas for ourselves, then worry about what people will think if we want to do something differently. But Isaac, you're *allowed* to change your mind. Deciding to pursue a physical relationship with Sophia, or anyone else for that matter, doesn't alter who you are as a person.'

'I can't imagine having a physical relationship with anyone *other* than Sophia.'

'And doesn't that tell you all you need to know?'

Isaac didn't know how to reply. Everything Eveline had said was right.

'Are you worried about what people might think? Your guru?'

'Yes.'

'Don't be. Don't let other people dictate your happiness.'

'But I don't even know if Sophia likes me that way.'

'Then ask her! You've got nothing to lose.'

'I don't want to make her uncomfortable. Anyway, I'm her teacher, so it's completely inappropriate. *And* I'm too old for her.'

'What? You're... Eight years older? I've got five years on Jack and neither of us care. Honestly, if we all went around following the so-called rules to the letter, then we'd be miserable. You're a man of the utmost integrity. I know you'll only say something to Sophia if you feel she might be receptive. And if you're concerned about what people in Foxbrooke are going to think, the only person who might have been a little disgruntled with you getting a girlfriend, is Estelle, but she's now madly in love with Sophia's brother.'

Isaac's insides twisted in turmoil. For the first time in his life, he understood temptation. His rational mind told him to stick to his life script, but every other part of him craved Sophia more than his next breath.

'Isaac?'

'Yes?'

'Allow yourself to be happy, and please, also consider this. If Sophia likes you as much as you like her, shutting down any possibility of a relationship will hurt *her* just as much as it's hurting you...'

AFTER HIS CONVERSATION WITH EVELINE, ISAAC SAT ON THE beach and mulled over her words as the stars faded and the pale edge of dawn glimmered on the horizon.

Whether through the cruel and unnecessary actions of others, family circumstances, or accident, Sophia had already been through enough for one lifetime. The thought he might be causing her pain made Isaac feel sick.

To his left, at the edge of the beach, the dark shapes of people were moving into the temple. Standing and turning away from the sea, he faced the private villas and a choice he never thought he'd have to make. Each morning and evening, whenever he was with his guru, Isaac was the one who escorted him to Satsang.

But now there was someone else his thoughts went to first —Sophia.

Torn with indecision and doubt, he forced his feet towards the far end of the beach and Swami Vishnu's house.

As he drew near, his guru came out onto the deck.

'Namaste, Hanuman.'

Isaac dipped his head in deference. 'Namaste Guruji.'

Swami Vishnu proffered his arm. 'Shall we?'

Isaac took it, and they made their way along the path in front of the villas.

'How's Sophia doing?'

'Okay, I think, considering the circumstances. She'll need time to rest and heal, and the bruising will come out more over the next few days.'

Swami Vishnu chuckled. 'Not so pretty now, is she?'

A sudden bolt of anger struck Isaac's chest, so fast and furious he lost all sense of the man he'd worked so hard to become. An icy wind of fear followed on, chasing the anger away and rattling the cages that held his darkest memories.

Am I still that person? Dangerous? Unhinged?

His guru seemed to take Isaac's silence as agreement.

'See, I was right. Youth and beauty are a transitory illusion. The soul is eternal.'

Isaac's jaw clenched. Yes, Sophia was beautiful, but his attraction to her wouldn't have grown into what it was now if she hadn't also been such a lovely person.

As they approached her small building, the door opened, and she hopped out unsteadily.

Swami Vishnu's arm tightened slightly around Isaac's, but he ignored it, pulling away and rushing forward to help.

Sophia gave him a grateful smile. 'Thank you.'

Isaac closed the door behind her and she came forward on the crutches.

'Good morning, Swami Vishnu.'

He gave her a nod. 'How did you enjoy sleeping in Hanuman's bed?'

Sophia's eyes widened with shock, and she stumbled on the step down from the wooden deck.

Isaac caught her before she fell.

'You okay?' he murmured.

Swami Vishnu chuckled. 'Hanuman gave up his accommodation for you.'

Why are you telling her this?

Sophia stared at Isaac, an expression of horror on her face. 'I've taken your room?'

'It's fine.'

'But where are you staying now?'

'He's in a tent that got left behind at the end of last season,' Swami Vishnu said. 'Don't be concerned. He's slept in a cave before. A tent is luxury.'

Sophia's features were pinched. 'You've already done so much to help me. You can't do this as well!'

Isaac's heart squeezed at her distress and he clenched his jaw. Why was Guruji stirring the pot? Sophia didn't need to know he'd given up his room for her.

Forcing a smile, he kept his voice calm. 'This is my choice, and Guruji agrees with my decision. I'm perfectly happy in the tent and that's where I'm staying.'

Swami Vishnu continued along the path.

'We're going to be late for Satsang,' he called over his shoulder.

Isaac stayed by Sophia's side as she hopped, her face set with determination, as if trying to be as fast as possible.

'Go on with him,' she whispered. 'Please?'

He glanced ahead to Swami Vishnu, now walking at a more spritely pace than normal.

'But I want to stay with you.'

Sophia shook her head. 'This situation is awkward enough already. I don't want the entire ashram seeing you abandon your guru for me. I promise I'll be okay, and if I fall, everyone will see. Please, Isaac. Just go.'

He gave her a brief nod, jogged up the path to rejoin his guru, then continued by his side in silence.

You should have stayed with her.

And gone against what she explicitly asked? Made her more unhappy?

Entering the temple, his eyes flicked to the back. Jessica was next to the two chairs he'd laid out with Sophia's name on them, glaring at anyone who tried to take one.

Isaac settled Swami Vishnu in his seat, then sat beside him, his gaze following Sophia as she manoeuvred around people who seemed oblivious to her, or disinclined to get out of the way.

Anger burned brightly inside him. He wanted to yell at them to open their eyes and have a care for someone who wasn't themselves. Was yoga really this self-centred?

How are you any different? You chose this path for you, not for anyone else.

Feeling Swami Vishnu's eyes on him, Isaac regulated his breathing, but only picked up the bell for his guru to ring once Sophia was safely in her seat.

ISAAC HAD NEVER BEEN SO ON EDGE DURING A SATSANG. ON the surface, things were mostly the same, but subtle differences scratched at what little equanimity he had left.

Mohan wasn't there, presumably driving the ashram's ferry, as the usual captain, Ganapati, was sitting on the other side of Swami Vishnu, his scowl stapled in place.

Swami Saraswati seemed out of sorts, fiddling with her robe and frowning. Anisha looked to be on the verge of tears.

What was going on?

As Satsang finished and people dispersed, Isaac stood and held a hand out to Swami Vishnu.

The older man waved him away, inclining his head towards Sophia at the back of the temple.

'I've already told you my wishes, Hanuman. Ganapati will assist me today.' He took one of Ganapati's ham-sized hands and got to his feet.

Isaac took a step back and waited as Swami Vishnu left the temple with Ganapati, Swami Saraswati and Anisha following, then crossed the floor towards Sophia, his heart lifting.

'Morning, Hanuman. You gonna take care of my best bud today?' Jessica asked as he reached them.

'I'd love to.'

Jessica turned to Sophia. 'There we go. I can paint the town red knowing you're in safe hands.'

Sophia's pale cheeks coloured as she glanced at him. 'You don't have to.'

Was this her way of telling him she'd rather be alone?

Isaac cleared his throat. 'I've got no other plans, and I'd really like to spend the day with you. But only if that's what you want.'

In the silence that followed, Jessica's mischievous grin grew bigger, and Sophia's blush deepened.

'Yes, please,' Sophia eventually said, her voice quiet. 'I'd like that.'

Jessica patted her shoulder. 'That wasn't so hard now, was it? Right, I'm gonna change out of these yoga pyjamas and get in line for the boat. If I'm not on the next one outta here, I might lose my goddamn mind.'

She grabbed her bag. 'Be good, kids. And if you can't be good, be careful.'

She winked at them, then strode from the temple.

Isaac's heart thumped louder in his chest. A whole day with Sophia. He couldn't remember the last time he'd felt such giddy excitement. He sneaked a glance her way. She was staring at the temple entrance, as if Jessica was still there.

Come on. You're just hanging out with her. How hard can this be?

He swallowed. 'So, er... What would you like to do?'

❦ 15 ❦

What would I like to do? Er, stare into your eyes as you tell me I'm beautiful? Kiss you for hours? Have your hot naked body—

'Sophia?'

A is for ashram, B is for bashed up from a nasty accident, and C is for celibacy. Remember?

Her gaze refocused, and she forced it to meet Isaac's.

He looked... *worried? Unsure?*

Still exhausted from the day before, Sophia could have done with going back to bed, but there was no way she was going to tell Isaac that. A whole day stretched in front of her, with nothing to do except spend time with him. Her answer was a no-brainer.

'I'd love to just hang out. Is there somewhere quiet where we could sit before breakfast?'

His concern melted into a smile that made her heart jump.

'I know the perfect place.'

. . .

Isaac led Sophia out of the temple and around the side, unlocking the gate to the private area.

'There's a meditation garden that Swami Saraswati designed behind the main building. I think she's in a meeting with Guruji at the moment, so we can see if it's free.'

Even though she now had access to this part of the island, Sophia hadn't explored. She followed Isaac carefully along perfectly level paths, flowers filling the beds on either side, and the morning light dappling through the palms above.

Ahead was a wooden gate between two hedges. Isaac peeked over the top of it, then opened it wide and extended his arm for Sophia to pass through.

Walls of bushes and bamboo made the space utterly private, a green border between the earth and the sky. In the centre was a little pond with a water feature at one end, made up of a tower of flat, round stones. Water bubbled over them from the top to the pool below, the sound filling the air. It was quiet here compared to the rest of the island, the main building and thick hedges insulating them from the noises of people and the sea.

'It's nearly as beautiful as your garden in Foxbrooke,' she said quietly, as if they were in a library or the temple.

'That's quite the compliment.'

A flat paved area lay in front of the pond, presumably for the Swami to meditate, with a wooden bench along the far edge. Meandering paths, greenery, and pebbles filled the rest of the garden.

'It's very Zen.'

Isaac nodded. 'Swami Saraswati's father was a French diplomat, and she grew up in Japan. Let's get you settled on the bench. Luckily, it's got sides, so your back will be supported.'

Sophia hopped over and Isaac took her crutches as she sat, before lowering himself to the floor beside the bench.

'There's room for both of us.'

He shook his head. 'You've got to elevate your leg. I'm fine here.'

Guilt prodded her chest. *First, he loses his room, and now he doesn't get a seat.*

Isaac's smile was warm and understanding. 'I'm perfectly comfortable, and if that changes, we can move elsewhere.'

'Would you *actually* tell me if you were uncomfortable?'

There was a tiny hesitation before he said, 'Absolutely.'

'Isaac!'

He grinned. 'I promise I will. Scout's honour.'

Heart lightening, Sophia lifted her leg to the bench, immediately feeling the relief.

'See? Listen to Doctor Isaac.'

She stuck out her tongue and his grin got wider.

Despite the aching pain in her head and knee, as well as all the other parts of her body that were battered and bruised, Sophia was buoyant and happy. There was nobody else around, and she felt completely at ease with Isaac.

Well, almost… Accompanying the relaxed feelings were ones that made her heart skip and her skin tingle.

Isaac Hayward likes me!

Whenever the thought sparked in her head, every part of her lit up. Each moment she spent with him felt charged with meaning and potential. Every second precious, like a grain of gold passing through an hourglass.

Tearing her eyes away before her smile grew too big for her face or she accidentally begged him to kiss her, Sophia gazed around the garden. Whenever she was with Isaac, her senses heightened. But here, in this little corner of paradise, her soul was singing louder than the birds overhead.

She focused on the details, imprinting every facet of the experience so deep into her memory that no matter what happened in the future, she could close her eyes and find herself once again in this perfect moment.

Isaac let out a contented sigh. 'There's something so calming about being in nature.'

Sophia nodded. 'Even if I'm on my knees in a muddy trench, I always feel happier there than back in the office.'

'I've read some great studies on the therapeutic benefits of spending time outdoors.'

'Forest bathing?'

He smiled. 'Also known as "going for a walk in the woods".'

She grinned. 'When I first heard the term, I did think it must have been coined by a researcher trying to pretty-up a grant application.'

Settling back onto the bench, Sophia thought about Isaac's house in Foxbrooke. Even though she'd only been there once, it had made such an impression on her that she missed it.

'This is such a lovely place, but I still prefer your garden.'

'You do?'

'Don't you?'

He nodded, then his expression became clouded.

'Isaac?'

He blinked. 'Sorry, my mind was elsewhere.'

'Is everything okay?'

There was a pause before he replied, as if he was weighing up whether or not to tell her something.

'There's a proposal for a bypass around Foxbrooke. If it goes ahead, my land will be compulsorily purchased.'

Shock shot through her. 'They can't do that! Can you stop it?'

A shoulder lifted in a half shrug. 'I'm doing what I can, and talking to other affected people, but I don't know if it will do anything.'

'Can I take a look at the proposal? I've had a decade in

academia. I might be able to add some weightier language to your appeal.'

'You'd do that?'

'Of course! Your house and garden should have world heritage status. I don't have my laptop with me, but I can work on it when I get home.'

'Thank you. I'd really appreciate that.'

Sophia tried to imagine Isaac's land disappearing under tarmac. If it happened, would he disappear too?

'If the worst came to the worst,' she began hesitantly, 'would you buy somewhere else locally, or...'

He looked away, staring at the pond. 'I thought I would leave.'

No! Adrenaline spiked in Sophia's blood. The thought of losing Isaac, even as a friend, flooded her with panic. But how could she get him to stay?

'I really hope you don't go.'

His body stilled, then he nodded. 'Me too.'

As they sat quietly in the garden together, Sophia's mind was whirling, spinning off on fantastical tangents where she left her job in Salisbury to move to Foxbrooke, saved Isaac's house, and he renounced his vow of chastity to be with her.

But she was never going to ask him to make that sacrifice. It was his decision what he did with his body, and she didn't want to be the kind of person who wafted a bacon sandwich under a vegetarian's nose.

The bell rang for breakfast, startling her from her daydreams.

Isaac stood, holding her crutches out for her.

'Thank you.'

Sophia took them and got to her feet. 'Jessica held my plate at dinner for me. Would you be able to do the same at breakfast?'

'Your wish is my command...'

If only...

'...Milady.'

'Oi!' She brandished a crutch at him. 'I wish you'd never seen my passport.'

He grinned. 'Your secret is safe with me.'

Bowing deeply at the waist, Isaac extended his arm towards the gate. 'Shall we?'

SOPHIA MOVED SLOWLY ALONG THE PATH AS STREAMS OF people overtook her, all heading in the same direction. Isaac was a protective wall by her side, not budging an inch as they brushed past him. Maybe they were just as starving as she was, because none of them were smiling.

'Isaac...'

'Hmm?'

'In general, people here don't seem particularly happy.'

'They don't?' He sounded genuinely surprised. 'Maybe they've got super-stressful lives and haven't decompressed yet.'

'It's not just the guests. The guy who usually drives the boat. He always looks so angry.'

'Ganapati? Yes, he does have a particular aura about him. He's originally from Australia and used to be at the ashram in India with Guruji.'

'Why did he move here?'

'Guruji sent him.'

'*Sent* him?'

'It's part of the Gurukula system. You follow the teachings

and direction of your guru. For whatever reason, Swami Vishnu wanted him here, so he went.'

'Maybe he was too grumpy for India.'

Isaac chuckled, then lowered his voice. 'Just be thankful he's doing mauna. It's better than him shouting at everyone...'

REACHING THE DINING AREA, ISAAC TOOK A PLATE AND Sophia pointed at what she wanted.

'You know, we can sit with the staff if you like? They've got food on the tables so you can help yourself without having to move.'

Sophia's head whipped from side to side. 'Thanks, but no way. I'm no good at small talk and don't want to draw any more attention to myself.'

There were a few people from the TTC who'd elected not to leave the island on their day off, and their glances prickled the back of her neck.

'Fair enough. Where would you like to sit?'

'Can we go to the bench at the very back?'

'Sure.'

Sophia followed him to the table, and Isaac placed her food down.

'Tuck in, don't wait for me.'

As he jogged off, Sophia kept her attention on her plate and the sargassum-covered beach through the trees. She hated being observed, and now there were too many reasons for people to look at her.

Even though she wanted to spend this time with Isaac, she missed the way Jessica unpicked the contradictory nature of the ashram and the inbuilt hierarchy and hypocrisies. Isaac either didn't seem to notice, or just accepted things for being the way they were.

'How did the Devanandara organisation get this island?' she asked when Isaac returned.

'Do you want the official or unofficial story?'

'Both please.'

He smiled. 'Well, you know Swami Devanandara founded the first ashram in the nineteen-fifties in Rishikesh?'

She nodded. The TTC manual spoke of westerners flocking to India to follow his teachings, then carrying them back to their home countries.

'Did you ever meet him?'

'Unfortunately not, however Swami Vishnu was very close to him and has shared a lot of stories with me. He was apparently intensely charismatic and popular with pop stars and people who had a lot of money but not much inner peace. One of these was a billionaire whose son was struggling with addiction. Swami Devanandara cured the son, and in gratitude, the billionaire gave Tranquillity Island to the organisation.'

'Wow. That's quite a gift. So, what's the unofficial story?'

Isaac leaned forward. 'Swami Devanandara won it off him in a game of poker.'

Sophia clapped a hand to her mouth as a shocked laugh escaped.

'Apparently he was a bit of a card shark and knew enough about people to play them. Coming across as a genial old yogi, then going in for the kill.'

'I like that story the best. How did Swami Vishnu get to be in charge?'

'The plan was to leave the organisation in the hands of the swamis who headed up each ashram, all of whom had been trained and appointed by Swami Devanandara. But on his deathbed, he changed his mind and gave it all to Swami Vishnu.'

In Sophia's head she could hear Jessica yelling 'yeah right'.

'Did anyone... I mean, er...'

Isaac smiled as if knowing where her mind had gone. 'There were two others who witnessed the decision.'

'And are they still at the ashram?' *Shut up, Miss Marple!*

'They left the ashram shortly afterwards, I presume devastated by their guru's death. By all accounts, the organisation was a bit of a mess when Swami Devanandara died, but Swami Vishnu really turned it around.'

Sophia nodded and took a mouthful of food, not wanting to ask any more questions and look like she doubted what had happened. Just because Swami Vishnu creeped her out, it didn't make him a bad person.

AFTER SHE'D POLISHED OFF HER SECOND PLATE OF FOOD, Isaac took Sophia's plate.

'I'd like to do something, but it's going to take about fifteen minutes. Do you mind waiting here?'

'Not at all. Do you need any help?'

He shook his head, then glanced towards the private dining area. 'Hang on, one sec.'

Striding away, he dropped off her plate, then disappeared from view, returning a moment later with a bowl.

'That wasn't fifteen minutes.'

'I got diverted by something more important.'

He placed the dish in front of her.

'Oh, my god!' she hissed. 'A chocolate brownie!'

He grinned. 'I hoped you'd like it.'

'But it's against the ashram rules!'

'And Swami Vishnu has a sweet tooth...'

Isaac hesitated, and Sophia had the oddest feeling he was about to lean down and kiss her.

But then he straightened. 'Enjoy the brownie. I'll be back in a bit.'

'What are you going to do?'

He flashed her a smile. 'If it works, you'll soon see...'

'A HAMMOCK!'

If Sophia could have put any weight on her left leg, she would have jumped up and down with delight.

'I found it in the shed where I got my tent. It's clean and in good condition, so I thought I'd rig it up here.'

'Thank you!'

He'd hung it above the wooden deck outside her chalet, sheltered from the sun under the overhanging roof. Sophia wondered how she could get in without immediately falling out the other side.

'I'll hold it steady and you turn around and sit. Then you should be able to get your legs in.'

She gave him a look. 'Knowing me, this could end really badly.'

'It won't. I've got you.'

The air crackled between them, full of words that couldn't be spoken and actions that couldn't be taken. Sophia longed to be back in the hospital, to have Isaac kiss her forehead and call her 'love'.

He moved, holding the hammock securely in place.

Sophia gingerly backed up to it and eased herself down.

So far, so good.

Clutching the edges of the fabric, she threw her right leg in, then lifted in her left.

'Have a shuffle about to get comfy. You can put this behind your head if you want,' Isaac said, holding a cushion.

Sophia wriggled about, then took it from him, letting out a happy sigh. 'Now all I need is a piña colada.'

He chuckled. 'I'm sure there's some alcohol stashed somewhere on the island, but unfortunately I don't know where.'

Taking one of the chairs on the decking, Isaac sat by her feet so they could see each other, then reached out and gently rocked the hammock.

Sophia closed her eyes. 'This is bliss, thank you.'

'My pleasure.'

His words ran through her veins like warm honey, pooling low in her abdomen. Why did men as wonderful as Isaac choose a life of chastity, when others such as Marcus couldn't keep it in their pants?

As she opened her eyes, his gaze dropped from her face to the floor.

A sudden flame of bravery flickered inside her. She wouldn't ever ask him to break his vow, but she could ask why he chose it.

Come on. What would Estelle do in this situation? Jessica?

Sophia smothered her smile. No doubt Isaac would have been tied up on the bed inside ten minutes ago if they'd have been in her place.

'Isaac?'

He lifted his head. 'Yes?'

'I was wondering why you chose to be celibate?'

His tanned cheeks flushed.

'You don't have to answer!'

'It's okay. I don't mind.'

He kept rocking the hammock, but his mind seemed elsewhere, his gaze unfocused.

Then he cleared his throat. 'As you know, I'm the youngest of four boys and we all became lawyers. I got a job at a brokerage firm in the City and thought I had my life sorted.'

'My brother used to work for a brokerage company, too.'

Isaac smiled. 'Which one?'

'Conqueror.'

'No way! Same as me.'

He paused, a frown furrowing his brow, as if this information was no longer a nice surprise.

'Was he there thirteen years ago?'

'No, he was there for the last six years.'

Isaac's face relaxed. 'Well, I'm sure you know what the hours are like and the pressure you're under. As the youngest in our family, I was always playing catch-up and wanted to be as rich and successful as my older brothers.' He gave her a rueful smile. 'But youth and working out at the gym will only prevent you from hitting the wall for so long.'

Sophia knew he'd been burnt out by his job. But what did that have to do with celibacy?

'I had a girlfriend, Daniella. She was in her early twenties and she moved into my place because we hoped it would make it easier to see each other with my long hours. But I didn't just work late into the evenings, I also worked weekends as well and so we hardly ever saw each other.'

'This was my life, and it was normal, but I couldn't see what I was doing to my mental health. I was a hamster on a wheel, surrounded by other hamsters running just as fast as I was. Daniella was unhappy, but I didn't notice. I was always working towards the next pay packet, the next bonus.'

He broke off, rubbing his jaw with one hand, the other still gently rocking the hammock.

'Daniella got a job at Conqueror, working for one of the partners, a guy called Victor Thornfield. He was in his fifties, big and bullish. The kind of man who has to be at the top of every pile. She kept telling me he was a creep, but I didn't pay enough attention to what she said. I knew he was an arsehole, but I was a bloke so had never experienced him acting inappropriately.'

Isaac hung his head. 'A few of us had been working on a big deal and were still at the office at ten o'clock one night. I got a hysterical call from Daniella and found her hiding in one of the disabled toilets at Conqueror, crying that Thornfield had groped her. She begged me not to say anything, and that she would handle it, but I ignored her and stormed through the building to confront him. It just made everything worse.'

'How?'

'It cost Daniella her job.'

'What? Seriously?'

He lifted his head. 'She was twenty-two and still on probation. Thornfield was one of the bosses and it was his word against hers. Daniella was furious. It had taken her so long to get this position, and now, because of me, she'd lost it as well as a positive reference from Conqueror. She said I'd ruined her life.'

'Isn't that going a bit far?'

Isaac shrugged. 'Maybe? But I'd let her down spectacularly. I hadn't been present in our relationship for a long time. I hadn't paid attention to her growing unhappiness, and when things came to a head, I ignored what she wanted me to do and got her sacked. After we broke up, I didn't feel ready for a new relationship, and when I met Guruji, he showed me the peace and freedom celibacy can bring. And anyway, all that aside, it's safer for me to be single.'

'Safer?'

'I can't take the risk of losing it like I did. I turned into a caveman.'

'But you're a completely different person from who you were then!'

Isaac let out a heavy sigh. 'Sometimes, even after years of

yoga, I worry it hasn't worked and I'm still the same. I can't take the risk of hurting someone like I hurt Daniella.'

Grief for what he and Daniella had been through in the past, and the future she and Isaac would never have, punched Sophia in the guts.

'But it's such a waste!'

'Huh?'

Tears filled her throat, and her words spilled out unchecked. 'There are so many horrid men out there, but you're not one of them. You're one of the good guys. I've never met anyone as kind and calm as you are. Women want and need someone like you.'

I *want and need someone like you.*

His expression was heavy with sadness.

'Just because things went wrong with Daniella, doesn't mean the same thing will happen with someone else. There's no way my next boyfriend is going to be anything like Marcus.'

'I hope not,' Isaac said softly.

Sophia held his gaze, willing him to say more, wishing he would act on how he felt for her.

But he didn't move, he just kept gently rocking the hammock, then turned to look at the sea.

Closing her eyes, she squeezed them tightly shut, willing the tears away.

If someone as nice as Isaac liked her, then she had to believe there was someone else in the world, as kind as he was, waiting for her.

The trouble was, she didn't want anyone other than Isaac.

❧ 16 ❧

The sound of the wind and water ebbed and flowed in Sophia's consciousness as Isaac rocked the hammock. Her mind drifted, floating along thought paths, then getting lost as fantasy and reality collided to become dreams. Was she falling asleep? Each time she asked the question, the answer slipped away.

She dragged herself into the present moment, her limbs stiff, and opened her eyes to see Isaac smiling at her.

'Did I sleep?' she asked, her voice scratchy and low.

He nodded.

She checked her watch. 'Four *hours*?'

'You needed it.'

'I can't believe it. I always seem to be dropping off whenever you're around.' Sophia glanced at his hand on the hammock, heat rising in her cheeks. 'Did you rock it the whole time I was sleeping?'

Isaac gave a half shrug. 'I didn't want to stop and have you wake up.'

'But... Your arm must be knackered!'

Lifting his hand from the hammock, he moved and flexed it, but not in the way that Sophia's brother would have done, in order to show off his muscles.

'Feels okay.'

'But wasn't that the most boring four hours of your life? Rocking me whilst I slept?'

'Not at all.' His face darkened, and he stood, facing away. 'Can I get you anything?'

'Could you possibly fill my water bottle? I'm really thirsty.'

'No problem.'

He picked it off the deck. 'Be right back.'

As soon as he'd gone, Sophia let out a strangled cry. Knowing that Isaac liked her whilst also knowing he would never touch her, was a form of torture she could never have imagined.

Her thoughts turned to home and Marcus. She couldn't stay in Salisbury and keep working with him and his student girlfriends. As soon as she was back, she'd have to look for another job. *And* somewhere permanent to live.

As she gazed at the sparkling blue water, a sour taste in her mouth, a wave of guilt moved through her. Here she was, in a picture-perfect paradise, but she was miserable.

Carefully holding the sides of the hammock, she swung her legs to the floor, grabbed the crutches and pushed to stand, going into her little cottage. She needed the bathroom, and she wanted to check what she looked like before Isaac returned.

Ten minutes later, her teeth were clean, her hair brushed, and she was relaxing in one of the chairs on the deck.

Isaac strolled towards her, a brown jug in one hand and her water bottle in the other.

'What have you brought?'

'A surprise,' he replied, stepping up onto the porch and passing her the bottle.

'What's in the jug?'

He pulled a glass from his back pocket. 'Close your eyes and hold out your hand.'

She frowned. 'Is this going to be a nice surprise?'

'Yes.'

'Okay.'

Closing her eyes, she heard him pour something into the glass, then felt the coolness of it against her palm.

As she brought it to her lips, the scents of pineapple and coconut filled her nostrils, and her eyes snapped open.

'You didn't!'

His grin was infectious. 'Minus the rum. I couldn't find any of that in the kitchen.'

Sipping the drink, Sophia's eyelids fluttered with the pleasure of it. 'Please tell me you're going to have some?'

Filling another glass, Isaac reached forward and clinked it against hers.

'Santé. To your health.'

'I'll definitely drink to that.' Taking another mouthful, she rolled the flavours across her tongue. 'You know, before I arrived, I thought I'd be spending so much time on the beach and swimming in the sea. But every beach apart from this one is covered in sargassum, and now I'm here, I can't walk on the sand, *or* swim.'

'You could always paddle?'

'You're joking, right? I can barely stand up straight in water when I've got both legs working. How do you think it would work now?'

'I'll help. You can hold on to me on one side and have a crutch on the other.'

Excitement fizzed in her tummy, as if her piña colada had been laced with rum.

'Are you sure?'

'Absolutely.'

'Right. Paddling here I come!'

Rolling up her baggy yoga trousers, Sophia grabbed one of her crutches, then took Isaac's proffered hand. Letting herself be drawn against him, she leant her weight through his arm.

Stepping off the path to the soft sand was an adjustment, but Isaac was her rock, stopping her from falling. Moving slowly forward, Sophia bit the inside of her cheek to stop a giggle from escaping. She felt like a tipsy teenager taking part in a three-legged race with her equally inebriated friends, all destined to end up on the floor in a fit of hysterical laughter.

But as well as this bubbling of childlike joy in her veins, she was also giddy about once again being this close to Isaac.

He appeared to be taking his role of human crutch seriously, going at her pace and taking so much of her weight he was almost carrying her.

Now there's a thought...

Sophia knew he would have done so in a heartbeat, but she didn't know who was watching them from the buildings by the shoreline and didn't want to fuel any more gossip. So she swallowed her smiles and focused on the warm sand until it turned damp and they reached the rippling edge of the water.

'You'll be fine to take your crutch in,' he said. 'I'll just give it a rinse when we're out.'

'Okay.'

The bay was on the lee of the island, so there were no waves, but Sophia still gripped Isaac's arm a little tighter as she hopped forward.

'Ooh! It's cold!'

He chuckled. 'Only because your feet are so warm from the sun. You'll get used to it soon.'

Going a little deeper, she wobbled as her foot sunk into the wet sand. Isaac lifted her as if she weighed nothing, and they continued forward until the water lapped at her mid-calf.

'Having fun?'

Turning to face him, she nodded, her smile too big to hold in. 'It's perfect.'

Isaac was so close she could make out every facet of his emerald-green eyes, the accents of amber and gold, his thick dark lashes. He was staring at her with such intent, as if on the brink of saying or doing something utterly life-changing.

Her smile faltered, and she swallowed.

His gaze dropped to her mouth, his lips parting.

Is he going to kiss me?

A fat drop of water splashed Sophia's arm, and she glanced at the grey clouds punctuating the blue sky. 'Is it going to rain?'

'I don't think so. We might get a few spots, but then it'll move on.'

Behind them, the tops of the palm trees moved faster as the wind picked up.

'Are you sure?'

'Do you want to go back in?'

She shook her head. 'We've only just got here, and anyway, we're British. We can cope with a bit of drizzle.'

'That's true. Have you seen any fish yet?'

'What, this shallow?'

'If we're still, they'll be drawn to us for shelter.'

Sophia looked down as the stirred-up sand settled.

'I see them!'

Tiny fish darted around and between their legs. She started counting, but heavy drops of rain splashed onto the surface, obscuring them.

'Isaac...'

'Yes?'

Sophia lifted her head. 'What would you call this level of precipitation?'

He frowned as a flurry of raindrops hit him. 'A light shower?'

She gave him a look.

'Er...'

Thunder rumbled.

'Isaac!'

He pulled an embarrassed face. 'I may have miscalculated.'

A bolt of lightning split the sky, then the heavens opened.

One moment, their upper bodies were a little damp. The next, they were standing under a waterfall, the surface of the sea a mist of spray from the pummelling force of the droplets.

'I'm sorry!' he shouted. 'Can I carry you out?'

'Someone might be watching!'

He nodded in understanding, then lifted and turned her so she was facing the beach.

'Ready?'

'Yes!'

As the rain poured down, Sophia hopped back towards her little cabin, Isaac holding her steady as she slipped on the sand. The situation was so comical she couldn't stop a snort from escaping. Isaac chuckled beside her, their laughter escalating until they couldn't stop.

Staggering onto the deck, the overhanging roof sheltered them from the rain, and they were cocooned on either side by the walls of the porch.

No-one could see them.

Dropping her crutch, Sophia hung onto Isaac as they laughed together. Each time she thought she'd got control of herself, she caught his eye and it set them off again until tears ran down her rain-soaked cheeks and her tummy ached.

Then the laughter ebbed, and every part of her was suddenly aware she was in Isaac's arms.

Lifting a hand, he gently moved a wet curl of hair from her forehead.

She shivered.

'Are you cold?'

Sophia shook her head. Pressed against the heat of Isaac, all she could think about was kissing him.

'Sophia...' The warmth of his breath felt like a caress.

'Yes?'

'I... I want to talk to you about something.'

'Okay.'

His gaze was so focused, so intense, it was difficult to breathe.

'I've been unsettled and unhappy for a while but couldn't work out why, because I'd created my perfect life. But then I met you... And the path I was on cracked.'

Sophia's heart thumped faster against her ribs.

'I've never questioned my vow, and no woman has ever challenged it. Being celibate was easy.'

His words were halting, his expression pained. Was she hurting him by being this close? Should she pull back? But no matter how many questions her mind threw out, her body refused to listen.

'I don't want to put you under any pressure, and I know my behaviour right now is unethical—'

'What?' she whispered.

'I'm your teacher.'

'And?'

'I don't just want a friendship with you. I want a relationship.'

Oh, my god.

'D-do you mean that?'

'Yes. My feelings for you bury deeper into my heart every moment we're together, and they're not going anywhere. I know you may not feel the same way about me, but I wanted to be honest with you as well as with myself.'

'You want to break your vow?'

'Only with you. If you aren't interested, then I'll stay celibate. But no matter what happens between us, meeting you has changed my life for the better.'

'How?'

'You challenge my status quo and make me question things I've never really thought about before. You inspire me to step out of my comfort zone and do more with my life.'

Sophia's head was filled with fireworks. All she could manage in response was 'Oh.'

Isaac's smile was tender, his expression one of resigned acceptance, as if this was the end of something and not the beginning. Shifting his arm, he tried to move her away.

She held onto him tighter.

His forehead furrowed. 'Sophia?'

Fingers trembling, she reached up and stroked his worry lines away.

'I want you too,' she whispered.

He froze.

'I've never felt like this with anyone else before.'

Sophia's heart was already thumping painfully fast, but when Isaac's shocked expression melted into fire, she was convinced it would burst from her chest. She cupped the side of his face, the softness of his stubble tingling against her palm.

Isaac's arm tightened behind her, his free hand threading through her wet hair, prickling her scalp with electricity. He gazed at her as if she were a feast prepared by angels and he'd been starving in the wilderness for years.

The drumming rain receded into the background. All Sophia could hear was the rushing of her breath, her lungs pumping in air as if to keep her afloat.

Any restraint drifting away, she grazed her fingers down the line of his jaw, feeling the heat of his skin, the wildness of his pulse. Every one of her senses thrummed with awareness of him.

Rising onto her toes, she moved closer.

Isaac swallowed as he stared at her mouth, his gaze hooded and heavy with heat.

Then he brushed his lips against hers.

Lightning crashed through her, shocking her with pleasure so sharp that she gasped.

He tensed as if he'd done something wrong, pulling away.

No!

Sophia's head was fizzing, her breathing rapid and frantic.

Don't stop!

But she was too stunned to vocalise her thoughts.

'I'm—' Isaac broke off, his expression anguished as if he'd taken something from her she never wanted to give. 'Sophia, I'm sor—'

Clutching the back of his neck, she dragged his mouth back to hers.

He didn't respond, his body stiff, but when she tentatively touched her tongue to the seam of his lips, they parted and a low groan reverberated from his throat into her.

Then Isaac kissed her back, and Sophia wondered if it was possible to survive such an experience. His tongue stroked hers with licks of fire until she was molten, white-hot pleasure pounding through every part of her, forging her into someone she never knew she could be.

She'd never encountered such feelings before. Not with Marcus, not even when on her own and fantasising about Isaac.

It was the difference between gazing at the stars and being thrust into the heart of one.

Her heart was pounding, her breath coming faster. It was too much, and it wasn't enough.

Breaking the kiss, her lungs heaving, she rested her forehead on his.

'You okay?' he asked, as out of breath as she was.

Sophia nodded, clutching him tighter to stop him withdrawing. Words had deserted her again, to be replaced with overwhelming emotion.

Isaac stroked her face, pressing tender kisses to her cheeks as love filled her throat and stung her eyes.

But despite her trembling body, she felt utterly safe in Isaac's arms. Getting her breath back, her lips found his again, and she slicked her tongue into his mouth.

He gave a feral growl, sparking a flash of lust between her legs, then kissed her with the confidence of a man who knew exactly how to make her weak at the knees.

Isaac tasted of fresh rain and piña colada, the sweetness wrapped in earthy masculinity and underscored by the rock-hard ridge of his cock pressing into her lower abdomen.

Sophia clung to him, gripping his t-shirt, his hair, as his kiss rocketed her higher. Blood was roaring through her veins, pressing on the inside of her skin, pulsing in her core. All she could think about was the desperate, aching need to be filled by him.

But despite the passion pouring off him in waves, the strength and hardness of his body, she felt the subtle vibration of Isaac's muscles as if straining to hold himself back.

Sophia didn't want him to hold back. She wanted him to take everything she had to give.

Reaching between them, she wrapped her hand around his cock through his loose yoga pants and squeezed.

He jerked his head away, a guttural cry escaping.

His trousers were so thin she could feel every glorious inch of him. Stroking his shaft, she leaned in and lightly bit his neck.

'God! Fu—' His eyes were wild, his cheeks flushed.

Sophia had never seen Isaac like this before. So beautifully untamed and teetering on the edge of losing it. She'd always been the good girl, doing what was expected without truly asking if it was right for her. And with Marcus, she always followed his lead and put his pleasure before her own. But now she was following *her* heart and *her* desires.

And all she wanted was to make Isaac come undone.

His breath was laboured and erratic, his cock hot, hard and huge in her hand.

He parted his lips as if to speak.

'I don't want to stop,' she whispered. 'But I will if you want me to?'

Isaac's gaze was desperate, as if agonising over what he thought he should do, and what he truly wanted.

'Do you want me to stop?'

He held his breath, and she stilled her hand.

There was a brief, electrifying pause, then, as if bending to the will of his body, he shook his head.

Exhaling her relief, Sophia reached up to kiss him again.

His response was immediate, his tongue tangling with hers, his cock thrusting in her grip as if finally giving himself permission to dive into pleasure.

She stroked firmer and faster, pressing him against the wall of the porch, her pussy clenching and her nipples aching. Pulling his hand from her face, she put it under her t-shirt and onto her breast.

Isaac cried out against her mouth, but his lips didn't leave hers, his kiss turning raw and ravaging.

The pad of his thumb found her nipple, and she gasped, sensation shooting down to her clit, so sharp and sweet that stars danced behind her eyes.

Isaac was shaking now, the fabric by the head of his cock wet with precum.

Power and pleasure surged inside her. Arching her chest forward, Sophia closed her eyes, losing herself in the feelings of Isaac's body as it built towards the point of no return, moving her hand faster as his breath shortened.

Suddenly he stiffened, his cock jerking into her hand, a harsh cry tearing from his throat.

Joy bursting inside her, Sophia kept stroking, feeling his trousers soaking with the warmth of his release.

Wrenching his mouth from hers, Isaac dropped his forehead to her shoulder, drawing in shuddering breaths, his hand still on her breast.

Now she was the one to soothe him, running her fingers down the nape of his neck, pressing soft kisses into his hair.

Raising his head, Isaac stared at her in wonderment, his pupils blown out, then kissed her again, his hand dropping from her breast to clasp so tightly around her back she could hardly breathe.

'Sophia, Sophia, Sophia,' he murmured between kisses. 'Sweet Sophia.'

It felt like *she* was the one who'd just orgasmed. Filled with such giddy happiness, she wasn't sure whether to laugh with joy or burst into tears.

A loud squawk sounded above them, and Sophia jumped, glancing to the beach.

The rain had stopped as quickly as it had started, the sun now beating down on the golden sand, the rainwater evaporating like steam.

In the distance was the ashram ferry, heading back towards the island.

Reality rushed in.

Turning back to Isaac, his expression stopped her heart. When had anyone, ever, looked at her that way?

'You're incredible,' he murmured, his gaze caressing her. 'That was...' He shook his head. 'There are no words.'

Then, as if he couldn't help himself, he kissed her again, nipping and sucking down her neck.

'Isaac... Isaac!'

Sophia tugged on his hair. 'The boat is coming back.'

Raising his head, he blinked, then gazed out to sea.

'Fuck,' he exhaled, as if his thoughts had accidentally escaped with his breath.

'We can be together when we're back in Foxbrooke?'

Sophia didn't mean to turn the statement into a question, but she still couldn't quite believe Isaac wanted to be with her.

His eyes flicked to the door of her cabin, as if wanting to lay her on the bed inside, then back to her.

'Are you going straight home after the course finishes?'

She nodded.

'Then I will, too.'

Her heart leapt, then froze at the sound of a faint click-click from down the beach that signified the gate opening and closing.

Isaac picked up her crutch.

Sophia took it, then hobbled towards the door. 'I'd better get showered and changed before dinner.'

His gaze raked her body, making her shiver. 'Will you be eating with Jessica?'

'If she's back in time.'

'The ferry is the last one before the evening meal. I'll grab a change of clothes and meet it. If she's not on board, I'll come back and collect you.'

'Thank you.'

Isaac paused, as if wanting to say more, but there was a creak as someone stepped towards them on the boardwalk in front of the villas.

'Go,' he said, then strode away.

Sophia entered the room and closed the door as another wave of lust and longing passed through her.

How was she going to bear being so close to Isaac but not being able to touch him for the next three weeks?

‏ ❧ 17 ❧

‘Hanuman!’

Swami Vishnu opened the door to his accommodation and beckoned Isaac in.

‘Guruji,’ he replied, dipping his head respectfully.

‘Take a seat.’

The house Swami Vishnu was occupying had a living room and kitchenette as well as a double bedroom and bathroom. Luxuriously furnished, it was used for the most important visiting speakers when Swami Vishnu wasn’t on the island.

Isaac perched on the edge of a rattan chair, glancing out the large window at the rain. The weather had turned, drenching the island in between the usual bouts of blinding sunshine.

‘You *can* relax, you know,’ his guru said, flopping down in the larger chair opposite Isaac then letting out a contented sigh. ‘My bones aren’t like they used to be, and I’d forgotten how intensive the TTC is.’

Isaac nodded. He and Swami Vishnu were now teaching most of it. Isaac wasn’t sure why they were involved and was concerned it was so that his guru could see how he interacted with Sophia.

Sophia.

Isaac's eyes briefly closed as desire pulsed in his chest. It had been nearly a week since she'd given him an experience to rival all others and altered him down to his DNA. Sophia had not only flipped a switch inside him, she'd permanently ripped it from the wall and thrown it away.

He was no longer Isaac, the yoga teacher. He was now Isaac, the eternally devoted acolyte to the goddess Sophia Hunter-Savage.

The only problem was that he'd had neither the time, nor the opportunity, to truly worship her...

Swami Vishnu reached forward and patted Isaac's knee. 'I'm glad my plan worked.'

Huh? 'What plan?'

The older man smiled benevolently. 'Sophia. Not so enamoured now, are we?'

Isaac stared blankly at Swami Vishnu as every part of him screamed that he loved her. The word no longer held any fear for him. He *had* changed. He wasn't the man he was over a decade ago, and attachments weren't to be avoided.

For weeks now, he'd hidden at the back of his mind the truth of his feelings. Now Sophia had told him she wanted a relationship, the floodgates had opened. His love for her was as natural as his next breath and as permanent as gravity. Before he'd met Sophia, he'd grown dissatisfied with life. Now he was excited about the future.

Swami Vishnu chuckled. 'You've forgotten about her already?'

Isaac rubbed his face as if to scrub away the heat rising in his cheeks. He knew he'd have to tell his guru he was breaking his vow to be with Sophia, but now didn't feel the right time.

What they had was so special, and Swami Vishnu clearly didn't understand. Sharing that news with him felt like it would soil it somehow.

'Even after how much time you've been spending together? Or has one of the other students caught your eye? They are a pretty bunch on this course and you've been very attentive to them in asana class.'

Only because you keep pushing me towards them...

Isaac bit his tongue as anger needled his stomach. Swami Vishnu had a much more hands-on teaching style than he did, and instructed Isaac to follow his lead.

Isaac always asked permission before touching any of the students, however they always said yes, then constantly called him over for more adjustments. Over a matter of days, some women had gone from adept yoga bunnies to incompetent yoga giraffes who'd lost all bodily awareness after a night on the tequila.

He gave what he hoped was a nonchalant shrug. 'I'm not interested in any of them like that.'

'Well, you're certainly giving them more attention than Sophia. It's like you don't notice her anymore.'

Isaac wanted to laugh. He did nothing *but* notice Sophia. Even if he deliberately kept his eyes averted, his body hummed with awareness of her.

Her time at the ashram had been tough enough, and he didn't want any more eyes drawn her way. When they were cleaning the temple together, they were technically alone, but they kept their distance in case anyone spotted them.

It was a torture like no other not to touch her.

Swami Vishnu adjusted his robe and smiled. 'Well, I'm glad the infatuation has taken its natural course.'

That's exactly what Eveline is going to say...

Isaac tensed his jaw to stop a wry smile from escaping.

Eveline would be ecstatic when he told her what had happened.

'And now you can devote all your attention to more important matters... I want to share some news about the organisation.'

'News?'

'Yes.' Swami Vishnu interlaced his fingers, clasping his hands in his lap. 'Swami Saraswati is moving on.'

'What?'

'It's time for a change.'

Isaac was sideswiped. Swami Saraswati had run the ashram on Tranquillity Island for over twenty years. He couldn't imagine the place without her.

'Where's she going?'

'Alaska.'

'*Alaska?*'

'We've been gifted a small estate and I want her to establish an ashram there. It's a tremendous opportunity for both her and the organisation.'

'And she wants to go?'

Swami Vishnu frowned at him, as if Isaac had just asked an English person what their favourite sexual position was, and how much they earned.

'Hanuman, we devote our lives to the organisation. This is her karma yoga.'

'Who's taking her place here?'

Swami Vishnu spread his palms. 'I am.'

'But what about the ashram in India?'

'I'm sending Mohan and Ganapati to act in my stead. They know the place well, and I expect both of them to be swamis in the not-too-distant future.'

Isaac's head was reeling.

'But Guruji. Ganapati is...' *A grumpy bastard at the best of times*. 'Not the most customer-facing person within the organisation, and Mohan is in a relationship with Anisha.' *Not to mention incapable of keeping it in his pants.*

Swami Vishnu sighed. 'Hanuman... Mohan and Anisha ceased intimacy years ago and I've instructed Anisha to follow Swami Saraswati to Alaska. As for Ganapati? Was not Arjuna a fierce warrior? In the Bhagavad Gita, Krishna himself counsels him to follow his dharma by fighting, even though it will mean the death of his cousins. Ganapati's devotion to the organisation should be commended.'

Isaac didn't know what to think. He'd always trusted his guru implicitly, but he couldn't understand the rationale behind these decisions.

'And I want you here, Hanuman, leading all the TTCs. You've become a wonderful teacher and your talents need to reach more people. The issue with your house and land is a cosmic sign. No matter what happens, your path lies here now, helping the TTC programme grow.'

Isaac froze, knowing this was the first direct commandment from his guru he was going to ignore. The Devanandara organisation had always been his sanctuary, but for the first time in his life, he was counting the days until he could leave the island. His home and heart were now wherever Sophia was.

Swami Vishnu patted his knee again. 'Keep this news to yourself. We're making the official announcement in a couple of months. I appreciate you'll need to return briefly to England to tidy up your affairs, but I want to have you back here by November. Mohan will take some pictures of you for our promotional materials, so make sure you're wearing one of his vests. You can't show off what yoga can do to the body in a shapeless t-shirt.'

The ashram bell sounded in the distance and Swami Vishnu held out his hand for Isaac to help him up.

They walked to the door together, and Isaac opened it.

'At least the rain has stopped again,' Swami Vishnu said as they passed onto the boardwalk. 'Is it tomorrow Sophia has the staples in her head out?'

Isaac nodded. 'We'll take the eight o'clock boat after Satsang to Tortula and return hopefully by early afternoon.'

'Good. She can then move back into the dormitory.'

No way.

'Guruji, she'll still be using a crutch, and those stairs are too narrow and steep. It's not safe.'

Swami Vishnu let out a dismissive snort in response, and Isaac's skin prickled with anger. Where was his guru's compassion?

'Please, can we wait until we hear what the doctor advises?'

'Humph. I suppose so. The last thing the organisation needs is a lawsuit on their hands.'

Isaac kept quiet. No matter what the doctor said tomorrow, Sophia was not being kicked out of her room.

'Are you sure it's safe?'

Sophia's eyes were wide, her face pale as she gazed at the ocean.

The brown layer of sargassum around the dock was rolling and crashing in the wind. Beyond it, the water was being whipped into whitecaps.

'Yes,' Isaac replied. 'It'll be a bumpy crossing, but I've seen worse.'

'Is this the storm that's forecast?'

He shook his head. 'That's not due till late this evening and is scheduled to miss the islands completely. We'll be fine.'

Sophia didn't look convinced, and all Isaac wanted was to take her in his arms and hug her worry away. But they were standing on the dock in a line of people waiting to get onto the ashram ferry, so he had to keep his distance.

Ganapati was back driving the boat and extended a huge hand to help Sophia onboard.

She was still using crutches, so Isaac went on the other side of her to make sure she didn't fall, then led her to a seat in the middle and at the back.

'We'll get the least bounce here and hopefully no spray.'

Sophia put her bag between them on the bench, then slid her hand underneath it. Isaac tucked his hand under his side of the bag, his fingers finding hers. This was the closest they'd been for a week, and her touch felt like fire.

He gazed at her, watching her cheeks turn pink and her pupils dilate. Secretly holding hands in plain sight of everyone was one of the most transgressive and erotic acts he'd ever performed.

Second only to Sophia giving him the most mind-blowing orgasm of his life a week ago.

The wind was howling above the noise of the engine, so Isaac leaned across to whisper in her ear. 'I can't wait to get back to Foxbrooke with you.'

Sophia squeezed his hand under the bag and nodded, the colour in her cheeks deepening.

Isaac wanted to kiss her, touch her, love her, but they were crammed in next to people with suitcases heading for the airport, so he stroked his fingers into the creases between hers, drew leisurely circles in her palm, and caressed her hand in a promise of what was to come when they were back home and truly alone.

As the boat cut through the choppy sea, Isaac communicated solely through the connection of their hands, tightening his hold when Sophia flinched at a particularly big bump, then soothing her stress away. In the past, he'd craved solitude, but now he dreamt of everyone else disappearing so he could be alone with her.

As they arrived at Beef Island, rain joined the weather party, gusting sideways and flicking water from the puddles onto their legs.

'I could probably try to put all my weight on my leg,' Sophia shouted against the noise of the wind and aeroplanes taking off and landing nearby.

Isaac shook his head. 'Wait and see what the doctor says.'

Holding an umbrella over her head as she hopped towards the row of taxis, he held open the door of one of them for her.

The inside of the cab felt like a cocoon, with a black leatherette cover over the seats and carpet up the walls and on the ceiling.

After giving their destination to the driver, Isaac turned to Sophia. Her cheeks were flushed, her face sparkling wet from the rain. The sight was a visceral reminder of the last time they'd kissed.

This time, there was no hesitation.

As his lips met hers, a bolt of lust struck him in the balls, making him groan with relief and desire. Electricity crackled across his skin, surging in power with every sweep of her tongue against his.

Sophia may have been shy and sweet in public, but this kiss was strong, hot and wild. It was a drug made from fireworks, volcanos and rainbows and he couldn't get enough.

Grabbing her bag, he dumped it in his lap to hide his impatient cock. The cab driver was probably used to people making out, but not to someone wearing loose yoga pants and sporting a huge hard-on.

Despite the visceral need to cup her breast and slide his

fingers under the waistband of her trousers, Isaac kept his hands still, pouring his love and need for Sophia through his kiss. Each touch of her tongue amplified the wattage surging through him until all he could see was light.

Time and space ceased to have any meaning. He was bound to Sophia, lost in her kiss. Nothing else existed.

Until there was a loud throat-clearing from elsewhere in the car.

Sophia leapt away from him, gasping, her lips swollen and wet.

His cock throbbing painfully, Isaac turned to the grinning driver.

'You sure you want the hospital?' he asked. 'Not a church?'

Isaac swallowed, the image of marrying Sophia making his heart expand even more.

'We're married,' he replied.

The older man chuckled, his eyes alight with amusement. 'No, you're not. But you're gonna be, mark my words!'

Isaac dared a glance at Sophia. Her cheeks were pink, but she was smiling, seemingly unperturbed by the driver's prophecy. Isaac's heart beat faster.

'We're here, lovebirds.'

The car came to a stop, and the driver got out to help Sophia.

As Isaac paid, he was passed a business card.

'I'm Benjamin. If you can't find a cab, give me a call. You staying the night on the island?'

Isaac shook his head. 'We should be done here in the next hour, then we'll head back.'

There was a screaming of sirens in the distance.

Benjamin glanced at the sky. 'Don't be late. There's a storm coming.'

'It's going to miss the islands.'

Benjamin pulled a disbelieving face and turned to Sophia. 'He always this optimistic?'

She smirked. 'He's less effective at predicting the weather than sargassum.'

Isaac's cock leapt at her unexpected sass, and Benjamin guffawed.

'She's going to give you a run for your money, yoga-boy,' he said, slapping Isaac on the shoulder before nodding at Sophia. 'Take care of yourself, Ma'am.'

'Thank you, Benjamin. It's a pleasure to meet you.'

The sirens were getting closer.

'And you. I'd better be going. They're probably coming here.' He gave them a wave and drove off.

ISAAC AND SOPHIA HAD ONLY BEEN IN THE HOSPITAL building a few minutes when two blood-covered patients were wheeled in on stretchers.

'Car slipped off the road in the rain,' a paramedic said to a nurse as they headed straight through the double doors to the treatment area.

Sophia squeezed Isaac's hand. 'That's so awful. I hope they're going to be okay.'

Leaning closer, he brushed a kiss across her furrowed forehead. 'They're in the best place to make that happen.'

She nodded and moved closer, letting him wrap his arms around her.

No matter where he was, if Isaac was with Sophia, his soul was content. A hospital may not have been the most romantic of settings, but it was away from the prying eyes of the ashram so he could touch and kiss her as he'd been dreaming.

Well, up to a point... His cock was still unsubtly reminding him that there were other ways to show her his love.

. . .

THE TIME FOR SOPHIA'S APPOINTMENT CAME AND WENT AND the wind picked up, buffeting the main door into the hospital.

'Will we be okay getting back to the island?' Sophia asked.

'I hope so. It depends on when we can get you seen. I can ring the ashram and find out, and also text Ganapati.'

Sophia chewed her bottom lip. 'I love nature, but not when it's being unfriendly.'

Isaac smiled. 'I know what you mean. I like a good thunderstorm, but only when I'm inside, looking out.'

'You're not worried about a tree falling on your house?'

'They're in good condition and young enough to stay upright. Plus, the other trees act as a buffer, lessening the force of any wind.'

'I love your house. It couldn't be more perfect.'

I could say the same about you...

Isaac's heart thumped louder. They hadn't spoken much about the future, only that they would keep their relationship platonic until they were home.

But now he'd made the decision to renounce his vow and knew he loved her, he didn't want to waste any more time.

'Sophia... When we get back to Foxbrooke, would you like to...' He swallowed, trying to find the words that wouldn't scare her off. '...stay with me?'

Her eyes went wide.

'Or not,' he added hurriedly.

Sophia shook her head rapidly, and Isaac's heart sank.

'Sorry, I was getting ahead of myself. We don't—'

'No! I mean yes!' she interrupted, her pale cheeks glowing. 'Yes, I would very much like to, er...' She lowered her voice. '*Stay* with you in your perfect house, with your perfect self, giving me perfect kisses.'

Relief flooded through him.

'For, um... for how long?' she asked shyly.

'If I'm honest, will you run away?'

She held up a crutch. 'For many reasons, that scenario will not be taking place.'

He grinned and took her hands. Her eyes were bright, but he could still see anxiety, her teeth biting into her plump lower lip.

'I'd like you to stay forever. Or as long as you're happy there.'

Sophia let out a little squeal of excitement, and Isaac's heart soared.

'Is this for real?' she whispered.

'Us?'

She nodded.

'Yes. It's the most real I've ever felt. You're incredible.'

Isaac wanted to say more. He wanted to tell Sophia he loved her, stand on the plastic chair and announce it to the waiting room, go outside and yell it to the wind.

But he stayed quiet, biding his time as he revelled in her happiness.

'I used to think I must have been a very bad person in a former life because of what has happened to me this year,' Sophia began. 'But now I know I must have been a saint. Nothing else can explain how lucky I feel right now.'

Isaac stroked her cheek. 'You're already a saint. And a goddess.'

She blushed. 'I feel different when I'm with you.'

'I want you to feel like that all the time. Be truly yourself and don't worry about what anyone else might say or do. That's on them. It's *their* crap. Don't allow them to make it yours.'

A shadow crossed her face, then she nodded. 'I was born shy and unsure, and life circumstances made the imprint deeper. But with you, I feel I could be as quietly confident as Eveline, and as badass as Estelle.'

'And with you, I can be fully in the world, rather than running away from it.'

The main doors opened, and the wind shrieked in, making Sophia jump. She glanced at the wall clock.

'You hungry?'

She nodded. 'I didn't think we'd be here past lunchtime.'

Drawing her forward, Isaac dropped a kiss on her lips. 'I'll go get some food. I won't be long, and Murphy's Law states that the moment I leave, you'll be called through.'

'Very true.'

'You okay to go in on your own if that happens?'

'Yes. It's different now. Everything's different.'

Isaac gave her another quick kiss, then left, taking out his phone as he passed into the main body of the hospital and ringing the ashram. He wanted to tell them he and Sophia had been delayed, and check the ferry was still running.

Five minutes later, he knew they weren't going anywhere.

18

'What's happened?' Sophia asked as she hobbled out of the treatment area, now only using one crutch.

Isaac was waiting for her, his phone in his hand and his expression tense. 'How did it go in there? Everything okay?'

'Yes, absolutely fine. There's just a small amount of paperwork to do, then we can leave. I'm going to hang onto this crutch for the next two weeks and I—*we* can drop it off when we leave the islands. What did the ashram say?'

'It's too rough, so they've cancelled the ferry. The storm has changed course and is headed this way.'

Sophia's eyes were drawn to the palm trees outside the main doors, their tops whipping in the wind. Stinging prickles of anxiety stabbed her skin.

'Is there another way back to the island?'

'Not tonight. All flights are cancelled as well. We've got to find somewhere to stay.'

'Oh.' *Oh...*

The realisation that they would stay the night together, far away from the ashram, seemed to be lost on Isaac. His brow was furrowed as he ran a hand through his hair.

'Have you been ringing places?'

He nodded. 'But everywhere's fully booked.' He took her free hand. 'Take a seat and I'll keep calling. Can I get you anything to drink?'

Sophia's heart flip-flopped. She wasn't used to this level of kindness and attention from a romantic partner. She'd only had one before Isaac, and he'd always put himself first.

'Thank you. Would you be able to find somewhere to refill my water bottle?'

'Of course.' He took it from her. 'I won't be long.'

Sophia sat facing the doors as rain threw itself angrily at the glass. Was this a hurricane? Whatever it was, or was about to become, she knew it could be lethal. Weather events like this in the UK were uncommon, and she had no frame of reference for what might be approaching.

It's okay. We can just stay in the hospital. It's safe here.

As if on cue, there was a loud bang from outside and a section of clapboard flew past the doors.

Focusing on her breathing, she thought of Isaac's house in the sunshine, the leaves rustling gently overhead. Her tummy fluttered with excitement.

My future home! With my new boyfriend!

The situation still felt so unreal, but she was going to lean into it. She wasn't the naïve eighteen-year-old falling in love with her professor anymore. She was nearly thirty and now knew enough about the world to make better choices.

Her phone pinged with a message.

Estelle: Just checking in to make sure you
haven't turned into a lentil. How's the knee?

Sophia hadn't told her family and friends the full extent of the accident, nor that she'd been to the hospital for it. And she certainly hadn't shared that Isaac was on the island or what had happened between them.

Sophia: Ommmmmmmmmmm…

Estelle: PMSL. Please, for the love of GOD,
when you first see your brother, can you wear
orange robes? He's already worried you've
joined some kind of cult

Estelle: It would be fucking hilarious if you did
that. Please? For me?

Sophia: I thought you were in love with him?

Estelle: Yeah, totally, but he needs to be kept
on his toes, and messing with him is top
drawer entertainment

Estelle: Oh! And shave your head!

Sophia: What? No way!

Estelle: Fair enough, that's probably a step
too far

Sophia: You think?

Estelle: Lolololololol

Estelle: So, two weeks left. Have you
achieved enlightenment yet? Done a
headstand? Started dreaming of
cheeseburgers with crispy bacon?

> Sophia: 100% the burger part. We only eat twice a day and I'm almost always hungry

> Estelle: Whaaaaat???? You didn't tell me that! Holy shit! Should we meet you at the airport with a bacon sandwich?

Sophia had already planned with Isaac for them to travel back to Foxbrooke together. Should she tell Estelle he was here? Lay the groundwork for a revelation none of them would expect?

> Sophia: I'm okay. I've got transport booked to get me home. And we're allowed one day off a week. I left the island the last time and had a mixed grill…

> Estelle: Amazing. Will you now be reincarnated as a slug in your next life?

> Sophia: Lol. We'll see

A door opened off the main reception area, and Isaac appeared.

> Sophia: Got to go xxx

> Estelle: Good luck. And if you can't find any orange robes, I'll see if I can nick any from Mammy. She's bound to have that kind of thing lying around XXX

Sophia pocketed her phone as Isaac approached. 'Any luck?'

He gave her a relieved smile. 'I rang Benjamin. His cousin's neighbour runs a small guesthouse and has one room left. He's going to pick us up in the next half hour.'

'Thank goodness.'

'Yeah. I've never been here when there's been a hurricane before, but I know how bad it can get.'

Panic squeezed her throat.

Rushing forward, Isaac took Sophia's clammy hand. 'It's going to be fine, love. The islanders know what to do.'

She nodded uncertainly.

Taking her in his arms, he kissed the top of her head. 'I'm not going to let anything happen to you, I promise. Everything's going to be okay.'

Sophia gripped Isaac's hand as the taxi drove slowly along the road, buffeted by the wind.

'Not far now!' Benjamin called over his shoulder.

There were still people outside, busy nailing boards across the windows of their houses.

Sophia's mouth was dry, her heart thumping against her ribcage. She was trying not to let Isaac know just how terrified she was, but he seemed fully aware, letting her squeeze the life out of his hand without complaint.

'The place is run by Margo and Anton,' Benjamin continued. 'Lovely people.'

He brought the car to a halt outside a large, two-storey house with a wraparound balcony on the first floor, then got out to open the door for Sophia.

The rain lashed at her skin like gravel flung by a petulant god, and she grabbed Benjamin's arm to stop herself from being blown over.

A large woman in her fifties bustled out of the house, her beaming smile at odds with the angry weather.

'Welcome, welcome! I'm Margo.'

'I'm Sophia, and this is my boyfriend, Isaac.'

'Nice to meet you both. Let's get you inside.'

Isaac pressed money into Benjamin's hand, thanking him profusely, then took Sophia's free arm and helped her into the house. Her knee was healing, but it still hurt putting weight on it, and the wind was making her even more unsteady.

Standing in the entrance hall, delicious smells percolated from elsewhere in the house.

'I'm afraid you've got the smallest room,' Margo said. 'We rarely let it out to couples because of the size, but you're in a bit of a spot right now.'

'We're so grateful. Thank you,' Isaac replied. 'Can I help with any of the storm prep?'

Margo hesitated, then nodded. 'That would be appreciated. I'm busy cooking in case the power goes out.'

'What can I do?'

'Anton's outside, boarding up the windows. If you could help him, I'll get this lovely lady to your room. You can borrow dry clothes from Anton when you're done.'

Isaac gazed at Sophia. 'You okay?'

She nodded, even as her tummy tightened with nerves. The storm sounded as if it was trying to blow the house down.

He brushed a kiss across her cheek, then left.

'What a handsome young man you've got there,' Margo said with a grin. 'Now come with me. Your room is on the ground floor, so there are no stairs to worry about.'

She led Sophia down a corridor. 'There's a shower room attached and plenty of towels. If you want to freshen up, I suggest you do it now in case we lose electricity.'

Opening a door, she gestured for Sophia to go in. 'I'll go get you some dry clothes.'

Sophia entered the room and suppressed a nervous giggle. The room was indeed small and dominated by the bed. It filled the space, leaving only a narrow gap on either side and enough room at the foot end for a slimline chest of drawers. The bedside tables were smaller than a piece of printer paper, and the attached shower room was tiny.

Even if Isaac *wanted* to sleep on the floor, there was simply not enough room. Thanks to the storm, they were going to be spending the night in bed together, and the thought made Sophia's knees weak with anticipation.

'Here we go!' Margo said as she entered the room with a pile of brightly patterned clothes. 'The dresses will be several sizes too big, but the style suits everyone.'

'Thank you so much.'

Margo put them on the bed. 'Now, you've got towels in the bathroom, and I've stocked it with toiletries and travel tooth-brushes we pick up each time we fly. They come in handy for guests who've forgotten theirs.'

Her forehead furrowed as if she was going through a mental list of what Sophia might need.

'It'll be dark soon, but I'll bring you lanterns for light just in case. I'll get you bottles of drinking water and I've made food for everyone which you can eat whenever you like. Is there anything else you need?'

'I don't think so. This is all amazing.'

A large bang by the window made her jump, and she turned to see nothing but wood.

'We've boarded up that window already. It should only be a category one storm, so we'll be fine. It's just good to be prepared.'

Sophia nodded, wishing she was the kind of person who might have relished this experience rather than being terrified by it.

Margo squeezed her hand. 'You're safe here, honey. If you need anything, or you're hungry, come find me in the kitchen. Just follow your nose.'

She left and Sophia had a quick shower, spritzed on a floral perfume she found in the bathroom cabinet, then put on one of Margo's dresses. It was indeed far too big, but the bold and colourful design was pretty. She smiled shyly at her reflection in the small mirror. Maybe it was the diet and exercise regime she'd been on for the past two weeks, or maybe it was being in love, but she felt beautiful.

There were no messages from home, so she turned off her phone to save the battery and went to look for Margo, finding her in a kitchen with glossy green units and the work surfaces covered with bottles of water and lanterns.

'Why, don't you look lovely!' she said to Sophia, then indicated the lanterns. 'I'll give you two for your room and one for the en suite. And extra candles. You hungry?'

'I am. I thought the nerves might stop my appetite, but it seems to have gone the other way.'

'That's music to the ears of a cook. Take a seat. The other guests are in their rooms, so you can eat first.'

Sophia sat at a table in the centre of the room. 'What's on the menu?'

'Pork Calaloo and Fungi then coconut tart. Nothing fancy, but it tastes good.'

'Fungi? Like mushrooms?'

Margo let out a peal of laughter. 'You aint had Fungi before? What do they feed you on the yoga island?'

'Rice and a lot of pulses, mainly. Bread, salads, that sort of thing. It's vegetarian, but they don't use eggs, garlic, onions or some spices because they're meant to stimulate the body too much.'

Margo was staring at her as if she'd just grown a second head. 'Well, that explains why you're so skinny. You can't come all this way and not eat local food. Fungi is cornmeal, and Calaloo is like a thick soup with okra, greens, and usually pork or seafood.'

She gave Sophia the side eye. 'Do I have to explain what a coconut tart is?'

Sophia smiled. 'I can work out what it is, but I've never had it before.'

'Well then, this storm is a blessing and your stomach's going to thank God.'

'Not the cook?'

Margo flashed her a grin and waved her hands. 'He works through these.'

AN HOUR LATER, THE LIGHT HAD FADED, AND THE STORM had strengthened. Sophia's stomach was full, but the rest of her was overflowing with anxiety. Other guests had entered the kitchen to eat, and each time the door opened, her pulse sped up, hoping it was Isaac.

Being sociable with Margo was easy because she was so warm and welcoming, but the other guests were quiet, seemingly as worried as she was. Their stress amplified hers.

'Well, aren't you handsome!' Margo said. 'Even in clothes that don't fit right.'

Sophia turned as Isaac entered the room, her heart quickening.

He was wearing a pair of cream trousers that were too big in the waist and too short in the leg. They were held up by a pair of braces, over an oversized white dress shirt. He looked like a hot Huckleberry Finn.

Coming straight to Sophia's side, he took her hand. 'You okay?'

She nodded. 'Have you finished now?'

'We certainly have,' an older man said as he entered the room. 'I'm Anton. And I couldn't have finished so quickly if I hadn't had this man's help.'

He slapped Isaac on the back. 'If this is what yoga does, I might have to take it up.'

Margo laughed. 'You can't even touch your toes.'

Crossing the room, he kissed her. 'But I can touch yours. Does that count?'

She playfully slapped him away. 'You must be famished. Come, eat.'

Anton took a seat and Isaac sat next to Sophia, still holding her hand.

'You look beautiful,' Isaac murmured.

'Doesn't she just?' Margo agreed. 'Now, please tell me you know what Fungi and Calaloo are?'

Isaac scrunched up his face as if in deep thought. 'Mushrooms?'

Margo put her hands on her hips and took a big breath.

He laughed. 'I know what it is.'

Margo's stance didn't change. 'What is it then?'

'Polenta,' he replied smoothly. 'And Calaloo is like a stew with leafy greens, okra and meat or shellfish.'

'You pass the test,' Margo said, going to the stove.

'My stomach is grateful,' Isaac replied. 'I'm—'

There was a loud bang from outside and all the lights went out.

Sophia flinched, and Isaac squeezed her hand.

'Well, that's that then!' Margo said. 'Anton, the lanterns.'

There was already one lit in the centre of the table, and Sophia held stock still as Margo and Anton moved confidently around in the shadows.

More lanterns were lit, and Anton went off, returning with a torch that he hung from a pan holder above the stove.

'Thank you, darlin',' Margo said, then dished up a plate of food and placed it in front of Isaac.

He kept hold of Sophia's hand as he ate.

'Thank you, Margo. This is the best Calaloo I've ever had.'

She laughed. 'If only this storm weren't raging, I'd take you over the road and get you to repeat that to my neighbour. Now, please excuse us. Anton and I are going to check on the other guests.'

They left the kitchen, and Isaac turned to Sophia. In the flickering glow from the candles, he looked like a god.

'You sure you're doing alright?' he asked.

'Not really, but I'm a thousand times better now you're back inside.'

'Anton says it's only a category one storm, so we'll be fine. You ate already?'

'Yes. Margo made sure I was well fed.'

They lapsed into silence, gazing at each other. Sophia's pulse was already racing, but when the tips of Isaac's fingers nudged indecently into the creases between hers, she thought her heart might explode.

Were they going to have sex? Did he want to wait until they were back in Foxbrooke? Did ashram rules still apply here? Did he have a condom?

The questions flew around her head until she was dizzy.

'Sophia…'

Margo re-entered the kitchen, grabbed two enormous bottles of water, then exited.

As soon as she'd gone, Anton appeared wearing a head torch and carrying a wooden box. He began filling the box with more lanterns.

'Can we help?' Sophia asked.

'No, no,' he replied. 'You stay with your man. Everything's in hand.'

My man…

She sneaked a glance at Isaac. His expression burned bright in the darkness.

Then Margo returned, and he resumed eating with the speed of a man who needed to be somewhere else, doing something far more important.

'Just leave it on the table when you're done,' Margo said to him. 'Your room has extra lanterns, water and matches. Anything else you need, just ask.'

'Thank you.' Isaac placed his cutlery down. 'You sure we can't help with anything?'

She shooed them away. 'We're fine. Go to bed and ride it out.'

Isaac opened his mouth to speak, but began coughing instead.

'You want some water?' Margo asked.

Shaking his head, he took a breath. 'I'm okay.'

Sophia got to her feet. 'Thank you, Margo. We'll go to bed —our room—the room now.'

She cringed at her own nervousness, but Margo hadn't seemed to notice.

'Okay, honey. We'll see you in the morning. Sleep well.'

Isaac stood, gave Margo his thanks, then led Sophia out of the kitchen.

Despite the howling storm, the silence between them felt just as loud as they made their way through the house.

Anxiety gnawed at Sophia's insides. She'd only ever slept with one man before, and the thought of being intimate with Isaac was as terrifying as it was thrilling. Marcus had been her entire frame of reference when it came to sex, but she knew without a doubt it would be a completely different experience with Isaac.

Would she do it right? Be good enough? Suddenly, she desperately wanted to talk to Estelle, someone overflowing with sexual confidence.

Isaac held the door to their room open, and she entered.

'Do you want to use the bathroom?' she asked tentatively.

'After you.'

The air in the room was thick with anticipation, but it appeared they'd reverted to being the most British versions of themselves, politely tiptoeing around each other and the very large elephant in the room currently disguised as a double bed.

Sophia used the bathroom, then stood in the small gap between the edge of the bed and the far wall as Isaac had his turn.

When he came out, he hovered on the other side of the room. 'Are you happy with that side of the bed?'

She nodded. 'Margo has left extra blankets in the chest of drawers, in case we need them.'

Now he nodded. Was he as nervous as she was?

Come on! 'Do you want to have sex with me?'

The candlelight cut across his cheekbones, heightening the flush.

'Do you want to have sex with *me*?' he asked, his voice low.

'You first.'

He swallowed. 'Yes, I do. It's just—' He broke off, his gaze searing into hers as he took a breath. 'I didn't think this would happen for a couple of weeks and I'm nervous.'

'So am I.'

'I haven't slept with anyone for twelve years.'

'And I've only slept with one person before.'

Silence.

Isaac took a deep breath. 'I don't have a condom.'

'Me neither, but it doesn't matter.'

His eyes widened.

'I've got an IUD fitted, and after I broke up with Marcus, I got tested, and everything was okay.'

'I, er, got tested after my last relationship, too.'

'So then, we're good to go?'

He nodded, but remained stock still, as if unsure of what to do next.

Despite knowing Isaac was way more sexually experienced than her, Sophia knew it was up to her to make the first move.

Pulling her dress up and off over her head, she dropped it at the end of the bed.

❧ 19 ❧

Blood roared inside Isaac's head and his mouth ran dry as he gazed at Sophia. The flickering light from the candles caressed her skin, burnishing it to gold.

He couldn't think. Couldn't act. All he could do was stare in wonderment, his heart tripping over itself.

'The underwear is what you bought me,' she said shyly. 'Do you like it?'

Get yourself together!

He nodded. 'I love you.'

Sophia's lips parted, and she inhaled sharply.

Isaac had meant to say 'I love *it*,' but his heart had overruled that decision and substituted the more appropriate word.

'I love you,' he repeated, doubling down.

He'd wanted to wait until he was sure he wouldn't scare Sophia off with the intensity of his feelings, but the words were now out and they were the truth.

Her eyes were liquid and shining. 'I love you, too. I love you, Isaac.'

Now it was his turn to be shocked.

Getting onto the bed, she crawled over to his side. The sight took him one heartbeat away from an aneurysm.

She knelt in front of him and put her arms behind his neck. 'I love you.'

Trembling, he reached forward, touching the smoothness of her skin, desire pounding through him.

Take it slow. Take it slow. Take it slow.

Sophia pressed her lips to his, and Isaac's whole body shuddered with pleasure.

Then, when her tongue touched his, he was convinced he was about to die.

Groaning, he wrapped his arms around her, running his hands across her back, down to her backside, slipping his hand under the lace.

She gasped, dragging the braces off his shoulders, then tugging up the bottom of the oversized shirt.

Breaking the kiss, Isaac pulled it over his head and stepped out of the pooling trousers.

Now Sophia's hands were on his boxers, lifting the waistband away from his cock and pushing them down. Taking them off, he then reached behind her, undoing the clasp of her bra.

She shook it to the bed and kissed him again, pressing her chest against his.

Electricity crackled across his skin from her touch. The pleasure was so bright it was blinding.

He wanted to take it slow, but when Sophia clutched at his hair, whimpering into his mouth, he couldn't hold back.

Laying her on the bed, his hand found her breast as their tongues tangled. Isaac had never missed sex, but then he'd never met Sophia. She was more addictive than life and more vital than his next breath.

Spreading her legs, she anchored him between her thighs, grinding her pelvis into his cock.

Stars danced behind his eyes and desire roared like a beast inside him. Nipping and sucking down her neck, he latched onto her nipple, rubbing the roughness of his tongue against the tip.

Sophia cried out, her voice echoing the storm outside.

Isaac wanted to give her the same pleasure that was coursing through his veins, the same ecstasy he'd experienced on the porch during the rainstorm. So he forced himself to focus, licking and sucking, learning how to make her cry out, how to make her as frantic with need as he was.

One of her hands clung to his head, the other fluttered down his back as she arched her body, her pussy rubbing against his cock. Then she shifted, reaching for her underwear, trying to pull her panties off even though his weight was pressing her hips into the mattress.

Shifting down the bed, Isaac dragged them off, then knelt above her, gazing at Sophia's outstretched form in wonder. Her hair ran in dark, curling rivers across the white pillows, her plump lips were parted, and her eyes were heavy with need.

He followed the shape of her incredible body; the candle-light illuminating the fullness of her breasts, the softness of her stomach, the curves of her hips.

Then he zeroed in on her pussy and his hands clenched into fists, forcing his orgasm down.

A tiny voice inside his head urged him to go slow, but when Sophia spread her legs wider and he saw her arousal glistening in the half light, all thoughts were burned to ash by the flames of his desire.

Falling to the bed, Isaac hooked his arms under Sophia's thighs and buried his face into her pussy with a groan. She cried out again, pushing herself closer, opening completely to him.

He dived into the sweet earthiness of her taste, her liquid heat and the softness of her lips. Worshipping her pussy with long licks, he vibrated his tongue over the hard bud of her clit, then thrust it inside her.

'Isaac! Isaac! Isaac!'

He held her still as she thrashed and moaned, letting every one of his senses drown in her pleasure and his. Nothing had ever felt so right. So world-alteringly perfect.

The storm faded into the background. It was no match for the power of his feelings, the chemistry between them that set every cell alight and changed the very fabric of his being.

Her thighs were shaking, her voice becoming incoherent. Isaac focused his attention on the centre of Sophia's pleasure, feeling the shifts in her body, the erratic movement of her breath, the vibrations as her cry got higher.

Sophia. Sophia. My Sophia.

Emotion flooded his veins, fuelling the speed of his tongue. He was the wind, pushing her orgasm on like a cresting wave.

Her hands clutched his hair, holding him to her as if afraid he would stop.

I love you. I love you. I love you.

Isaac had been content for most of the last twelve years. But now? Nothing would or could ever compare to this moment of truly divine ecstasy. Sophia was his goddess, and worshipping her was the ultimate pleasure.

She was gasping now, the space between each one getting shorter and shorter, until they cut off and she stiffened beneath him.

Yes.

His tongue kept flicking as the tension in her body changed

to shudders, then convulsions, as her breath returned with fitful cries.

'Oh, my god! Isaac! Oh my god, oh my god...'

Sophia's hands were still tangled in his hair, as if holding on for dear life as the aftershocks of her orgasm kept coming.

Love and lust diffused in and out of each other, creating a feeling so profound his heart felt like it would burst.

As her muscles relaxed, he nuzzled her soft curls and pressed kisses onto the inside of her thighs. She stroked his hair, as if trying to put it back into place.

'I love you,' she murmured.

'I love you too,' he replied, his breath ghosting across her pussy. Then he licked up her length, flicking the tip of his tongue across her clit.

'Oh!' She sounded surprised, as if this was not what she was expecting.

He smiled and did it again.

'Oh, my g—'

She broke off, her thighs tightening once more as he thrummed his tongue against her.

How could he have lived without this taste? Without the exquisite pleasure of making Sophia come? It was as if he'd been living his life in a palette of muted tones and now the future lay before him in a kaleidoscope of colour.

'Yes! Yes! Yes!'

Isaac prided himself on being a fast learner, and now he'd made Sophia orgasm once, he knew some of the ways to make her respond. Licking faster, he chased her climax on, feeling her reach her peak, then sucking her clit hard into his mouth.

She screamed, her hips bucking, her fingernails digging into his scalp as she ground her pussy into his face.

The waves of her orgasm kept coming, rippling through her, until she collapsed with shaky gasps, her hands trembling.

'Isaac,' she breathed, as if finally finding him after a lifetime of looking.

He went back to kissing the soft skin of her upper thighs, sucking the flesh into his mouth, feasting on her.

She tugged on his hair and he kissed his way slowly up her body until she yanked his head higher to bring his lips to hers.

Isaac groaned into Sophia's mouth as their tongues clashed. There was nothing else in existence apart from the two of them and their love. Nothing could beat this feeling.

But then she angled her hips, pushing an inch onto his cock and his body exploded with light.

Breaking the kiss, he dropped his head to her neck, his jaw tight as air hissed in and out through his gritted teeth. The pleasure was so intense he could barely stand it.

Heart thumping painfully against his ribs, he regained control of his breath, then pushed up onto his hands, gazing down at her.

Sophia was achingly beautiful, with her face flushed with desire. Isaac stared at her sensuous body beneath his, feeling her clenched around the head of his cock.

'I love you,' she whispered, her eyes shining.

How had he got so lucky? How did he deserve such a gift?

Reaching to his backside, she pressed gently on his skin, encouraging him deeper.

He pushed in another inch, sensation shooting out from his cock, sparking through every nerve.

She sighed, pulling him into her further.

'I love you,' he choked out, his throat tight with emotion.

Angling her hips, she took him deeper. 'I love you,' she murmured.

'I love you,' he repeated, filling her completely.

They breathed together, eyes locked. There was nothing

else, only her. Sophia was the beginning and the end. His alpha, his omega, his everything.

He moved slowly, withdrawing an inch, then pushing back into her tightness.

Her breath was like the edge of the ocean, moving with the rhythm of his thrusts, rushing in and out like water over pebbles.

A great wave was building deep inside him, pleasure upon pleasure, flooding through his cells. It was too much for one body to contain. He couldn't take any more.

But then it began.

The darkness of the room around Sophia fractured into light, spinning around her body as the wave moved up his spine. It went beyond a physical release. It was a cosmic orgasm, rolling through his body in a never-ending expansion of energy and light.

Sophia's eyes widened as she stared at him. She could feel it too.

Isaac kept moving, holding her gaze as her face changed into that of Devī, then back again, morphing into goddess after goddess until her eyes were golden orbs and light sparkled from her skin.

Breathing together, electricity flowed around and through them. Sophia's body was rippling beneath his as climax after climax tumbled through her.

Time and space lost all meaning. Pleasure became a first principle, underpinning their entire existence. They were one with each other and the universe, in limitless bliss.

This was a divine union that transcended anything Isaac's rational mind could comprehend. His connection with Sophia was as intimate as the one he had with himself. He didn't stop moving, his cock filling her tight pussy, joining them physically as their souls entwined.

He was her, and she was him. They were the storm outside, the sun behind it, and the galaxies beyond that.

Isaac had no idea how much time had passed. There was just the faint feeling of fatigue in his arms, and a bodily sensation that told him he needed to ejaculate.

Sophia seemed to sense this, her breath coming quicker, as if she was on the same trajectory as him.

His hips pistoned faster, pounding into her, and she began keening with pleasure.

Lightning struck the base of his cock and he let out a harsh cry, the physical release shooting up his spine and blowing through the top of his head.

Isaac could no longer keep his eyes open as he tumbled into his climax. It shattered through every cell, breaking them apart until he was reduced to a collection of glittering particles.

As he collapsed onto Sophia, her pussy continued contracting, milking him dry. She clung to him, holding him in place as she gasped for air.

His own breath was ragged, his body still pulsing with light and pleasure.

Shifting to the side of Sophia so she could breathe more freely, Isaac gazed at her. Iridescent light still shimmering around her like phosphorescence. Tracing his finger across her skin, the colours swirled around his touch, eddies of energy in all the colours of the rainbow.

He'd spent nearly a third of his life in search of a deeper connection with himself and the universe, and now he'd found even more than he could have ever imagined in the most unlikely of circumstances.

Sophia was smiling at him, her expression radiant. Raising his hand, Isaac pressed his palm against hers. Light pulsed between them.

'It's so beautiful,' she whispered. 'I can't believe it's there all the time, but we can't see it.'

'I've only ever seen it twice. And both times were with you.'

Intertwining her fingers with his, she brought their clasped hands to her lips and kissed his knuckles. 'I never thought it was possible to feel this way, to experience what we just have. Will it always be like this?'

Reaching forward, he kissed her hand. 'I don't know if we'll always have a tantric experience, but the physical one was enough to blow my mind. And I know it will keep getting better and better.'

A line appeared between her brows. 'It's going to be really difficult being back at the ashram and not being able to touch you.'

He dropped his head to her shoulder. 'I know. It's going to be the hardest thing I've ever done.' He nuzzled up her neck. 'But it won't be for long. And then nothing can keep us apart.'

Sighing happily, her lips found his.

Isaac sank into Sophia's kiss. *Two more weeks*. That was all. Then their lives together could start.

❧ 20 ❧

'Where's the ferry?' Sophia asked as she stood with Isaac on the dock.

He frowned at the churning sargassum and slate-grey water. 'I don't know.'

Still holding her hand, he took out his phone, then held it to his ear.

She squinted at the horizon. 'Is that it?'

He followed her gaze. 'I'm not sure. I think your eyes are better than mine.'

No-one picked up his call, and a couple of minutes later the shape in the distance got close enough for her to make out the ashram speedboat.

Sophia gave Isaac's hand a squeeze, then dropped it, moving a foot away from him. The space between them felt brutal, like a chasm ripped into the ground after an earthquake.

His eyes held hers as silent words of love, reassurance and patience passed between them more easily than breath. Her stomach was already beginning to tighten, tendrils of anxiety stretching up to wrap around her lungs.

Just breathe. It's okay.

But the stench of the sargassum made her nauseous.

'Do you want to sit?' Isaac asked, concern creasing his brow.

Sophia nodded and lowered herself onto the wooden bench, splaying her fingers on her thighs to stop them clenching into fists.

Ganapati pulled up alongside the dock in the speedboat and threw Isaac the bow line.

'Where's the ferry?' Isaac asked. 'And how did the island cope last night?'

Ganapati didn't reply, instead holding out a hand for Sophia to get onboard.

Isaac passed him his phone and Ganapati typed out a message before handing it back, then turned the boat towards the open sea.

'They've cancelled the ashram ferry and the regular schedule, and roped everyone in to clean up,' Isaac said to her.

'But what about the day off for everyone doing the TTC?'

Isaac rubbed his face as if trying to remove his frown. 'It's not happening.'

Sophia was silent. She didn't know if the situation was worse on the island, but they'd seen little damage on the mainland apart from palm fronds and other minor debris on the roads.

'Will there be another day off instead of this one?'

He let out a weary sigh. 'Probably not.'

Sophia's heart sank. Jessica had been counting the hours until she could leave the ashram. Her friend's stock of extra food was running low, and she, like everyone else on the course, was shattered and stir-crazy.

Isaac gazed at her, his hand reaching across the space between them.

Sophia glanced at Ganapati's back, then took it.

'*Two weeks*,' Isaac mouthed.

She nodded and tightened her grip on his fingers. They could do this.

'HANUMAN!'

Mohan was striding along the dock towards them as Ganapati moored the speedboat. He held out a hand for Sophia to help her off the boat.

'Everything okay at the hospital?'

'Yes, thank you. I only need one crutch now'

He nodded, then turned to Isaac. 'Where did you stay?'

Sophia's heart thudded painfully in her chest. Lying made her acutely uncomfortable. What would Isaac say?

His expression was bland as he smiled at Mohan. 'Our taxi driver found us a guest house with rooms.'

Mohan nodded. 'Good. We took your tent down with all the others before the storm hit, but some roofs have damage.'

'Anyone hurt?'

'No, but the place is a mess. Guruji needs you in charge of a group doing the clean up.'

'Can I help?' Sophia asked.

Mohan glanced at her crutch, then nodded. 'Drop off your bag, then find Anisha.'

'Okay, thanks.'

She started along the dock.

Isaac came to her side. 'You need any help?'

'No, thank you, Hanuman,' she said with as much detachment as she could muster. 'I'll be fine. You find Swami Vishnu.'

Isaac looked torn, his brow furrowing again.

'Go,' Sophia said, a little more forcefully, trying to convey with her tone the need for him to treat her the same as anyone else on the island.

'Yeah, come on, Hanuman,' Mohan said to him. 'She's fine.' Putting a hand on Isaac's shoulder, he pulled him away, Ganapati following.

Taking a deep breath, Sophia squared her shoulders and hobbled down the dock towards the island. The sargassum seemed even worse than normal, so far up the beach that it was now under the trees.

However, the private beach with her accommodation was on the lee of the island, and when she got there, apart from leaves and the odd branch on the sand, everything looked the same.

Letting herself into her room, Sophia sat on the bed and let out a sigh. Her body ached, and she was dizzy with tiredness. The previous night, she and Isaac had made love until the sun rose, too desperate for each other to sleep. She'd dozed in the taxi on the way to meet the boat, but it was nowhere near enough to take the edge off her exhaustion.

Could she have a nap now? It wasn't like she was mobile enough to clear seaweed or any other physical task. Guilt gnawed at her insides. Logically, she knew she wouldn't be much help, but the idea of sleeping whilst everyone else worked on their day off didn't sit right with her.

Her phone buzzed in her bag with a call, and she took it out.

'Estelle?'

'Aha! You're alive then. Jolly good.'

'Did you know about the storm?'

'I was just checking the weather, and I'd left the location on the BVI. I didn't want to tell James or your folks before I'd tried you, as I didn't want them to worry.'

'Thanks, I really appreciate that. I'm fine.'

'But it was still a hurricane. It can't have been much fun on that tiny island.'

'Oh, we were on the mainland.'

There was a short silence, and Sophia's sleep-deprived brain went slowly back over her words, trying to figure out what she'd just said.

'*We?*'

Oh dear…

'Who's "we",' Estelle continued, 'and why were you on the mainland?'

'Um…'

'Sophia? Is everything alright?'

Tiredness rolled through her, pushing tears into her eyes. She was emotionally wrung out and desperately needed to talk to someone about what was going on.

'Sophia? You still there?'

'Yes, sorry.' She swiped at her eyes and sniffed. 'Isaac was with me.'

'Isaac? As in *Isaac*, Isaac?'

'Yes. He came here from India with his guru.'

'Has he been there the whole time you've been there?'

'Uh-huh.'

'Why didn't you say anything? Is he okay? He left Foxbrooke so abruptly. Have you seen much of him?'

Sophia's mind flashed with images of Isaac's naked body on hers, their limbs entwined as orgasm after orgasm rolled through her. The memories were viscerally fresh, but also starting to feel like a fevered dream.

'Sophia? Is he okay?'

'Yes, kind of.'

Sophia struggled to think of the right way to tell Estelle. She'd have to break the news to everyone anyway in two weeks. Could Estelle pave the way? Make it less of a shock for her parents? They'd already been through so much this year, and she didn't want to add to their burdens.

'Did you know Isaac used to work at Conqueror?'

'Er, no.'

'That was the job he left to become a yogi.'

'O-kay... That's super not-interesting and happened a million years ago. I want to know if he's alright *now*. And what the fuck you were doing on the mainland? Did you make a break for freedom and he came to get you like a sexy yoga bounty hunter, armed only with the power of his om?'

Despite her tears, Sophia let out a small laugh, then steeled herself. 'I didn't tell you all the truth about my little fall.'

'Go on...'

'I fell into a statue with really sharp edges, and then it toppled onto me. As well as pulling my knee, I cut my hand and my head and needed to get it stapled at the hospital.'

'What the fuck? *Stapled?* You're not a fucking document!'

'Apparently that's normal.'

'For what? Paper or people? Jesus, Soph!'

And this is why I didn't tell James or my parents...

'So you went back to the hospital for what? So they could pull the staples out, then chuck you in the recycling bin?'

'Everything minus the recycling.'

'Are you okay?'

'Yes, and by the time I'm home, I shouldn't need the crutch anymore.'

'Crutch?!'

'Please don't tell James or my parents. I don't want them to worry.'

Silence.

Estelle took a deep breath. 'Okay, I won't tell them the extent of your accident, but you need to text them to say you're okay in case they check the news and find out about the storm.'

'I will.'

'So, what's up with Isaac? Did he tell you why he buggered off to India early?'

This was it. Time to let the biggest secret Sophia had ever had out into the open.

'Isaac and I are a couple.'

'What?'

'He said he's in love and wants to spend the rest of his life with me.'

More silence.

Anxiety flashed across her skin. Did Estelle still have feelings for Isaac? Was James a poor replacement?

'I'm sorry,' Sophia said, her fingernails digging into her thighs.

'Huh? For what?'

She bit the inside of her cheek. 'I know you were... You liked him a lot.'

Estelle snorted. 'You think I still fancy him? God no. I haven't thought about Isaac like that for nearly a year, and now it's a physical impossibility for him to give me the horn. I love your infuriatingly awesome brother far too much.'

Thank god.

'But Sophia...'

'Yes?'

'I don't want to rain on your love parade, but are you sure this is the right thing for you?'

Ice pierced her heart. 'What do you mean?'

Estelle sighed. 'I know Isaac's super nice and super hot, but are you just rebounding from Marcus? I know your ex was a complete fuckwad and you're not getting back with him, but you were together for ten years. That's a lot to unpick and process.'

It *was* a lot, but each time Sophia thought of Marcus, it was with revulsion, sadness, and disbelief that she'd been with him for that long.

And when she thought of Isaac, her heart grew three sizes and her soul sang.

'I'm not doubting that Isaac fancies you. It's just his vow was one of the things that defined him. What if he changes his mind and then somehow blames you for leading him astray?'

Was that going to happen? She wanted to throw up.

'Shit. I sound like a total arse. I'm sorry, Soph, I'm just gobsmacked and should have processed the news without sounding my big mouth off. Ignore me. Honestly, I don't know what I'm talking about. Please forget what I've just said.'

But how could she?

AFTER GETTING OFF THE CALL, SOPHIA LEFT HER ROOM AND went to find Anisha, mulling over Estelle's words. Isaac had been so clear back in January that he didn't want to break his vow, but now he had.

Would he regret it when they got back to Foxbrooke? He'd asked her to move in with him, but he'd been living alone for longer than she'd been with Marcus. Would Isaac change his mind once there were two toothbrushes in the bathroom and her clothes in his wardrobe?

Doubt and misery churned in her stomach. It had taken a massive leap of faith to believe Isaac wanted to break his vow with her. Apart from Marcus, she'd never been aware of anyone else fancying her before.

And Isaac was beyond hot. No matter what he'd said to her,

or how he'd worshipped her, old insecurities were crawling from the woodwork to bite chunks out of her happiness.

Sophia knocked on the admin block door and Anisha opened it. Her face was pale and her eyes dark and hollow.

'Mohan said you'd arrived back.'

'How can I help?'

'Can you go to the kitchen and help prepare breakfast? It's been delayed till lunchtime now. You can chop while sitting down.'

'Yes, of course.'

'Thank you.' Anisha gave her a tight smile, then went back inside the building.

Ten minutes later, Sophia was sitting on one of the picnic tables outside the kitchen, peeling vegetables. The faint smell was not enough to cover the sargassum stench as it drifted up from the beach.

People moved slowly through the calf-deep seaweed like zombies, heaping it into piles, then transferring it onto trolleys that were wheeled past her.

'Where are they taking it?' she asked a chef when she came to collect the carrots Sophia had just chopped.

'They're putting it on the ferry then dumping it offshore on the other side of the island.'

'Won't it just float to the mainland then?'

The woman shrugged, seeming too exhausted to care. 'Give me a yell when you've finished these and I'll give you something else to do.'

Sophia continued working, her heart beating faster as she watched Isaac shifting sargassum at twice the speed of everyone else.

There was a yell in the distance and he suddenly sprinted right, disappearing from view.

Standing, Sophia grabbed her crutch and went to see what was going on.

Isaac was lifting Blake's lifeless body from the seaweed.

Xander rushed to help, and they carried him to the edge of the beach and laid him on the ground at the edge of the dining area.

'What's happened?' Sophia asked as she got to them. 'Can I do anything?'

Isaac glanced at her, sweat beading across his brow. 'He's fainted. Most likely from a mix of exhaustion, dehydration and the fumes from the decomposing sargassum.'

He turned to Xander. 'Can you go to the kitchen and get them to make jugs of electrolyte solution? If they're not sure how to do it, use half a teaspoon of salt and three tablespoons of sugar per litre.'

Xander nodded and dashed off.

Blake was breathing, but his eyes were closed and his skin was grey.

'Isaac, this isn't safe. They're probably as exhausted, if not more, than we are. When on earth are they going to get a break? And anyway, can't it just be left where it is?'

His gaze went down the beach and she turned her head to see what he was looking at.

Swami Vishnu was applauding everyone working. He then brought his hands together in a prayer position and bowed his head.

'Please speak to him,' she said, trying to find words that wouldn't overtly criticise Swami Vishnu's behaviour. 'It's dangerous what they're being asked to do. These people paid thousands of pounds to do a yoga course. They didn't spend all that money to do hours of dangerous manual labour.'

As if agreeing with her, Blake's eyes fluttered open. 'What happened?' he slurred.

'You fainted, buddy,' Isaac said. 'We're getting you a rehydration drink, then I'll take you back to your room.'

Blake's eyes filled with tears. 'I'm sorry, man.' He turned his head away, a hand covering his face as if embarrassed. 'Fuck!'

Isaac held his shoulder. 'It's okay. We're all struggling a bit right now.'

Xander came running back with a jug and a glass. 'It hasn't all dissolved yet, but I thought you'd want it, anyway.'

Isaac nodded and Xander poured a glass, then gave it to Blake, who gulped it down.

'Take the next one slower,' Isaac said. 'You don't want to—'

Blake threw it all back up. 'Fuck! Sorry, man.'

'Xander, can you help me get Blake back to his room?' Isaac asked. 'I want you to stay with him and get him to sip the water. You also need to drink half of what you've got there. If he keeps it down, go and get another jug and the two of you keep going until your pee is pale yellow. Okay?'

Xander nodded, and they helped Blake to his feet.

Sophia caught Isaac's eye, inclining her head towards the figure of Swami Vishnu, cheering everyone on.

Isaac gave her a brief nod, then helped Blake away.

SOPHIA CONTINUED CHOPPING VEGETABLES, NOT STOPPING Isaac to chat when he returned.

He carried a tray filled with jugs of electrolyte solution and glasses to the beach, called everyone to drink them, then disappeared, presumably to talk to Swami Vishnu.

It must have worked, as no-one went back to the beach. Some people went to help in the kitchen, the others lay on the ground and fell asleep. Sophia continued doing what she could to help, her stomach angrily demanding to know why she wasn't eating what she was preparing.

'Sophia?'

She turned to see the lead chef. 'Yes?'

'Grab yourself food now before we call everyone. I'm expecting it to be a bit of a bun fight and I don't want anyone accidentally knocking you over.'

'Thank you.'

Getting to her feet, Sophia filled her plate, then carefully carried it to the furthest picnic bench and started eating as the ashram bell rang.

Five minutes later, she spotted Jessica and gave her a wave.

Coming to the table, Jessica sat down with a thump. 'Give me five minutes, then I'm all yours.'

She shovelled food into her mouth, hardly chewing before taking another forkful. Her face was pale, sweaty and streaked with dirt. She looked as shattered as Sophia felt.

'I'm sorry I couldn't get any food from the mainland. We were delayed at the hospital, then everywhere was shut.'

Jessica waved her hand as if it didn't matter, then pointed at Sophia's leg with her fork and gave her a questioning look.

'It's much better. I'll probably be on one crutch for the next week, then I should be able to bear weight.'

Jessica gave her a thumbs up.

'I've been helping in the kitchen and they've made two huge trays of chocolate brownies. There should be enough for everyone.'

Her friend clapped her cutlery together, then swallowed. 'Hoo-ee! Now that *is* something I can get behind in this hellhole.' She swallowed a few more mouthfuls, then pushed her plate to one side. 'I'll get some more in a minute. I need a break so I don't just upchuck.'

'How was last night?'

Jessica shrugged. 'I was fine with it, but everyone in the dorm freaked the fuck out, especially when half the roof blew off.'

'Oh, my god!'

Jessica puffed out her cheeks. 'We still had power 'cos of the generators, so I just did my usual thang, stepping up and sorting out everyone's shit. We moved the beds and stuff out of the way of the rain, then went downstairs and joined the people camping out in the asana halls.'

'The ones usually in tents?'

'Yeah. I don't think anyone got much sleep. Then, as soon as it was light, we all went off to Satsang to hear Swami Fuckwad announce that everything's cancelled and we've been conscripted into the Devanandara Peace Corps.'

'Have any other buildings been damaged?'

'Not much, I don't think. The asana hall roofs will need a bit of attention, but our dorm got hit the worst because it's the highest building.'

'Where will you sleep?'

'They're gonna cram us into other rooms.'

'Why don't you stay with me? There's space for another bed.'

As soon as the words were out of her mouth, Sophia knew it meant there was no way she could be alone with Isaac.

Jessica's confident expression flickered. 'Thanks. That would be freaking awesome.'

Sophia rubbed her eyes, trying to wipe away some of the tiredness. 'This wasn't what I imagined this experience to be like.'

'You're telling me. A couple of the girls have been to other ashrams and said the Devanandara ones are the most hard-core. This course may be the quickest way to get from zero to yoga teacher, but it's the most brutal. Although half the class seems to think the weight loss makes up for everything else.'

'I hate being this hungry.'

'Me too. And some fucker stole the rest of my food.'

'Oh no! When?'

'Sometime last night. They took the jerky and the rest of the chocolate.'

Sophia got to her feet. 'Let me see if they've brought the brownie out yet.'

'No, I'll go. You need two hands for this job. Want any more curry? Salad?'

She shook her head. 'I'm full enough and can't face it, to be honest. Not when there are brownies to go around.'

'I know what you mean. The moment I'm back onboard a mega-yacht, I'm gonna seduce the chef and live off fillet mignon, Cheetos and cream puffs.'

'I don't know what cream puffs are, but they sound delicious.'

'Oh my god, girl, you haven't lived. Google it later when you're back in our crash pad. Right, I'm off.'

Sophia watched as Jessica got two plates, then walked up and down the lines of trestle tables, searching for the brownies.

Surely they would have been put out by now?

Stopping with a frown, Jessica eyeballed the private dining area where the Swamis and ashram staff were seated.

Oh no.

Her friend marched straight up to the table and leaned forward.

Anisha stood, pushing her away.

Jessica pushed back, her yell of 'hey!' loud enough to be heard by everyone.

Then Isaac was by their side, his head bent as he spoke to

Jessica. He led her out of the area, then returned and dropped to a crouch beside Swami Vishnu.

Jessica stood to one side, her arms crossed, the white plates looking like weapons in her hands.

Swami Vishnu came forward into the main dining area and spread his arms.

Everyone fell silent.

'Yogis and yoginis,' he began with a benevolent smile. 'We have weathered the storm, and all worked tirelessly to repair our beautiful ashram. In recognition of your karma yoga, I have two announcements.'

He paused for dramatic effect, and a murmur of anticipation passed around the tables.

'We would, of course, appreciate any help you can continue to give today, for example, clearing up after this beautiful feast, preparing dinner, and relocating those who were sleeping in the top dorm room. However, if you feel you need to rest, you may take the afternoon off.'

He spread his hands as if bestowing the most generous of gifts, and people glanced at each other with hopeful excitement at the prospect of sleeping for the first time in over thirty hours.

'And that's not all,' Swami Vishnu continued. 'As a special treat, I have asked the chefs to make beneficially rajasic chocolate brownies.'

A collective gasp went around the tables.

Isaac and Mohan came forward, each carrying a huge metal tray. Isaac approached Jessica first, then went with Mohan to serve everyone else.

'Enjoy!' Swami Vishnu cried, clapping his hands.

People burst into applause, some cheering Swami Vishnu as he beamed at them with his hands in prayer position and his head inclined regally.

'Sanctimonious motherfucker,' Jessica growled as she sat opposite Sophia and passed her a plate, on which sat an enormous chocolate brownie.

'What happened?'

Jessica leaned in and lowered her voice. 'Greedy arsehole wasn't going to give these to anyone but the chosen few. Your boyfriend had a few words, and he changed his tune.'

Sophia bit into the brownie and moaned as the taste exploded on her tongue. 'Thank you.'

'No problem. He knew if he hadn't shared them, I was going to go full Pedersson on him, and at least half the ashram would have mutinied.'

The two women chewed in happy silence.

'Hey,' Jessica began. 'You think we get tomorrow off now?'

Sophia hesitated, then shook her head. 'Is—Hanuman said it's unlikely.'

Jessica's forehead hit the table. 'Fuccccckkk!'

'I know. Let's get your bed to my room and have a nap. I think we'll feel better once we've slept.'

Jessica's head raised. 'Right now, I'm counting the days till this is over. The moment I've got my qualification, I'm outta here for good.'

Sophia nodded. When she left the island on the ferry for the last time, she wasn't planning on looking back.

❀ 2 1 ❀

'**S**wamiji!'

Isaac jogged the last few feet to Swami Saraswati's side as her hand dropped from the door to her meditation garden.

She turned, her expression neutral. 'Hanuman?'

'Er...' Now he could speak to her in private, he wasn't sure what to say.

'Can I help you?'

He ran both hands through his hair. 'Guruji told me you were leaving here, and he was...' he trailed off, not wanting to say the words 'replacing you'.

'And?' Her features were a bland mask. He couldn't read her.

'Is this what you want?'

There was a flicker of surprise in her eyes. 'It's not about what feeds my ego, Hanuman. It's about what is right for the organisation.'

'Yes, but...'

He stopped before voicing the heretical thought that

maybe it was better for the organisation that Swami Saraswati continue running the ashram she'd shaped and led successfully for the past two decades.

The sound of rustling leaves filled the silence.

'Hanuman...'

'Yes, Swamiji?'

She placed her hand back on the door. 'You chose your path a very long time ago and I do not believe it is possible for you to step off it.'

Giving him a small nod, she went into the garden and shut the door behind her.

Isaac stared at the brown wood, his gaze unfocused.

What did she mean? How did his decision to be celibate have anything to do with her leaving the ashram?

Closing his eyes, he tried to empty his mind, but it was too full of Sophia. And behind the all-consuming awareness of her, his head was filled with noisy confusion.

Turning away from the meditation garden, he made his way slowly down the stone path, tiredness weighing heavily in his limbs. It had been three days since the storm and he'd worked nonstop fixing what had been broken and toiling at the Sisyphean task of clearing sargassum from the beaches. Swami Vishnu and Mohan had been teaching the TTC, so he hadn't even had a chance to speak to Sophia. And now Jessica was staying in her room, there was no opportunity to see her at night.

Isaac knew he was dangerously fatigued. His brain was slower, his movements clumsier. He'd slipped on the dorm roof the previous day and nearly fallen to his death. After that, he'd refused to go back up or let anyone else, telling Swami Vishnu that the ashram had to pay for craftsmen from the mainland.

His guru had nodded and patted him on the arm, telling

him he needed to slow down. But that statement was quickly followed by a list of other tasks he wanted Isaac to attend to.

'Hanuman!' Mohan was hurrying down the path towards him. 'I've been looking for you everywhere.'

'Everything alright?'

'Guruji wants you to finish teaching the main lecture today.'

Isaac glanced at his watch. It had started twenty minutes ago.

'Why does he want me for the lecture? I thought you and Guruji were now teaching the whole course?'

Mohan didn't meet his eye as they strode through the ashram. 'I've already taught the first section. I'm going to help out at the beach now. They're in hall five. I'll see you later.'

He jogged off, and Isaac paused, watching his retreating figure. What on earth was going on?

Then he stepped into the asana hall and his heart sank into the pit of his stomach.

Kriya day.

'Ah! There you are!'

Swami Vishnu sat on his throne, beaming from ear to ear, the course participants on the floor in front of him.

Isaac forced himself not to look for Sophia.

'Mohan has already demonstrated Kapalabhati, Tratak, Nauli, and Jala Neti for our students. We're running a little behind schedule, so I thought we could skip Sutra Neti and move straight onto Dhauti.'

There was a table to the left of Swami Vishnu, on which stood eleven buckets of salt water, sections of plastic tubing, strips of cotton gauze and drinking glasses. Isaac stared at it as if looking at the tools of a torturer's trade. Out of the corner of his eye, he caught the worried glances of the students, all sitting with small plastic neti pots beside them.

There were traditionally six yoga kriyas, designed to accelerate one's spiritual progress. Most schools of yoga didn't touch the more physical practices, believing that a kriya was an internal action, achieved through breathwork or postures.

However, the founder of the organisation, Swami Devanandara, believed they were cleansing practices that could rid the body of everything from asthma to leprosy.

Isaac had only done the more extreme ones once before, on his own Teacher Training Course. It had been an experience he'd never seen the point of repeating, and had reduced most of his fellow students to hysterical wrecks. Since that day, whenever he'd taught the TTC, he'd neither demonstrated, nor prescribed, that students should do them.

'Why don't we start with Plavini?' said Swami Vishnu.

Isaac resisted the urge to ask if his use of the word 'we' meant that his guru was also going to be joining in.

Clearing his throat, he faced the group. 'Plavini is wind purification. For this exercise, you need to take a mouthful of air, then swallow it. Keep doing this until your stomach is full, then slowly burp it out.'

'What's the point?' Jessica asked.

Isaac let his gaze be drawn to the back of the room where she was sitting next to Sophia, her expression hard with challenge.

Keeping his eyes on Jessica and not allowing them to drift to Sophia, he replied. 'By doing Plavini, you remove the foul gases from the stomach along with the air.'

'The gases caused by breaking down the food we eat?' Jessica continued.

Isaac didn't know what to say. He'd never believed in the science behind the exercise.

'Maybe we wouldn't have such "foul gases" if we weren't living off lentils, beans, and cabbage? Surely the most effective way to purify the excess wind in my body is to stop eating rabbit food? If we didn't sleep with the window open at night, then Sophia would be gassed to death by morning.'

One of the men hid his snigger behind a cough.

'Jessica,' Swami Vishnu said, articulating each syllable as if they were something bitter he was spitting from his mouth. 'The yoga sutras were laid down thousands of years before your soul graduated to human form. You are here to learn secrets that go beyond your narrow, reductionist, western belief system, and have chosen to partake in the authentic ashram experience. I suggest you have more of an open mind.'

'Oh, don't get me wrong,' Jessica replied with a smirk. 'If there's gonna be a burping competition, I'm the one to beat.'

Swami Vishnu ignored her, turning to Isaac. 'Hanuman?'

He nodded and cleared his throat again. The last thing he ever wanted to do was burp an entire bellyful of air in front of Sophia.

Keeping his focus on the front row of students who were staring at him with morbid fascination, Isaac swallowed mouthful after mouthful of air until his tummy ached.

Then, before his guru could instruct him otherwise, he turned his back on everyone, went to the edge of the platform and burped it all out towards the bushes.

'Whoop whoop!' Jessica cried. 'Go Hanuman!'

'Now your turn everyone,' Swami Vishnu said.

Isaac kept his back to the group, focusing on the dark green leaves as a cacophony of burps, shrieks and giggles erupted behind him.

This was the fun part. No-one was going to like what was coming next, and the thought of forcing anyone to do Vastra Dhauti or Kunjar Kriya made him sick to his stomach.

'Okay, my children,' cried Swami Vishnu. 'Settle down.'

The room quietened, and Isaac turned to face everyone.

'Now,' his guru continued, 'next up is—'

Jessica interrupted his words with an enormous belch. 'I win!'

'Vastra Dhauti and Kunjar Kriya,' Swami Vishnu carried on, as if she didn't exist. 'Form into groups of three or four and take a glass and a strip of gauze each, along with one bucket per group.'

Isaac's feet seemed made of stone, rooting him to the spot as he watched the students follow the instructions, their faces still bright from the comedy of the previous exercise.

'Take the gauze and knot it at roughly ten centimetre intervals. You, too, Hanuman.'

Heart thudding, Isaac took a strip of gauze, a glass and bucket of water, then did as instructed. The pieces of cotton were only two inches wide but several feet long, and he could tell from the students' faces that they had no idea what they were meant to do with them.

Swami Vishnu clapped his hands. 'Wonderful. Now Hanuman will demonstrate Vastra Dhauti followed by Kunjar Kriya.'

Isaac knew that in the next two weeks he was going to go against his guru's direct orders and remain in the UK with Sophia. Guilt about refusing to do what was asked of him was plaguing his thoughts and dreams.

Right now he wanted to say 'no' to demonstrating the kriyas, but didn't want to defy in public the man who'd done so much for him over the years. He knew Swami Vishnu was already irritated with him after he'd said that the students cleaning the beach needed to rest, then that the brownies should be shared with everyone.

Isaac had done these two kriyas once before and had lived to tell the tale. He could do it again.

'I'll show Vastra Dhauti first, then Kunjar Kriya, also known as Vamana Dhauti. Then, *if* you want—'

'Everyone will perform the exercises,' Swami Vishnu interrupted.

Taking a deep breath to fortify himself, Isaac reached forward and soaked the wad of gauze in his bucket of salt water.

'These kriyas are traditionally used to help with asthma, gastric issues and excess stomach acidity. They cleanse the intestine of impurities or obstructions, improve liver function and remove worms,' he began, then paused, as every part of his body yelled 'this is utter nonsense' at him.

He'd always taken the justification behind these practices with a pinch of salt, but now he could see zero scientific rationale or benefit behind them, as well as huge physical and psychological risk to anyone performing them.

As Isaac brought one end of the gauze strip to his mouth, a sad realisation settled on him that this moment marked the end of a chapter.

He would always teach and practise yoga, but going forward, he would withdraw from such a close association with the Devanandara organisation, and wouldn't spend at least a month a year at one of their ashrams. Isaac had always believed he would follow his guru for life, but now he was willingly stepping off that path and choosing a different life. With Sophia.

'I'm going to swallow sections, one knot at a time,' he said. 'Then slowly pull it out.'

He kept his focus on the floor as a collective gasp of shock filled the silence.

Breathing slowly in and out of his nose to stay calm, Isaac swallowed knot after knot, his eyes streaming, and his irritated oesophagus trying to vomit the cotton back up.

He took his mind back to his house in Foxbrooke, imagining Sophia in the garden, laughing in the sunshine, diving into the pool. Cooking with her in the kitchen, curled up on the sofa, reading together, making love in a room filled with starlight.

The images helped him take the entire strip of fabric. Then he exhaled a long breath and slowly pulled it back out, discarding the gauze into an empty bin by the side of the table.

The space was so quiet he could hear the rapid thudding of his own heart. He couldn't meet Sophia's eyes. He couldn't look at anyone. He just needed to get through this.

'With Kunjar Kriya,' he said, his voice rough and his throat in pain, 'we swallow glasses of salt water, then put pressure on our stomach with our left hand and stimulate our gag reflex with the fingers of our right, until we forcibly remove the water we've just drunk.'

Dipping a tumbler into the bucket in front of him, he gulped five glasses, then turned and immediately vomited it over the edge of the wooden platform onto the ground. As his stomach heaved and his eyes watered, he felt lighter, as if he wasn't just getting rid of the salt water, but also his deep attachment to the Devanandara organisation.

Turning, Isaac met the eyes of the people directly in front of him.

Their faces were white. Some women were quietly crying, and Grace was shaking. There was no way he was going to make any of them do what he'd just endured.

Then he risked a glance at Sophia.

Tears tracked down her cheeks. They felt like acid dripping onto his soul.

Jessica took hold of Sophia's hand, an expression of fury on her face. 'What are the bits of plastic tubing for?' she asked, her free hand pointing at the table.

The answer stuck in Isaac's throat.

'They are for Basti,' Swami Vishnu said. 'You'll go into the sea and insert the tube into your rectum. Then you'll engage Uddiyana Bandha, followed by Nauli to draw water into your colon through your anus. After that, you'll withdraw the tube, do another couple of rounds of abdominal churning, and expel the water from your intestines.'

Silence.

Swami Vishnu clapped his hands, an excited expression on his face. 'Okay, everyone! Dip your gauze into the bucket and start swallowing.'

'Hell to the no,' Jessica called out.

Grace was shaking so hard, Isaac was certain she was having a panic attack.

He dropped to his knees in front of her. 'You don't have to do any of this,' he murmured. 'Nobody does,' he continued, a little louder.

Letting out a gasping sob, Grace grabbed his hands. She was trying to speak, but couldn't get her words out.

Isaac squeezed her ice-cold fingers. 'It's okay, Grace. You're okay. No-one is being forced to do this. It's optional.'

'It's all part of the authentic ashram experience,' Swami Vishnu exclaimed over the murmurs of discontent.

His words seemed to send a shock through Grace. Eyes wide with panic, she fell forward, her fingers clawing at Isaac's t-shirt as if to hide in his arms.

Sitting, he held her small body on his lap, his arms tightly around her as she shuddered and sobbed.

The prospect of these exercises was terrifying enough, but Isaac also knew just how many people came to this course with an active or prior eating disorder. These practices could trigger PTSD as well as create fresh trauma, and so he'd never pressured anyone to do them.

'Come along,' Swami Vishnu said testily.

Still holding Grace, Isaac played the only trump card he currently had, other than outright mutiny. Nine years ago, he'd edited the TTC manuals and added an addendum in the kriya section.

'If you turn to page two hundred and eighty-five of your manuals,' he said, making sure everyone could hear him. 'You'll see these exercises should not be done if you've ever suffered from an eating disorder. If this applies to you, you may sit all of them out. If the sight of people doing the exercises is triggering, then you may leave the class.'

Jessica immediately dragged Sophia to her feet and led her out of the asana hall.

There was a brief pause as everyone else realised the sky wasn't about to fall on their heads, then there was a hurried mass exodus. Grace crawled off Isaac's lap and dashed after everyone else for the entrance.

Within twenty seconds, the only people left in the space were Isaac and Swami Vishnu.

Isaac turned to face his guru and took a breath.

'Hanuman,' he interrupted, holding up a hand to silence him. 'I am disappointed in you. Over the years, you have been my most diligent student and staunchest supporter. You've been like a son to me.'

Guilt sat in Isaac's stomach, weighing him down.

'There is an ugly dissonance growing within the organisation and I am relying on people like you, people I trust, to stand beside me. I cannot have you go against my teachings.'

'Guruji, I am sorry, but we cannot traumatise people who are paying—'

'The path of yoga is not meant to be easy. If it were, then every couch potato would be a Buddha, a Jesus, or a Swami Devanandara. By confronting the darkness within, we find our light. I think it would be appropriate for you to practice mauna until the end of this TTC.'

Every cell in Isaac's body screamed 'no' to that directive. He would not be silenced by order. It was time to cut the cord, no matter if it meant the end of his close relationship with Swami Vishnu.

'Guruji, I'm sorry, but I can't stay here after the TTC.'

'I know that. You have to tie up your affairs in the UK.'

'No. I mean I've decided to stay in Foxbrooke. If I lose my house, then I'll find somewhere else to live. My dharma lies there, teaching my classes.'

Swami Vishnu didn't even pause to assimilate Isaac's words, continuing with a clipped tone.

'That is not your dharma. You can reach thousands of people a year by staying here. Who do you touch in England? A handful of menopausal women, and the odd yoga bunny who's only there because they think they can bed you?'

Isaac thought of all his wonderful students. About the octogenarians at Foxbrooke Haven who could hardly manage any posture but loved what he taught and made him laugh like a drain. Anger pulsed through his veins at his guru's dismissal of them.

Swami Vishnu leaned forward, steepling his fingers. 'Is Sophia behind this decision?'

Was she? Sophia was the reason he was breaking his vow, but even if he'd never met her, he knew he'd choose his life in Foxbrooke over one at the ashram. Sure, he would teach more people within the organisation, but the connection would be transient. Impermanent.

Before leaving for India, Isaac had decided to move on from Foxbrooke if he lost his land. But now, thinking of the relationships with his students, with Eveline, the thought seemed ridiculous.

'Sophia isn't the only reason I wish to remain in the UK.'

His guru threw his hands in the air and leaned back in his chair. 'So, you still cling to the hope you will be together? You should think about your next life. Your next incarnation. Not chasing what is as meaningful and fleeting as the existence of a fruit fly.'

'I want to be happy in *this* life, Guruji.'

'What you feel isn't real. Sexual desire is a flame that can be snuffed out in an instant.'

Isaac kept quiet. His love for Sophia burned hotter than the sun, and he was positive it would last longer.

Swami Vishnu's eyes narrowed. 'Have you been intimate with her?'

Isaac froze. He'd wanted to be honest with his guru, but right now it felt wrong, like he was tarnishing something private and perfect.

'Hanuman?'

He settled for a partial truth. 'When I return to the UK, we'll begin a relationship.'

A long silence followed.

'I'm sorry to disappoint you, Guruji, but I've made my decision.'

Swami Vishnu got to his feet.

Isaac stood and held out his arm, but the older man shook his head. 'I will make my own way back.' He flicked his fingers at the abandoned buckets of water and gauze strips on the floor. 'Ensure this is cleared up.'

Repositioning his robe across his shoulder, he walked off.

Isaac let out a breath. It was done. The worst was over, and he could focus on the next phase in his life: a bright and blissful future with Sophia.

❀ 22 ❀

'**B**urger and fries, jerk chicken, chocolate fudge sundae, piña colada and a beer,' Jessica said to Sophia as they went through the ashram on the way to their next class. 'And that's just for the appetiser. For my entrée, I wanna find an all-you-can-eat buffet and smash it.'

'Can we look for some local food as well?'

'Sure. In two days from now, you and I are gonna gain twenty pounds in less than eight hours.'

Sophia's hand moved reflexively to her stomach. Like most women she knew, she'd always wanted to lose a bit of weight. However, she didn't like the aching feelings of hunger she now felt so much of the time, nor the dizziness.

Jessica lowered her voice. 'Have you spoken to Hanuman at all since kriya day?'

She shook her head. Isaac had been taken off teaching most of the TTC, now only leading one asana class a day with Swami Vishnu. The older man kept him on a tight leash, making Isaac demonstrate the poses, then correct the pretty women who appeared to have forgotten how to even stand upright without hands-on help.

If that wasn't bad enough, Sophia was now cleaning the temple with Ganapati, the surliest yogi she'd ever met, and Isaac had been moved to helping the other women with their chores.

'I swear to god, something's not right in paradise,' Jessica muttered.

'What do you mean?'

'Swami Saraswati still comes to Satsang, but she never gives the lecture or leads the chanting, even though she's meant to be the boss of this place. Mohan and Anisha don't seem to be talking at all, and Anisha looks like she spends half the time crying. And as for the rest of the staff? They seem even more miserable than we are. The only person who appears happy is Swami Vishnu.'

'I really don't like him,' Sophia whispered.

'He's a grade-A asshole and I don't understand why your man thinks the sun shines out his butt.'

Unease coiled in Sophia's stomach. From how Isaac had talked about his guru when they'd been back in Foxbrooke, she'd imagined him to be a cross between the Dalai Lama and her childhood teddy bear.

She loved and trusted Isaac, but how did he not see how creepy Swami Vishnu was? The kriya day was still giving her nightmares. What kind of person expected people to torture themselves?

Sophia's limbs and brain were moving slower than normal thanks to the combination of a sleep and calorie deficit, and her anxiety had gone into overdrive. She desperately wanted to talk to Isaac, but there hadn't been an opportunity.

It wasn't just the reassurance she needed that things between them were still okay. She needed to have a harder conversation about his guru's behaviour. She'd considered sending Isaac an email, but there had been no time to give it proper consideration and she wanted to speak to him in person.

Jessica linked her arm with Sophia's. 'Ten days to go, that's all. We're on the home straight now.'

Sophia nodded. She was counting the hours.

'I'm gonna get some water. Does your bottle need a refill?'

'Yes, but let me do them.'

'No, lady. You're still on a crutch. I'll see you in class.'

Before Sophia could protest, Jessica took her bottle and strode off.

The asana hall was a few yards away, slightly hidden under the trees. Taking a deep breath, she made her way carefully towards it and up the steps.

'Sophia!'

Tyger was beckoning her forward from her position in a huddle with Fearne, Khloe-Narcisse, Paisley, and Grace.

'Take a seat.'

Sophia lowered herself to the floor, her pulse quickening. What did they want?

Tyger leaned in. 'We wanted to talk to you about Hanuman,' she whispered.

Oh god. What do they know? Panic flashed across her skin.

'Don't look so worried,' Paisley said. 'We know he isn't into you.'

Sophia clamped her lips shut to stop a manic laugh from escaping.

'Mohan told me Hanuman has taken a vow of chastity,' Tyger continued. 'But we think it's bollocks, and he only said that because he's jealous.'

The other women nodded in agreement.

'Do you know anything?' Khloe-Narcisse asked. 'It's

obvious Hanuman thinks we're hot. He touched my butt when I was in downward dog.'

Paisley nodded. 'And he fondled my boob when he didn't think anyone was looking.'

Sophia dug her nails into her palms as the urge to be sick smashed into her stomach.

It's not true. You know *it's not true.*

'Was he handsy when he took you to the hospital?' Tyger asked.

Biting the inside of her cheek, Sophia shook her head.

'Course he wouldn't be,' Paisley said crossly to Tyger. 'He doesn't fancy her.' She turned to Sophia. 'Did he say anything to you about a vow of chastity?'

What should she say? Unsure, she shook her head.

The other women's faces lit up.

'See,' Khloe-Narcisse said to the group. 'Mohan's full of shit.'

They nodded.

'I'd still shag him,' Fearne said with a grin.

'Well, it's less than forty-eight hours until our day off. Then we'll have time to take them up on what they're offering,' Khloe-Narcisse said. She raised her hands for the other women to high-five her. 'May the best woman win.'

BY THE TIME JESSICA ARRIVED AT THE ASANA HALL, SWAMI Vishnu was clapping his hands to signal the start of the lecture.

'Sorry! Just needed to fill my bottle and empty my bladder,' she said cheerfully, before plonking herself down on the floor next to Sophia. 'Carry on! Don't mind me!'

Swami Vishnu gave her a look designed to ensure she was born as an amoeba in her next incarnation, then turned his smiles to the women sitting at his feet.

'Yogis and yoginis, today's lecture concerns the twenty spiritual instructions handed down to us from Swami Devanandara. Practising these daily will lead you down the path to enlightenment and grant you freedom from the bonds of rebirth. Turn to page three hundred and five in your manuals.'

Sophia did, noting the first instruction to always get up at four a.m. every morning. Did Isaac do that? Would he expect her to? She flicked her eyes down the list. It was so prescriptive and onerous. There seemed no time to have a job, rest, or chill out watching rubbish on the telly.

'Your practice should begin with meditation whilst facing east. Begin with one hour, then extend this to three hours. To save time, you may also repeat your mantra in multiples of one hundred and eight, up to two thousand and six hundred times daily,' Swami Vishnu continued.

'Not gonna happen,' Jessica murmured under her breath.

'After meditation, practise your asanas for two hours. Do not skip a day of this.'

Jessica's hand went up.

Swami Vishnu ignored her. 'A sattvic vegetarian diet will help promote spiritual discipline.'

'Guruji,' Jessica called out. 'Do *you* practise asanas for two hours daily?'

There was a collective shocked intake of breath from the group, and Mohan tensed as if waiting for the order to attack.

Swami Vishnu gave Jessica a condescending smile. 'I do.'

Sophia could almost hear the cogs in everyone's head whirring as they compared Swami Vishnu's physique with Mohan's.

'I do them in my mind,' Swami Vishnu continued. 'When you are as spiritually evolved as I am, it is a more profound way to experience the asanas. They work at a cellular level.' He closed his eyes. 'Right now, I am doing sirsasana, the headstand.'

Jessica tapped Sophia's leg, then made the hand gesture for 'wanker'.

Sophia bit back a grin as Mohan frowned at them both.

Swami Vishnu opened his eyes, his expression bright as if he'd just stepped up another rung on the ladder to enlightenment.

'Learn Sanskrit and study the Gita and the Vedas daily, memorising them gradually until you know them by heart.'

'All ten thousand, seven hundred verses of them?' Jessica spluttered.

Swami Vishnu winked at the women in front of him. 'It may take you a while.'

They tittered.

'Observe mauna for a few hours daily,' he continued, 'not making any gesture or noise during this period.' He eyeballed Jessica. 'Some of you may need to extend this silence to several hours a day.'

A few people snorted.

His gaze now flicked to Sophia. 'And remember, you will die.'

Her brain stuttered to a shocked halt as her blood turned to ice.

Swami Vishnu smiled benevolently at everyone else. 'If we are cognisant that death awaits us at every moment, we will never fail to fulfil our spiritual duties.'

Anisha ran up the steps into the hall. 'Please excuse me, Guruji.'

'Yes?'

'A call has come through for Sophia from her brother. He says it's important.'

Sophia couldn't breathe. Had their dad had another heart attack? Died?

Jessica helped her to her feet. 'Do you want me to come with you?'

'That will not be necessary,' Swami Vishnu answered.

Jessica ignored him. 'What do you want me to do?'

'It's okay,' Sophia stammered. 'You stay here.' Leaving her bag with her friend, she followed Anisha out of the hall, her heart thudding and her eyes stinging.

Anisha was silent as she led Sophia to the admin block and a room at the back where a phone lay on a desk.

'I hope everything is okay,' she said, her expression sympathetic, then hesitantly reached out to squeeze Sophia's arm. 'Take as long as you need. I'll be out front if you need anything. And don't worry, I can't hear you with the door closed so you'll have privacy.'

'Thank y-you,' she stuttered, collapsing into the chair behind the desk.

Anisha left, quietly closing the door behind her.

Sophia picked up the old-fashioned receiver. 'James?'

'Char! Fuck, it's good to hear your voice.'

'Is it Dad? Mum?'

'They're fine. Everyone's fine.'

Sophia let out a gasping sob as her emotional wall collapsed and tears flowed down her cheeks.

'Shit. Did you think something had happened to them? Char, I'm a fucking idiot. I said it was serious because they didn't want to get you out of class. I'm so sorry.' Her brother sighed. 'Estelle is going to flay me alive when she finds out.'

Sophia hiccupped a small laugh at the image of Estelle whacking James with her riding crop.

'So, what's happened?'

'Nothing. I needed to speak to you about Isaac.'

What? 'Isaac?'

'Yes. He's not who you think he is.'

Sophia gulped in a breath, lights flashing behind her eyes.

'Don't be cross, but Estelle told me he was at the ashram and that something had happened between you. Is that true?'

'Isaac... He's my boyfriend,' she said, trying to speak with conviction even though her voice was wobbling.

Her brother sighed heavily. 'Char, I know this year has been a clusterfuck for you, and I'm glad you want to move on from Marcus, but I want to keep you safe.'

'What are you talking about? I don't think I could be any safer than when I'm with Isaac.'

'You don't know him. You only met him, what, eight months ago? You've got no idea what he's capable of.'

Sophia clutched her free hand to her pounding head. 'Isaac's a yoga teacher, not a serial killer. I trust him completely.'

'Look, when Estelle told me you were seeing him, I did some digging, made a few calls.'

'You did *what*?'

'Char, I'm your overprotective older brother. I felt like I'd failed you with Marcus and I didn't want to see you hurt again.'

'I don't care who Isaac was in the past. I only care about who he is now.'

'Do you know why he left Conqueror?'

'Yes. His boss was a creeper who tried it on with his girl-friend, and Isaac kicked off.'

Silence.

James took a deep breath. 'Char, Isaac put Victor Thorn-field in hospital.'

'W-what?'

'He didn't just "kick off", Isaac kicked the living shit out of him. The only reason Victor Thornfield isn't dead is that other people intervened and dragged Isaac away.'

Sophia's head was reeling. 'I... I...'

'Charges weren't brought against Isaac because Thornfield made a deal with HR after other women came forward saying they'd also been felt up by him. He promised to keep his hands to himself and not press charges as long as Isaac and his girlfriend lost their jobs.'

'But... That's not fair!'

'I know, but Isaac went fucking psycho, Char, and I don't want you to be with anyone who could flip out and harm you like that.'

'James! For god's sake! Back then, Isaac was burnt out, sleep deprived and stressed out of his mind. That's why he left all of that and became a yoga teacher. He's a completely different person now, and the most gentle and caring man I've ever met. And anyway, Isaac attacked a *man* who'd harmed a *woman*. If *you* were strung out, and Victor Thornfield attempted to assault me, Mum, Estelle. How would *you* react?'

'Look, I hear what you're saying, and I don't deny I'd want to kill him, but I genuinely don't think I'd attack him like Isaac did. I'm just worried for you, Char, and I don't want to see you hurt in any way.'

'Will you respect my decision to be with Isaac?'

James let out a heavy breath. 'Yes.'

'Have you told Mum and Dad?'

'No, they don't even know he's there with you.'

'Please don't say anything. We're coming back in ten days and I want to introduce him to them myself. And please never tell them what you know. It happened over twelve years ago. Everyone deserves a second chance.'

He didn't reply.

'Promise me?'

He huffed. 'Okay.'

AFTER THE CALL ENDED, SOPHIA SAT IN THE QUIET OF THE room, trying to organise her thoughts. She was overwhelmed with information and the pressure of writing and submitting homework every day in order to pass the course.

Inside her aching head was a whirr of hamsters on wheels. She was overthinking everything. Her brain didn't have enough food to fuel it, nor enough sleep to make it function properly.

Was this how Isaac might have been feeling all those years ago? Like he couldn't think straight and was running on unstable emotion and adrenaline?

And *had* she been wrong about him? Was Isaac just as bad as Marcus, just in a different way?

Getting to her feet, she went to the door. She had to find him.

She had to reassure herself that he wasn't who James, or any of the women at the ashram, thought he was.

'**S**ophia! Wake up!'

Crawling out of the darkness of sleep, Sophia couldn't even find the energy to open her eyes.

'I didn't hear the frikking bell and we're gonna be late,' Jessica continued, pulling Sophia's covers off. 'Shake a leg, Sugarplum. Only twenty-eight hours until burger time.'

Dragging herself out of bed, Sophia staggered to the bathroom.

'Just pee and brush your teeth,' Jessica called through the door. 'Everything else can wait.'

THE SKY WAS PALE, THE AIR COOL AS SOPHIA AND JESSICA left the room.

Up ahead, Swami Vishnu was almost at the temple, Isaac on one side of him and Ganapati on the other.

Sophia hurried on, her crutch thudding on the boardwalk with every step. She hadn't managed to talk to Isaac, and her insecurity and anxiety were now beginning to win the war against her logical self. Tears pricked her eyes as she watched Isaac's graceful movements as he opened the low gate and helped his guru into the temple.

Will I always be second to Swami Vishnu? Is it Isaac's judgement that's off about him, or mine? Was anything with Isaac even real?

Right now, a week on from their last trip to the mainland, it all felt like a dream.

Jessica pushed a tissue into Sophia's hand. 'You win.'

'What?'

'The prize for being the first person to cry today. If you need to howl it out, go to the toilet ten minutes into meditation. If you're a long time, I'll tell Anisha you've got the shits.'

Sophia smiled and wiped her eyes. The previous day, she'd told Jessica that James had rung to give her an update about their father's angina. She still didn't feel comfortable sharing what had happened with Isaac. Her fledgling relationship with him now seemed more precarious and fragile than a newborn baby attempting to tightrope walk over a crocodile-infested swamp.

Just get through the next nine days. Then sort it all out in Foxbrooke.

They'd almost reached the temple when a piercing scream rang out from inside.

Forgetting her injured knee, Sophia ran forward after Jessica.

'Turn the lights on!' Isaac yelled.

The inside of the temple was dark, but Sophia could still make out his figure as he ran from his position at the front to the main entrance on the other side.

Another scream rang out.

As Sophia followed Jessica through the side door, the lights went on, but people were now standing, blocking their view.

'Why the fuck has the statue been put back there?' Isaac

roared. 'Anisha! Get the first aid box. Ganapati! The keys for the boat.'

Sophia glanced over her shoulder at the ocean. The ashram ferry was already a few hundred yards out on its first trip of the morning.

Elbowing her way through the crowd, she stopped, her heart in her mouth, memories cutting into her skin and down to the bone.

Grace was on the floor of the temple, blood on her hands as she clutched her ankle. The statue of Shiva was lying face down on the floor. Isaac was holding Grace and trying to talk to her as she sobbed.

Swami Vishnu waved a bell, and people's heads turned his way. 'Who is she sharing a room with?'

A couple of hands went up.

'Go as quickly as you can and pack her a bag.'

Anisha barrelled into the temple carrying a green box and dropped to Isaac's side.

'Anisha,' Swami Vishnu continued loudly over the sound of Grace's cries. 'Get whatever Hanuman needs for another trip to the hospital.'

Leaving the box with Isaac, Anisha ran off.

'Satsang will reconvene in fifteen minutes. Everyone, please leave the temple immediately.'

Sophia couldn't move, her eyes glued to Grace and Isaac, her heart pounding and her breath ragged.

Jessica took her hand. 'Come on, let's go back to ours.'

Tearing her gaze away, Sophia followed Jessica out and along the beach to their little chalet.

Sitting on the deck, Sophia stared at the low building of the temple on their left and the edge of the dock behind it.

'You okay?' Jessica asked.

Sophia shook her head, numb with shock.

'Hang on.'

Her friend disappeared back inside the room, then reappeared with two tiny bottles and handed one to Sophia.

'The Caribbean's finest rum, and hidden well enough so that my food thief didn't find them. I was saving these for our last day on the island, but I think we should drink them now.'

Sophia unscrewed the cap. 'Thank you. I feel—' She broke off, her emotions too fractured to vocalise.

Jessica clinked her bottle against Sophia's. 'Don't think. Don't feel. Let the alcohol do its job.'

The liquid burned Sophia's throat and warmed her stomach. Almost immediately, she felt it enter her bloodstream, heating the back of her neck and melting the sharp edges of her emotions.

In the distance, Isaac was carrying Grace along the dock, Anisha by his side. Ganapati helped Isaac lift Grace into the speedboat, then Isaac took two bags from Anisha, got onboard, and Ganapati started the engine.

'What a fucking shitshow,' Jessica murmured as the boat roared away.

Sophia nodded, a tiny part of her brain glitching, as if she'd forgotten something really important.

Jessica turned to her. 'I thought the statue had been moved away from the door?'

Oh my god, yes!

She nodded. 'It had. And last night, during Satsang, it was still against the back wall. I always check.'

'Hoo-ee... I bet Grace moved it.'

'No!'

'Aw, come on, Soph. All the girls can talk about is our day off tomorrow and how it's open season on Mohan and Hanuman. Grace knows she hasn't got a chance against Paisley or Khloe-Narcisse. I bet the farm she snuck in last night and moved it so she could recreate your accident, just with more screaming and less blood.'

'You really think she would do that?'

But even as Sophia asked, she knew it was a logical explanation.

'Grace isn't a klutz and the ashram bell went off at the right time, so there wouldn't have been a crush entering the temple. She knew what she had to do to get Isaac to take her off the island.'

Sophia sighed. 'This actually makes me feel a little better. I hope it means she hasn't hurt herself badly.'

'Nah. I think a few scrapes on her hands is all she'll have. There was almost no blood compared to when you fell, but she was still doing her best to smear it all over herself.'

The rum was wearing down Sophia's inhibitions, and she let out a little giggle, then slapped a hand to her guilty mouth.

Jessica grinned. 'That's more like it. And don't worry about your man giving in to Grace's charms. If he didn't break his vow with you, there's no way he's gonna do it with her.'

Jessica's words sat in Sophia's stomach, sloshing around like undigested food. Isaac *had* broken his vow with her. Would he break it again with Grace?

Shut up! You know he wouldn't! Stop torturing yourself!

But no matter how much her logical mind yelled one narrative, her subconscious reminded her how she'd been clueless about Marcus's affairs, even though they lived and worked together for ten years, and she'd known every woman he'd slept with.

'Ooh! Wanna know a silver lining to this morning's drama?' Jessica asked.

'There is one?'

'Uh-huh. If Gana*twati*'s with Hanuman and Grace, he won't be doing karma yoga with you.'

· · ·

Sure enough, a few hours later, Sophia entered the temple to find it blissfully empty.

Retrieving her cleaning supplies from the cupboard, she went to the statue, now back against the far wall. Breathing slowly through her nose to calm herself, she rubbed at the stains of blood. Jessica had been right, there wasn't much, and she couldn't see any on the floor, either.

When the statue was gleaming, she pushed a dry floor-mop across the white tiles, wholly focused on the job as a form of mindfulness, allowing the rest of her turbulent thoughts time to rest.

'Sophia!'

Dropping the mop handle in shock at the sound, she whirled around.

Swami Vishnu was standing at the entrance.

He raised his hands and smiled. 'I didn't mean to startle you.'

Flustered, Sophia bent to pick up the mop. 'I didn't hear you come in.'

'You were multitasking. Meditating whilst performing your karma yoga.'

He strolled towards her. 'Leave that and sit with me.'

Carefully lowering himself to a step on the side of the temple, he patted the space next to him.

Putting the mop to one side, Sophia sat. What on earth did he want?

'This morning's incident must have given you a bit of a scare,' he began. 'How are you feeling?'

'Um... A bit better now. I just hope Grace is okay.'

'I'm sure she will be. I've seen far worse accidents in my time. Did you know before I became a Swami, I used to coach gymnastics back in England?'

Sophia shook her head.

'I was County Champion in my teens, but not quite good enough for the Nationals. And anyway, I found my calling in teaching rather than competing. I've seen far more serious incidents than what happened earlier.'

Swami Vishnu's expression was affable. He seemed so different to the man who'd taken the kriya class the day before.

'What made you decide to become a yogi?' she blurted, trying to imagine his life in gymnastics before leaving for India.

Something flickered in his eyes, and he adjusted the hem of his robe.

'Several things. Politics, burnout... The British weather...'

He winked, and Sophia forced a smile.

'But I found my calling and have never looked back.' He stared intently at her, his glacial blue eyes shrewd and assessing. 'I've spent my life learning people. Seeing their demons and setting them on a better path. I see you, Sophia. I know you.'

Her stomach lurched. Had Isaac told him what had happened between them?

His expression was sympathetic. 'You are a sweet soul, but also a young one. Fresh and innocent. Easily led.'

'W-what do you mean?'

Letting out a sigh, he took her hand.

Sophia was too shocked to pull it away, then embarrassed about the thought of doing so. She didn't like Swami Vishnu, but he was still a spiritual man and the revered leader of the entire Devanandara organisation.

'My child, I know what happened to you back in the UK. Hanuman shared your story with me.'

What? How much had Isaac told his guru?

Swami Vishnu sandwiched her hand between the two of his

and squeezed. 'You were taken advantage of, and I do not want it to happen again.'

This was like James. Yet another man warning her off Isaac.

'I am deeply sorry, Sophia, to have to tell you this, but you are not the first woman Hanuman has deceived for his own ends.'

Her throat was dry. 'I don't understand.'

His smile was benevolent. 'The easiest way to get a woman into bed is to make her believe she is the only one with the power to break his vow.'

No. No, no, no, no, no.

'This is why I asked him to leave the ashram in India all those years ago. During each Teacher Training Course, he identified a new target. But once he'd bedded them, he got bored and moved on. I thought he'd changed, but....'

Sophia's hand shook in between his, sending a tremor up her arm, and tears spilled uncontrollably down her cheeks. She didn't want to believe a word Swami Vishnu was saying, but her exhausted mind was spiralling out of control. She desperately needed to see Isaac. To be held in his arms and know down to her soul that none of these words were true.

Pulling her closer, the older man put an arm around her, pressing her cheek against his chest.

'I know you are drawn to Hanuman, but he cannot offer what you need.'

Even though Swami Vishnu was acting sympathetically, Sophia didn't feel comforted. This was the man who'd told Isaac his feelings for her were transient. The man who'd pushed them together and was now trying to pull them apart.

One hand held tightly to hers, the other stroked up and down her back, pushing her nose against his robe. It smelled of incense and body odour.

Years of conformity to societal structures and behavioural norms ran so deep, Sophia couldn't work out how to break away from Swami Vishnu without causing offence.

'You need more,' he continued, his voice hypnotic. 'You want more.'

Her breath was coming faster, panic blooming in her chest.

'Hmmm... Yes, you feel it.'

Ice filled her veins. What was he doing? How could she get away?

Tugging her hand between his legs, he folded her fingers around something hard and stubby.

Lights flashed behind Sophia's eyes. She was outside her body looking at the scene, screaming at herself to run, but her limbs had frozen with fear.

'Yes, that's right,' he murmured. 'This is what you really need.'

'Get the fuck away from her!' came a scream as Jessica ran full tilt through the temple towards them.

Pushing Swami Vishnu over, she grabbed Sophia and pulled her away.

'Disgusting fucking perve. Back the fuck off!'

Falling to her hands and knees, Sophia threw up.

Over her retching, she could hear a bell being rung, Swami Vishnu shouting for help and Jessica yelling that he was about to have his balls served to him on a platter.

'Predatory asshole. I'm gonna make it my life's work to make sure the rest of your miserable existence is spent as some serial killer's pet.'

Ganapati came running into the temple, his eyes on Swami Vishnu, who was now lying on the floor.

'They attacked me!' he cried pitifully.

'What the fuck?' Jessica screamed as Sophia crawled away from her own vomit, sobbing and shaking.

'That creeper sexually assaulted Sophia. He put her hand around his pathetic excuse for a cock.'

Going to Sophia's side, Jessica hauled her up. 'Come on, we're calling the police.'

'Ganapati!' Swami Vishnu wailed.

Ganapati advanced towards them, his eyebrows drawn down and his expression thunderous.

'Stop!' Sophia cried, her stomach still rolling as blinding fear shot through her.

Jessica shoved her back and grabbed the mop, pointing it at Ganapati. 'Don't come any closer!'

Stalking forward, he tore the mop from her hands and threw it to the floor.

Anisha ran into the temple, and Ganapati froze.

'I heard shouting,' she said. 'Is everything okay?'

'No, it fucking isn't,' Jessica snarled.

'They attacked me!' Swami Vishnu moaned, still lying prone on the floor.

Anisha's eyes bugged out, her gaze going from her guru to the splatter of sick on the white tiles, then to Sophia and Jessica.

'He, he tried to—' Sophia began, her teeth chattering.

'He put her hand on his dick,' Jessica spat. 'You need to call the police.'

Anisha's expression flickered with shock, then indecision.

'Sophia and Hanuman were intimate,' Swami Vishnu said. 'I was counselling her, then she attacked me.'

'The fuck she did!' Jessica yelled.

'They need to be removed from the ashram immediately.'

Ganapati stepped towards them, and Jessica and Sophia stumbled back.

'I can hold him off,' Jessica murmured under her breath.

'You run for our room, lock yourself in the bathroom, and call the cops. Okay?'

Sophia nodded.

'Ganapati!' Anisha cried. 'Stop! There's no need to threaten them. We can get this sorted out calmly.'

'Please call the police,' Sophia managed. 'Please, Anisha.'

Mohan now entered the temple and took in the tableau. 'Guruji?'

'They attacked me. Get them off the island.'

'Bullshit!' Jessica snarled. 'He sexually assaulted Sophia.'

Sophia glanced between Mohan and Ganapati. They were outnumbered, and neither her, nor Jessica had the strength to take them on.

'I'm afraid you'll both have to leave the ashram immediately,' Anisha said, her voice unsteady. 'We'll escort you to your room to pack, then Ganapati and Mohan will take you by speedboat to the mainland.'

'No way,' Jessica shouted. 'We paid for a yoga course and qualification, not sexual assault. And how much is it going to cost us to change our flights if you kick us out now?'

'You'll both receive certification for the course,' Anisha said quickly. 'And...' Her eyes flicked to Swami Vishnu's, and he gave a brief nod. 'A thousand dollars each in cash. Whatever happens, the two of you will leave the ashram in the next hour. It's your decision what you choose to take away with you.'

Jessica turned her back to them and faced Sophia. The fight seemed to be draining out of her. 'What do you want to do?' she whispered.

Sophia gripped her hand. 'I want to get out of here,' she replied, her voice wobbling. 'I want to go home.'

Jessica turned to Anisha. 'Two thousand dollars each and

our certification, and we go quietly. If not, I'm gonna make sure every motherfucker on this island knows what he did.'

Anisha quickly glanced at Swami Vishnu, then nodded. 'You've got fifteen minutes to pack. Mohan and Ganapati will accompany you. I'll meet you at the boat with the money, your certificates and your passports. Do we have an agreement?'

Sophia nodded. Right now, she was desperate to get away from Swami Vishnu and everyone associated with him.

Isaac's face suddenly came to mind. She clutched her stomach as another wave of nausea rolled through it. Who would he believe? Her or his guru?

Anisha picked up Sophia's crutch and handed it over, then stepped back as Sophia and Jessica exited the side door of the temple, Ganapati and Mohan behind them.

'ADIOS, FUCKERS!' JESSICA YELLED AT GANAPATI AND MOHAN as they pushed the speedboat away from the dock by the airport.

'Make sure you think of us each time you look in the mirror, assholes! Shame on you! I hope your dicks fall off and you get reincarnated as cockroaches! Ever considered what your mothers would think of your crappy behaviour? Eh? Eh?'

Sophia collapsed onto the bench by the water's edge and stared at the wooden boards beneath her feet. This was where she'd met Jessica three weeks ago. Back then, she never could have imagined how their ashram experience would have turned out.

Jessica took her hand. 'You wanna call the police?'

She shook her head. 'There's no evidence. It's our word against all of theirs. And I never, *ever* want to go back there.'

'What about Hanuman?'

Rubbing an errant tear from the corner of her eye, Sophia

shrugged. 'Even if he believed me, which is unlikely considering how he worships Swami Vishnu, what could he do?'

Jessica was silent. No matter how laws may have changed to protect women, they both knew that most abusers remained unpunished. Here they were, hoping to change the ocean by tossing in a pebble.

'What are *you* going to do?' she asked Jessica.

'Probably hop up to Fort Lauderdale and stay with a girl-friend until I get another job. You going straight home?'

She nodded.

Jessica put an arm around her. 'Promise you won't forget about me?'

Sophia leaned into her hug. 'That would be a complete impossibility.'

'Maybe I'll come visit Foxbrooke one day.'

'You definitely should. Although when you meet Estelle, the universe might implode. You look completely different, but she's your spiritual other half.'

Jessica cackled. 'You think England can cope with the two of us?'

'Definitely not, but I can.'

'And that's all that matters. Okay, let's get you into the terminal and find you a flight home.'

SITTING IN A CORNER OF THE DEPARTURE LOUNGE, SOPHIA stared at her phone as it rang. She hadn't yet told anyone she was on her way home, but she'd called Isaac repeatedly.

Where was he now? Had he noticed her absence? What had the ashram staff told him?

Every cell felt drugged with exhaustion, but her nervous system was too wired to let her sleep. That could wait until the flight from Miami back to the UK. With the money Anisha had given her, she'd upgraded to business class so had a flatbed. Sophia knew she'd sleep the moment the plane left the ground. It wasn't just the bed, it was the fact she was leaving the continent far behind.

'Sophia?'

She jolted as Isaac's voice came through her phone. Nerves, excitement, anxiety, anger and grief all fought for her attention.

'Sophia?'

'Yes, it's me.'

'I've just got back to the ashram. Is everything okay?'

Despite everything Sophia needed to tell him, her inherent nature made her think of someone other than herself. 'How's Grace?'

'Good. Just a few scratches on her hand. Luckily, her ankle isn't broken or swollen. She's got a Tubigrip bandage on it, but they didn't give her crutches. Aren't you meant to be in class now?'

Getting to her feet, Sophia went to the wall of glass overlooking the runway so nobody seated nearby could hear her.

'I'm at the airport. Jessica and I got kicked off the island.'

'What? Why?'

Sophia's hand shook as she gripped the phone. 'Swami Vishnu found me when I was doing karma yoga. He put his arm around me and said you'd broken your vow with women before.'

She gulped in breaths to stay calm as the memories flashed through her.

'Then he put my hand on his... on his penis,' she finished with a rush.

Silence.

'Isaac?'

'Are... Are you sure that's what happened?' His voice sounded calm. Measured.

Everything from the past year tumbled onto Sophia like a collapsing building. Marcus cheating on her, undermining her on the dig, stealing her credit for the find, misreading the evidence, making her out to be a hysterical, scorned woman. Humiliation after humiliation with nobody taking her seriously or believing her.

'Why on earth would I make something like that up?' she said, fighting to get the words out through her chattering teeth. 'I was so petrified, I couldn't move. I just sat there, frozen.'

Sophia dropped to the floor and pressed her forehead against the cool glass as lights flashed behind her eyes. 'Jessica came in and rescued me. Then Swami Vishnu rang the bell and said we'd attacked him.'

More silence.

'Isaac, I was so bloody terrified, I threw up!' she cried, her voice rising. 'Ganapati, Mohan and Anisha made us pack and took us to the mainland in the speedboat.'

Sophia breathed heavily, trying to stay afloat. 'Are you even listening to me?'

'You need to call the police.'

She let out a manic laugh. 'What's the point? It's our word against all of theirs. And I'm not going back there.' Her voice broke. 'I'm never going back.'

'Tell me exactly what happened. From the moment Swami Vishnu entered the temple.'

Sophia wasn't sure if Isaac was being so calm in order to bring her down off her psychological ledge, or if he wanted to trip her up because he didn't believe her. Whatever the case, she was falling into a hell where nothing made sense, even her own thoughts.

'I know what you did to the man at Conqueror. You lied to me.'

'I didn't. I told you I lost it.'

'You didn't tell me you'd put him in hospital! Are you going to attack Swami Vishnu?'

There was a brief hesitation before Isaac replied.

'No.'

With her free hand, Sophia clutched her pounding head. 'Of course you won't. Because he's your guru and can do no wrong.'

'No, that's not why. My reaction back then made everything worse. I want—'

'So, you'll just let him get away with it? Do you even believe me? I thought you were different. I thought...'

'Sophia! Love, just breathe. I'm going to come to you now.'

But she was spiralling, her face and hand soaked with tears.

'Was any of it real? What happened between us? Or are you just like Marcus? Your guru? Do you tell women you're celibate to get them into bed? You *knew* how vulnerable I was.' She gulped in a shuddering breath. 'I must have been your easiest mark.'

'Sophia, no! Please! That's—' Isaac sounded out of breath, as if he was running.

The tannoy went off, announcing the final boarding for her flight.

'I can't, Isaac,' she sobbed. 'I have to get on the plane.'

Cutting the call and turning off her phone, Sophia got to her feet and limped away, her mind a tangled mess.

The only truth she knew for certain was that she had to get back to Foxbrooke.

✻ 24 ✻

I saac stared at the silent phone in disbelief, his heart hammering.

He redialled, but it cut off with no voicemail option.

Standing at the end of the jetty, he stared past the undulating sargassum to the mainland on the horizon. There was no way he could make it to Sophia in time.

Black horror pulsed through his veins. It was like Daniella all over again. He'd failed to see what was in front of him, and the woman he loved had been violated.

Hanging his head, hands braced on his knees, Isaac breathed deeply as his stomach rolled, trying to vomit up his guilt.

He'd put his guru on a pedestal, never for a moment contemplating he could behave in a way that wasn't aligned with the spiritual principles of yoga. Reading in the news about heads of other yoga organisations being arrested for assault, Isaac's first thought had always been, 'thank god Swami Vishnu isn't like that'.

How could you have been so blind? So ignorant?

Isaac knew grief would come knocking soon. Grief for Sophia, and for the loss of the relationship with his guru that had shaped the last twelve years of his life.

But right now, rage roared through Isaac's blood, demanding vengeance.

He was going to make Swami Vishnu pay.

Running through the ashram, Isaac leapt up the steps into the asana hall where his guru was sitting on his gold throne, addressing the students.

The moment Swami Vishnu's eyes met his, Isaac knew, with sickening dread, that Sophia had not been his first victim.

Fear flashed across his features, but it was soon replaced by arrogant disdain. This was a man who was used to denying his actions.

Ganapati and Mohan were seated either side of him, and stood the moment Isaac entered. The students turned their heads, expressions of confusion on their faces.

'Hanuman—' Swami Vishnu began.

'That man sexually assaulted Sophia in the temple earlier,' Isaac interrupted, pointing at Swami Vishnu. 'Jessica interrupted the attack and both her and Sophia were forcibly removed from the ashram by Ganapati and Mohan.'

People gasped, their eyes wide.

Ganapati ran forward, his shoulders hunched, his fists raised. Students scrambled to get out of the way as he launched himself at Isaac.

Muscle memory from mixed martial arts training kicked in. Dodging Ganapati's fists, Isaac smacked his own into the Australian's face with a vicious one-two punch that sent Ganapati sprawling on the floor.

Mohan was dithering by Swami Vishnu's side, as if not wanting his pretty face re-arranged.

'Did you know?' Isaac snarled at him.

'They attacked Guruji,' he said quickly. 'We had to protect him.'

'Bullshit! You've sold your soul for control of the Indian ashram.'

Isaac turned to the students, who were staring at him with a mix of shock, awe, and sexual arousal.

'Take the rest of the morning off. I'll find you all later and let you know what's happening.'

Swami Vishnu stood. 'Hanuman! Enough! You will leave the ashram immediately.'

'No. And I'm no longer Hanuman, I'm Isaac. You gave me the name Hanuman and I'm renouncing it. And you don't deserve the name Swami Vishnu or Guruji. You're Jeremy Brunting—'

Swami Vishnu sucked in a shocked breath.

'And you're a sexual predator.'

Isaac looked back at the students, who were slowly gathering up their notebooks, manuals, and water bottles. 'You need to get out of here.'

Ganapati got to his feet and ran again at Isaac.

Isaac got the first punch in, then kicked Ganapati's feet from under him.

'Hanu—*Isaac*, do you need a hand?' Blake asked, a hopeful expression on his face as if wanting permission to join in.

Isaac shook his head. 'I've got this. Just make sure no women are ever alone with any of these three.'

Blake's chest puffed up, and he nodded at the other men on the course. 'We've got this.'

He and Xander hung back, ensuring they were the last students to leave the asana hall. Some women waited for them on the path outside, their admiring glances now transferring from Isaac to Blake and Xander.

When they disappeared through the trees, Isaac turned

back to face the man who had betrayed him, Sophia, and the entire Devanandara organisation.

'This is a witch hunt,' Swami Vishnu spat. 'Just like when I was coaching gymnastics. Surely you can't believe her.'

Isaac stared him down. 'I will make it my life's mission to ensure you're removed from the organisation like the cancer you are.'

Swami Vishnu's laugh was cold and brittle. 'I *am* the organisation. Ten ashrams, forty centres, thousands of people loyal to me. What are you? A small-town yoga teacher. You came to me, broken, and I fixed you. I created you, Hanuman, and now I will tear you apart.'

Isaac turned to leave. He didn't know what to do next, but he couldn't be in the same space as his former guru.

'Look at what you're throwing away, Hanuman,' Swami Vishnu called after him. 'Your life for a whore.'

Isaac's feet faltered as the words struck his back like a knife. Blinding rage powered through every nerve, making his muscles twitch. The urge to rip Swami Vishnu limb from limb was so powerful he took a breath and held it, forcing his fury down.

Find another way. Don't let this end like before.

He strode towards the admin block. Did Swami Saraswati know?

Only one way to find out…

Isaac found her in the meditation garden, seated on the bench next to a puffy-faced Anisha.

Swami Saraswati stood as he approached. 'Can I help you, Hanuman?'

'You believed *him* over Sophia and Jessica?' Isaac said to Anisha.

She started sobbing.

'Hanuman! Enough!' Swami Saraswati shouted. 'What was she meant to do? Take on the head of the organisation, Ganapati and Mohan? She did what was necessary to defuse the situation and get them away.'

Isaac paused, shame lancing his heart. Swami Saraswati was right. Anisha was small and slight. She didn't have the strength to go up against any of the men, let alone all three.

'I'm sorry, Anisha,' he said softly, then took a breath and addressed Swami Saraswati. 'Swamiji, what did you mean when you told me I'd chosen my path a long time ago and you didn't think I could step off it?'

The older woman inclined her head, as if acknowledging both her words and the seismic shift occurring inside Isaac.

'I believed you were blind in your devotion to Swami Vishnu. Since taking control of the organisation, his true nature has emerged from the darkness of his heart. However, he has built around him a wall of supporters that I do not believe it is possible to breach.'

'Were you trying?'

She nodded, her pale blue eyes holding his.

'Why did he leave India?'

Swami Saraswati let out a sigh. 'Let us go to my room. We can talk freely there.'

FROM: ISAAC HAYWARD

To: Sophia Hunter-Savage

Subject: I'm sorry

Sophia, I've tried to leave a message, but you don't have voicemail enabled on your phone, so I'll do my best here.

I'm so sorry for what happened and plagued with guilt that I could have stopped it. I've been blind and will never forgive myself for not realising sooner that Jeremy was not the man I thought he was. I've stopped calling him Swami Vishnu, as he doesn't deserve that name. He's Jeremy Brunting, and assaulting you was not his first offence.

Swami Saraswati told me the reason he left India was that he'd been accused of touching other women and the police had been contacted.

That's why he fled to Tranquillity Island.

If, and *only* if you feel able, could you and Jessica write witness statements and email them to me? Jeremy is still at the ashram with Ganapati and won't leave. However, so far, they're not leaving his accommodation.

Mohan is full of self-recrimination and wants to apologise to you and Jessica. Anisha is also distraught about what happened, and wants you to know she got you off the island for your own safety.

I'm going to speak to every person Jeremy has come into contact with since we arrived here, then fly to India to see what I can do there. I'm not sure how long I'll be, but there are some leads I want to follow up which might take time.

I hope you get back safe and sound. If you don't want to reply, please can you ask Estelle or Eveline to let me know you made it home okay?

Please, can you also pass my email address on to Jessica along with my apologies? Your time within the Devanandara organisation should have been wonderful and positively life changing. What you experienced is unconscionable.

I hope you can believe the truth of what happened between us. My love for you is so deep-rooted in my heart, nothing can shift it. I hope you can one day forgive me.

Isaac xxx

❦ 25 ❦

Sophia stared at Isaac's email for the hundredth time, blinking as tears blurred his words.

Lying in bed at Shoscombe Manor, the physical tiredness was slowly abating, but she was still heavy with sadness. She hadn't told her parents what had happened, only that she'd had enough and wanted to come home.

Sophia had only told James the truth after he'd assumed Isaac was to blame and had an alpha-older-brother reaction, threatening to 'make him wish he'd never been reborn'.

There was a knock at the door and Sophia put her phone down.

'I'm awake,' she called out.

Estelle's head appeared. 'Up for a quick visit from your favourite sister-in-law-probably-at-some-point-because-I-love-your-brother-so-much?'

The corners of Sophia's mouth twitched as if learning how to smile again, and she nodded.

Pushing open the door, Estelle carried a round tray in and

put it on the bedside table, then sat cross-legged on the end of the bed.

'Care package,' she said, lifting her chin towards the tray. 'Cappuccino from your brother with a heart in the foam because he loves you and is sorry for assuming Isaac was to blame, French Fancies from your mum and dad, and Chelsea buns from me. Well, I got Perry—*Jan*, the cook at Foxbrooke Manor, to make them for you. If I'd actually made them, then they wouldn't be so delicious.'

Sophia sat up in bed. 'Thank you. There's rather a lot. Do you want one?'

'Do bears shit in the woods?'

Estelle leaned forward and grabbed a Chelsea bun, tearing a strip from the side and popping it in her mouth.

'Although you need to eat the rest. Everyone's fretting that you're wasting away.'

Her tummy gurgling with happy anticipation, Sophia took a bun and pulled a piece off, dunking it in her coffee.

'Good call,' Estelle said. 'Ooh, I wonder if I could get Perry to make coffee Chelsea buns?' Holding the rest of her bun between her teeth, she took out her phone, tapped out a message, then dropped it to the bed. 'Done! I'll let you know if they work.'

Sophia smiled. Estelle was a force of nature, and the perfect person for her equally powerful brother.

The two women ate in silence, but Sophia knew she was being softened up before her friend spoke her mind.

Estelle finished her bun, sucked the ends of her fingers, then cleared her throat.

Sophia braced herself.

'Oh, come on now. I'm not *that* bad!'

Sophia raised an eyebrow, and Estelle cackled.

'Okay, okay,' she said, raising her hands in a gesture of surrender. 'I'll be gentle.'

Cradling her coffee mug for support, Sophia waited.

'Have you heard from Isaac at all?'

She nodded.

'What did he say?'

Opening Isaac's email, Sophia handed her phone over.

Estelle's eyes widened as she read. 'Fucking hell...' She glanced up. 'Have you replied?'

Sophia shook her head.

'Are you going to forgive him for something that isn't his fault, and he was obviously clueless about?'

'Well, when you put it like that...'

Estelle pulled a face. 'Sorry. Do you think Isaac could have stopped Swami Fuckface from assaulting you?'

She hesitated. 'No, I don't think so. But that's not all of it. I don't trust my judgement anymore. Look how wrong I was with Marcus. Is Isaac just another great actor?'

Estelle's eyes bugged out as she stared at her.

'Did he say he was celibate just to get me into bed?' Sophia continued. 'Was it real? Or am I just being a naïve fool all over again? Maybe I'm just not cut out for any relationship.'

Estelle placed her hands on her knees, palms facing up and her thumbs and index fingers touching. Lifting her face to the ceiling, she let out a long 'ommmm'.

'What are you doing?'

'Trying to centre myself before I reply. Ommmm...'

Sophia huffed.

'Hang on, three's the charm. Ommmm...'

Lowering her head, Estelle gazed at Sophia. 'Do you think that Eveline would ask Isaac to be godfather to her baby if she thought he was a dodgy fucker? And do you really believe that if Isaac wanted sex, he wouldn't have shagged me, or any of the other women who've thrown themselves at him over the years?'

Reaching forward, Estelle squeezed Sophia's knee through the duvet. 'Look. Men can be right numpties, sometimes. They're not as infallible as the patriarchy would have us believe. Isaac gave this Jeremy arsewipe too much credit for the transformation he made to his own life. And when you've elevated someone that high in your estimation, it's very hard to see their faults.'

Sophia was quiet, taking in Estelle's words. She'd blindly worshipped Marcus for almost as long as Isaac had idolised Swami Vishnu.

'Isaac is one of the good ones. And the fact he's going to India to try and get justice shows that. You can't compare Marcus to him. You were only eighteen when you met him, an adult in name only. How on earth were you to know he was a cheating dickhead? Yes, I understand you're worried about making the same mistake, but I trust Isaac.' Estelle took a deep breath. 'You know what I think?'

Sophia shook her head.

'Part of you is still that teenager. Star-struck that Professor Cockwomble noticed little-old-you. Not quite believing someone so amazing was actually interested in shy Sophia. It must have been like being at school and the hottest and coolest guy asking you to the Prom.'

Sophia's cheeks heated. It had felt *exactly* like that when Marcus had made his move.

'And then Isaac professes his love for you. Says he wants to break his bloody vow of *celibacy* to be with you. Out of all the women in the world, he chooses *you*. And so your insecurity rears its head again, telling you it can't be true, that you don't deserve it, that there has to be some kind of catch. An ugly lie hiding behind the curtains, waiting to pounce.'

Unbidden, tears spilled from Sophia's eyes.

Estelle's face creased with concern. 'We all deserve love, and nobody right now more than you. Don't let what Marcus did to you in the past dictate your future. Don't allow whatever bullshit lies Guru Gobshite told you to lodge in your head as the truth. Isaac's a good man and he loves you. If you love him, then don't stand in the way of your own happiness.'

WHEN ESTELLE LEFT, SOPHIA LAY BACK, STARING AT THE plaster moulding on the high ceiling, mulling over her friend's words. She felt as if she'd been battered by a storm that had lasted months. It had finally blown over, but left her life in pieces. It was now up to her to rebuild it, but this time it was going to look very different.

She emailed Jessica, then started a detailed account of Swami Vishnu's assault. But as her fingers rattled over the keys, she didn't just recount what had happened at the temple.

Sophia wrote about Swami Vishnu's behaviour during the class on chakras, how he never asked for permission before touching people, how fucked up the kriya class was, and the way he'd pushed her and Isaac together, then pulled them apart as if they were pawns in a sick game he was playing.

When she finally finished her statement, she emailed it to Isaac and Jessica, then started another message to the Vice Chancellor of the University and the board of trustees. Her experiences at the ashram had shone a spotlight on Marcus's behaviour. No matter if the students he'd seduced were willing partners, he'd abused his position of trust. The women were young, and Marcus was responsible for their grades and future job prospects. Pursuing them for sex was unethical, and encouraging them to smoke heroin with him was unforgivable.

As well as detailing his affairs, Sophia also asked for a peer review of his assessment of the Iceni find, stating the facts, her interpretation of them, and why she believed that Marcus was wholly wrong in his assertion that the warrior was Roman.

Then she tendered her resignation. No matter what happened with Isaac, she wasn't going back to Salisbury University. She couldn't face all the memories of her life there with Marcus, nor face him, their students, and the other lecturers and admin staff who'd stood by and said nothing as she was humiliated.

She would live with her parents until she found another job in academia, or look for freelance or consultancy work. It was time for a fresh start.

But one bit of her old life kept whispering to her, like an ear worm that could cut through everything, even sleep. Opening the folder with the survey data from the dig site, Sophia scanned the numbers and images. Marcus hadn't let her lay a trench across the most promising area, but she couldn't let it go.

Before she could second-guess herself, she took out her phone and dialled.

'Sophia? You back?'

'Hi Maggie. Yep, I came home early.'

'Everything alright?'

'Not really, but I'll tell you all about it when I see you. How do you fancy a bit of digging?'

'Do I get a prize for guessing where?'

Sophia laughed. 'You already know exactly where.'

'Weather's looking good for tomorrow, if you fancy it?'

'Definitely. I'm going to ring Richard now to get permission to go back on his land. As soon as he's given us the okay, I'll let you know.'

. . .

THE LATE SUMMER SUN BLAZED HIGH IN A BRIGHT BLUE SKY, and the air was heavy with heat as Sophia stood with Maggie at the edge of the escarpment.

So much had changed since January. Back then, Sophia believed herself happily coupled with Marcus and secure in her job. Now those chapters in her life were coming to a close, and it was time to finish another.

'Are you going to make a speech?' Maggie asked.

'Huh?'

The older woman shifted her metal detector from her shoulder. 'You look like you're either composing a poem or about to recite one.'

Sophia huffed out a short laugh. 'I was just thinking about how much has occurred since the start of the year when you found the coins.'

Maggie nodded. 'Mostly good stuff.'

'Yeah...' Sophia lapsed once more into silence. Her time with Isaac was one of the best and most surprising things ever to have happened in her life. Could she still dream of a future with him?

'Come on then! We're not going to find anything moping around.'

Sophia scanned the data again, even though she knew it better than the back of her own hand. 'You're right. Okay. I'll mark out three test pits and record everything as we go. The first one is actually right under your feet.'

'Okey-Dokey.'

Taking a step back, Maggie carefully cut the turf away, placing it to one side.

Sophia took another GPS reading just to double check the position, then Maggie removed a few inches of soil and scanned the bare earth with her detector.

Nothing.

'Take that look off your face,' Maggie scolded. 'If there *is* anything down here, you know it wouldn't be this shallow.'

Sophia took a big breath. 'I'm just a bit on edge.'

'I know, love, but don't count your chickens till they've laid the golden egg. Okay?'

She burst out laughing. 'Since when has *that* ever been a phrase?'

Maggie grinned. 'Since I said so.' She removed more soil and scanned again, even though the dirt didn't look any different.

Sophia bit the inside of her cheek as Maggie worked down through four more silent layers. Was this going to be yet another thing she'd been wrong about this year? Was her gut as faulty as her head?

Shut up! Isaac isn't Marcus! Or this dig!

A loud burst of sound from the detector made Sophia jump. She refocused on the bottom of the hole but couldn't see anything.

Maggie handed her a trowel. 'You do the honours.'

Taking it from her, Sophia knelt on the warm grass, reaching down and carefully scraping the soil away. The tip moved almost effortlessly until it snagged on something solid.

Maggie held out a smaller tool as if assisting a surgeon in an operation.

Heart racing, Sophia took it, gently feeling around the harder object.

A flash of gold below made her gasp.

'Go on, love.'

Brushing the dirt away, Sophia saw a rounded edge. 'It's a torc,' she stammered. 'A huge one.'

Torcs were large golden rings worn around the neck or arm, and created by twisting wires together. Sophia could already tell this one was too large to be worn as a bracelet.

'Around her neck was a large golden torc; and she wore a tunic of diverse colours over which a thick mantle was fastened with a brooch,' Maggie murmured, reciting the only description of Boudica on record, made by the Roman historian, Cassius Dio.

Fingers trembling, Sophia carefully removed more soil, finding the ornate ends of the torc. She'd never seen one this size and weight before. Whoever wore it was as high a status as you could be in ancient Britain.

Then she uncovered vertebrae.

Sitting back, she breathed heavily, trying to keep her emotions at bay. She thought she'd scream with excitement at this moment, but instead she burst into tears.

Maggie clasped her weathered hands around Sophia's muddy ones and squeezed.

'You found her, love. You did it.'

❧ 26 ❧

From: Isaac Hayward
To: Sophia Hunter-Savage
Subject: Re: Witness statement

Dear Sophia,

Thank you for taking the time to write this. I can only imagine how hard it was to relive what happened. I've forwarded it, along with the witness statement Jessica sent me, to Swami Saraswati, who is overseeing the investigation within the organisation and liaising with the police here in India.

I'm thinking of you all the time and hope all is well.

Isaac xxx

FROM: SOPHIA HUNTER-SAVAGE
To: Isaac Hayward
Subject: Re: Witness statement
Dear Isaac,
I admit I'm still finding it hard to process everything that

happened at the ashram. Do you know how long you might be in India for?

Sophia x

Isaac stared at the screen, fixating on the small x after Sophia's name, hope blooming like a flower inside his chest. He clung to that one letter like a life raft, keeping the faith that one day it might bring her back to him.

'We're here,' the taxi driver called over his shoulder.

Handing over a wad of dirty bills, Isaac got out and stood in front of the smart residential house.

His heart beating faster in his chest, he pulled the collar of his shirt away from his neck. The humid Indian summer made his clothes cling to him in a way that was as familiar as it was unpleasant, but he refused to let it bother him. It was penance for what Sophia and many other women had endured, thanks both to his blindness, and that of others who'd put their devotion in the wrong man.

Sophia's witness statement, then the one from Jessica, had made Isaac's blood run cold and his stomach turn over. He couldn't get the images out of his head, and at night they made every dream a nightmare.

He was desperate to return to the UK, to see Sophia in person, to know if there was still a chance they could be together. But that could only come when he'd done everything in his power to right the wrong he'd unwittingly been a part of.

And part of that journey had led here.

Isaac pressed the doorbell, then stood back, straightening his shirt.

A small, older woman answered the door and glanced at him suspiciously.

Putting his hands in a prayer position, Isaac bowed his head. 'Namaste. Is Mr Sharma in?'

She moved her head in the gesture Isaac knew to mean 'yes', then beckoned him in.

Slipping off his shoes, he padded through the house after her to a living room with brown leather-effect sofas adorned with colourful embroidered cushions.

A thin, older man stubbed out his cigarette as Isaac entered, then stood and shook his hand.

'Mr Sharma, I'm Isaac Hayward. We spoke on the phone.'

The man gestured to the sofa. 'Please sit. Can I get you some tea?'

'Thank you.'

Isaac sat, knowing that the reason for his visit might remain undiscussed for most of the time he was there. He had to remain calm and hope that Rajesh Sharma eventually opened up about what happened one night, fifteen years ago.

The woman brought tea and kalakand, milk cakes that Isaac had a particular fondness for, then left, closing the door behind her.

Rajesh lit another cigarette, the tips of his fingers trembling slightly.

Isaac noted the overflowing ashtray in an otherwise spotless room and wondered just how much the man had smoked in anticipation of this meeting.

Sucking hard on the cigarette, Rajesh held his breath, then exhaled the smoke towards the slowly beating ceiling fan.

'Do you have a wife? A family, Mr Hayward?'

Isaac cleared his throat. 'I hope to. I have...'

Was Sophia still his girlfriend? He remembered the thrill of calling her his wife.

'I'm very much in love with a woman and hope to marry her.'

'And you would do anything for her?'

'Yes. She's the reason I'm here.'

Rajesh's eyes flicked to Isaac as if surprised by this information. 'I thought… I thought…'

'Swami Vishnu assaulted her last week.'

The cigarette dropped from the older man's fingers and he fumbled to pick it up.

'Swami Vishnu was my guru for twelve years,' Isaac continued. 'But he's done many terrible things, and shamed the organisation Swami Devanandara founded.'

Rajesh dragged on his cigarette, his movements tight as if he was a puppet with failing limbs, trying to hold himself together.

'I'm not here to find someone to blame,' Isaac said. 'I'm trying to find a way to remove him from his position. All that matters is making sure he doesn't hurt anyone else.'

The cigarette now hung from Rajesh's fingers as if he'd completely forgotten about it. Then his eyes drifted to a photo of him and three women who Isaac presumed were his wife and two daughters.

Isaac held his breath as he waited to see what the older man would do.

A solitary tear ran down Rajesh's leathery cheek, and he stubbed the cigarette out.

'I will tell you what me and Sunil did,' he said quietly. 'And ask for forgiveness.'

ISAAC SAT BY THE GANGES AS IT FLOWED, DEEP AND WIDE IN front of him. He'd had no expectation of finding the two men who'd been with Vishnu Devanandara when he'd supposedly signed his organisation over to Swami Vishnu.

However, he'd not only found them, but they'd agreed to

tell the truth about what happened that night in return for no charges being brought against them.

Isaac didn't begrudge them for making the decision they did. Swami Vishnu had offered them more money than they could ever have expected to make in a lifetime. Money that had done so much for their families.

The past couldn't be undone, but the future could be moulded into something better.

Arriving in India, Isaac had been surprised by how much the police had already done to gather evidence against Jeremy Brunting. No wonder he'd decided to move permanently to the ashram on Tranquillity Island.

After Sophia's assault, Swami Saraswati could speak publicly about what had happened, and any support Jeremy had maintained at the Rishikesh ashram had melted away like snow in the spring.

Now that Isaac had helped find another piece of the puzzle, he had nothing more to offer. He was free to go back to Foxbrooke and try to win Sophia back.

His phone rang, and he stared at the screen.

She's still got the same number? After all these years?

He took the call. 'Daniella?'

'I can't believe you still have the same number!'

'I was just thinking the same about you. You got my email?'

'That's why I'm ringing. You okay? I don't think we've spoken for, what, over a decade?'

'Yeah. It's been a long time. How are you?'

'Good. I'm in Sevenoaks now, working part time due to the kids.'

'Kids?'

She laughed. 'Yep, I've been busy. Got married to a doctor called Adam and we've got three kids. Maisie's one, Ada's three, and Wilfred's five.'

'Wow.' Isaac was completely stunned.

'You?'

'Er...' How empty his life sounded in comparison. 'I've just been teaching yoga in Somerset. Haven't done the marriage or kids thing.'

'Sounds like the quiet life you were after.'

'It was, but I don't think it's right for me anymore. I met someone this year and I really hope it can work out.'

'That's great, Isaac! What's her name? What's she like?'

The smile spread naturally across his face. 'She's an archaeologist. Called Sophia. She's shy and sweet, and just... utterly lovely.'

'You *are* in love.'

'Yeah. I didn't think it would ever happen again.'

'Well, I'm glad. I can't have you moping after me for the rest of your life,' Daniella said, the humour clear in her voice. 'So, what can I do for you? I've got a few minutes before Maisie wakes from her nap and demands feeding.'

Isaac rubbed a hand across his face, memories flooding into his mind as if they'd happened yesterday.

'Last week, Sophia was assaulted in an almost identical way to how you were by Thornfield.'

Daniella gasped.

'She's going to be okay, and I'm working with other people on getting him removed from the organisation and prosecuted. At least for what he's done to other women in India.'

'Who was it?'

Isaac hesitated, guilt and shame catching in his throat. 'It was my guru.'

'Oh, Isaac... Shit. I'm so sorry.'

He took a deep breath, acknowledging the pain of betrayal and how deep the wound went.

'It just brought back everything that happened to you, and I needed to apologise again and check you were okay.'

'Me? Honestly, I'm more than fine. I don't even know the last time I thought about it, but it must have been years ago. It feels like I was a completely different person back then, so young and so bloody unhappy.' Daniella sighed. 'I'd got what I thought was my perfect job, but then I absolutely hated it and didn't know how to tell you. Our relationship was on the rocks, and you were so overworked and stressed out. God, Isaac, it was a perfect storm. And when it all went to shit, I blamed you. I'm sorry for everything I said.'

'Huh? You had nothing to be sorry for! I cost you your job!'

'Yeah, but that turned out to be the best thing for me. Don't forget, you lost yours, too. And you want to know one of my deepest, darkest secrets?'

'I don't know... Do I?'

Daniella laughed. 'I'm going to say something terrible now and you must promise to keep it to yourself.'

'I promise.'

'Okay... I'm glad you kicked the shit out of Victor Thornfield. He was a smug, predatory arsehole, and he deserved every bruise you gave him. I know you regretted what you did, but I kept in touch with some of the girls from Conqueror, and when Thornfield came back to work, he was different. He didn't touch anyone up again. It might not have been the best way to get him to stop sexually assaulting women, but it worked.'

Isaac was flabbergasted. He'd had no idea that anything positive had come out of his actions.

A baby cried in his ear.

'Right, my time's up. I've got to reassure Maisie I haven't abandoned her.'

Isaac heard the cries getting louder.

'Maisie-Moo, I'm here, sweetheart. Mummy's here,' Daniella crooned.

Emotion punched Isaac's heart. Daniella was happy. She had a family. He hadn't ruined her life.

'Sorry, Isaac, I've got to dash. I hope it works out with Sophia. Let me know, okay?'

'I will do. You go. And thanks, Daniella.'

'No worries. Speak soon, bye.'

The call cut off.

Isaac let out a long breath, his gaze unfocused as the vast river moved in front of him. He should have spoken to Daniella years ago. Or maybe just now had been the perfect time.

His mind returned, like a tight rubber band, back to thoughts of Sophia. He'd emailed to say he might be a couple more weeks, but he was done here earlier than expected and free to go home.

Time to return to Foxbrooke.

Even if Sophia wouldn't take him back, he had his life there, and now it felt new, fresh and exciting. And if he managed to hold on to his land? He had plans for it.

Taking out his phone, he gazed at it. Should he tell Sophia he was coming back? Ask if he could see her? His guts twisted. He didn't want to put her under any pressure. Nor did he want to turn up unannounced and make some grand public gesture.

Sophia was shy and private and such a move would no doubt have the opposite effect of what he hoped for. Not to mention the fact Isaac had no idea what she might have told her family about him. The last thing he wanted was to show up at the door of Shoscombe Manor to find James and Kevin Hunter-Savage's fists waiting for him.

He gazed at the ancient temples on the far bank, the even older mountains rising behind them. What would archaeologist Sophia make of it all? An idea whispered into his mind, as if the spirit of a sage from Rishikesh was still trying to help people.

Isaac smiled. He didn't know if it would work, but it seemed the right way to let Sophia know he was waiting for her. Whenever she was ready.

❧ 27 ☙

The waiting room was stuffy and smelled of cleaning products and age. Sophia crossed and recrossed her legs, trying to get comfortable on the plastic chair as she focused on her breathing. The Vice Chancellor of the University, Michael Granger, had called her in for a meeting, and she knew it would be about her complaint against Marcus.

Her heart beat faster in her chest, however for the first time in her adult life, she was confident she could control her anxiety. This was all thanks to yoga, and Isaac.

Sophia tried to imagine him in India, and her heart ached. Now she was rested and had talked to Estelle, her head was in a better place. She could look at what had happened at the ashram with conscious clarity.

When she thought of what Swami Vishnu had done, she understood how Isaac must now be feeling. Just as she'd believed in Marcus and made her life serve his, Isaac had put his faith and trust in a man who'd betrayed him completely.

It's just like what happened to his last girlfriend. All over again.

Sophia had been so exhausted and traumatised, she hadn't

fully grasped how her situation would have brought to the fore some of Isaac's darkest memories.

Now she needed to see him. Email was too impersonal and even a video call hid someone's micro expressions. She wanted to speak to him in person, to apologise for flying off the handle and doubting him. To hold his hand and know they could have a future together.

She smoothed the skirts of her dress, the one Isaac had bought for her on Tortula island. She felt feminine, grown up, a woman in charge of her own destiny. No matter what the Vice Chancellor threw at her, she could handle it.

The door to his office opened and a man with short white hair came out to greet her, his hand outstretched.

'Sophia, thank you for meeting me. I don't think we've met before, but I'm aware of your sterling work. I'm Michael. Please, come on through.'

She followed him into a brightly lit room, sunshine flooding through the tall windows.

'Take a seat,' he said, indicating an area of sofas away from his desk arranged around a low coffee table. 'We're out of the sun here. Water? Tea? Coffee? I've even got ice. It's the only thing keeping me sane in this heat.'

'Water, thank you.'

After filling two tumblers with ice, he poured water over.

'Here we go.' He smiled genially at her as she took the glass. 'I'm practically eating it at the moment. If I didn't have to keep up appearances, I'd be behind my desk with my feet in a bucket of the stuff.'

Sophia smiled back at him. If he was in this good of a mood, it couldn't be that bad what he was about to discuss with her. Could it?

Michael took a big gulp then leaned forward, elbows resting on his thighs, palms facing each other like a politician about to make an important point whilst also appearing to be one of the people.

'I got your letter.'

Sophia nodded, remembering her brother's words of advice.

'*If in doubt, don't say anything. The quieter you are, the more they'll reveal their hand.*'

'I'd like to speak to you in complete confidence, if I may?' he continued. 'Man to—' He broke off and pulled an embarrassed face, his cheeks reddening. 'Oops. I think I just failed my gender bias assessment. Please accept my apology.'

Sophia nodded again, trying not to giggle as she imagined James high-fiving her.

Michael cleared his throat and tugged at the collar of his shirt. 'I got your letter. However, it hasn't been the first communication I've had regarding the conduct of Professor Thwaites. Normally I wouldn't share with you what concerns have been raised, however due to your, er, *personal* as well as working relationship with him, plus your letter of resignation, I thought it prudent we had a conversation as soon as possible.'

Someone else has complained about Marcus? But who?

Michael's expression grew grave, his eyebrows drawing together.

'I was first contacted by the parents of Kiera Thomas. Their daughter has become addicted to heroin and they claim Professor Thwaites is to blame.'

Sophia gasped, her hands flying to her mouth.

'Would you know anything about this?'

Eyes filling with tears, Sophia told him about the night she came home early from the conference back in January and found Marcus smoking heroin with Kiera and Darcie.

Michael sighed heavily. 'This concurs with what Kiera told

me. It would seem she fell out with Darcie and the shine wore off her relationship with Professor Thwaites. She's made a formal complaint against him and is currently in a rehab centre.'

'That's so awful.'

'Indeed, indeed, but at least she's now getting professional help. She also drew my attention to the exciting archaeological find your department made, earlier in the year.'

Sophia nodded, uneasy again.

'She told me it was actually yourself who'd made the discovery, not Professor Thwaites, and that he ignored your assessment of the findings in favour of his own conclusions.'

She shrugged. It was true, but what could she do about it?

'I put in a call to the museum and the curator of the upcoming exhibition told me she was also unconvinced by his hypothesis. Then, yesterday, she rang to inform me of another, far more significant find...'

Sophia's eyes widened. How did they already know?

Michael smiled. 'After you contacted the Finds Liaison Officer, he spoke to the curator directly, concerned that the exhibition should be put on hold until another excavation could be made.'

'Oh.'

Sophia's head was spinning. This was even better than she could have hoped for.

'And this brings me neatly on to your resignation letter.'

She stiffened, her guts crying 'no!' She couldn't go back to the department or work with Marcus ever again. Even though she had no job to go to, that chapter of her life was over.

'I've been acquainting myself with your career, Sophia. You're a brilliant academic and responsible for the most exciting archaeological discovery in my lifetime. You're going to put Salisbury University on the map and attract students from all over the world. I fully understand your reticence about working with Professor Thwaites, however I want to let you know, in strictest confidence, that he won't be returning to the department.'

What?

'The police are already involved, and we're undertaking our own disciplinary proceedings against him. I want to ask if you would rescind your resignation and come back to the department at the start of next term. I want to promote you to a senior lecturer position and make sure you're in charge of the team excavating your find. You'll take full credit for it and be the public face of the university when we unveil it to the press.'

Sophia sat in stunned silence. Marcus was gone. She was being promoted and would have full control of the dig. She was being offered more than she'd ever dreamed of. It was like winning the lottery on your birthday.

But the university was in Salisbury, and Isaac was in Foxbrooke. If they could restart their relationship, then committing to her job would mean she hardly ever saw him. Whatever choice she made, she would lose out.

'*Char?*' Her brother's voice came to her mind, deep and confident. '*Take a breath. There's always a plan C...*'

'BABE! HOW DID IT GO?' BEVERLEY WAS ON SOPHIA THE moment she entered Shoscombe Manor, her kohl-rimmed eyes crinkling with concern.

'Hi Mum. Good, I think. I'm just a bit frazzled from the drive.'

'Ice tea?'

'Thanks, that would be lovely.'

'Chuck your bag down there and come into the sitting

room. I've got a jug on the go already and a box of French Fancies on the sideboard.'

Sophia followed her mum through the house and into the high-ceilinged living room, overlooking the formal gardens behind the manor.

'Anyone else around?'

'Your dad's in his office with Elyse, and James is helping Estelle train with her horse riding archery thing. He's entered her into her first-ever competition next year.'

Sophia sank into a deep armchair, the feather cushions covered in leopard-print velvet fabric, and frowned. 'Did Estelle know he was entering the competition on her behalf?'

Beverley hesitated. 'No, babe.'

'Oh, my god! Is he still alive?'

Her mother cackled. 'Only just. She threatened to use her riding crop on him.'

Sophia snorted. 'And what did he say in reply?'

'What do you think? Cheeky bugger told her he'd been waiting for her to do that for months.'

Sophia shook her head. 'Those two were made for each other.'

'I know. I'm so happy he's finally found someone.'

A tight silence descended on the room. Her mum had never liked Marcus, but she'd never voiced her concerns, and Sophia knew she'd been secretly holding out for grandchildren. Sophia didn't want to tell her mother about Isaac because everything was still up in the air.

'Oh, I forgot, a parcel arrived earlier for you.' Beverley got up. 'It's in the kitchen. Two secs.'

Sophia took a long drink of water and ran the day over in her head. She was still processing all the news and what it might mean for her and Isaac.

'Here you go, babe.'

Her mum passed her a six-inch squared box with Sophia's name and address on the side. It was heavy.

'You expecting anything? There's no return address.'

Sophia shook her head. She didn't recognise the writing.

'It's too big and heavy to be jewellery and too small to be a severed head or anything.'

'Mum!'

'Sorry, babe, I watched *Seven* last night with your dad and it scared the shit out of me.'

'Why on earth would you watch that?'

'It was his choice for date night. Next time I get to choose. I'm gonna make him watch *Barbie* again.'

Underneath the plain brown paper was a nondescript white cardboard box. What was inside?

Opening it, the first thing Sophia encountered was crinkled packing paper. She removed it to reveal a large Plaster of Paris heart.

'What the devil is that, babe? A paperweight? Who's it from? You got an admirer? He's a bit late. Valentine's Day was months ago.'

Sophia lifted it out. It was a little rough around the edges, as if it had been made by hand. She wanted it to be from Isaac, but he was in India. And anyway, why would he send her a plain plaster heart with no note or explanation?

'Is there anything else in the box?'

She rummaged around and pulled out a tiny metal mattock.

Oh, my god. There's something inside the heart!

'What's that for? You meant to smash it? Bugger me, Soph, it's not some sick thing from Marcus, is it? Some funny way of saying you've broken his heart or summat?'

Sophia shook her head. She just knew it wasn't from her ex. 'Mum, I'm going to take this up to my room, okay?'

Beverley pulled a face. 'If you want a bit of privacy, could you break it in the garden, babe? It'll make such a mess and I don't want plaster dust all over the carpet.'

'Yes, of course. Sorry, I should have thought.'

'That's alright doll, you know how I get.'

She nodded. Her mother was obsessed with cleaning and had been known to follow Sophia around the house with a vacuum cleaner.

Getting up, Sophia took the box to the French windows and went through into the garden. It was late afternoon, but the air was warm, heat still radiating out from the pebbled paths between the box hedges.

Going to the edge of the gardens, she sat on a bench behind a tall yew hedge and placed the heart on the ground. Her heart was beating faster than when she and Maggie had discovered the golden torc and grave site.

Please let this be from Isaac.

Raising the mattock, she carefully chipped away at the plaster. Flakes fell to the ground, but nothing was revealed.

There has to be something inside! Why else include a mattock with it?

She tapped harder.

Still nothing, and now she'd nearly reached the centre.

Tears threatening to fall, Sophia gave it one final whack.

The remains split in two and a small plastic bag fell to the ground.

Hands trembling, she lifted it up. Inside was a set of keys on a ring with a sterling silver letter 'S' and a note.

Sophia, my heart will always be yours and I'll wait as long as you need. Isaac xxx

He'd given her a set of keys to his house.

She took a shaky breath. *Oh my god, oh my god, oh my god.*

Isaac had said he wanted her to stay with him forever and

this showed her he meant it. But did this also mean he was back from India?

Sophia's hand went unconsciously to her face, her hair. She needed a shower. Should she pack a bag? Was he really back? What was she going to tell her mum?

She ran towards the house. The only way to find out if Isaac had indeed returned was to go to his house and see for herself.

❧ 28 ❧

Parking in the area outside the five-bar gate into Isaac's property, Sophia left her overnight bag in the boot.

What if he wasn't there? What if she was being presumptuous by bringing her pyjamas, clothes and toiletries? No matter how explicit Isaac's invitation had been, Sophia was still a reserved Englishwoman down to her core and a tiny part of her was braced for disappointment.

She gazed at the lighter coloured areas of wood on the gate. The aggressive signs telling people to keep out of his private property had been removed.

Butterflies danced in her tummy to the rapid beat of her heart as she went through the gate, the metal latch clicking into place behind her.

Standing for a moment, she took it all in. The rustling leaves above her were changing colour with the fading of summer, but the warmth from the day still lingered. Birds noisily went about their business, with no awareness of just how much had changed since her last visit. Clutching the keys

Isaac had given her, Sophia took a deep breath and set off down the path.

Every step forward was a meditation and a commitment to a future with Isaac. She'd never been so aware of her own agency as she moved through the world. This was the beginning of a brand-new chapter in her life, and she was consciously choosing her own destiny.

Her feet crunched softly on the track as it curved to the right, Isaac's house still obscured from view by the thicket of evergreens. Despite her nervousness, Sophia's pace didn't slow, and her breathing was steady and controlled. Squaring her shoulders, she rounded the bend and looked for her dream man inside his dream house.

She couldn't see him, but the bi-fold glass doors separating the living space from the deck were open, and the sight pushed her pulse higher. He *was* here.

Going to the front door, she knocked.

Nothing.

Even though she could have walked through the glass doors a few yards to her left, Sophia took the keys Isaac had given her, slid the top one effortlessly into place, and entered the house.

'Isaac?'

No reply.

On the wall to her right were two hooks. One had a set of keys hanging from it and the letter 'I' above it. The other was empty with the letter 'S' above. Heart jumping with excitement, Sophia hung up her keys, then continued into the house.

It was just as she'd remembered; clean, tidy, and so beautiful. Like walking into an upmarket interiors magazine. On the kitchen island was a woven willow trug, filled with salad leaves and fresh vegetables. Was Isaac in the garden?

Making her way through the silent house, Sophia pushed

open the back door, stopping dead as she spotted Isaac in the distance.

He hadn't noticed her, his attention on picking flowers from a bed of wild colour, his movements graceful and measured. Dressed in a plain t-shirt and loose linen trousers, Sophia half expected a photographer to appear, shooting the next Ralph Lauren advertising campaign.

Her gaze ranged over his tanned arms as he moved, the tips of his tousled brown hair bleached lighter by the Caribbean sun. He was the most beautiful man she'd ever known. And he'd given her the keys to his heart and home.

Sophia didn't want to move, held in a liminal space between the end of something and the beginning of everything. She just stood, revelling in the perfect moment of stillness, knowing that the man before her was the one she would spend the rest of her life loving.

Then Isaac straightened, noticed her and froze, his shocked expression easing into a tentative smile.

Sophia raised a hand, and he started towards her, his strides determined and confident.

She ran to meet him, stopping, out of breath, a couple of feet away.

Isaac's eyes raked over her. Concern, insecurity, then hope flitting across his features as she smiled at him.

Sophia wanted to fall into his arms, but all she could manage was a breathy 'hi'.

He seemed as tongue-tied as she was, thrusting the flowers he was holding forward like a five-year-old presenting them to his grandmother.

'These are for you.'

As she took them, her fingertips grazed his, and a tingle of electricity ran up her arm.

'Thank you,' she said softly. 'They're beautiful.'

Isaac swallowed. 'Are you okay?'

Sophia nodded. Despite her inability to express herself with words, she'd never felt happier. It wasn't just the exhilarating rush at seeing Isaac again, nor the way her body ached for his touch. It was the love that underpinned all other emotions, as constant as the tides and as deep and fathomless as the ocean.

'I'm sorry,' he continued. 'I'll never forgive myself for not noticing sooner that something wasn't right. *He* wasn't right. I was just so close to him, and—' He broke off, shaking his head, his face pinched.

Reaching out, Sophia took his hand and squeezed. 'I spent ten years *living* with Marcus and didn't see what was right under my nose. It's not our fault. People who do bad things are very good at hiding what they do, and we're so trusting because it would never occur for us to behave the same way.'

Isaac's nod was hesitant, as if remembering that he'd said something similar to her, many months ago.

'Thank you for my present.'

His cheeks coloured. 'I... I didn't want to put you under any pressure, but...' He took a deep breath. 'Every word I said to you when we were abroad was true. I love you, and I want to be with you for as long as you'll have me.'

Sophia's heart was running faster than a sprinter, pumping so much emotion into her blood she didn't know whether to laugh with joy or cry. Suddenly, the space between them was too much to endure. Dropping his hand, she threw her arms around his neck, holding him tightly.

'I love you, Isaac. I don't want to be anywhere else than with you.'

He hesitated for a millisecond, as if processing her words, then embraced her, kissing her neck and murmuring how much he loved her, over and over again.

Closing her eyes, Sophia melted into the heat of his body, letting her senses drown in his clean and spicy scent, the feel of his powerful muscles, the soft pressure of his lips on her skin, the texture of his words wrapping themselves around her heart. She'd found her home in Isaac's arms. Here, she could be unconditionally herself and bathe in his love.

Tugging on his hair, she brought his mouth to hers, their tongues meeting with a jolt of electricity, sparking fires that blazed along every nerve.

The surrounding garden disappeared. There was nothing but Isaac and the burning need to have him covering her, filling her, taking her to places she could never have imagined before.

Breaking their kiss, he reached down and lifted her into his arms.

Sophia let out a squeak of surprise and clutched the back of his neck. 'I'm too heavy!'

'No, you're not.'

Isaac grinned at her as he strode towards the house and Sophia grinned back, dazed with lust and happiness. Turning sideways to enter the back door, he kicked off his flip-flops and Sophia let hers drop to the floor.

'Where are you taking me?' she asked, breathless with anticipation.

'Where would you like to be taken?' he replied, walking her to the kitchen where a vase stood on the counter, already filled with water.

Sophia dropped the flowers she was holding into it, then focused on Isaac's sparkling green eyes. 'Well, I haven't seen your bedroom before...'

'Don't you mean *our* bedroom?'

Biting her lip to stop a squeal of excitement escaping, she nodded.

Isaac carried her to the right of the building, down a short corridor, then into a room.

Sophia was briefly aware of dark wood floorboards and furniture, dove grey curtains and creamy sheepskin rugs. But when Isaac laid her on his enormous bed, the only thing she cared about was him.

Crouching above her and pressing kisses to her face, he ran his hand up her leg and under her dress.

'Sophia, Sophia, Sophia,' he murmured, sucking and nipping down her neck.

Every brush of his fingers left a tingling trail of goose-bumps in their wake, each gentle bite an electric shock. She was already gasping, trying to keep track of the swirling, whirling pleasure as every cell lit up, her body turning into an ever-changing kaleidoscope of colour and light.

Growling, Isaac pushed the hem of her dress to her waist, zeroing in on her underwear. Sophia had picked her nicest pair, however Isaac appeared to view them as an unwanted barrier between her pussy and his mouth.

Tugging them down and off her legs quicker than she could draw breath, he lowered his head and sucked her clit hard into his mouth.

Sophia cried out, her chest lifting off the bed with the whip-cracking pleasure, her fingers tangling in Isaac's hair to let him know she was alright and wanted him to stay right where he was.

His tongue was hot, wet and fast, licking her pussy with fire until she was burning with the need to come. There was no way to quantify or track the sensations. They just kept layering over each other, exponentially building until all she could do was hold on tight and hope she survived the onslaught.

Every inhale was a gasp to stay afloat, every exhale a plea for more. Without breaking the movement of his tongue, Isaac eased two fingers inside her, curling the tips and pressing hard against her swollen flesh.

'Wha—oh my go—'

The climax hit with such intensity it slammed the breath from her, smashing the atoms of each cell apart in an explosion of light. She was no longer conscious of anything except blinding pleasure, radiating out from her core, taking her to the edge of the universe and beyond.

Over a high-pitched ringing in her ears, Sophia heard her breath return with gasping cries of ecstasy. Shaking, she grabbed Isaac's hair, desperate to have his body on hers, holding her together before she completely fell apart.

Moving up the bed, he held her tightly, stroking her face as she trembled.

'Shhh... It's okay. I've got you, love,' he whispered, nuzzling into her hair. 'I've got you.'

But as Sophia floated down from the orgasmic high, the edges of her body drifting back together, there was an emptiness in her core. A desperate, yearning need to have him inside her.

She fumbled for the fastening of his trousers. 'I... Isaac, please...'

He leapt up, tugging off his clothes as if every second of his body not touching hers was an eternity of agony for them both, and she pulled her dress off along with her bra.

Then he lay on top of her, bracketing her head with his forearms and gazing at her with such reverence that tears stung her eyes.

'I love you,' he said, his breath a caress. 'I love you.'

'You too,' she choked out, spreading her legs and shifting her hips to guide him inside her.

As his cock pushed an inch into her tightness, she gasped,

the sweet stretch sending prickling pleasure shimmering out inside her like moonlight on water.

Isaac paused, his golden-green eyes holding hers, his jaw tight.

'You okay?' he whispered.

Sophia nodded, adjusting to his size. He was big, but being filled by him was a sensation like no other. One that touched her soul and made her body sing.

Angling her pelvis, she pushed herself further onto his cock, her heart pounding through her skin and vibrating against his.

He was breathing faster, his lips parted, staring at her in fearful wonderment, as if she held his life in her hands.

'More, Isaac,' she whispered, her love for him flooding her chest and spilling from her eyes.

'Sophia...' He held still, his expression agonised, as if worried he was hurting her.

Lifting her mouth to his, she sucked on his lower lip and scored her fingernails down his muscled back.

'Ah!' His hips jerked reflexively, his cock thrusting deep inside her. 'Sophia!'

She cried out at the sharp pleasure, locking her legs around the back of his, her arms around his waist to hold him in place.

'God, Sophia!'

Drawing in a laboured breath, Isaac stared at her, his pupils overrunning the irises till only an edge of emerald remained.

Through her glistening tears, he was shining like an angel.

She smiled to reassure him, her heart overflowing. 'I love you, Isaac. Every part of me loves every part of you.'

Cradling her face, he gently wiped the corners of her eyes with his thumbs. 'I love you.' His lips brushed hers. 'God, I love you.'

He kissed her again and Sophia slanted her head, opening

to him, her tongue tangling with his and sending shivers of light down to dance with the heavy beat of pleasure in her pussy.

As Isaac's cock slowly withdrew, she pulled back, then snapped her hips forward to meet his as he thrust.

Tearing her mouth from his, she gasped. 'Oh... Oh my god, yes!'

He did it again, his gaze roaming her face, as if drinking in every breath, every tremble, every cry.

His expression, the emotion behind it, and the hard heat of his body on her, filling her, was all-encompassing.

Isaac, Isaac, Isaac, her mind repeated like a mantra. He was her everything, taking every layer of her being, from the solid to the ephemeral to places she could never have believed possible.

He thrust rhythmically, circling his hips into hers, grinding against her clit, stoking the flame of her orgasm. It was building deep inside her, a white-hot, molten pressure, with enough power behind it to break her apart.

But she welcomed it. Wanted it. She was safe within Isaac's storm, running towards the point of no return, knowing he would be with her, keeping her safe even as she dissolved into bliss.

This time there were no visions, no out-of-body experiences. The love they shared, the knowledge that they were truly together, was enough.

Trembling with emotion, breathing faster and faster, Sophia clung to him, her eyes anchored to his as the blinding force of her climax bore down on her.

With one last, frantic gasp, she cried Isaac's name.

Then the wave hit, crashing through her, stealing her breath, her vision. She was rolling, tumbling in a boiling surf of sensation and light.

Isaac pounded faster. The feelings of him losing control pushed her orgasm on and on, swells of pleasure sweeping through her as he fell into his own release with a tortured cry.

Clutching his shuddering body to hers, the feelings continued, flooding every cell, rippling across her skin, ringing in her ears. Her lungs laboured to get air in and out fast enough, her fingertips tingling and stars flashing behind her eyes.

Isaac collapsed to the bed beside her, his arms still wrapped around her.

Sophia pressed her lips against the hot, damp skin of his neck, feeling his wild pulse, hearing the rush of his breath as if he'd just sprinted a marathon.

Warm honey ran through her veins, an oxytocin glow suffusing her with utter contentment.

Turning on his side to face her, Isaac's mouth met hers. His kisses were long, sweet and soulful, inundating her heart with love.

This man...

Happiness bubbled up, escaping with a giggle.

Isaac drew back, an eyebrow arched.

'I don't think I've ever been happier,' she said.

His smile shone brighter than the sun. 'Me neither.'

Taking her hand, he placed it on his chest. 'This is yours, and—' he broke off and inclined his head at the room around them, '—this is yours. Everything I have, I want to share with you.'

Anxiety prickled like a thistle against Sophia's skin. How could they find anywhere as perfect as this if the bypass went ahead?

His forehead creased. 'What is it? What's wrong?'

She swallowed. 'You might lose your beautiful home...'

He grinned and leapt off the bed.

'Where are you going?'

'Two secs,' he replied, disappearing out the door.

He returned a moment later with a tri-folded piece of paper and passed it to her.

Sophia scanned the text, her pulse quickening. 'They're not going ahead!'

Isaac sat beside her. 'I could pretend that all the letters worked, but I think what swung it was the fact it would have also affected Foxbrooke Haven. One of the residents, Shirley, got the bit between her teeth and organised a campaign effective enough to win a general election.'

Sophia stared at him, excitement fizzing through her.

'Shirley's husband, Robert, wrote the kind of legal correspondence that would make anyone pause for thought, and the two of them led a protest at the council offices, culminating in around twenty of them storming a private meeting.'

'What? But aren't they...' she trailed off.

Why would they lose their fire just because their hair is white?

Isaac laughed. 'I don't think there's a situation more terrifying than a bunch of octogenarians with placards and Zimmer frames. Doris doesn't even need to use a walker, but she borrowed it to help block the door and prevent the councillors from escaping.'

'Oh, my god!'

'Shirley said they hadn't had that much fun in years. She told me they were chanting "we shall not be moved" louder than football supporters.'

Sophia held her tummy as she giggled.

'Erica, the manager of Foxbrooke Haven, filmed it and sent the video to the local press. It went viral and I think that was the final nail in the coffin for the project.'

Isaac shook his head. 'To think, I spent so much time talking to big-shot City lawyers, when all it took was a bunch of rowdy eighty-year-olds to make everything go away.'

'That's amazing. I hope I get to meet them.'

'You will. The moment I tell them about you, they won't stop badgering me until I bring you over. And also, if they know you're real, maybe Doris will stop pinching my bum.'

Sophia's cheeks were hurting from laughing so much. 'They sound incredible.'

Isaac grinned. 'They are. They're my naughtiest students by a country mile.'

'Well, thanks to them, your peace and quiet in paradise is guaranteed.'

He hesitated. 'About that...'

Her eyes widened. 'Oh god, am I too noisy? Too much?'

'What?'

Isaac appeared completely confused, as if she'd just informed him she was a werewolf and had to be locked in a silver crate every full moon.

'I...' she stammered.

Surely he wasn't going to go back on everything he'd said?

Isaac clasped her hands as if to prevent her from bolting. 'I'm going to apply for planning permission to turn the derelict barn into a studio,' he said in a rush. 'If I get it, then I'll sell my London flat to finance it.'

'Oh!' Sophia sagged with relief.

Pulling her onto his lap, Isaac cradled her in his arms. 'I want you here more than my next breath. Now I've met you, living on my own doesn't hold any appeal.'

'Sorry,' she mumbled into his chest. 'After everything I've been through, this level of happiness is going to take some getting used to.'

Isaac nuzzled her cheek. 'All I want is for you to be happy. You promise to tell me if I annoy you?'

Sophia didn't reply. Right now she couldn't imagine any situation where Isaac and her might fall out.

'Sophia?'

'I will, but I can't see it ever happening.'

'Even with all the dad jokes?'

She smirked. 'They're endearing.'

He huffed. 'Tell that to my brothers.'

'Gosh, I hadn't even thought about meeting each other's families. I told my mum I was going to see a friend this afternoon and might stay the night.'

His smile lit up his face. 'Will you stay?'

She nodded shyly. 'Yes, please.'

Isaac looked so happy, Sophia's heart was suddenly too big for her chest. This was her life now. Joy and contentment with this incredible man.

'I know we won't always get time together with your job being in Salisbury. But when we do, I want to make the most of every minute.'

She stilled, her hand flying to her mouth. In all the uncertainty and drama of the last few days, Isaac had no idea what had happened in her work life.

'Sophia?'

'I forgot... You don't know.'

'Know what?'

She shuffled off the bed, pulling on her dress. 'It's a good thing, I promise! Give me five minutes. I just need to get my bag from the car.'

Dashing down the track between the trees, Sophia's heart sang louder than the birds overhead.

This is my life!

Grabbing her bag, she ran back to the house.

Isaac met her at the door, wearing his linen trousers slung indecently low on his hips.

She kissed him loudly on the lips, then pulled out her phone.

'I went back to the dig site with Maggie. She'll *adore* you, by the way, and we dug a test pit in the area I'd always wanted to excavate.'

Sophia was so excited she was bouncing on the balls of her feet. 'And we found this!'

She showed him a photo of the torc sticking half out of the soil.

'Holy shit! Is that gold? What is it?'

'It's a torc, an ancient necklace or bracelet made by twisting strands of metal together. This is the largest and most valuable ever found.'

'That's incredible! Do you know why it's there?'

Sophia nodded and squealed with excitement. The importance of the find was finally sinking in. 'I uncovered vertebrae, so it was around someone's neck when they were buried.'

She flicked through more photos on her phone, showing them to him. 'We stopped right there and rang the landowner and the council's Finds Liaison Officer. We'll be starting a formal excavation as soon as possible.'

'Love, this is fantastic! But what will it mean for the exhibition of the other grave?'

'It's on hold. And...'

'Ye-es?'

'Marcus has lost his position in the department and won't be going back. The Vice Chancellor offered me a promotion and the job of leading the dig.'

'That's amazing!'

'But I said no.'

Isaac's ecstatic expression crumpled. 'What?'

'If I took the promotion, then I'd hardly ever see you.'

'But this is your career! Your life's work! I can't take that from you.'

Taking Isaac's head in her hands, Sophia smoothed away the furrows in his brow and kissed the end of his nose.

'You're not. I negotiated a better deal.'

'You did?'

She nodded. 'I've enjoyed teaching undergrads, but it's time to move on. I want to try something different. Maybe do consultancy? Write a book? I'm not totally sure yet. But I'm staying on at the Uni in a freelance capacity to lead the dig and work with Salisbury Museum on a new exhibition. I'll stay over with Maggie during the excavation, but after that I can commute from here whenever I need to.'

Isaac blinked a couple of times as he stared at her, as if processing the information, then lifted her into his arms and spun her around.

Laughing with pure, unrestrained delight, Sophia clung to him, holding on tightly as he slowed to a stop, the room still spinning around them.

'This calls for a celebration,' he said with a grin.

'What do you have in mind?'

'Dinner, make love, hot tub, make love, champagne, make love. You choose the order.'

She giggled. 'Sounds pretty perfect to me.'

'And you are completely perfect to me,' he replied, bringing his lips to hers.

Sophia sank into the kiss, tingling warmth spreading to the tips of her toes. Isaac was her happy ending and her even happier beginning, and she couldn't wait to spend the rest of her life by his side.

EPILOGUE

NINE MONTHS LATER

'A year and a half ago, Maggie Howard, a renowned local detectorist, rang me to say she'd found an Iceni coin hoard...'

Poised and relaxed, Sophia's voice was clear as she addressed the journalists and local dignitaries.

Isaac had only ever seen this many cameras and microphones at press conferences on the television. Now they were zeroing in on the love of his life. The lights were almost blinding, and the constant camera shutter noise sounded like someone had kicked a box of Lego down the stairs.

But this was not Sophia's first rodeo. She'd been the warm, engaging, and beautiful face of the whole dig. She'd announced the discovery of the grave and torc the previous year, handling the media attention with a confidence Isaac could not have guessed she had the first time they'd ever met.

Lacking a scraggly beard, ratty jumper, or arrogant sense of her own importance, archaeologist Sophia was a tabloid editor's dream. Attractive, wholesome, and utterly non-threatening, she was also the perfect counterpart to the legend of Boudica, and a none-too-subtle way for the mainstream media to remind women how they should conduct themselves.

Isaac held Sophia's phone steady, taking photos to send to Jessica. Jessica couldn't attend the event, but was arriving in the UK for a visit in a couple of weeks' time and Sophia was over the moon at the prospect of seeing her friend again.

'It's important to remember that, although the evidence tells us that this woman was a tall female of the highest status, buried with a sword, a mirror, pottery, Iceni coins and jewellery at the time of the uprising against the Romans, we cannot say definitively that she is Boudica,' Sophia continued.

Isaac smirked. That was the official line, but everyone, Sophia included, believed they had found the warrior queen.

The exhibition had even been titled 'Queen Boudica?', and the signage for each exhibit had text that steered the reader into forming the same conclusions. 'A warrior's sword', 'A necklace fit for a queen', 'The history of Boudica', were some display titles, along with a life-sized painting of what she might have looked like.

Maggie stood by Sophia's side, her face sweaty and red, her smile fixed and slightly manic. She hadn't wanted any recognition for the find, but Sophia had insisted, and the two of them had shared the credit.

And the money... Fifty per cent had gone to the landowner, with Sophia and Maggie sharing the rest. It was enough for Maggie to pay off her mortgage and spend more time outside with her metal detector, and Sophia now had a nest egg and freedom and choice in what work she did.

She'd used some of the money to remodel the barn into a

yoga studio. Sophia's suggestion had horrified Isaac. However, she'd calmly explained that it was more sensible to keep his London flat as an investment. Isaac only went along with her idea after adding Sophia's name to the deeds for the flat and his house in Foxbrooke. Whatever he had was also hers, and that made it official.

His hand sat on the outside of his trouser pocket, the small item inside burning through the material into his palm. This was another way to ensure whatever he had was hers, but Sophia knew nothing about this particular plan.

'Thank you all so much for coming,' Sophia said, beaming at everyone as if they were her closest friends and had trekked across the country to celebrate her birthday. 'I'll be on hand for the next two hours, but if you have any questions, I'd be glad to answer them now.'

The horde of journalists started yelling, but were quickly interrupted by Isaac and Sophia's family, clapping and whooping. Estelle stuck her fingers in her mouth and wolf-whistled loudly, and James marched forward into the throng like a scary cheerleader, the percussive slap of his hands and his bullish body language informing everyone in no uncertain terms that they should follow his lead.

'That's my girl!' Kevin Hunter-Savage roared.

Sophia blushed, and smiled shyly in their direction.

Isaac's heart swelled with love and pride as he gazed at her. No words could describe how amazing she was, and how much brighter and happier his life was with her in it.

As Sophia began answering questions, Maggie shuffled off the stage and hot-footed it behind the crowds towards the drinks table.

Meeting her there, Isaac passed her a glass of water.

'Thanks, love.' She downed it, then fanned her face. 'Bugger me. I don't want to do that ever again.'

'You did great.'

She gave him the side-eye. 'I stood there sweating like a pig in a bloody sausage factory.'

'Did you want to say a few words?'

Raising both eyebrows, Maggie stared at Isaac as if he'd just asked the stupidest question of the day.

'You know I didn't. I'd rather impale myself on Boudica's sword than have the spotlight on me.'

'It's only fair you share the glory.'

Maggie harrumphed, but couldn't hide her grin. 'I'd have been happy with bragging rights down the pub, but the fame has also come with a small fortune, so I'm not going to look a gift horse in the mouth.'

They smiled at each other, then turned to where Sophia was deftly answering questions.

'I never thought she had it in her,' Maggie said quietly.

'The confidence?'

She nodded. 'Last January, she left a conference she was speaking at early rather than have to sit through the dinner and socialise with people she barely knew. Now look at her.'

Isaac did, warmth filling his chest.

'It's all thanks to you, you know.'

He shook his head. Sophia had said the same thing to him, multiple times, but he wanted no credit.

'It's all her. I'm just along for the ride.'

'Maybe, but she wouldn't have had the courage to do any of this before meeting you. You've brought her out of herself. Given her room to breathe and space to shine.'

Isaac's throat tightened. At the start of the previous year, Sophia wouldn't have said boo to a goose. Now she was out front and in charge, channelling Boudica in her own unique way.

'And want to know something else?'

Isaac raised an eyebrow. Maggie looked like a naughty schoolgirl with an enormous secret she was bursting to share.

'News has got out about the TV show Sophia's going to do, and that twatmuffin, Marcus, is spitting blood about it.'

'He's not going to cause any trouble, is he?'

'Nah, no-one takes him seriously anymore. He's been black-listed by production companies, and can't get another job. He's just sounding off on forums filled with disgruntled men who still live with their parents and can't get laid.'

'Good.'

Isaac never mentioned Marcus to Sophia, but Maggie had filled him in on what her ex had been up to after being released from prison. Isaac was relieved to know he wouldn't be hassling her, nor the TV companies who'd passed on working with him, yet were actively courting Sophia.

'You think we've got another five mins before they finish?' Maggie asked.

Isaac glanced at the throng of journalists. James was standing next to Sophia, one hand raised to keep the crowd quiet, the other pointing at the next person who was allowed to ask his sister a question.

'I think so. Did you bring it?'

'Yep. It's in the boot of my car. Come on, we can transfer it to yours now and she'll be none the wiser.'

SOPHIA'S EYES WERE CLOSED, HER LIPS CURLED INTO A contented smile as Isaac drove them home.

'Tired?'

As if on cue, she yawned, then giggled and glanced at him. 'Exhausted. It's been a really long day.'

'We're nearly home.'

She nodded. 'Good. I'm just about ready for bed.' She let out a happy sigh. 'I actually really enjoyed myself.'

'I'm glad. You were incredible.'

Reaching across the centre console, Sophia squeezed his thigh. 'All thanks to you.'

'Rubbish. You're the expert, not me.'

Was this the right segue into telling her what was in the boot? Isaac's hands gripped the steering wheel tighter and he took a steadying breath.

'Did I tell you the editor from that big publishing company was there?' Sophia asked, interrupting his thoughts.

'No. What did they say?'

'They definitely want me to write a book about the find.'

He shot her a quick glance. 'That's brilliant!'

She did a jiggle in her seat. 'It's so exciting! With that, the TV show, and the exhibition tour, it's going to be a busy couple of years.'

'It certainly is, and when it eventually calms down a bit, you'll be people's first choice for consultancy work.'

Sophia nodded. 'I'm so lucky. I could never have imagined my life would turn out this way.'

'You put in the work and never gave up, even when everything was against you. You deserve this.'

Isaac eased the car to a stop outside the gate to their house, a wooden sign on it reading 'Shady Acres House & Yoga Studio'.

Sophia leaned over and kissed his cheek. 'I'll open the gate. You go on and I'll follow you up to the house.'

ISAAC WAS LIFTING THE METAL DETECTOR HE'D BORROWED from Maggie from the boot of his car when Sophia strolled around the corner.

'What on earth is that for?'

He rubbed the back of his neck. 'I lost my necklace somewhere in the long grass near the pool and can't find it.'

'Oh. Do you know how to use that?'

'Turn it on and wave it about?'

Sophia smirked. 'According to Estelle, that's how most men approach a problem... Did Maggie show you how to ground balance it? How to set the thresholds, the modes, the sensitivity?'

'Er...'

'Did she run through *any* of the setup and functions with you?'

Isaac pulled an embarrassed face. 'I think she just expected...'

Sophia rolled her eyes. 'Me to use it?'

Giving her a sheepish smile, he nodded.

She glanced at her watch, then at the blue sky.

'There's nearly an hour and a half before sunset. Want me to have a quick look?'

Isaac's tummy turned over with relief and excitement. 'Yes, thank you.'

Sophia took it from him. 'Near the pool? Right side or left?'

'Left. Where we usually get in.'

He took her bag from the car and opened the house. 'I'll come and help.'

'Cool.'

Sophia was relaxed and at ease, but Isaac's stomach was now tangled in knots.

Breathe!

In the back garden, she fiddled with the controls of the metal detector, put the headphones on, then started sweeping from side to side at one end of the natural swimming pool.

Standing a few metres away, Isaac dropped what was in his pocket to the ground, took four careful paces to the side, and waited.

Sophia's gaze was focused on the grass, her brow furrowed slightly as she listened.

Suddenly she stopped and bent over, her fingers separating the stalks.

She straightened, waving a hair clip. 'Lost this last week!' she said triumphantly.

Isaac forced a smile, but his heart rate was rising uncomfortably high.

Sophia continued on towards him and the words he'd rehearsed ran around his head until he was dizzy.

Now she was sweeping right next to him.

She stopped again and bent down.

Isaac swallowed, rubbing his palms dry on his trousers. This was it.

Straightening, Sophia gazed with a confused frown at the band of gold between her fingers, then pulled her headphones off and turned to him.

He dropped to one knee. 'Will you marry me?' he blurted, the beautiful speech he'd polished over months vanishing into thin air.

Sophia blinked, glancing between him, the ring, and the metal detector as if struggling to fit the three pieces of his proposal puzzle together.

Then her shock snapped into delight. 'Oh, my god! Oh my *god*, Isaac!'

'Is that a "yes"?'

She tugged him up to stand. 'Of course it is! Yes, yes, a thousand times yes!'

Sophia stared at the ring as if seeing it for the first time.

'I commissioned a torc design to remind you of the one you found. And I added the diamonds because if they'd been around in Boudica's time, I'm sure she would have worn them.'

Her eyes filled with tears. 'It's the most beautiful thing I've ever seen.' She brought her gaze to his. 'It's perfect.'

'Just like you. You're my perfect person and I would be honoured to be your husband.'

Sophia threw her arms around his neck. 'I love you, I love you, I love you!' she cried, peppering his face with kisses.

Isaac smiled with joy. 'I love you too, my sweet Sophia.'

She drew back. 'I need to see if it fits.'

'The jeweller took a guess...'

Pushing it onto her finger, she held up her hand, the ring glinting in the evening sun.

'Perfect! Oh, I can't wait to show this off!'

'Just to forewarn you, I did tell your parents I was going to ask you to marry me.'

'Did Mum cry?'

Isaac nodded. 'And your dad slapped me so hard on the back I nearly popped a rib.'

Sophia snorted. 'James and Estelle will probably hug you to death when they find out.'

'Yep, and that's why you're going to be there to protect me. I've invited them and your folks for lunch tomorrow if that's alright with you?'

'Of course it is. Why don't we invite Eveline, Jack and baby Robert as well?'

'That's a wonderful idea.'

'Fabulous!' Sophia paused. 'I know we're not traditionally religious, but how would you feel about asking her to marry us in Saint Saviour's?'

'I'd love it. Shall we ask if she's got a free slot in the next couple of weeks?'

She grinned. 'I'd be up for it, but I think both your parents and mine will expect a little more lead time than that...'

'Fair enough. I just can't wait to call you my wife.'

Sophia squealed with excitement and threw her arms around him again.

'I love you, Isaac. Thank you for today, yesterday, and all the days before that. I'm the happiest and luckiest woman in the world.'

His eyes roamed her face, in awe that this incredible woman was choosing to spend the rest of her life with him.

'I'm the lucky one,' he murmured, then brushed a kiss across her soft lips.

She let out a breathy sigh and kissed him back, her tongue darting into his mouth.

Groaning with desire, Isaac tugged her closer, deepening their connection, losing himself in her hot sweetness, joy filling his veins.

Sophia had given his life a new meaning and purpose. She'd opened his eyes and his heart, enriching and expanding his life, and he was going to spend the rest of his days supporting and loving her right back.

THE END

Thank you so much for reading The Love Position! If you want to read Sophia and Isaac's very sexy and unexpected **extended epilogue,** which takes place in the natural swimming pool in their back garden, then join my newsletter list at **www.eviealexanderauthor.com/subscribe**

☙❧

Leo and Ella's fabulously festive story is up next in Christmas off Script...

Get Christmas off Script in print, audio, or eBook format now from **www.eviealexanderbooks.com**

REVIEW THE LOVE POSITION
WRITE A REVIEW & MAKE MY DAY!

Thank you so much for reading The Love Position! I hope you enjoyed reading it as much as I enjoyed writing it!

Even if just a few lines (or star rating), writing a review is the most amazing thing you can do! It helps people find my books, and lets them know what you loved about them.

You can review The Love Position at:
Apple
Amazon
Bookbub
Goodreads
Kobo
Barnes & Noble
Google Play

And any other storefront or platform you use!

And, if you want to share more about The Love Position on social media or your blog, please **help yourself to our library of graphics, elements and more by going to:**

www.eviealexanderauthor.com/the-love-position/

Thank you!

READ CHRISTMAS OFF SCRIPT

Next up is Ella and Leo's story!

CHRISTMAS OFF SCRIPT

Leo Foxbrooke is Ella Chamberlain's best friend, her rock, and the one person who is absolutely, 100% off-limits.

Kind, charming, and unfairly gorgeous, he's the heart of Foxbrooke Manor. Meanwhile, she's the girl who just got dumped, lost her apartment, and landed on his doorstep days before Christmas, looking like the ghost of bad decisions past.

Moving into his family's fairytale home is supposed to be her chance to regroup, not lose her heart. But then she ends up in the room right next to his and somehow gets roped into the town Christmas play as his Cinderella. Those 'practice kisses' on stage? They're setting her world on fire.

Leo's always been her steady, unshakable constant. The one person she can count on, no matter what. But risking everything to follow the spark growing between them? That could cost her the one thing she can't live without – him.

Christmas off Script *is a messy, magical, and oh-so-steamy story of risking it all for love. If you're looking for festive fun, fiery chemistry, and a guaranteed happy ending, this standalone romcom is the perfect holiday escape!*

Get Christmas off Script in print, audio, or eBook format now from www.eviealexanderbooks.com

NEWSLETTER SIGN-UP

Want to read Sophia and Isaac's sexy and unexpected extended epilogue in their natural swimming pool? Sign up to my newsletter to get it today, plus so much more...

In my newsletter you get Evie news before anyone else, as well as exclusive content and goodies.

Newsletter subscribers are my extra special friends, and get everything from bonus epilogues, 19,000 words of deleted sex scenes from Highland and Hollywood Games, free stories, free audiobooks, extracts from my current work-in-progress, and exclusive offers and giveaways.

Sign up now!

www.eviealexanderauthor.com/subscribe/

SEX INDEX
(AKA THE GOOD BITS)

There have been many great contributions to the world of literature. Gutenberg invented the printing press, Shakespeare invented romantic comedy, and J K Rowling invented Harry Potter. However, all of these achievements pale into insignificance compared to my contribution – the sex index.

Using this sex index, you can easily find the steamier moments from The Love Position. Enjoy...

Page 207 – Well, that escalated quickly...
Page 241 – This is how you break a vow
Page 342 – Home is where the heart is

And if that wasn't enough, don't forget I've got nineteen thousand words of super-hot deleted sex scenes from Highland and Hollywood Games as well as Isaac and Sophia's extended epilogue available exclusively for newsletter subscribers.

If you want some extra action, then sign up to my newsletter today!

www.eviealexanderauthor.com/subscribe/

ACKNOWLEDGMENTS

Yoga has been an intrinsic part of my life since I was a teen, and after I qualified as a yoga teacher, I taught hatha, pregnancy, and mum and baby yoga for over a decade, as well as yoga nidra. And now, even though I rarely teach, I still attend classes four times a week.

This book is dedicated to Jennifer Peterson and all the people I did my own yoga teacher trainer course with, many years ago. Fortunately the ashram I attended did not have a Swami Vishnu character, however *un*fortunately, neither did it have an Isaac...

Jennifer arrived onto our course (and into my dorm room) a day after the rest of us and was a whirlwind of sass and humour. If I'm the most English of Englishwomen - reserved, uptight, and rule-following, then Jennifer is the most American of Americans. She's loud, confident, gives zero fucks and takes zero shit. Whilst I was hobbling around on crutches after falling over in the temple (no statues or blood were involved), and losing my mind through lack of sleep and overwhelm, she was getting on with it and trying to make our lives easier (hence her plan to wash our clothes whilst we were in Satsang).

Jennifer is wild, hilarious, and has the wickedest laugh. We speak weekly, and even though it feels very long ago, I still thank her for getting me through our yoga course with my sanity intact...

If you're interested in learning yoga, then my recommendation is to start with Iyengar yoga as they have the most rigorous teacher training qualifications (it takes years to be a qualified teacher) and have a forensic approach to how the body works. This gives you the best foundation for then exploring the many different yoga schools that are out there if you wish.

Keeping with the yoga-related thanks, I want to give a HUGE thank you to Leem, my current yoga teacher for making sure I got the yoga terminology spot on, even if the interpretation of it was down to Swami Vishnu, and not any other school of yoga. I'm so lucky to have found Leem, not just as an incredible teacher, but also as a very special friend.

Moving onto archaeology, I want to thank the archaeologists who have helped me write this book - Marie-Claire, A. M. and Ashleigh. From early research, to reading the final draft, these people have helped ensure that what I have written is at least sixty per cent accurate, as poetic licence was used in some instances to make the story work... If you are an archaeologist and find a bit that is not exactly true to life, then blame me, not them.

A massive thanks go to my medical advisors, Dr Beth in the US, and Dr Tonya in the UK. It's always great to chat to doctors who read romance as they know just how to make an injury or illness dramatic *and* sexy...

Thanks as ever go to my fabulous alpha reader, Pash Baker, to whom I write multiple Easter eggs, knowing that she is the only person in the world to recognise them as such, and my epic editing team - Margaret Amatt and Mike AF. Thank you to Matt Wellsted for designing this wonderful cover and Mark Karasick for taking such fabulous photos of me.

Thank you to my sensitivity readers, in particular Hime and the ever awesome Tori Ross.

My team at Emlin Press: Victoria, Mandy, and Liezl. Thank you for doing everything I can't, won't, or don't have time for. Thank you for tolerating my foul mouth, laughing at my unfunny jokes and sticking around.

Thank you to my husband—the best decision I've ever made, and to my daughter—the best luck I've ever had. I love you both to the ends of the multiverse and back.

And last, but by no means least, I want to thank my fabulous ARC team, the incredible online community of book lovers and, once again, YOU, the reader. Thank you for your continued support and for reading the fourth book in the Foxbrooke series. Each time you read my books, write me a review and recommend me in countless different ways, my heart gets a little fuller. Thank you!

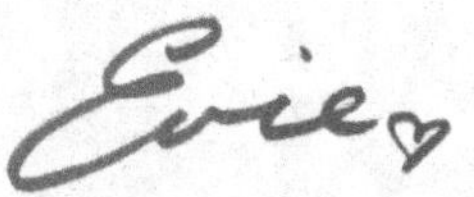

PS - I love, love, LOVE hearing from my readers, so please get in touch via email or social media to ask me anything or just tell me about your day!

ALSO BY EVIE ALEXANDER

Get all of Evie's books in print, audio, or eBook format, as well as special offers, early releases, and exclusive deals at www.eviealexanderbooks.com

THE KINLOCH SERIES

HIGHLAND GAMES

Zoe's given up everything for a ramshackle cabin in Scotland. She wants a new life, but her scorching hot neighbour wants her out. As their worlds collide, will Rory succeed in destroying her dream? Or has he finally met his match? Let the games begin...

Tropes

Small Town, Enemies-to-Lovers, Grumpy/Sunshine, Fish-out-of-Water, Opposites Attract, Forced Proximity

HOLLYWOOD GAMES

In a last-ditch attempt to save Kinloch castle, new lovers Rory and Zoe throw open the doors to a Hollywood superstar. But when it all goes south, it's up to them to rewrite the script, save the castle's future, and find their own happy ending.

Tropes

Small Town, Soulmates, Grumpy/Sunshine, Fish-out-of-Water

KISSING GAMES

Bodyguard Charlie has a new mission: teach workaholic Hollywood actress Valentina how to play, one wild adventure at a time. But when no-strings fun turns into something more, they have to face some hard truths. Can they find a future together, or will their love remain a Highland fling?

Tropes

Small Town, Dark Secrets, Bodyguard/Actress, Forced Proximity, Alpha-roll hero, Dating Game

MUSICAL GAMES

After lying to a Hollywood megastar, Sam needs Jamie to write an album with her in just ten days He's got the voice of an angel and the body of a god, but fame is the last thing on his mind. Will he help make her dreams come true?

Tropes

Small Town, Grumpy/Sunshine, Male Virgin, Cinnamon Roll Hero, Opposites Attract, Fish-out-of-Water, Forced Proximity

WEDDING GAMES

Rory and Zoe want to get married. Not easy when their mothers are mortal enemies and Rory's step-father is a Hollywood star with a death wish. Can they unravel the tangles in time to tie the knot, or is eloping the only answer? Get ready for Scotland's wedding of the year!

Tropes

Small Town, Grumpy/Sunshine, Opposites Attract, Soulmates, Fish-out-of-Water

CHRISTMAS GAMES

Having a baby's easy, right? Until wayward in-laws, an out-of-control cow and mad Santa get in the way. All Rory and Zoe want is a relaxing Christmas before their baby arrives, but straightforward is not their style...

Tropes

Small Town, Grumpy/Sunshine, Opposites Attract, Soulmates, Fish-

✦

THE FOXBROOKE SERIES

ONE NIGHT IN FOXBROOKE

When chef Ben 'Kenobi' Walker gets the call to help save a VIP dinner at Foxbrooke Manor, he doesn't expect to run into old flame Leia Perry. She's all grown up and even more attractive than when they were teenagers – but she hasn't forgotten what happened ten years ago, and she *definitely* hasn't forgiven him. Will one night give Ben the second chance he needs to prove himself and win back Leia's heart?

Tropes

Small Town, Second Chance, Return to Hometown, Enemies-to-Lovers, Bet, Brother's Best Friend, Work Colleagues, Forced Proximity, First Love, Reverse Grumpy-Sunshine, Opposites Attract

LOVE AD LIB

Shy and reserved Lord Henry Foxbrooke needs a fake girlfriend. Free-spirited actress Libby Fletcher needs a job. But when they arrive in Somerset for Henry's birthday celebrations, neither are prepared for their reception. As friendship blurs and faking it starts to feel a little too real, disaster strikes. Can Libby and Henry stick to the script, or has their entire act just bombed?

Tropes

Small Town, Fake Dating, Grumpy/Sunshine, Opposites Attract, One Bed, Different Worlds, Fish-out-of-Water

AN UNHOLY AFFAIR

Gorgeous Jack Newton has fallen in love with Eveline Shaw. But she's a female vicar dreaming of marriage and kids, and he's a male escort heading out of town. Can Jack show Eveline heaven and keep his secret safe, or are they both headed straight for hell?

Tropes

Small Town, Forbidden Love, Love at First Sight, Sworn off a Relationship, Priest, Different Worlds, Opposites Attract, Dark Secret

THE UPPER CRUSH

James Hunter-Savage is a cocky city boy who isn't used to anyone else taking the reins. Lady Estelle Foxbrooke is a fiery country girl who's about to show him who's boss. Can they learn to fight for love rather than with each other, or will their love hate relationship destroy everything they're working for?

Tropes

Small Town, Enemies-to-Lovers, Alpha Hero, Love/Hate, Playboy in Love, Different Worlds, Workplace Romance, Fake Dating

THE LOVE POSITION

Beautiful academic, Sophia Hunter-Savage, has run away to an ashram to reinvent herself. Hot yoga teacher, Isaac Hayward, has left town to avoid the only woman able to tempt him off the spiritual path.

But karma sucks.

Now Isaac's teaching Sophia and they're finding themselves in all kinds of unexpected positions. Will their forbidden love bring inner peace and happiness, or end in a tangled mess?

Tropes

Forbidden Love, Opposites Attract, Teacher/Student, Sworn off a Relationship, Forced Proximity, Love at First Sight, Different Worlds, Fish-out-of-Water

CHRISTMAS OFF SCRIPT

Best friends, Leo Foxbrooke and Ella Chamberlain, have never been single at the same time. Until now... Playing Cinderella and Prince Charming in the Christmas pantomime, their on-stage chemistry kindles an unexpected spark behind the scenes. Can they rewrite their friendship this festive season and finally unwrap true love?

Tropes

Small Town, Friends-to-Lovers, Best Friend's Ex, Oblivious to Love, Unrequited Love, Fake Relationship

ONE NIGHT ONLY

Pop star Avery Taylor craves a break from her public life, and a one-night stand with a stranger feels like the perfect escape. A year later, while recovering from an injury, she's stunned to find her nurse is Connor Foxbrooke, the man who touched her soul that night. Avery is ready to break the rules for love, but Connor, who values his quiet life, fears heartbreak. With Avery set to return to the spotlight as soon as she's recovered, can they bridge their worlds and turn their one night into forever?

Tropes

Second-Chance, Mistaken Identity, One Night Stand, Different Worlds, Opposites Attract, Injury, Forced Proximity, Fish-out-of-Water, Celebrity, Pop Star, Small Town

RIGHTING MR WRONG

Mooning a party of nuns is bad for anyone, but for TV star Aiden Wilder, it's catastrophic. Enter Willow Foxbrooke, a quiet PR worker who's tasked with saving his reputation through a fake relationship. As Willow teaches him how to recover his image, they start to fall for each other. But how can true love grow from something that was never real to begin with?

Tropes

Small Town, Fake Dating, Grumpy/Sunshine, Celebrity, Opposites Attract, Different Worlds, Fish-out-of-Water

UNDER THE INFLUENCER

Sunny Summer Foxbrooke's career as an Influencer is over. Now she's forced to work with grumpy Finn Oakley, the man who's avoided her for years. Will Finn finally return her love, or will she always just be his best friend's little sister?

Tropes

Brother's best friend, Grumpy/Sunshine, Beauty and the Beast, Age Gap, Unrequited Love, Rivals, Different Worlds, All Grown Up, Small Town

৩৯৫

By Evie Alexander and Kelly Kay

EVIE & KELLY'S HOLIDAY DISASTERS SERIES

Evie and Kelly's Holiday Disasters are a series of hot and hilarious romantic comedies with interconnected characters, focusing on one holiday and one trope at a time.

CUPID CALAMITY

Featuring **Animal Attraction** & **Stupid Cupid**

Patrick and Sabina have ditched their blind dates for each other. Ben's fighting a crazed chimp for Laurie's love. Insta-love meets insta-disaster in these laugh-out-loud Valentine's day novellas.

COOKOUT CARNAGE

Featuring **Off With a Bang** & **Up in Smoke**

Cute farm boy Jonathan clings to a love ideal, blissfully ignoring what the universe has planned, while keeping track of his pet pig. Posh Brit follows his heart into the American Midwest in search of Sherilyn, his digital dream love.

CHRISTMAS CHAOS

Featuring **No way in a Manger** & **No Crib and No Bed**

In Scotland, Zoe and Rory attempt to have a civilised and respectable rite of passage, but straightforward is not their style. In Sonoma, Bax and Tabi attempt to throw a meaningful Christmas celebration. But there are too many people involved and it's nothing like they expect.

Get Evie's books in all formats as well as special offers, early releases, and exclusive deals direct from her website:

www.eviealexanderbooks.com

ABOUT THE AUTHOR

Evie Alexander is a multi-award-winning author of sexy romantic comedies, blending snort-laugh humour and panty-melting chemistry into unputdownable stories that will steal your heart.

When she's not dreaming up swoony heroes and relatable heroines, Evie can be found in the beautiful West Country of the UK, where she lives with her ridiculously patient husband, miracle daughter, and two dogs who think they run the show.

eviealexanderbooks.com

www.eviealexanderauthor.com

instagram.com/eviealexanderauthor
facebook.com/eviealexanderauthor
x.com/Evie_author
bookbub.com/authors/evie-alexander
amazon.com/Evie-Alexander/e/B08ZJGLP29?ref=sr_ntt_s-rch_lnk_1&qid=1630667484&sr=8-1
pinterest.com/eviealexanderauthor